The Reich Device

Richard D. Handy

Matador
9 Priory Business Park,
Wistow Road, Kibworth Beauchamp,
Leicestershire. LE8 0RX
Tel: 0116 279 2299
Email: books@troubador.co.uk
Web: www.troubador.co.uk/matador
Twitter: @matadorbooks

ISBN 978 1784623 456

British Library Cataloguing in Publication Data.
A catalogue record for this book is available from the British Library.

Printed and bound in the UK by TJ International, Padstow, Cornwall
Typeset in 11pt Aldine401 BT Roman by Troubador Publishing Ltd, Leicester, UK

Matador is an imprint of Troubador Publishing Ltd

For FGH and the bravest of the brave

CHAPTER 1

Leipzig, Germany, 7th May 1933

Professor Gustav Mayer trembled as equations flowed from his pen. Ignoring his aching fingers and the hunger knotting his stomach, he rubbed his eyes and pressed on, desperately scribbling to transfer his new theory to paper. His heart missed a beat. 'My God,' he whispered. 'That's it… ' He clung to the logic steps in his head as mathematical hieroglyphs cascaded from his pen.

A rush of sweat soaked his skin: the delicate construct forming in his mind could unravel in an instant, and would be lost forever. 'No, no… that's not right… ' Mayer mumbled to himself out of habit. 'Think… think… think… yes… yes… the speed of light is constant… we know that… Einstein's equation says $E = mc^2$… energy and the speed of light… energy and the speed of light… '

More frantic note-taking pushed the boundaries of science to the next level.

'Arghh!' Mayer smacked his forehead and momentarily stared at the ceiling. 'No! How could I be so stupid!' He crossed out the last two lines of equations like a frustrated child, then continued. 'Come on… come on… go over it again… the energy is right… the mass does not add up… so… '

A sudden flood of new equations went onto the paper as Mayer worked the pen. His eyes scanned back and forth, checking each equation for mathematical accuracy. 'Yes, yes! That's it!' he whispered.

His mind's eye saw atoms, elegantly dancing with each

1

other, not the chaos everyone else predicted – but order where order should not exist. If physics was music, then this was Mozart – thousands of atoms coming together to play the Requiem – but only if you knew the rules. Newton gave us rules for dealing with gravity. Einstein created rules for dealing with light. This was something different – a new set of rules that would change the world, and the course of humanity forever.

A knock at the office door startled Mayer from his thoughts. He instinctively covered his notes with a blank sheet of paper.

'Who is it?'

A head appeared around the door.

'Professor… sorry for the intrusion… I know it's late, but… '

'Nico, I must work. Please, can this wait until the morning?'

'Sorry… of course, Professor, I've just finished the experiment you asked me to do… it worked… but the data doesn't make any sense.' His assistant wore a grubby laboratory coat. Bloodshot eyes and several days of stubble completed the look.

Mayer was intrigued, but fought back the urge to see the new data. 'Sorry, Nico, it sounds great, but I have something to finish.'

Nico's face brightened. 'Oh, what is it? A new set of calculations?'

'It's nothing to concern you!' Mayer snapped.

The assistant took a step back. 'Forgive me. I'll come back in the morning.' He edged sheepishly for the door.

'Nico, no, I am sorry, leave it with me. I will read it later.' Mayer gave a consolatory smile.

Nico walked slowly up to the desk with the laboratory notebook in hand. Involuntarily, Mayer hunched over his papers, using his elbows for good measure to cover his work.

'Here, the second page is especially interesting.' The assistant thrust out an arm, glancing Mayer up and down. Crumpled pages stuck out from his well-worn laboratory book.

'Thank you. Now I should get on... ' Mayer forced another smile as he took the volume.

'Alright... tomorrow then... I'll lock up on my way out... ' The assistant turned back towards the door, then hesitated. 'Professor, are you alright?... Well, I mean, it's very late... can I get you something to drink before I go?'

'No... ' Mayer remained perched over his notes like a vulture, protecting them from prying eyes. 'Nico, I am fine, go home.' He gave a brief grin. Nico was a good assistant. It was hard not to like him.

Mayer stared absently at an old photograph on his desk while he waited for Nico to leave. The grainy picture showed a beautiful, athletic young woman sitting on horseback. A lump formed in his throat as his fingers gently caressed the edge of the picture frame and then ran over the date embossed in gold at the bottom: 1912. Those had been happier times.

The door clanked shut, snapping Mayer back to reality. He grabbed the pen from his desk and after snaking it through the last few lines of calculations, he picked up the thread. Numbers whirled around in his mind again.

'Focus... focus... if *alpha* is the sum of *theta*... then... ' Gradually a steady rhythmic flow in the maths emerged; almost taking a life of its own, one logic step leading to another. Mayer's mathematical symphony flowed onto the paper.

The old building on the street corner provided a shadowy refuge. No one saw the agile figure, chameleon-like against the sooty, pock-marked brickwork. The grey of his worn overcoat concealed a lean, but muscular physique, with the flesh honed by long experience of combat. The grey man stooped and picked up a small handful of damp soil. He rubbed it methodically on the backs of his hands and, for good measure, streaked some dirt across his face.

He pulled up the collar of his overcoat; it was going to be a long night. Keeping out the chill was easy, but breaking into Leipzig University was a different matter. The place was swarming with troops. Another two-man patrol appeared around the corner, only five minutes since the last one. It wasn't much of a time interval, but it would have to do.

He moved off, stooping low, and in silence he half ran across the cobbled street. He pressed himself into the perimeter wall on the other side. Crouching, he listened. Good – no boots approaching. He strained his eyes in the darkness, but still nothing. A mist was starting to form. Any help Mother Nature could give tonight was welcome.

The wall looked high; at least fifteen feet, and there was no telling what was on the other side. He swung the grappling hook and prayed the rope was long enough. It whistled through the air, and a sudden clank announced contact with the top of the wall. Instinctively, he hunkered down, but there was no alarm. A tug on the rope confirmed it was secure. His arms took the strain, and with his breathing steady, he heaved upwards.

Clip, clap, clip, scrape.

There was no avoiding the sound of his boots against the stone wall, but there was nothing to be done about that now. Climbing was all that mattered.

He pulled himself onto the top of the wall, breathing deeply, and surveyed the scene below. At last some luck: bushes. At least some decent cover – and with the main gate to the University campus only fifty yards away he needed all the luck he could get. He pulled up the free end of the rope and dropped it down the inside edge of the wall. He tried to turn the grappling hook around, but it was stuck. He gripped the wall with his thighs and strained silently; with his teeth gritted, he sucked in air, working to release the hook. Suddenly, the hook gave way. The grey man braced against the sudden loss of balance, but slipped. A jolt of pain ripped through his shoulder as he dangled by one arm on the inside of the wall, but snorting through his nostrils, he managed to hold on. Miraculously, the grappling hook was still in his free hand. With a well-timed throw, the hook was re-set on top of the wall, with the rope dangling into the bushes. He grabbed the rope, relieving the pressure on his shoulder. The hassle was worth the effort: it was always good to have a planned exit route. A job could go to pieces quickly, and getting out alive was the name of the game.

He dropped to the ground, squatting for a moment, and listening to the night. After several lungfuls of the cold night air, he gathered his breath, and then peered through the prickles of the nearest holly bush. The lawn out front was fairly wide; maybe fifty feet. Suddenly voices came from the left.

The sentry post!

He glanced in their direction, and exhaled, his shoulders relaxed. It seemed as if the guards were giving in to idle chatter. He clicked a round into the chamber, then ran across the lawn in an awkward monkey run. Keeping one hand curled around the pistol, he bounded silently into the cover of the rhododendrons on the far side. He rolled up onto one knee, pistol at the ready, and searched the darkness for a target.

Mayer finished the last equation and stretched in the chair to relieve the pain in the small of his back. He gave a few involuntary yawns. The annoying ache persisted. He stood up and massaged the muscles with his fingers, whilst surveying the pages that were now covering the desk. The equations seemed to be right, but that was just a question of algebra and maths. It was the *idea* that made all the difference. The threads of knowledge had somehow come together at the right moment. Perplexed by his own ingenuity, Mayer started to pace around the office. He mumbled while rubbing his chin, 'What to do with it?… What to do with it?'

The sudden click of jackboots on the concrete outside penetrated his thoughts. He peered cautiously through the window. Two troopers patrolled the gardens below. 'Who can I trust?… *Who* can I trust?' The question rammed home like a freight train. These were deviant political times. There were rumours of people disappearing. It was impossible to tell friend from foe. The Brown Shirts were everywhere. Even members of the University Senate were paid up members of the Nazi Party.

A wave of nausea made him lightheaded. Sweating, he leaned on the window sill to steady himself. 'Safe… I need to keep this safe… no, I need help, but from whom? Damn it! Why me?… Why now?'

The grey man adjusted his position in the undergrowth. He rubbed the mud off his newly acquired German Navy *Kreigsmarine* wrist watch. The previous owner wouldn't be missing it. The glow on the radium dial said four a.m. The Professor was evidently still working. The light was on in his study and he hadn't left the building. This was a lot of surveillance for some obscure academic. Still, it didn't matter; orders were orders. The job description was simple – protect one Professor Gustav Mayer and find out what he knows.

The file on Mayer was impressive. A theoretical physicist, connected with the great and the good in the scientific community, and by all accounts, close friends with Albert Einstein. Mayer had done some work on the new theory of relativity, whatever that was; probably cobblers. Much more interesting was his work on propulsion systems and high-octane fuels. So, Professor Mayer was making rockets; no wonder military intelligence was interested. These were not the overgrown fireworks of the Great War, but an altogether new beast: metallic monsters designed for an impressive payload of high explosives.

Crack!

The sound of a breaking twig ripped the grey man back to

reality. Footfalls through the undergrowth approached steadily. He froze. A pair of shinning boots stopped inches from his face.

There was the sound of a zip opening, whistling, then the splash of warm, rank liquid on the soil. The stench of urine filled the grey man's nostrils. Ignoring it, he reached for his knife. With luck the German would finish and wander off none the wiser.

'Scheisse!'

Too late! The grey man lunged.

The German caught a flash of the blade as the grey man drove it home, deep into the soldier's chest. Piling on top, he tried to silence the trooper as they fell to the floor.

'Scheisse… ' the German sentry cursed repeatedly through clenched teeth, gasping, snorting, tensing every muscle in his body and bucking up and down, trying with steely determination to rid himself of the vice-like arm around his throat. His head throbbed as panic started to set in.

'Come on… come on… die, you bastard,' hissed the grey man, steadying his grip and pulling hard under the German's chin. He could feel the neck starting to stretch. Instinct took over as the grey man locked his legs around the German's waist to get more purchase. 'Jesus… come on… you big bugger… ' He heaved harder, arching his back for good measure, holding on as waves of cramp flushed through his arm. He wasn't sure how much longer he could keep the pressure up, but a final burst of effort gave the required result. The telltale *click-clack* sound announced the collapse of his victim's windpipe.

The German went limp.

He kicked the corpse off, and silently cursed himself. How could he have been so stupid? He'd been all eyes on the Professor's window and totally absorbed.

Not good enough!

Taking a piss in the bushes had cost the German his life. He conceded the point: he'd had to kill him. Secrecy was everything. Nobody could know he was here. The dead German marked a premature end to the night's surveillance, but that was the nature of the game. You could never tell how things would go on any mission. He recovered the knife from the dead man's chest and wiped it clean on the soldier's lapel. He checked himself over. The mud was useful camouflage for now, but he would never pass as a civilian in daylight. Hopefully, the forming mist had muffled the sound of the struggle.

He checked his weapon and quickly scouted around the immediate undergrowth. Nothing else had been dropped – it was time to move off. He worked silently through the bushes. There was no point running the risk of bumping into any more German soldiers tonight. They would surely come looking for their missing comrade soon enough.

The grey man expertly worked his way across the campus, keeping to the undergrowth, pausing every now and then to allow yet another patrol to go past.

This was madness. Why so many soldiers in a place like this? It just didn't make sense. But then, nothing in Germany made any sense right now. The whole country was a mess. After all, there was a new regime in town: the Nazis. To add to this screwed-up mission, he'd been dropped into a hot zone. Leipzig was a major showpiece for the Nazi propaganda machine. Most weekends there were parades, rallies and grand speeches. More to the point, wall-to-wall Nazis made surveillance difficult. Sooner or later his luck would run out – and when it did, the powers that be back home wouldn't be mounting any rescue. He was on his own.

The main gate loomed out of the darkness. He settled down into cover, observing the scene. The two guys at the entrance looked bored. He smiled at the thought: *same old army the world over*. He'd done his share of square bashing. The sentries would have been on shift for some five hours now, and it was a fair bet their minds were focused on a warm billet and hot food, the local whorehouse, whatever – anything but stag duty. The nearest German sparked up a smoke and passed one to his friend.

Perfect timing.

The grey man made a short run across the lawn, and slammed into the wall on the far side. The rope was just where he had left it, concealed by the shrubs. A quick glance confirmed that the Fritz brothers were still enjoying their cigarettes. He took the strain on the rope and began pulling himself slowly, like some kind of mud-soaked praying mantis, onto the top of the wall. He stopped.

Still no Fritz.

Now was not the time to be spotted. Dropping off the top of the wall into the lap of another patrol would be bad news – after all there was a curfew on.

He listened hard and squinted into the mist, tensing his fingers to maintain a hold on the brickwork. He gingerly dropped down the wall, then kneeling to keep a low profile, he listened again.

Nothing.

He was good to go. With that, the grey man disappeared into the night.

CHAPTER 2

Einstein

Professor Mayer pulled up the collar of his coat and held the leather satchel containing his precious papers tight against his chest. Hunched over, he struggled to keep the papers dry in the pouring rain. Lost in his thoughts, he trudged along the narrow cobbled street in the darkness. Miraculously, he had managed to get this far on foot from the University without bumping into any Brown Shirts. Surely his luck could not hold out? There was no excuse for being on the streets this late at night. What would he say if the Nazis stopped him? What would happen to his precious cargo?

A chill ran down his spine. He wasn't made for this kind of excitement, but at least it wasn't far to go to Einstein's house.

He squinted through the gloom as he turned the corner into Einstein's street. Nothing was out of the ordinary. It was just an unremarkable suburban street like any other in Leipzig. Fame had not yet driven Einstein from the comforts of a normal domestic life.

Mayer glanced up and down the road. Shadows played tricks in the torrential rain. A wave of adrenalin flushed his face crimson pink. It was all too much. He broke into a run for the last few metres, hastily dashing up the steps to the front door. Welcoming the relative darkness and cover of the porch, he thumped on the door, hoping that Einstein's housekeeper would let him in.

'Who is it?' a timid voice whispered through a crack in the now open door.

'It's me, Gustav. I mean Gustav Mayer, I… I am sorry to disturb you so late, is the Professor home?'

'Yes, yes, come in,' came a soothing reply.

Mayer stepped into the hallway, thankful to be out of the rain, but still panting and flushed. He took off his coat.

Suspicious, but polite, the housekeeper dutifully hung up the coat. 'I will see if the Professor is ready to receive you.'

'No, no, I know my way…'

Unable to contain himself, Mayer leapt up the stairs two at a time, bursting through the door into Einstein's study.

'Albert! Albert! I know it is late, but I must speak with you!'

'Hello Gustav, what brings you here at this hour? What's wrong? You look terrible my friend.'

With a strange mixture of excitement and concern, Mayer stood in the doorway for a few seconds trying to catch his breath, absently wiping the rain from his face.

'Well, come in, sit down my friend.' Einstein shifted a pile of papers, gesturing Mayer to the now vacant chair.

The two scientists sat staring at each other for a few seconds. The single oil lamp burning on the desk cast eerie shadows amongst the piles of documents around the room. Einstein leaned forward into the light. The crumpled sleeves of his threadbare tweed jacket contrasted with his neatly trimmed, thick, black moustache. His wiry dark hair seemed to randomly occupy his scalp.

Mayer finally broke the silence.

'Albert! I have been working on something: a new theory! There is so much I want to tell you! My ideas, the University, and, and…'

'Slowly, slowly my friend… this sounds interesting, but take your time.' Einstein scanned the worry lines on Mayer's face. 'Gustav, are you alright?'

'Yes, well… I think so… actually… I…'

Mayer straightened out his damp notes on the desk, and

took a deep breath to gather his thoughts. This was it! Now there would be two men in the world who knew his extraordinary idea! *His* secret.

'Albert, I… I need to tell you something important. It is potentially wonderful, but also it's been a terrible burden… and playing on my mind.'

Einstein lifted an eyebrow.

Mayer continued. 'Let me explain… ' He grabbed a sheet of paper and pencil from the desk; he started sketching out his idea for Einstein. Mayer always found it easier to draw and think. It was an automatic habit, picked up after many years of mentoring students. The fact that his 'student' for this discussion was Professor Albert Einstein seemed irrelevant. The two men shared a ferocious appetite for knowledge.

'Alright, we start with the Brownian motion of particles. Consider the random movement of particles that enables simple physical processes such as diffusion to occur… '

Einstein nodded encouragement.

Mayer continued. 'Then, we consider quantum theory: the idea that matter at the atomic level can have both mass, and at the same time, be an electromagnetic wave.'

Einstein nodded again as Mayer sketched away furiously on the notepaper.

'Well, what if we add energy to these particles at the precise moment when the matter transformation occurs… ' He scribbled a series of equations, even more intensely.

Einstein grunted his understanding, and leaned closer to the paper.

'You see… these equations show that adding a small amount of energy will create a force… a huge force… and a monumental release of energy.' Mayer looked at Einstein for approval.

Einstein scrutinised the maths. 'Yes, I can see that you need to add some energy to start off the reaction, but I don't understand… how do you get so much energy back?'

'Quantum energy is the key… and the right materials with the right properties… '

'What materials?'

'This… ' Mayer made another cartoon showing a series of carbon atoms joined together to make a hexagonal ring.

'A flat hexagon of carbon atoms? This chemistry is well known. You need to do something with these rings to make a bigger structure. Am I correct?'

Mayer smiled and made a new diagram of dozens of hexagons joined together like a sheet of atomic chicken wire.

'I see, a high conductivity surface. Fascinating!'

'That's not all.' Mayer picked up the sheet of paper and tore off the edges, then he curled the sides of the paper together to make a hollow ball. The hexagons decorated the outside, just like a soccer ball. Mayer held the ball up to the light.

'Look at the arrangement of the atoms… stable, yet in a configuration that will make a tiny sphere with quantum properties. You see… a new material with the potential to create an unlimited supply of energy and unimaginable levels of force.'

'The structure is very elegant, I agree,' Einstein smiled then shook his head. 'No, I've almost lost the thread, Gustav… in fact you've lost me. How do you manipulate the quantum properties of this material? This substance… whatever it is… how do you harness it to make such vast amounts of force?' Einstein rubbed his chin, his brow furrowed.

'It needs to be contained in a particular way with some clever but elegantly simple engineering.' Mayer started another diagram. He drew a long cylindrical tube with carbon spheres on the inside.

'I see… it's an interesting technology… ' Einstein pointed at the sketch, 'What do you call this device?'

Mayer shrugged. 'I haven't got a name for it yet.'

'How do you start it up?'

'A standard power supply should do it, just like any other

electric motor. The electricity cranks the engine – only this one has no moving parts, and it will run indefinitely renewing itself with its own particle energy.'

'Remarkable... perpetual motion. How fast do you think it can go?'

Mayer opened his hands, palms uppermost. 'I am not sure exactly, way beyond any propulsion systems we have now. Ten, to maybe... a hundred times the speed of sound. Probably more...'

'A hundred times! My God! A rocket with such a motor could reach escape velocity and go into space! A hundred times the speed of sound!' Einstein made a quick piece of mental arithmetic. 'That's... Mars and back in... seventeen days!' His jaw dropped for a few seconds, then he shook his head. 'Gustav, are you sure? What's your mathematical proof for this limitless energy and force?'

Mayer picked up a blank piece of paper, and hovered over it with his pen. 'If I am right, then this explains the resulting phenomena...' Suddenly in full flow, Mayer threw several lines of fresh equations onto the page.

Einstein gasped – it was beautiful.

The housekeeper sat quietly on the stairs outside the study, and with one ear to the door, she listened intently. The extra income from the local Nazi Party officials was useful; easy money in these hard times and all for simply keeping a watching brief on Professor Einstein. The instructions were clear: report everything, no matter how trivial.

Words drifted through the door. Impossible words. Strange words: like diffusion, quantum and momentum. What did they mean? It didn't matter. The tone of the voice and urgency of the conversation conveyed their importance. Her brow furrowed with intense concentration as she struggled to keep up with the muffled voices coming through the door. Fearful of her masters, she reached into her apron to find a piece of paper and a pencil. All she could do was write down what seemed like key phrases and dutifully pass the information on. After a few minutes, the crumpled paper was full. She thrust the precious scrap back into the apron, annoyed at herself for not bringing more notepaper. It was too late now to get more paper. The slightest creak on the stairs might give the game away; she would have to manage just by listening.

Mayer rubbed his forehead while tapping the pencil on the paper. He massaged his forehead again. 'Albert, do you see the main steps in the logic? Do you agree that they are right?'

Einstein took the pencil and traced through the equations again, grunting and shaking his head at each checkpoint in the logic.

'You see, it should work?' Mayer looked at Einstein.

Einstein paused, absently sucking the top of the pencil while considering his reply. 'Gustav, yes… yes, I believe it will work.'

The approval strengthened Mayer's resolve.

'In that case, I will type up my notes into a formal manuscript.'

'Of course Gustav… but keep it safe… keep it *very* safe.' Einstein stared hard at his friend, and suddenly gripped his arm. 'You *must* keep this safe.' Einstein relaxed into a brief smile, easing his hold on Mayer's arm.

'I will guard it with my life.' Mayer gazed back at his friend.

'Now you're being too serious.' Einstein risked a smirk.

Mayer let the frown drift from his face.

The two men stood. Mayer clasped Einstein's hand in a solemn but also strangely triumphant handshake. The idea was wonderful, but also potentially deadly.

'Albert, what are the chances?… Do you think anyone else could work this out? You know… stumble on it by accident?'

'No… not likely.' Einstein shook his head. 'It's extremely

improbable that anyone else would come up with the right sequence of logic by chance. No, this is a once-in-a-lifetime discovery.'

Mayer forced a smile, humbled.

'... And it's all yours. Yours alone, Gustav. Congratulations! This is of monumental importance.' Einstein shook his hand firmly again.

The sudden scrape of chairs on the wooden floor sent heavy vibrations to the housekeeper's ear – movement inside the study! Wearily, she rubbed her eyes. Had she fallen asleep? She wasn't sure. Suddenly alert and breathing rapidly, she tried to move her limbs from the uncomfortable awkwardness of crouching outside the study door, but it was no good. Pins and needles flushed down each limb. Moving like a semi-anaesthetised manikin, her numbed limbs tottered down the stairs. A floorboard creaked under her weight. Perspiration erupted on to her brow and her breathing become more erratic. Anything was preferable to discovery and the wrath of her masters.

The bottom of the stairs didn't come soon enough. Wincing at the pain, but with feeling returning to her legs, she crossed the lobby to the dining room door. She gingerly pushed the door open, and resolved to lurk in the dining room at the front of the house. It would be useful to hear the visitor leaving, and note their time of departure. Anyway, at least there was some hard information: the technical jargon, as well as the flow and tempo of the discussion. It would all make a good report. She was a conscientious little spy.

Voices emerged from the study, followed by footfalls on the stairs, and then the clunk of the front door latch. An adrenalin rush gave the housekeeper a newfound alertness as she peered through the curtains – yes, it was definitely Professor Mayer now outside on the doorstep. She noted the time and the direction – downhill – the Professor must be returning to his lodgings near the University. She waited a few more minutes, and when the coast was clear, headed for bed. This seemed far too important to wait for her weekly meeting at the Commandant's office. She would report first thing in the morning.

Mayer hurried towards home, with his head down into the driving rain, lost in his thoughts. It would be light soon, and the authorities would ask questions. There was no explanation for being out at this hour. Fear took over, and utter loneliness. It was the way of things now, he had been alone for *so long*.

She had been so beautiful. A Polish girl with a clean white complexion and fiery red hair. Slim and athletic, she had a mind as sharp as a razor. An involuntary smile of happier times crossed his face. He could still see her now, working in the laboratory just after the Great War; but it was not to last. The Spanish influenza took her in 1919. Mayer flushed with a sudden bout of melancholy. It still hurt. The grief was undiminished after all these years, but that was to be expected. She was the one, the only one. Tears formed in his eyes.

There was only room for work and his students now. There was nothing else. When was the last time he had socialised? He couldn't remember. He never went out; except for now.

Mayer snapped back to reality after subconsciously registering a familiar sight: his own street on the edge of the University campus. How had he got home so quickly without being stopped?

Suddenly, the clatter of a rubbish bin down the street shattered the silence. Mayer jumped around in startled terror.

A cat dived into the hedgerow with some easy pickings.

'Relax you old fool,' he muttered to himself.

He exhaled, pausing for a second, before glancing up and down the street. The coast was clear. He headed up the steps to the front door, and after fumbling with his keys, made it inside. He bolted and locked the door shut, and slumped with his back against the woodwork. He fought back tears. The tension of the day's events had simply been too much. There would be more trouble to come. But for now, only sleep mattered. Mayer went up the stairs, and after carefully placing his notes in the top draw of his bedside table, collapsed into bed.

The grey man folded his binoculars away, placing them carefully into his coat pocket as the bedroom light went out. 'Sleep tight Professor, your Guardian Angel is watching... '

CHAPTER 3

Commandant Kessler

'I need a name. Give me a name now!' Commandant Kessler grunted with exertion as he punched the prisoner in the face. The prisoner garbled an inaudible reply through snot, blood and broken teeth. Not good enough. 'Come on, I don't have all fucking day! Give me a name now!' Kessler's tall but muscular frame delivered another left hook.

This time the prisoner, and the chair he was tied to, toppled to the floor. 'Fuck… ' Kessler cursed as he bothered to drag the prisoner upright. 'Now, how many times do I have to repeat myself?! Give me a name!' Teeth ground together as the fist made contact with the prisoner's jaw.

Kessler worked up the next blow, and was only just getting into his stride, when a knock on the cell door interrupted proceedings.

'Commandant, forgive me, but… '

'What is it? Can't you see I am busy?!'

It was his corporal from the office up stairs. 'Forgive me sir, but there is a woman waiting for you. She says she has some vital new information… she's one of your informants, sir.' The corporal waited, hoping not to unsettle his master too much with his intrusion.

'Fuck!' Kessler kicked the prisoner, chair and all, on to the floor and paced urgently out of the prison cell.

'This had better be good.' He glanced daggers towards the corporal as they went briskly up the stairs towards the office.

The corporal swallowed hard and nodded.

He had good reason to worry. Commandant Kessler was not a man who took being displeased lightly. He was also worth keeping on-side for other reasons. Kessler was a man rising rapidly through the ranks of the Nazi Party. He had the ears of his commanders in Berlin, but that was no surprise; it was common knowledge that his father was a war hero. A man of legendary proportions. He had served during the Battle of Verdun, one of the bloodiest engagements of the Great War. Tens of thousands of men had died in the bloodbath; but not Kessler senior, who had led a successful counterattack, breaking the French lines. Rumour had it, that he had single-handedly taken a heavily defended machine gun post. Kessler senior had been decorated by the Kaiser himself. Kessler junior had a lot to live up to.

Kessler swept into his office and took up position behind the desk. He paused for half a minute, combing his jet black hair. It was good to keep the minions waiting.

'Fräulein Hirsch to see you Commandant,' explained the corporal.

'Enter,' commanded Kessler.

Einstein's housekeeper moved briskly and business-like, coming to halt in front of the desk. Kessler deliberately ignored her, and carried on with some paperwork for another minute to illustrate his inconvenience to the unscheduled visitor.

'What is it?'

'Please, Commandant, forgive my intrusion,' the housekeeper hovered, palms sweating. 'I have a report to make.' She went on to explain the meeting that Einstein had with Professor Mayer the night before.

'I made these notes,' she thrust out a hand holding the scrap of paper.

Kessler examined the note: interesting. Technical phrases, jargon – something to look into?

Carefully maintaining a neutral expression, Kessler replied.

'Thank you. Please continue your vigilance Fräulein. The Party is grateful for your efforts. You may go.' He waved his hand in a gesture of dismissal, and the housekeeper left the room as briskly as she had arrived.

Kessler sat, drumming his fingers on the edge of the desk.

There was so much to do, and priority had to be given to the next rally. It was probable that the Führer himself would attend. The extra dignitaries and the crowds all added to the security headache. Kessler exhaled.

Still, it was curious about the Professors. Einstein had some international connections; not the sort of person you could lock up without explanation. However, Mayer was a different matter. He would be watched more closely, and it was time to increase security checks at the University. From now on, the sentries on all the routes into the University campus would be doubled. Anyone with the slightest errors on their identity papers, found wanting for any reason, would be arrested. After all, it was a justified precaution with the party leader due in the city, and the University was certainly a 'risk area' with all those visiting foreign intellectuals – damned troublemakers. A night in the cells would sort them out. There was always room for one more.

Kessler smiled to himself. There was still a name to get from the prisoner in the basement. The security preparations for the coming rally could wait a few more hours. He grabbed a fresh knuckle duster from the desk drawer and headed for the stairs.

The grey man shuddered off the cold, and repositioned the stock of the modified Mosin-Nagant Model 1891/30 sniper rifle into his shoulder. The barrel of the Russian weapon was heavy, but the new Zeiss telescopic sight made up for that. He had to admit, the Soviets were in the habit of evolving some pretty nice hardware. The weapon would leave no forensic trail given that half the Bolshevik Army, and the Germans, used the firearm.

He wiggled his toes to keep his circulation going. How long

had he been lying here? Two hours, maybe three; and not very much to show for it so far. At least it wasn't raining, but there was the cold wind gusting across the rooftop to contend with. Nonetheless, it was a good vantage point for observing the comings and goings at the local headquarters of the National Socialist Party.

The building seemed to double up as an administrative centre and a military command post for Leipzig, but that wasn't so unusual for the Nazi Party. Flexing his fingers against the cold, the grey man adjusted the telescopic sight and zeroed in on the office window. The cross hairs came into focus on a slim, immaculately dressed German officer – a commandant from the insignia on his uniform. That had to be Kessler, and by all accounts, the information in the Leipzig file had indicated he was a hard bastard. Not one to be trifled with.

He adjusted telescopic site for windage and fine focus on the cross hairs, bringing Kessler's forehead into sharp relief. He slid his finger under the trigger guard, gently increasing tension on the trigger mechanism. He held his breath, ready to take the shot.

At this range the weapon would blow his head clean off; and Kessler certainly deserved it. With one hand Kessler organised the legitimate security for visiting dignitaries, and with the other killed off enemies of the state. How very convenient.

The grey man moved the cross hairs on to Kessler's left eye – a dead centre shot. He increased the tension on the trigger. Should he kill him now? Or was there some more intelligence to gather? His gut told him the latter, resisting the urge, he moved the scope.

A woman emerged into view, standing at the desk, looking subservient. Where had he seen her before? Then it came – Einstein's house. She was the housekeeper! The telescopic sight worked over her body. She held out a piece of paper. Kessler took it. So, was she a willing informant? Or was there some coercion? Either was possible. Lips moved silently in the telescopic sight. The woman seemed agitated, and within a few minutes she walked briskly from the room.

The grey man moved the gun sight back to Kessler, who was leaning over a large paper chart on the desk, no – not a chart – but some kind of diagram or floor plan. It was no secret that Hitler would be in town, so perhaps this was the security plan for the stadium?

The grey man clicked a few notches on the telescopic sight, spreading his elbows some more for stability, then adjusted the fine focus. At this distance it was hard to read the papers on the desk. Definitely a floor plan though. The south and north entrances to the stadium were clear, a red pen marked the secure access area for the VIPs, and green crosses on the map seemed to mark the position of the sentry posts – what a gift! But should he call it in to London? The whole situation in Germany was about to boil over and here was a chance to pop the top brass; including Hitler himself.

The Nazi regime had ignored the Treaty of Versailles and re-occupied the strategically important Rhineland of Germany. This defiance of international law had gained popular support from the masses. Herr Hitler was in a strong position.

But one bullet could put a stop to all that.

Alas, he conceded that these were not his orders – just to observe, report back, and protect the life of one Professor Gustav Mayer at *any* cost. He could hardly do that by assassinating the leader of the Nazi Party.

What about Kessler? In this game you had the advantage if you could get inside the mind of your adversary, but what was Kessler *really* like? The files back in London told a familiar story. After graduation from the military academy, he joined the local Nazi Party and got involved in paramilitary activities.

Kessler had the opportunity to prove himself on the 9th November 1923 when Hitler attempted to seize power by raiding the government buildings in Munich. The coup failed; but during the fighting Kessler had gallantly protected his leader. He was quickly promoted to a captain in the *Sturmabteilung* or stormtroopers, and after a couple of years was transferred to the new *Schutzstaffel*, the SS. When Hitler eventually came to power in January 1933, he remembered the loyalty of Kessler and promoted him to commandant. Kessler became a member of *Liebstrandarte Hitler* – the Führer's personal bodyguard.

It was an impressive CV. It also explained why Kessler was in Leipzig. What could be more appropriate than a member of your own personal bodyguard to arrange your security? Kessler was responsible for the Führer's security during public engagements in Leipzig. That inevitably gave him certain latitudes with the natives, but how much? Was the brutality and murder in Leipzig just sanctioned by Berlin? How much of it was Kessler?

The grey man got an answer to his question, with sudden movement at the side of the building.

A blood-soaked body fell into the back of a truck, and in plain view of the public. Brutality and fear were the tools of Kessler's trade. With the finances at his disposal, Kessler could dish out a fair chunk of misery to the masses. The gun sight zoomed back to Kessler's office – the grey man might have pulled the trigger – only Kessler wasn't there.

'Another time my friend, another time… ' The grey man always kept a promise.

CHAPTER 4

Disappearances

Mayer paced up and down the study. The situation had changed dramatically in the last forty-eight hours. 'Albert, I think I was followed! It may not be safe for me, or for you!'

'Oh, you worry too much, that does not seem likely. Who would want to follow you?' Einstein gave a reassuring shrug, palms upwards.

'I don't know… well, I am not exactly sure, perhaps you are right.'

'You know I am making sense, Gustav, relax… please,' Einstein smiled.

Mayer shook his head. 'Things seem out of kilter and you've heard the rumours… '

'Rumours?'

'Yes, people are disappearing… ' Mayer paced even faster, '… and there are more sentries on the campus. *It is* dangerous for me.' He stopped and gave Einstein a hard stare.

Einstein shook his head. 'No, people are inherently good. Gustav, trust me on this, it cannot be as bad as you imagine.'

'Albert, but *it is*! Look at the evidence, the increased security is everywhere. Then there's this new Enabling Law – the Nazis have the legal power to detain anyone without recourse… and for as long as they see fit! I say again, people *are* disappearing and we could be next!'

'You really think so? Give me a concrete example.'

'Oh, there are plenty! I heard only yesterday about the

construction of a labour camp! In the forests – near here! Something about detaining certain criminal elements… '

'No, this cannot be. Exactly who are these criminal elements, and what forests? These are just rumours. Surely, just rumours?' Einstein shifted awkwardly in his chair; maybe his friend was starting to make sense.

'Wait a minute. Have you seen Nico, my technician?'

'Not for a few days, but then I've been working here. Why?'

'It's just unusual. I'd arranged to meet him this morning to go through our most recent experiments, but he didn't arrive.'

'So? Maybe he was just late?'

'Albert, I don't think so, Nico is never late. Besides, he would normally leave a telephone message if he was behind schedule.'

'So call him.' Einstein gestured towards the phone on the desk.

'Do you think I should?'

'Why not? Perhaps it will put your mind at ease?' Einstein raised an eyebrow.

'Alright, I will.'

Mayer picked up the receiver and dialled the number. Static filled his ears.

'I can't get through… ' Mayer tapped the mouthpiece. 'I… I… can't get anything… ' He rattled his index finger on the receiver, white noise crackled down the line. Mayer rang zero. 'Hello… hello… operator?'

'Yes sir,' an efficient female voice spoke back.

'Get me Leipzig, four, seven, two, please.' Mayer stared with a blank expression towards Einstein.

Einstein sat back in his chair, with his arms folded.

More static.

'I am sorry sir, the line is disconnected,' the female voice replied.

Mayer gently replaced the handset. 'There's no answer. His number's been cut off.'

'You jump to conclusions, perhaps he is visiting a relative?'

'No Albert, I don't think so.'

The phone suddenly rang. Mayer picked it up with lightning speed.

'Hello?'

A brisk German voice cleared the line. 'A call was just made to Leipzig four, seven, two, from this number. What business do you have… '

Mayer hung up, sweat seeped onto his brow.

'They have him!'

'What?' Einstein unfolded his arms.

'The authorities!' Mayer gulped.

'It's probably something minor, I am sure they'll let him go.'

'No! Likely as not, he is already dead! He is Jewish. You know the Nazis are discriminating against some ethnic groups. The Jews, the Poles… '

'… and the Germans?' Einstein finished for him. 'No, I just don't believe one human being could do that to another.'

'I wish I shared your faith in humanity, Albert, but I don't.'

'Look, there's nothing you can do right now. It is best to wait.'

'I suppose so… ' Mayer looked at the floor.

Einstein stood, placing a hand on his friend's shoulder. 'We should wait… at least until the end of the day. There's nothing to be done until then.' Einstein spoke gently.

'I guess you are right.' Mayer rubbed his eyes.

'That's the spirit Gustav,' Einstein patted him on the shoulder. 'Well, Gustav, I see you have finished your manuscript!' Einstein made a poor attempt at changing the subject.

'Yes… yes, I have. Well, at least what I think is a robust draft; but it needs a lot of checking.' Mayer spoke with humble modesty.

Einstein sat back at the desk, turning the pages, scanning

through each one for a few seconds to build up a mental picture of the layout and content. 'Gustav, it looks good,' Einstein smiled. 'I tell you what; why don't we go through it now?'

Mayer nodded gratefully, and pulled up a chair.

Commandant Kessler stepped from the Daimler into the mud. He glanced disdainfully at the glutinous detritus that squelched onto the pristine black leather of his boots, and buttoned his overcoat against the morning chill. The brand new chain mail fence, sporting fresh rolls of barbed wire, was at odds with the squalor in the rest of the work camp. Soldiers barked orders at the inmates as they hurried with buckets of cement and lengths of timber. The camp was evidently still under construction. A whiff of excrement, rank urine, and the foul body odour of the prisoners drifted on the breeze. Kessler lit up a cigarette to mask the smell, and took a long drag.

'What a fucking shithole. Are you sure this Nico van der Kemp is here?' Kessler took another gasp of his smoke.

'Yes, Commandant. He is here. The duty log back at the police station indicates that one Nico van der Kemp was arrested yesterday morning and, along with some other ethnics, delivered here in the afternoon.' The detective shoved his hands into the pockets of his cheap suit in an effort to keep them warm. He ignored the freezing, wet mud seeping over the top of his regular shoes, and regretted his lack of a warm coat; but decided to say nothing about the somewhat impromptu visit to the camp.

A stocky trooper plodded through the mud towards them, with a German shepherd straining at the leash.

'About bloody time, let's get on with it!' Kessler took a quick drag on his cigarette, and exhaled sharply.

'Good morning Herr Commandant, welcome. We were not expecting you.' The dog suddenly jumped forward with a snarl. The trooper gave a sharp tug to bring the dog to heel.

Kessler eyed the dog up and down, and returned a menacing

look to the trooper. 'You have a political prisoner here. He arrived in a batch yesterday afternoon. His name is Nico van der Kemp; take me to him.'

The dog pulled again at the handler's arm; the trooper held firm. 'Arrived yesterday you say? The fresh ones we put on heavy duties. He'll be digging foundations for the barracks. This way Commandant, sir.'

The trooper wheeled about, and trudged back towards the various buildings that were under construction. Some were near completion with roofs in place and wooden cladding being secured to the walls. Others were simply concrete plinths, waiting for the timber frames to be made. A stack of timber punctuated the site, a barrel of hot tar stood burning near one of the less complete buildings. Kessler and the detective kept a discrete distance from the snarls of their canine friend.

The trooper suddenly stopped at the edge of a concrete foundation. Groups of prisoners were busy nailing together timber to make sections of the frame for the hut under construction. Curls of black smoke drifted across from the adjacent barrel of tar.

'Nico van der Kemp,' the trooper shouted, 'which one of you is Nico van der Kemp?!'

The gang of bodies stopped working momentarily. A voice piped up from the middle of the group. 'I am van der Kemp.' Nico stood upright, putting his cement-covered spade to one side. He jumped down off the plinth and slid a few paces across the gloop, his clothes were already filthy and torn from the labour. He stopped in front of the trooper and took off his cloth cap.

'I am van der Kemp, sir,' he repeated.

Kessler flicked his eyes over the inmate, taking in every detail as he dragged on the last of his cigarette. 'Nico van der Kemp? You worked for Professor Mayer at the University of Leipzig?'

'Yes, sir.' Nico began to shiver, suddenly registering the cold through the remains of his brown woollen shirt. His black trousers were ripped at the knees, revealing a congealed wound on one of the kneecaps. Bruises marked his face.

Kessler revelled in the prisoner's discomfort, but kept a blank expression. 'You are a Jew and have spoken out against the Party?'

'Sir, no I...'

Kessler slapped him hard across the face. 'Did I give you permission to speak?!' He abruptly punched the inmate in the gut.

Nico curled up towards the floor, holding his gut and gasping for breath. Suddenly, Kessler gave a well-placed kick with his heel, sending Nico sprawling face first in the mud. The dog snarled.

Kessler flicked his spent cigarette end at the prisoner. 'Now answer, yes or no. Did you work for Professor Mayer?' He rammed a boot home into the side of Nico's ribs.

'Argghh! Yes! Yes!' Nico squirmed onto his back trying to fight the pain.

Kessler placed a boot on his chest, pinning him to the floor.

'Fucking marvellous! An intellectual Jew!'

The trooper and detective laughed nervously.

'Your Professor Mayer has been seen working very late at the University. What is so interesting to keep him at his desk half the night?'

'Err... I don't know, sir. He simply likes his work...'

Kessler interrupted with his boot. 'Indeed, as you can see, I enjoy my work!' He gave another kicking. 'But, I don't spend half the night in my office!'

'Arghh! Please, sir! I don't know, we are just physicists.'

'Tell me something I don't know!' Kessler suddenly grabbed Nico by the scruff and dragged him towards the barrel of tar. The trooper and detective followed, casting glances between each other.

'You are all the bloody same! Too intellectual for your own good! Well, not any more!' He dumped Nico unceremoniously against the side of the hot barrel.

'Arghh!' A splash of the scolding liquid spilt over the lip of the barrel, catching Nico's right hand. He cushioned the wound with his left, hyperventilating against the searing pain.

'Why is Mayer working so late?!'

'Please, sir! I don't know, some new calculations! Really, I don't know!'

Kessler gave his companions a withering look. 'Hold him down.'

'What?' The detective struggled to compute the request.

'Hold him down! Open his shirt!'

The detective glanced nervously at the trooper, then back at Kessler. 'Commandant... I... '

'Get on with it!'

The subordinates duly complied by heaving their victim onto the edge of the nearest pile of wood. They ripped open his shirt, and each held an arm down across a convenient length of timber with their heels. The dog jumped and snapped at the prisoner. The trooper only just held the dog short of its target.

Kessler picked up a bucket of tar and a brush from the side of the barrel. Acrid smoke drifted from the vessel, heat radiated from the tar-encrusted metal bucket. He walked slowly towards the prisoner, making a theatrical show of dipping the brush into the volcanically hot liquid. He knelt on a log, being careful to keep his distance from the canine, and dangled the brush over Nico's chest.

The handler pulled the dog to heel.

'Let me refresh your memory.'

'No, please! I... No! Please!'

Kessler dabbed the brush onto bare flesh.

'Arghh! Arghhh!'

The tar set quickly, cooking the underlying pectoral muscle.

Kessler dipped the brush again, applying it to the other side of the Jew's chest.

'No! Arghhhh! Arghhhh!' Nico bucked violently.

'What is your Professor doing?'

'I don't know! Arghhh! Probably some calculations on fuels! His normal work!'

Kessler shook his head and wiped the hot brush across his victim's stomach.

'Arghh! Arghh!' Nico thrashed.

Kessler waited for the pain to take full effect, then continued. 'Now, last chance... what is so interesting about Professor Mayer's work? Why is he so busy? Why is he meeting colleagues in the middle of the night?!'

He dabbed the brush again.

'Arghh! Arghh! I don't know! Christ! I would tell you if I did! But I just don't know!' Nico sobbed.

Kessler weighted up the response. It was a lot of pain, and most would have talked freely by now. Perhaps the young prodigy really didn't know what his boss was up to? It seemed that way. But what should he do with the young scientist? It would be easy to dispatch him now.

Kessler gave the brush a good coating in the boiling tar, and moved towards Nico's face.

'No! No, please! I'll do anything... anything at all!' Nico bucked, but was unable to break free. Kessler grabbed his chin, holding the brush firmly over his eye, he paused.

On the other hand, this Jew might be useful in the short term, and he could always kill him later. How many men had he murdered? He could not remember – save the first one – his own father. The old man had it coming, and died fairly easily for a war hero. He could still feel his father's blood-soaked iron cross turning over in his hand. It had been a pivotal moment: from that day he'd wanted an iron cross of his own.

Kessler snapped back to reality as a drip of tar landed in Nico's eye.

'Arghhh! Arghhh! Please!' Nico snorted snot and tears.

Yes, he could live for now.

Pleased with his morning's work, Kessler headed back to the car. So, Mayer was working on something secret, skulking around the city after dark, and keeping things from his own staff. Interesting, very interesting – it was clearly time to pick up Professor Mayer – catching him in the act on one of his nocturnal strolls.

CHAPTER 5

Brown Shirts

Einstein reflected quietly on his friend's work as he added his final comments to the margins. It was magnificent, a work of pure genius. The pencil notes were just finishing touches. It was a groundbreaking piece of science; but it was also dangerous, very dangerous.

Einstein looked up from his desk and smiled. 'Well, well, well, Gustav… your mathematical proof is beyond compare. You should publish it of course.'

Mayer stopped pacing up and down the study and exhaled. 'Albert, are you mad?! I don't think the world is ready for this. At least not now, not with things as they are in Germany.' Mayer rubbed his forehead, and shook his head. 'No Albert, this is a bad idea.'

Einstein's expression suddenly hardened. 'You *must* let the whole world know of this new carbon technology and its application to propulsion systems. This represents a step-change in human capabilities.'

Mayer whispered in a harsh tone. 'Albert, people *are* disappearing, and who knows what the National Socialists would do with this technology? They *cannot* have this… they *must not* have this technology.'

Einstein sat firmly, with his arms crossed. 'That is *precisely* why the world should know. It would be dangerous for any one individual, or nation, to keep this a secret. However, think of the future. It is worth the risk: the chance to alter the course of human history for the better.'

'Or to destroy... total annihilation!' Mayer reeled at the thought of handing his work over to the Nazis, but Einstein was also right. On the one hand, it could do a great deal of good for mankind: creating new lives and futures, spawning commerce and industry. There was more – much more! Mankind *could* literally reach for the stars. However, the alternatives were devastating.

'Albert, what if the technology got into the wrong hands?'

'With this device, and appropriate modifications, it could enhance existing weapons. Rockets could go into space and be used to target anywhere on the planet in an instant.' Einstein rubbed his chin, choosing his words carefully, '... Or used to find new ways to unlock the energy of the atom. You've heard the rumours about the heavy elements like uranium... ' Einstein furrowed his brow and, rubbing his temple, he exhaled, '... or something much worse. A new weapon based on the limitless and uncontrolled release of energy from your device itself. An army would be truly invincible. The destruction of one's enemies would be assured. The owner of your device, with a few adjustments and upgrades, could simply dominate the planet.'

Mayer gasped. 'My God, my God! There are plenty of madmen out there with world domination in mind... Stalin... you've heard the rumours of mass murder in the Soviet Union. Then, there's Herr Hitler.'

'Gustav, then we are in agreement. The political situation is too unstable to risk one group, or nation, having exclusive access to this knowledge.'

'But what should I do?' Mayer conceded. 'Human nature has a habit of turning ugly; the risks are too high.'

Einstein shrugged. 'You have a simple choice my friend: share this knowledge on the international stage so that stewardship of the technology becomes the responsibility of all nations; or admit the idea is just too much for mankind right now and bury it. Hide it away forever.'

'Albert, knowledge can't be undone… I… I would have to burn my notes, destroy the manuscript. Dispose of everything, so there was no trace or record of my work.'

'Yes, you would,' Einstein nodded.

'But that would leave only one source of information: me!' Mayer shuddered at the notion. Would he talk if he was tortured?

'Gustav, going public is the correct course of action. Think of all the good it will bring; it is new science, a frontier. You must publish your manuscript.'

'No, it's not safe. The Nazis are controlling every printing press in Germany. We would be picked up by the security forces in an instant.'

'Then we should go to a mainstream publisher overseas. Write it up in English and ensure they publish it quickly. It *can* be done.'

'Albert, no! Besides, what makes you think it would be any different elsewhere? We don't know how long the reach of the Nazis will stretch.'

'We can go to England.'

'What? But how?! I can't even get to the main street without being questioned or followed!' Mayer sagged.

Einstein stood and touched his friend gently on the shoulder. '*You* can't go, but *I can*.'

'Albert, you would do that for me?'

'Yes, I am reasonably well known, and would be missed by friends in the international community; some with significant political standing. The Nazis would have a hard time explaining my disappearance.'

Mayer shook his head. 'No Albert, I should not put you in danger. I am sorry, I cannot ask this of you.'

'There is a meeting of the Physics Society in Oxford. We could present your work there… ' Einstein paused to let his friend digest the information. 'It is a big decision, only you and

I know about this technology.' Mayer did not need reminding, they both knew things were at a pivotal point. 'But, once we present this theory… this new technology, there will be no going back… '

Both men stared at each other, firm lines etched on their faces.

Einstein finally broke the silence.

'Gustav, be brave. The world's media will be present in Oxford, and the paper could be delivered simultaneously to governments around the world.'

'Alright… alright. I agree.' Mayer closed his eyes and prayed that he had made the right decision. Then another realisation hit home. 'Albert, the authorities here will pick me up as soon as this goes public. I need to get out of Germany!'

'Yes, and where would you hide for the rest of your life? No, the Nazis will have no power over you once the information is published.'

Mayer's face drained to an ashen grey colour. 'If I follow that logic, the moment after the press release I would make no difference to them. I could be murdered all the same.'

The click of the door latch and a sudden crack of light announced Professor Mayer's emergence on to the street. He pulled up his collar and, clutching his leather satchel close to his chest, headed up the street in a strange zigzag. He kept to the shadows, and with his stomach churning, tried to get a good pace going, despite the rain. Taking a precautionary detour, rather than the direct route home, suddenly seemed like a bad idea.

After a few hundred metres, he glanced back down the street: a lone figure followed.

A Brown Shirt?!

Bile moved up into his gullet, and a burning sensation filled his chest. He erupted in sweat, despite the chill and increased the pace to get round the next street corner. He stopped, and, using the cover of a hedgerow, squinted back down the hill into the drizzle; but it was no good. The figure was too far away to tell. Was it a Brown Shirt or not? He risked waiting a few more seconds.

No, not a Brown Shirt, but a tall man in a dark grey overcoat. Even worse! Gestapo?

Mayer turned, lengthening his stride along the pavement, and with his heart pounding, nausea filled his belly. After a hundred metres or so, he risked another look over his shoulder. The figure had just turned the street corner!

Mayer took the next left. Still sweating and with his throat on fire, the pain in his chest got worse. Regardless, he broke into a jog. It was a bad decision – the pain intensified – and the left turn narrowed quickly into an alleyway, strewn with rubbish bins and old packing crates.

What would he say if the authorities stopped him here?

A fresh wave of crushing discomfort filled his rib cage. His mouth went dry as he fought against rapid shallow breathing. Mayer collapsed into a doorway clutching his chest. The rain intensified to a heavy shower. He closed his eyes and tried to take deep breaths, regretting his decision to be out on the street at night.

More deep breaths, in, out… slowly… slowly.

His head started to clear. He listened to the rain clattering off assorted metal dustbins. It was impossible to hear anything else, but the weather was somehow comforting. His heart rate began to steady. He stood up, using the doorway for support, and poked his head around the wall.

Thank God! He's gone. No sign of anyone.

Mayer squinted into the lashing rain. There was no point hanging about.

He stepped onto the narrow cobbles, and stumbled to the far end of the alleyway. He glanced around the corner.

All clear.

He moved quickly onto the pavement, walking, then almost jogging at times, for two blocks parallel to the main street.

Breathing heavily, he peered around the next corner.

A patrol!

Mayer dashed backwards for a few metres and, falling off the kerb, he landed hard into the gutter. Pain shot through his shoulder. Still clasping his satchel, icy rainwater flooded down his back. His diaphragm gave a spasm. He coughed.

Ignoring the discomfort, he gingerly placed the satchel upright on the relative dry of the pavement. He rolled over onto his belly, and started to get up.

Two Brown Shirts appeared on the street corner.

Mayer dropped flat into the gutter, lying motionless, the cold water soaking through his shirt.

The Brown Shirts looked tall and athletic; each man wore a pistol, and held a large cosh. Predatory eyes systematically scanned the junction for any signs of disturbance. One of the men produced a flashlight.

The beam edged down the street towards his position. Mayer pressed himself as low as possible against the kerbstone, ignoring the gurgling rainwater washing through his clothing.

The patrol paused as the light picked up his silhouette.

Mayer screamed and buried his face into the cobbles. Paralysed by the torch beam, his body turned to jelly.

Suddenly, he heard something.

Whistling? Yes, someone is whistling a tune?

Mayer raised his eyes slightly from the gutter and, holding one hand to shield his vision from the bright light, he took in the scene perplexed. The tune – he recognised it.

It's a Long Way to Tipperary?

The grey-coated figure stood whistling on a street corner, opposite the Brown Shirts. They turned to meet his gaze. The grey-coated man stepped casually into the street, still whistling as he sauntered towards the patrol. The man suddenly threw his coat back and in one fluid movement, the nearest Brown Shirt dropped to the floor.

Mayer gasped.

The Brown Shirt momentarily coughed blood around the knife protruding from his neck, and then went limp.

The second Brown Shirt dropped his torch. It clattered on the cobbles, but somehow remained alight, casting a spotlight over the deadly scene.

Mayer gulped in air, transfixed by the spectacle.

The whistling continued.

The remaining Brown Shirt fumbled for his pistol and, realising he wasn't going to make it, turned to run.

The thud of the second knife struck home. The Brown Shirt stopped sharp, shuddering as the blade penetrated his back. He keeled over face first onto the wet cobbles, motionless.

Mayer rubbed his eyes, blinking. He rubbed them again to clear the rainwater from his face.

The grey-coated figure nonchalantly placed a boot on the first Brown Shirt's chest, and recovered his knife from the man's throat. He wiped the blade clean on the corpse. He wandered over to the second body, collecting the second blade. He flipped up his coat, and stowed the weapons.

Mayer gulped back his terror and wretched into the gutter as the grey-coated man turned towards him.

The man simply stood there and, with a tip of his non-existent hat, resumed his tuneful rendition of the Tipperary song.

The man's voice suddenly commanded clearly in well-spoken German through the rain. 'Go home.'

The Tipperary song resumed, drifting away into the night as the man disappeared around the street corner.

Mayer lay stunned in the gutter.

What just happened? My God!

He waited, shivering. Would the man come back? He decided to stay put for another ten seconds. He counted in his head.

Nothing.

He rolled to his feet, grabbing his bag as he stood. He hobbled to the far end of the street, and turned the corner like a frightened rabbit. He found himself back onto the main road. Recognising the location, and with no sign of the mysterious figure, Mayer turned downhill, heading for home and the University campus as briskly as he could manage.

Mayer moved down the path into the courtyard outside the Physics Department, still clutching his now sodden leather satchel. He glanced back and forth, shaking as he fumbled with his keys. The door suddenly gave, he slipped inside the lobby, being careful to close the door. He leant against the woodwork, taking deep breaths, thankful to be off the street and out of the rain. Then, overcome with a sudden dread, he ran up the stairs to his office.

Mayer threw his soaking-wet coat onto the hat stand, and heaved the leather satchel onto his desk. He slumped, dripping into the chair, numbed by the evening's events. Who was the grey-coated figure? Why did he kill the Brown Shirts? What did he want?

Mayer rubbed the flats of his palms across his face, massaging some warmth back into his cheeks. He stared at the leather satchel. Did his manuscript have anything to do with it? Maybe?

Finding a sudden resolve, Mayer opened the bag, and gently removed the completed scientific paper. It was a work of art, a thing of beauty. He caressed the pages, marvelling at the elegant equations and logic steps, this really was a milestone that would change the world. He had been so careful, and the last few days had been well spent meticulously re-typing the pages that Einstein had marked for corrections. It *was* perfect.

But where to hide it?

Keep it safe, Einstein's words echoed through his mind.

Locking it away in his desk drawer would be secure, but also the first place the authorities would look. Hiding the manuscript amongst the many books and papers on the shelves of the office was too risky. The laboratory was out of the question: too many students. His apartment on campus was too obvious; the authorities were certain to look there.

Where should he conceal it?

Somewhere safe where it will not be disturbed, somewhere that no one else is likely to look.

Mayer looked around the office for inspiration. The bottom of the bookcase caught his eye, raised just half an inch from the floor by some ornately carved mahogany feet.

Perfect!

He quickly sealed the manuscript in an unmarked brown envelope; almost with indecent haste. Then, with the greatest precision, as if making an offering to the Gods, he carefully slid the envelope underneath the bookcase.

He stood back and inspected his handiwork. The manuscript seemed to be well hidden; he couldn't see it, even when stooping. He ran his finger under the edge of the bookcase – nothing – all cleverly concealed in a place that only he was likely to find.

Mayer, pleased that the deed was done, grabbed his coat and headed for the door, pausing momentarily to switch off the lights. He carefully locked the door, checking the handle twice. Patting his waistcoat pocket to confirm the office key was secure, his thoughts turned to the welcome comfort of his own bed.

In the twilight, the earlier draft of the manuscript containing the pencil mark corrections from Einstein sat neatly on top of a pile of papers; right next to the typewriter and in plain view for anyone to find.

CHAPTER 6

Theft

Commandant Kessler stared at the visa application with suspicion. It was from Professor Einstein – a request to leave Germany for England, and then onto the United States of America on some lecture tour. What should he do? The timing was definitely suspect, but then it might also be very convenient. He could just process the visa application in the normal way. After all, one of the administrative roles of his office was to complete such tasks for the districts of Leipzig; and with an internationally renowned University in the city, such applications were not uncommon.

Or he could deny the visa, but that might draw unwanted attention.

The visa application contained a supporting letter. It was an invitation from the Royal Society, inviting Einstein to attend a physics conference being held at Oxford University. Kessler held it up against the light: definitely official-looking notepaper embossed with a logo. It probably wasn't a forgery.

But what should he do? On the one hand, it was an opportunity to get a potential troublemaker out of the way for a while; for several months in fact. But on the other hand, Einstein was known to speak openly against the political situation in Germany; and while he was careful not to specifically direct adverse comments at the Nazi Party, the inference was there.

Kessler made his decision. It was better to have Einstein out of the way.

He called in his orderly to process the visa application immediately, with the necessary stamps and signatures. It would eliminate any administrative foul ups and get Einstein on his journey.

'The morning post, sir... ' the orderly handed over a pile of envelopes, '... and this has just come in. It's a telegram from Berlin.'

Kessler opened the telegram and sat bolt upright in his chair as he read the contents.

'Detain Professor Gustav Mayer for questioning. STOP. Hold in isolation until further orders from Admiral Dönitz. STOP. Immediate action. STOP.'

Kessler smiled; things were looking up; two pieces of good news in the same morning. He could get shot of two troublesome academic types in one go.

'Corporal! Have my car ready at once and include an armed motorcycle escort.' There was no time like the present.

The orderly clicked his heels in acknowledgement, and dropped what remained of the morning post back into the in-tray as he headed for the door. A trip out in the car was always more interesting than shuffling paper. He attended to his new task with gusto.

Kessler considered the situation. Professor Mayer was in his late fifties, and would not present any problems. It would be a simple matter – his car with two police officers, a few minutes to quietly collect the Professor from his office at the University. There would be no fuss, and the Professor would be detained. The motorcycle escort would deter the Professor from doing a runner on foot.

But where to put him? The most pragmatic solution, and low profile, would be house arrest. The Professor could be detained at his own home until the orders from Berlin were clarified. It was odd that such a senior figure in the Reich Chancellery was interested in Mayer. Admiral Karl Dönitz was a highly respected naval officer. He had come to fame for his gallant service on the cruiser *Breslau* in 1914, and had been instrumental in bringing Turkey into the Great War. He was a brilliant commander – but that was at odds with the situation – why was an academic of importance to a navy man like Dönitz?

Kessler hurried down the stairs to the waiting escort. His orderly revved the engine of the brand new Daimler to warm it up. Kessler paused at the passenger door, and used his reflection in the gleaming metal to adjust his uniform: it was important to look neat and authoritative when making an arrest.

The Daimler fitted his status with a very spacious interior. The rear of the car was divided from the driver by a glass screen to give the passengers some extra privacy. One could ask probing questions in private. It was all part of the show. Kessler opened the door and was greeted by the rich smell of polished leather. He took a seat. A police officer was already waiting in the back for him.

'So glad you could make it, Detective,' sneered Kessler.

The detective ignored the sarcastic tone of his superior; he knew his place in the pecking order. 'Not at all, where are we going?'

Kessler tapped on the dividing glass impatiently. 'Drive!' He didn't bother answering the detective's question. The local police were under the control of the Party, but nonetheless, Kessler liked to take the precaution of giving minimal information.

The journey to the University only took a few minutes, and the car stopped directly outside the front door of the Physics Department. Kessler stepped quickly out of the car, without waiting for his orderly or the detective, and walked briskly into the lobby. His steel toe-capped boots echoed on the flagstone floor, announcing their arrival. A quick inspection of the notice board identified the Professor's office on the first floor. Kessler headed for the stairs.

Mayer sat at his desk, absently doodling on the notepad. His shoulder throbbed. He rubbed his aching muscles, and exhaled.

It had been a close-run thing. Wandering the streets at night like that… how could he have been so stupid?! He dropped the pen on the desk, and rubbed his eyes with his palms. He took a deep breath and gave a long slow exhalation.

It didn't help.

Things *were* too dangerous. Who was the strange figure last night? Not a Nazi judging by the way he dispatched the two Brown Shirts, but what did he want? The damned Brown Shirts! They prowled everywhere. There were more guards on the campus now; and where was Nico?

Poor Nico.

It was certain the authorities had him. He'd been gone nearly two days now. It was only a matter of time before they came asking questions.

Mayer gazed at the photograph on his desk. She'd had an inner strength, his beloved Sophia. How she had thrashed on the bed, defiant, as the fever took hold. Her blue-green eyes burned into his soul as he held her clammy, blanched hands.

Suddenly, the door burst open.

'Good day Professor Mayer.'

A neatly dressed German officer stood in the doorway, smiling. Seconds later, two other men appeared, one in a corporal's uniform, the other in a dark suit. The three men formed an intimidating reception committee.

Mayer swallowed down his fear. Who were they? What did they want? It seemed best to do nothing and play ignorant. He remained seated at his desk, frozen to the spot.

'Good afternoon Commandant, forgive me, how can I help?' Mayer, struggling to maintain his composure, forced a polite smile.

'Let me say for now that your assistance is needed.' Kessler swaggered forward towards the desk; proximity was always more intimidating.

'I see, well… er… what assistance can I give?'

'If you would accompany me, please… ' Kessler gestured politely, but with authority.

Mayer, seeing that he had no choice, started to rise from his chair. Suddenly his heart missed a beat – the draft manuscript – on his desk! Mayer coughed in a vain attempt to draw attention away from the papers. Involuntarily, Mayer glanced down at the manuscript.

Kessler registered the concern. His eyes darted around the room. What was it? His eyes scanned the shelves and desk area for anything out of the ordinary – nothing. Kessler went with his gut instinct: something was out of place. The Professor was agitated, for sure, but there was also fear.

Mayer decided to play the bumbling academic. 'Let me get my coat.' He fumbled with his jacket. At least it would buy some time to think.

Suddenly a plan popped into his head, idiotic, but worth the risk.

He feigned a coughing fit and theatrically struggled into his coat. It flapped about, taking a perfect arc over the desk. Piles of papers cascaded across the floor. With seemingly lightning reflexes Mayer grabbed handfuls of the papers and dumped them back on the desk. It did the job; the manuscript was now at least hidden in an anonymous pile.

'Professor… ' Kessler gestured his impatience by offering Mayer the door.

He didn't bother to introduce the detective, or the orderly. They simply fell in on either side of Mayer and marched him briskly to the waiting car.

The orderly opened the rear passenger door of the Daimler, the detective climbed in first. Kessler pressed close to the Professor. The body language was enough for Mayer to understand that he was to get in next. Kessler stepped into the car, quickly bringing up the rear, to ensure his guest was sandwiched in the back with no chance of escape. The orderly took to the driver's seat and with typical efficiency started the engine and closed the cab window to give his Commandant some privacy.

A crushing chest pain and the taste of bile rose in Mayer's throat. He breathed deeply through his nostrils, forcing an outward facade of calm; but the illusion wasn't working.

Kessler came to an easy conclusion. The Professor wasn't just scared, he *was* hiding something. The furrowed brow, the small beads of sweat forming on his temple, and the look in his eyes – yes, the eyes – they always gave the truth away.

Kessler decided to let him stew in his own thoughts. The silence would make his captive uncomfortable for a while, and then there would be some small talk to give his prey some sense of security. He knew all the tricks of the trade when it came to softening up a prisoner for interrogation. It was a matter of psychology, tailoring the approach to the psyche of the individual. If that didn't work, some straightforward pain and suffering would always do the trick. Kessler was mildly amused by the idea; there would be plenty of time for the interrogation.

Mayer stared despondently at his surroundings. The interview room, if you could call it that, sat deep in the bowels of the district headquarters. Things were not looking good. Everything about the room screamed interrogation. The cold tiled floor, the spartan furnishings of just a small table and two chairs was all very functional. Then there was the waiting. How long had he been here now? It was hard to tell – they had taken his watch – no doubt all part of the process of softening him up. Well, it was working! The guard had made a show of firmly locking the door; the iron grill on the window confirmed things. There was no means of escape. The orderly was still on duty outside the door. The telltale noise of shuffling feet, and the click of a heavy rifle butt on the floor gave his position away.

The situation could not be any worse.

Mayer gazed at the floor in a fit of depression and wished he hadn't: bloodstains! The pinky red discoloration in the grouting of the floor tiles told an ugly story. He wanted it to be floor polish, but it wasn't. God only knew how many beatings had taken place in this room. The crushing pain returned to his chest as he began to hyperventilate.

Kessler's tactics were proceeding exactly as planned. He skipped down the stairs into the basement. The Professor had been wallowing for some hours now. Things would start with the usual cryptic questions to further unsettle the captive – then who knows what next?

Kessler entered the room. Mayer sat compliant in a chair at the small wooden table.

'Ahh… Professor Mayer… Professor Mayer… Gustav isn't it?' It is always more effective to extract information if one is on first name terms with the captive. It was just another standard procedure from the Interrogator's Handbook.

'How long have you lived at your address?' asked Kessler. Mayer replied.

'And you have worked for the University all this time?'

'Some twenty years. Most of my working life.'

'So Professor, tell me, when were you last in Berlin?'

'Let me see… a meeting at the University there, about two years ago.' Mayer was being truthful; he really could not remember the exact time of his last visit.

'And who do you know in Berlin?'

'Just my fellow academics at the University. A small group of physicists, some engineers and a few chemists.'

'So please explain why I should get this from Berlin!' Kessler hissed as he showed the Professor the telegram.

Mayer flushed with sweat. Was he about to become another statistic? Another disappearance? It wasn't looking good.

'I am sorry Commandant, please… I am just an academic…

I teach at the University. I do not know.' Mayer realised he was grovelling, but decided to put life ahead of dignity; at least for now.

Kessler raised his voice for a controlled effect. 'Again! Who do you know in Berlin?!'

'Only my colleagues at the University, they are just academics like me. Please, I really don't know what this is about!'

'I want names! Who do you know? How long have you known them?'

Mayer tried to comply, giving the names of one or two old colleagues in Berlin who could vouch for him: the Head of Physics, and a couple of engineers. The Commandant would find them anyway, so he risked nothing by giving some names.

Kessler lowered his voice, but kept the tone firm. 'What did you last speak of with your colleagues?'

'Only engineering matters, our last meeting was to discuss some mathematics of projectiles, and the energy content of different fuels. We just discussed the things we would normally talk about… ' Mayer was telling the truth.

'So, why do I get such requests from Berlin?!' shouted Kessler.

'Please, I am just an academic… I do not know.'

'Professor… ' Kessler paused for effect. 'I am trying to help you, but I cannot help if you do not answer my questions. What have you been doing in Berlin?!'

'I have only visited the University to discuss physics. That is all. Our meetings take place every two years. The University of Berlin is one of the venues we use for our scientific meetings as part of the physics community. This is well known, it takes place in Berlin every other year. You can check with the University… ' Mayer babbled.

'We will Professor… we will… ' Kessler played the menace. Satisfied that his prisoner was suitably softened up, it was time to try a different tack to extract information. Kessler adopted a calm and caring tone. Always test the prisoner; then be their friend.

'Professor, tell me, what you are working on now?'

'Um... err... just the usual things. Some work on fuel combustion... and... and on the aerodynamics of projectiles.'

Kessler smiled. The Professor was lying, but why would he lie? Kessler pondered the situation for a few seconds before asking the next question.

'Tell me about fuels, Professor... do you like to see things burn?' Kessler lit a match and held it close to the Professor's face; close enough so that he would feel the heat, but without burning his skin. There would be plenty of time for that later. He blew out the match, smoke went into Mayer's eyes.

'Fuels! Professor, what can you tell me about fuels?!' The nasty tone was back with a vengeance.

'We are researching high energy fuels, the idea that a fuel can have a high burn rate but still remain stable when it's stored. We are just working on the safety of new aviation fuels. It is just a practical problem for engineers.' Mayer knew he was replying to save his life.

Kessler expertly read the situation. This time Mayer was telling the truth, but why the initial hesitation? No matter, they could play this game for hours, question after question until the Professor was tired. Men make mistakes when they are fatigued. He would find out what was really going on.

'Aviation fuel? I don't think so! I have done my homework too Professor.'

'Yes, well... I mean... the fuel is high octane... volatile... it can be used for many types of high-speed propulsion.'

'Propulsion? Sounds interesting, what kind of propulsion?!' Kessler suddenly lashed out, thumping the table.

Mayer flinched. 'Rockets! The funding is for rocket fuels... ' Gasping a breath, Mayer stared down at the table, shoulders slouching.

'So Professor, we know about fuels, and we know about projectiles… what did you call them? Rockets? But I sense there is something else?'

'I have told you again and again, I am just a humble physicist working on an engineering problem and when I am not doing that I am teaching the students at the University. Please, I am just an academic… please… I have told you everything I know.' Mayer sunk back into the chair even further.

'Tell me about your colleagues.' Kessler gave a theatrical pause. 'I understand you know Professor Einstein?' He searched Mayer's face for the telltale signs of deception.

'Yes, I know him. He is a visitor in our Physics Department.' Mayer used all his resolve to give a bland but accurate answer.

'So, you work together?'

'We discuss physics together, as I do with many other colleagues in my department.' Another factually correct answer.

'Very good Professor, that will do for now.' Kessler smiled, and with a snap of his fingers, the orderly opened the door. Kessler marched out the door as briskly as he came. Mayer slumped forward in the chair, with his forehead almost on the table, and tried to breathe.

The orderly snapped to attention, after locking the door.

'No food for the prisoner, no water, no toilet – are we clear?'

'Yes sir.' A crisp salute followed.

Kessler went back to his office, and sat at his desk. There was plenty of time. The Professor would be uncomfortable soon enough. He was telling the truth about his job and his visits to Berlin. But he was also holding something back, and the occasional lie during the interview confirmed this. Perhaps headquarters would reveal some more background in due course? In the meantime, it was worth having the Professor's office searched. Despite the late hour, Kessler dispatched a squad to the University.

The grey man knelt outside the office door and gave a quick glance at the wooden plaque: 'Professor G. Mayer'. At least it was the right place. He tensed on the doorknob, it turned partially and then stopped – locked.

A subtle change in air pressure brushed the hairs on the back of his neck. He froze, and stared down the long first-floor corridor of the Physics Department, but saw nothing moving. He scanned the doorways for activity. They looked all the bloody same, but still no movement. He closed his eyes to listen.

It's just an old building, things creak.

He turned his attention back to the lock, and carefully inserted the skeleton key into the mechanism. Feeling the flex of the key, he inserted a thin strip of copper wire; then tried the key again. It still wasn't right. He eased a second strip of wire gently into the lock; then applied pressure on the key, flexing his wrist trying to feel the mechanism.

Why the hell won't the door open?

The door gave a sudden loud click. The grey man froze.

Nothing.

He applied gentle pressure to the doorknob, and slowly eased the door ajar. Moonlight flooded the door frame, revealing the shape of the room. Holding his breath, he quietly slipped into the room, closing the door behind him.

Crouching behind the door, breathing gently, he listened.

His vision gradually adjusted to the moonlight. Scanning the room, details of the layout started to come into grainy focus. It was a fairly typical academic office; an untidy desk in front of the fireplace, the shelves covering the walls were heaped with books, and piles of papers sat everywhere. This was going to take a while.

Moving off cautiously, instinctively rolling his feet to gently apply his weight on the old floorboards, he scanned the room for anything obvious. A first pass revealed nothing. He picked up a paper from the desk and squinted at the text. The words just danced in the haze. He produced a small torch from his pocket and, using his fingers to partly cover the bulb, he switched it on. A small glowing beam revealed the contents of the page. A student's essay – great – how was he meant to find the all-important documents amongst this crap? He grabbed the next piece of paper; the torch reported nothing interesting.

This could take forever and the place is crawling with sentries!

A systematic three-dimensional search was the only way to be sure; efficient and methodical. He treated the room like a big box, mentally dividing it up into one-metre cubes. The deal was straightforward; you searched the room a cube at a time taking in everything from floor to ceiling. He started on the first mentally constructed cube. The orders from London were clear: find the manuscript that the Professor was working on and make sure you find it first! No pressure then. The bureaucrats in Whitehall really didn't have a clue. The first few cubes revealed nothing. He shrugged it off and moved on, but the clock was ticking with only two hours to sunrise.

He focused on the next mental cube: an ornate bookcase. His eyes, starting on the bottom shelf, flicked from left to right. More bloody books! Suddenly, the lip of the bottom shelf caught his eye. *What's this?*

He rubbed his fingers along the rim, revealing a clump of dust. Then, down on all fours, he carefully shone the light under the bookcase – and stopped dead.

A solitary crisp brown envelope, and stuffed with something?

He moved the torchlight around the envelope and tracked the skirting board at the back of the bookcase. Nothing, at least no wires he could see. The envelope looked smooth and flat, with no telltale protrusion of a timing device or detonator; but there was only one way to find out.

He carefully lifted the envelope, shining the torch underneath it. He held his breath – no explosion. Pocketing the torch, he carefully slid the envelope out from under the bookcase. He pressed gently with his fingertips around the edges of the envelope.

Nothing suspicious so far, perhaps it's just paper?

He flicked open his pen knife, and opened the envelope; not at the seal, but by rolling back the front cover, just like opening a can of sardines. The first rule of counterespionage: never use the main entrance. He smiled to himself – a manuscript. A quick scan of the pages didn't help much, just meaningless numbers and equations, but it had to be the right document. Why else hide it under a bookcase?

He carefully placed the envelope into the inside pocket of his grey coat.

There was one last task.

It took a few seconds to find an identical blank envelope. He stuffed it with paper, taking care to achieve the same thickness and weight, then placed it in exactly the same position under the bookcase. To the untrained eye at least, the room would appear exactly as he had found it.

He moved back to the desk, making a final sweep across the room. Everything seemed in order. Then, something on the desk caught his attention. Fishing for the torch, he switched on the beam.

This cannot be?! A document with the same title page?

He flicked through the first few pages. It looked the same; only there were lots of pencil marks on the margins.

Suddenly the distant clank of keys, and locks turning, echoed down the corridor. Visitors!

Multiple footfalls, coming up the stairs from the lobby – and fast! At least four, maybe five men, definitely in boots.

The grey man did a double take at the papers in his hand.

Definitely the same as the manuscript in the envelope!

Boots approached the office door.

He grabbed the papers from the desk, stuffing them into his outside coat pocket, and headed for the window.

The latch gave after a heavy thump on the wooden frame, but the window opened under protest. Heaving himself onto the window sill, he glanced down at the silhouette of the bushes far below – not good – but then, not much choice.

The door burst open.

With the familiar sight of German uniforms out the corner of his eye, the grey man jumped to the deafening noise of automatic fire. Flecks of broken glass and masonry splintered across the window, as a searing pain erupted in his back.

Instinct took over as the ground rushed up to meet him; feet together, ready to take the impact, and roll. The bushes also did their job, and after bouncing off them, he hit the ground hard.

Breathing in deeply, his head jarred from the impact, he tried to move his legs – success – nothing seemed to be broken. He staggered to his feet, with pain lancing through his back.

The sound of distant shouting penetrated his skull.

Stooped in pain, he stumbled across the lawn, and glanced back down the footpath; shadows moved quickly in his direction. A dap of warm liquid soaked into his shirt. Escape and evasion were the priorities now. Holding onto the wound as best he could, he ploughed forward into the undergrowth. Twigs snapped under foot and, with branches tearing at his face, the grey man pushed for the perimeter.

The squad leader looked up at the broken window, sweating and panting. Broken glass crunched under his feet as he cocked his weapon. 'Find him! Two-man teams! Move it!'

With renewed vigour, men moved haphazardly around the lawn. 'You and you! Search over there!' Two teams scurried off towards the tree line. '… And you! Along the edge of the building: move!'

There was a slim chance their man was lying injured in the bushes.

The squad leader allowed his men to disperse. He bent

down, breathing heavily, trying to recover from the chase. A flap of paper came into view, and then another. He stooped into the bushes, recovering the two sheets. Typewritten text, equations and numbers stared back at him. He squinted at the paper in the poor light. It was hard to tell, but maybe there were pencil marks in the margins? Whatever it was seemed important.

The soldier folded the pages and placed them carefully in his tunic. At least his superiors would get the consolation prize of knowing what the intruder was trying to steal.

CHAPTER 7

London

Oliver Heinkel paced up the gangplank, coming to a stop expectantly on the grubby deck of the tramp steamer. His tall, lean, muscular physique, elegant good looks and neatly combed blond hair, were at odds with the surroundings. He surveyed the scene with contempt. Of course, security dictated that travelling at night would be best. At least the dilapidated wharf in the sidings of the busy industrial port of Hamburg would go unnoticed. He handed his bag over to the awaiting deckhand, but couldn't help curling up his nostrils at the stench of diesel oil and barrels of salted mackerel.

'If you would follow me please, sir.'

Heinkel dusted down the lapels of his jacket and checked the position of his silk tie as they walked. The deckhand moved busily along the starboard gangway and flung open a steel door leading to one of the berths. 'Thank you sir, this way.' He beckoned Heinkel inside and closed the door so his superior had some privacy.

The steel floor of the cabin vibrated in tune with the idle of the ship's engines. Heinkel automatically stooped to miss the sharp metal bulkheads. The robust smell of expensive cologne suddenly mingled with the stale air of the confined space. The narrow room contained two bunks and a small fold-out table with a slim, almost skeletal, German officer perched behind it.

'Dr Goebbels, I am… I am… honoured.' Heinkel tried to keep his facial expression formal to conceal his surprise.

'Forgive me, the location is a little unusual,' Goebbels

smiled. The brass buttons on his crisp tunic reflected in the electric light. 'I have your orders from High Command. In fact, from the Führer himself!'

'I am humbled. I am at the Führer's service of course.' Heinkel nodded a dignified salute and clicked his heels gently together.

Goebbels threw open a leather satchel, pulling out a thick manila file onto the desk. 'Study these documents – you're going back to America.' Goebbels suddenly hissed as he lowered his voice. '*It is time.*'

'Tell me Herr Doctor, will we hit the Americans where it hurts the most this time – Wall Street?'

'Of course… and more… much, much more.' Goebbels gave a sadistic smirk.

Heinkel nodded slowly. 'At last the waiting is over, I am ready to do my duty.'

'You are tasked with obtaining funds, substantial investment shall we say… in the interests of the Reich. Charm the rich Americans out of their money. Take advantage of their greed.'

'It will be done Herr Doctor.'

'That's not all. The Reich has lost far too many of its great intellectuals, engineers and physicists to the disgusting excesses of America. Bring back the technological advances that are rightfully ours!'

'Yes, Herr Goebbels, I already have some weapons technology in mind.'

'Good, I see you are prepared.' Goebbels unfolded a crisp white handkerchief from his breast pocket, and wiped his hands. He continued. 'Any German-American that will not return will be deemed a traitor… and we know what happens to traitors.'

'Of course, Herr Doctor, they will be dealt with most severely.' Heinkel gave a click of his heels.

'Everything is in the file.' Goebbels folded his handkerchief back up into an immaculate square and returned it to his pocket.

He looked Heinkel directly in the eye. 'Use your influence with these dim-witted Americans. Relieve them of their funds, steal their secrets, kills the ones that will not cooperate – kill them – kill them all!'

Sir Hugh Sinclair, head of the fledgling Secret Intelligence Service (SIS), considered the intelligence reports; it made grim reading. He stood at the head of the large ornate table in the cabinet office briefing room. The elegant fabric of his pinstriped suit, fresh from his tailor at Saville Row, easily accommodated his wiry frame. Hawk-like, he took in every detail of the men flanking each side of the oak monolith.

'Gentlemen, welcome.' The hubbub of the meeting room suddenly turned to silence. Sinclair had summoned his key field operatives and technical experts from SIS, and given the delicate political situation, the British Ambassador to South Africa, Lord Elgin-Smyth, also attended. General Gort, Commander of the British Army, sat next to the Ambassador.

'Gentlemen, I hope you have done your reading, this intelligence is fresh information courtesy of my man just back from Leipzig.' His sharp eyes flicked at the grey man, then went back to the report. Sinclair lifted the first page. 'The situation in Germany is deteriorating.'

All eyes focused on Sinclair.

'It is now clear that, since the Enabling Laws, Adolf Hitler has more or less complete control over the German people. Reports are coming in of Nazi brutality against minority groups. People are being murdered, and the police are doing nothing. In fact, it seems that some of the *disappearances* are being sanctioned by the state.'

'I agree,' the British Ambassador cut in with a polite smile, flashing his pristine white teeth momentarily, before pulling a gold pen from the pocket of his silk shirt. 'If you don't mind Sir Hugh... '

Sinclair shrugged, offering the floor to Elgin-Smyth.

'Gentlemen, the diplomatic situation could not be more fragile. The apparent lack of civil liberty in Germany is abhorrent. The idea of an undemocratic regime in any country bothers me. It's morally objectionable. Also, I fear it will create regional instability, and the last thing we need is another war in Europe.'

'I agree,' Sinclair nodded, 'and for that reason alone we are stepping up the number of field agents in Europe. The Prime Minister has already decided to support the democracies of Austria, Poland and others in Europe through diplomatic means. The intelligence services will, shall we say, supplement the diplomatic effort as and when required.'

Sinclair paused to pick up his pipe, he flicked a match into the bowl and took a couple of long slow drags to get the embers burning, then continued. 'Hitler has a security service, the newly formed SS, that seems to have no accountability to the army or police. We need to keep a close eye on this SS, and for all its lack of subtlety, it does seem to nurture a certain malevolence – and a new breed of German spies.'

'From a diplomatic viewpoint the German state and the judicial system seem to be one. That has to be bad news for the civilian population.' The Ambassador tapped his gold pen on the notepaper. 'This is why the Prime Minister is keen to open up diplomatic channels with Chancellor Hitler. We will be seeking assurances… '

'Thank you Mr Ambassador,' Sinclair took the chair. 'Gentlemen, nonetheless, it would be foolish of us not to increase our intelligence gathering within Germany. We cannot let the situation spill beyond Germany's borders, and we must understand the details of how this new regime is operating.'

'Our island is well protected.' General Gort crossed his arms, and scowled across the room. 'The army has reasonable reserves, albeit mostly inexperienced young men on their national service, but they're feisty and eager. If the Hun want to kick off again, we will be ready.' Sweat trickled from his short grey hair, running down his chubby face onto the over-starched shirt collar of his uniform.

'Sir, if I might make an observation… ' The grey man leant forward.

'Danny, go ahead… gentlemen, Major Nash has been our eyes and ears on the ground in Germany for some time.'

'Leipzig is crawling with German troops. These are not conscripts or boy soldiers, but in the main, seasoned professionals. The security services are utterly ruthless with the civilian population. I have personally witnessed summary executions; and in broad daylight. Both the regular army and the SS seem to be driven by a single purpose: to impose Hitler's ideology on the masses. The Nazi Party has become a ruthless killing machine. This situation is repeated in towns all over Germany as far as I can tell.'

Murmurs of disapproval went round the room.

Nash paused, absently rubbing his brow. 'My gut feeling tells me there's something else. I don't know exactly… the SS are showing a particular interest in civilian engineers and physicists, but for what purpose? It doesn't make any sense.'

'I dunno man, that would tie in with goings on in South Africa.' Rudy Temple, a weather-beaten and grizzled Africaan in his early fifties piped up. His muscular stocky frame stretched the fabric of his worn lumberjack-style shirt.

'Go on… ' Sinclair furrowed his brow.

'Yep, the bloody Germans are messing with us. What they do at home is their business; but there are too many of them running around the Transvaal these days. It's making some of the diamond traders a bit edgy; it's not good for business.'

The Ambassador nodded. 'I agree, it just isn't cricket. We're reliant on both the diamond and the precious metal trade in the region. The Germans are posturing, they want their old colony back – well they can't have it! At the end of the Great War, the reparations were very clear. German West Africa, or *Deutsch-Südwestafrika* as they liked to call it, became a British territory. The west-coast diamond trade and other mineral rights in the colony are ours.'

'But why do you think this is aggravating the Germans now?' Sinclair probed the Ambassador.

'I don't know. The influence of the National Socialists is spreading, they're finding sympathy with unsavoury types. Stirring up trouble in the colonies, as it were.'

'So what are the Nazis up to?' Sinclair spoke for everyone.

'The intelligence reports make some bloody interesting observations. Several reasonably senior figures from the Nazi Party have made journeys to Cape Town via banks in Geneva; but what the hell for? Anyways, the visits have been all too damned regular for my liking.' Temple spat his disgust, pausing to let the information sink in.

'Are these confirmed reports?' interrupted Sinclair.

'Yes,' the Ambassador nodded vigorously. 'Signals experts have deciphered the code used by the diplomatic arm of the Nazi Party. We know the dates of intended arrivals of party officials, and who they are; what's more they're bringing large amounts of gold with them.'

'Gold?' Sinclair stood upright.

'Yes, for several months now.'

'I've seen it myself,' Rudy Temple picked up the thread. 'I purchased one of the gold bars on the black market, Swastika stamp an' all. They're selling the stuff like it's going out of fashion.'

'Yes, but why are they selling gold?'

'Gentlemen, my diplomatic sources confirm some very large deposits of gold in the banks in Cape Town, and elsewhere. There is also evidence that the gold bars are being used to purchase supplies,' reported the Ambassador.

'Supplies? What kind of supplies?'

'All kinds of crap. Industrial materials, large quantities of chemicals.' Rudy Temple shook his head.

'If I may, Hugh. I have an inventory of some of the materials… ' the Ambassador flicked through his notes, '… including titanium, sodium permanganate, and mercury. Also… an assortment of dried goods… coffee beans, sugar, and the like.'

'Is there cause for concern about these industrial materials?'

'It's hard to tell. The materials could be used in construction, for any number of legitimate peace-time activities. The chemicals are a bit of a worry, but again, they could be used as catalysts in several industrial processes. It may all be legitimate,' concluded the Ambassador.

'Legitimate? I don't think so,' Nash shook his head. 'It doesn't stack up. These materials can be used for armaments, and the chemicals in the production of high explosives. I believe the Germans are up to something.'

'That may be so, but I don't understand; the Germans have access to minerals and they are in the heartland of European industry. Why get these materials from Southern Africa?' mused Sinclair.

'I would like to bloody know, that's for sure!' Rudy Temple pulled out a smoke and lit up.

'Alright, Rudy, we will need more intelligence on these activities in South Africa. Find out the connection to Berlin, it may be nothing more than state-sponsored money laundering, but we need to be mindful that such large quantities of gold might interfere with the money markets. Look for a motive.'

Temple nodded as he puffed on his cigarette.

'Major Nash, I need you back in Leipzig, find out what connects the SS to these chemicals; it must be some kind of technological ambition.'

The grey man acknowledged his orders.

'To work gentlemen, find the pieces of this Nazi puzzle.'

With that the meeting was over, and the assembled team began to disperse. Sinclair gathered his papers and waited for the men to file out the door, leaving Nash at the back of the queue.

'Danny, hold back a second… thanks.' Sinclair gave a gentle smile.

Nash hesitated.

The two men waited for the door to close. Silence engulfed the empty room. Nash dropped his heavy grey trench coat over the back of the nearest chair and exhaled.

'Emily is asking after you.' Sinclair gave a knowing look.

'It's been a while… ' Nash shuffled his feet involuntarily.

'Look, I know my own daughter. She can be stubborn at times, and I don't want to interfere; but while you're here in London… '

'Okay, okay! I get the message,' Nash raised his hands in mock surrender. 'She still at the Admiralty office?'

'Personal assistant to the first Lord of the Admiralty, no less.'

'Why doesn't that surprise me? It would take a woman like Emily to keep that cantankerous old git, Churchill, in line!'

'Just go and see her, that's all.' Sinclair raised an eyebrow.

'Okay, don't worry, I will.' Nash gave a wry smile as he picked up his grey coat. It was only a short hop on the number seven bus across town, and he had to face the music sometime… and it may as well be now.

A quick glance at the Rolex told him that everything was on schedule. That was just as well. Heinkel was bursting with inner pride at the task bestowed upon him by his beloved leader, Adolf Hitler. The Americans would be relieved of their wealth on a grand scale, but guile and cunning were needed. Subtly, insidiously, the USA would fall to the superior might and intellect of Germany.

A shout from the bridge snapped Oliver Heinkel back to reality. The Captain barked orders to cast off and, with a scurry of activity from the crew, the boat lurched into life. The engine revved, causing a cloud of smoky soot to engulf the deck. Heinkel instinctively choked on the smog. The sooner he could get off this old tub the better; he did not want to be distracted by his filthy surroundings. There was so much work to be done, secret work.

He straightened the gold Nazi part pin on the lapel of his jacket as a second rush of patriotic fever swept over him. He shuddered, a tingling sensation worked through his body; was it excitement at the prospect of what was to come? He dismissed it. Who wouldn't feel this way? After all, this was going to be the single most important event in the last two thousand years. *He* would live on in the hearts and minds of Germans, long after his mortal body had died of old age. More importantly, what *he* did now would secure the Reich's place in history for all eternity. Despite the stench of diesel oil, smoke and rotting fish, a sadistic smile etched across his face.

The world was about to change forever.

CHAPTER 8

Interrogation

Mayer sat, slumped against the table in the interrogation room. He slowly lifted his head as Kessler entered the room. He blinked, unable to focus. His head throbbed with a mixture of thirst and fatigue. The bags under his eyes and a day's worth of stubble were testament to his ordeal. An uncomfortable pain in his bladder registered as the door slammed shut.

Kessler walked briskly to the desk and punched the Professor hard on the jaw. Mayer spiralled to the floor, his head spinning, with the fresh taste of blood in his mouth.

Kessler spoke in a matter-of-fact sarcastic tone. 'Good morning Professor. A fine morning don't you think?'

Floundering, Mayer groped for the chair and, slowly, painfully, hauled himself back onto the seat.

Kessler landed another blow.

Mayer found himself lying on the floor again; this time coughing blood and sputum.

'Yes, a fine morning indeed!' Kessler dragged Mayer back to the chair, dumping him like a sack of potatoes at the table. It was all part of the show as far as he was concerned.

'No time for idleness this morning Professor. There is work to do; now where were we?' Kessler pulled a face of mild amusement.

'Ah, yes! Visits to Berlin and your work at the University! Tell me again about your work. Tell me about the work you are doing now.' He suddenly reverted to a calming tone. 'You may answer Professor… '

'I work on fuels and the math… '

Kessler delivered a harsh slap across Mayer's face. 'No Professor! I said tell me about the work you are doing now!'

'My work at the University is on high-octane fuels and the propulsion of rockets. You can check this with my colleagues here and in Berlin. I have published many papers in this field of research.' Mayer looked inwardly, mustering his resolve.

Sound authoritative and convincing. Stay alive! The Wehrmacht must not *know,* cannot *know…*

'Go on!' Kessler paced impatiently.

'In the last year we have been working on a new fuel that would be more stable. One that is very powerful, but safe to handle.' His eyes flickered involuntarily around the room, and despite his thirst, beads of sweat started to form on his brow.

Kessler read the signs.

So the Professor is trying to give an answer, but also lying.

Or was it just fear? Kessler wasn't sure.

'Continue,' demanded Kessler, with genuine curiosity this time.

'Well… ' Mayer paused, choosing his words carefully. 'The safety aspect is quite important. We want to make a fuel that is safe to handle. For example, so that it can be put into oil drums and transported on trucks without the risk of fire or explosion…' *So far so good, at least no punch in the face.* Mayer continued, 'However, to get fast acceleration the fuel also needs to be volatile and burn quickly. These properties are often mutually exclusive. A fast-burning fuel is usually unstable and explosive, not safe. So our work is trying to move forward with new, safer fuels.' Mayer prayed that the story sounded convincing.

'I see, an interesting idea… ' Kessler lashed out. Mayer absorbed the punch this time, rocking back on the chair. Bruising erupted on his face. More blood trickled from his mouth and nose. Mayer coughed to clear his airway in readiness for the next blow.

'Very interesting Professor, but we are not quite there yet are we?' Kessler switched to his patronising tone. 'For example, what does the phrase *Delta Pi* mean?'

Mayer stiffened, his heart missed a beat; did Kessler have his manuscript, or was it a lucky guess? Coughing to hide his concern, Mayer tried to buy some time.

Think! The story needs to be more elaborate. Christ! If Kessler has another physicist to hand, he will be checking the answers!

Another scientist could easily discern if the explanation was too simplistic and unconnected to the notes on the paper. He needed to give some new and accurate information on the physics of propulsion; something that would stand up to scrutiny but, equally, send his adversary into a dead end. It needed to be more elaborate, but plausible. He *had* to throw Kessler off the scent. Mayer steeled himself.

'*Pi* is a mathematical constant. We use it for calculating the rate of burn of fuel. *Delta* is a common notation for *the rate of change*. In this case, it is the rate of fuel consumption.'

Mayer gave a factually correct answer.

Kessler paced the room considering the reply.

So… he is telling the truth this time, but also being evasive?

Kessler trusted his gut instinct, it was usually always right. It was time to give the Professor some clarity of thought; something to give the prisoner a little more motivation.

The systematic administration of pain always worked.

Kessler grabbed the Professor by the wrist and twisted his arm to expose the inner part of the wrist, with the main artery facing uppermost. The skin is always thin and tender here, and sensitive to pain; with the added bonus of a major blood vessel just beneath the surface to add to the victim's anxiety.

Kessler tightened his vice-like grip. Mayer instinctively pulled back, but it was pointless. For good measure, the orderly came in behind the chair and pressed down firmly on Mayer's shoulders. Clearly a well-rehearsed routine. Mayer broke into a fresh sweat, with his heart racing.

Kessler produced a cigarette lighter with his free hand; the robust kind that ran on petrol. A spark soon produced a nice hot flame. Kessler studied the flame for a second or two, then moved the lighter closer to Mayer's wrist.

Mayer stiffened, and pulled back, snorting through blood-soaked nostrils, his eyes wild. 'Arggghhhhhhhhhhhh!... Arggghhhhhhhhhh!... Arggghhhhhh!'

Kessler counted in his head to the smell of burning flesh... *one... two... three... four... five.*

Click: the lighter closed.

Kessler smiled. The timing was perfect; just enough to raise a nasty blister, and burn deeply into the skin; but above all, to allow the victim to register the pain, scream, and then register the pain all over again. Kessler surged with satisfaction.

'Now we begin to understand the burning of fuels, Professor. How are your equations working now Professor?'

The lighter was reapplied. 'Arrrghhhh!... Arrrrgghhhhh!'

Kessler took a long, slow, deep breath, and released his grip. Mayer recoiled to protect his injured arm, gritting his teeth against the pain.

'Now that I have your full attention Professor, I would like you to decipher this document for me.' Kessler placed the last mud-stained page of the manuscript on the table and waited for Mayer's reaction.

'What is it?' Mayer kept a blank expression, but his eyes flickered involuntarily.

Kessler said nothing. He just shook his head in disappointment and sparked up the cigarette lighter. Mayer gritted his teeth, and tried with all his strength to hold back his injured wrist; but it was impossible against Kessler's superior might.

'Arrrgghhhhhh! Arrrrgggghhhh!' Mayer screamed. Flesh sizzled.

Kessler spoke with mocking sympathy. 'Focus... focus... Professor. I want to help you, but I can only do that if you help yourself.' It was just another routine method for getting inside the victim's head; another gem for the Interrogator's Handbook.

'Now tell me what is written on this paper.'

Mayer slowly took the page, his arm throbbing, eyes watering, and a dampness forming in his groin. The smell of urine mixed with burnt flesh.

'This page,' he coughed up some blood. 'This page,' he muttered again. 'Appears to be some calculation… err… '

Buy some time! Give Kessler something, but just stay alive!

'… It looks like some simple gas calculations.' Mayer lied as he firmly fixed Kessler's gaze. The two men looked each other in the eye for several seconds.

'A pity, such a pity.' Kessler shook his head. He then nodded to the orderly, who promptly left the room and returned seconds later with a hack saw.

Mayer gasped. An involuntary burst of urine dampened his trousers.

'Now we are going to play a little game. The rules of the game are simple.' Kessler spoke calmly. 'If you answer my questions truthfully, you will get to keep your fingers. If not…' Kessler paused to let his victim soak up the new horrific information. 'Well, each time you lie, you will lose a finger, and so on and so forth until they are all gone.' Kessler gesticulated with his hands for effect.

'Do you understand the game, Professor?!' hissed Kessler.

Mayer nodded.

'So Professor, my first question… ' Kessler picked up the hack saw and held it up to the light, pretending to inspect the blade. He turned the saw over slowly and feigned adjusting his grip, making a show of his new toy.

Kessler signalled to the orderly, who immediately grabbed Mayer firmly by the shoulders as before. Kessler pulled out the Professor's good arm. After all, why leave a working arm when you can double the agony? Pleased with the decision, Kessler tightened his hold as Mayer fought back.

Good… good… it looks like the prisoner will provide some sport.

'Now Professor, please answer my next question. Remember, I will accept only your first answer to each question; only one chance to keep each finger – simple.' Kessler smiled as he placed the blade in position.

He rested the blade lightly on Mayer's little finger.

Mayer stiffened at the coldness and touch of the blade and hyperventilated through clenched teeth. Sweat trickling down his face. Small uncontrolled bursts of urine came from his bladder.

Kessler spoke as if he was bargaining for the price of sausages at a market stall. 'Please explain *Delta Pi* and the other mathematical symbols on the page. One symbol for one finger, agreed?'

Mayer took a deep breath. He needed to keep a clear head, and give a technically plausible explanation. He needed to speak with conviction.

'Fuels are liquids which, unlike gases, cannot be compressed. Liquids occupy a finite space. In our case, this space is the fuel tank of a rocket. When the fuel burns, the residual volume of fuel remaining in the fuel tank will steadily decrease. That is, the fuel will be gradually used up. The *Delta Pi* relates to the shape of the fuel tank. The tanks are long cylinders. They need to be this shape to fit inside the rocket. *Delta Pi* describes the rate of decline of fuel in the cylindrical fuel tank over time.' Mayer spoke with all the academic authority he could muster, and waited for the pain.

'I see,' Kessler drew the hack saw blade across the Professor's little finger. It cut to the bone and blood oozed from the flesh wound. He always liked to verify the quality of the information he was receiving. He moved the blade back to take another cut.

'It is the truth, *Pi* measures diameter! The diameter of the fuel cylinder! So that we can calculate the volume of fuel used!' Mayer howled as the next cut went through the bone. Blood spurted from the open wound as the finger dangled on a sinew of the remaining flesh. Kessler twisted the partially severed finger and ripped it viciously away from the stump.

Mayer screamed. 'The truth! It's the truth! I am telling you! Please!'

Blood pulsated from the stump onto the edge of the table. Kessler ignored it and moved into position for another cut. He put the blade against the next finger and, pressing down, the blade started to bite.

'My next question for the next symbol. What is it? Explain what it is for? See I am being fair. Two questions for one finger, Professor.' He put more pressure on the blade. 'You may answer… '

Mayer was just about to speak, but was interrupted by an urgent knock on the cell door.

A voice called through the closed door. 'Herr Commandant! Herr Commandant! Forgive my intrusion, but there's an urgent phone call for you. It's Berlin!'

'I am busy! Take a message.' Kessler turned back to his prisoner.

'Herr Commandant! Sorry, you do not understand… the phone call… it is Admiral Dönitz… in person… sir!'

Kessler sighed and, pulling open the door, he looked the office clerk up and down.

'Admiral Dönitz you say?'

'Yes… err… yes, Herr Commandant, sir… waiting on the telephone now, sir.'

'Very well, I will take the call in my office,' Kessler conceded; he would have to take the call. One does not keep an Admiral of the Reich waiting.

'You!' Kessler pointed at the orderly. 'Clean him up, dress his wounds.'

Confused by the sudden change in the Professor's fortunes, the orderly snapped his heels together as he stood to attention. 'Yes, Herr Commandant!'

CHAPTER 9

Rockefeller Plaza

Oliver Heinkel walked briskly from the New York subway and headed towards Rockefeller Plaza. The square consisted of a collection of new buildings, in the heart of New York. This included one of the world's largest tower blocks: the Rockefeller Centre. The tower was meant to impress with its art deco facade and attention to detail, and it did. The building was an amazing centrepiece to a state-of-the-art civil engineering project.

The top floors were still being finished off, although the lower floors were now occupied by big businesses. These included investment banks, the offices of various international chemical companies, and of course the oil business that had made Rockefeller his fortunes. Rumour had it that the construction of the plaza and the associated buildings was the largest and most expensive building project ever financed by the private sector; or rather, financed by one man, John Davison Rockefeller.

Rockefeller was the richest man in the world. He owned the Standard Oil Company and its subsidiaries to more or less control the entire global production of oil. He also managed copper and smelting industries around the globe, and had interests in the US Steel Corporation, as well as the railways. He used his great wealth to obtain shareholdings in major financial institutions; including America's National City Bank, and insurance companies like New York's Equitable Life. The Rockefeller influence even extended to the Federal Reserve.

Heinkel stepped out of the elevator onto the tenth floor of

the Rockefeller Centre, and walked smartly across the plush carpet to the reception desk. The smell of the new carpets and fresh paint assaulted his nostrils.

'Mr Oliver Heinkel for Mr Rockefeller.' Heinkel handed his business card to the receptionist at Standard Oil.

'Please take a seat sir, Mr Rockefeller is a little behind schedule, it will be a few minutes before he can meet you.' The receptionist smiled.

Heinkel gave a sharp nod, and took to one of the leather armchairs in the reception. Irritated, he started to tap his fingers on the arm of the chair; and then immediately stopped. It would not do to let his composure slip, even in the company of allies. He went over his strategy. If he played it right, he could walk away with some substantial investment for the Reich; and all legitimate, at least on the surface.

The receptionist suddenly interrupted his train of thought. 'Mr Rockefeller will see you now.' She ushered Heinkel into the office.

The room was elegantly furnished in the art deco style. Rockefeller sat behind a large, teak desk that had ornately carved legs, and was covered in gold leaf. In front of the desk sat two high backed chairs that were similarly carved. Rockefeller was in his late nineties, and while his body was frail, relatively speaking, he was in good shape for someone who was nearly a hundred years old. Despite his great age, his mind remained as sharp as a razor. He gestured for Heinkel to take a chair in front of the desk.

'Ah, Mr Heinkel, it's nice to see you again. How is my little science project going in Germany, all good I hope?'

'The research and development has progressed very well. We are most grateful to the Rockefeller Foundation for supporting our scientific research.' Heinkel gave a cautious smile.

'Good, good, tell me more. What have you made of your scientific endeavours?' Rockefeller showed genuine interest.

'Your generous and substantial funding has enabled us to bring together some of the greatest scientific minds in Germany. Our physicists are working on a new type of engine and propulsion system that may revolutionise transport. The potential for faster travel around the globe will have obvious benefits to industries, such as yours. The German government is also grateful for your support.'

As far as the Rockefeller Foundation was concerned, this was just a pure physics and engineering project to make high-performance engines. The military application of rocket technology was of no interest to the American sponsor. Heinkel could see no point in bothering his benefactor with this detail.

'I am pleased this project has put German science on the international stage. It is vitally important for every country to take pride in its scientific works, and the technical skills of its people. The German people, in particular, achieve through hard work. This is something my father taught me at an early age, and I have remembered that lesson throughout my life. I got where I am today through hard work, not by luck. Science and technology in Germany can achieve the same great heights, and you have a strong leader to help you. Herr Hitler shows you the way by his good example. Germany has gone from strength to strength in the last decade, grasping new technology, and now has the potential to lead the world into a new age,' Rockefeller lectured. He was preaching to the converted.

'I too share this ambition for German science and technology, and this is why your generous funding is so important to us. We are on the cusp of a great new technology.' Heinkel talked up the idea.

'Actually, Mr Heinkel, to increase my collaborations with German industry I've just signed an agreed on behalf of one of my oil companies – Exxon – with two of your country's leading chemical corporations; BASF and I. G. Farben.'

'This is excellent news indeed, and I am sure the Reich Ministry will do all it can to smooth trade between these companies.' Heinkel gave a polite smile.

'Yes, and in return, perhaps the Ministry can renew our contract with your aviation industry?'

Standard Oil had struck lucky in the Middle East at Bahrain and was directly supplying Hitler's Luftwaffe air force with aviation fuel.

'Yes, I would be delighted to make this suggestion to the Reich Ministry,' Heinkel smiled, giving another polite but cautious answer.

Rockefeller was deeply involved with Germany's affairs. He had established the Schroder Investment Bank. The board of directors included senior members of the Nazi Party, Rockefeller, and German financiers who were close to Hitler. This included the German industrialist Fritz Thyssen, arguably the biggest financer of the Nazi Party, and a man on personal terms with the Führer. The list of connections went on. Rockefeller was a Nazi supporter and, by default, so were many American institutions controlled by the Rockefeller Empire.

'My dear Mr Heinkel, the Foundation is pleased to fund your research for another two years with a further five million dollars. I hope this will speed progress.' Rockefeller leant back in his chair with a satisfied grin.

'We are of course delighted with this news, sir! We will make swift progress indeed, and the Rockefeller Foundation can share the glory of this new technology!'

'Good, good... ' Rockefeller smiled, but then he changed his tone to a more hushed and personal voice. '... but there is something of a personal nature that you might do for me... '

'Anything, anything at all, I am at your service.' Heinkel leaned forward to get closer.

'It is a small favour; a little bit of trade union trouble you understand. The American work ethic has been infiltrated by communists and layabouts. You can imagine that trade unions cost me a great deal of money. It is time the unions changed, and took on the German work ethic. I believe you have some colleagues, German-Americans, who might take a greater interest in the affairs of our unions... ' Rockefeller looked Heinkel directly in the eye.

'Of course, I am pleased to help with this personal matter. There are many Germans working overseas, and my office in Berlin takes a special interest in their welfare.' Heinkel was happy to comply with the request; after all, he'd just been given five million dollars.

He smiled inwardly. Much of the union trouble that Rockefeller was experiencing was in part due to the activities of the German-American Bunde; a network of activists that enjoyed the full support of the SS and other parts of the Wehrmacht. It was just unfortunate that the Rockefeller Empire was affected. The German-American Bunde occupied positions in government departments, the road and rail networks, in industry, as well as commerce. Heinkel was amused. Using this network he could shut Rockefeller down in an instant; but for now the old goat was useful.

'There is one more thing... give my regards to Herr Himmler,' Rockefeller smiled.

'Of course, I would be delighted.'

Heinrich Himmler was the Minister for the Interior in Germany, with legitimate ties to Rockefeller through the Schroder bank. Germany was in a growth phase, and fleecing rich Americans was all part of the plan.

The meeting was evidently over. Heinkel stood and extended his hand. 'You will have my every assistance on these matters.'

'Thank you Mr Heinkel, tell Minister Himmler that I personally appreciate his help.'

Heinkel headed for the door. He would enjoy reporting to

his commander. After all, Herr Himmler was also the head of the Gestapo and could arrange any number of arrests.

Danny Nash stood on the street outside the Admiralty building, staring at the ornate facade and whitewashed mock Grecian pillars. He mumbled under his breath.

'Jesus... what the hell am I doing?'

He leapt up the steps two at a time and suddenly found himself in the lobby, breathing rapidly, sweat welled up on his palms. A wave of heat flushed from his pounding chest. He unfastened the buttons on his grey coat, and momentarily flapped the heavy fabric to get some cool air circulating against his skin.

He caught his own reflection in the shimmering glass facade: not great. The grubby marks on his regulation khaki shirt stuck out a mile. He grinned like an idiot and shoved his left hand deep inside the pocket of his grey coat, pulling out an old metal comb. He quickly slicked back the edges of his dark hair.

'Okay, here goes nothing... '

He walked straight for the closed double doors that marked the entrance to the Admiralty office. His boots echoed on the marble floor. He grasped the door handle, taking a deep breath of the bees wax polish on the pristine ash panels, and then stepped inside.

There she was.

Emily sat busily tapping away on the typewriter. Her golden brown hair was tied back, but a few stray locks had escaped to frame her perfect complexion. Nash soaked up her slim, elegant features. The white blouse and business suit concealed an athletic, but feminine physique.

Nash walked quietly up to the desk and waited. The delicate fragrance of lavender filled his senses.

'I will not keep you a moment, sir.' Emily, head down, kept typing. The letter for Mr Churchill was urgent.

Nash smiled as he took in the view of her cleavage for a second, then stopped himself.

'How are you Emily?'

The clatter of typewriter fell silent. Emily looked up.

Nash dropped the smile, and searched the blank expression on her face.

He spoke quietly. 'So, how are you?'

Her eyes filled with tears.

'Emily?'

She stood up abruptly, pushing back her office chair. It coasted gently back on its rollers, sinking into the lush carpet.

Silence filled the room.

Heart pounding, Nash moved slowly around the desk.

'Emily, I… '

'Where have you been? I thought… I thought… '

'I am alright. I… '

'Father said you were on another mission.'

'Yes.' Nash shrugged.

'You just vanished without saying goodbye.'

'I am sorry, it just happened that way. You know how it is. King and country and all that.'

Nash stiffened against the crushing lump forming in his gullet.

'Danny, I thought you were lost.'

'I was in a manner of speaking, but I am back now.'

'Oh, Danny!'

She flung her arms around his neck.

Nash hesitated. Lifting his arms robotically, he found the curve of her waist and pulled her in. He closed his eyes, and soaked up the moment.

She was the only one who could take the pain away.

CHAPTER 10

Dönitz

Kessler sat at his desk, making involuntary adjustments to his tunic. He cleared his throat before picking up the receiver.

'Admiral Dönitz, this is Kessler, how may I be of service?'

'You received my telegram I trust, and have located Professor Mayer?' The Admiral's voice crackled down the long-distance phone line.

'Yes, Admiral, I received your telegram and personally took charge of the situation. The Professor was detained within an hour of your orders arriving.'

'That is good Commandant. I have some new orders from Berlin. From the Führer himself!'

'Of course, I am at your disposal.' Kessler sat up sharply.

'The Professor has some skills that are essential to the Wehrmacht. He will be moving to Berlin and you will accompany him. You are responsible for his safe passage. Please report to the Armaments Corp on the outskirts of Berlin by 21.00 hours tomorrow.'

Kessler registered the new orders. 'Yes Admiral, it will be done; but what of my preparations here for the Führer's visit?'

'These must continue in your absence, but you will return in a few days. Now the priority is to deliver Professor Mayer to Berlin,' clarified Dönitz.

'May I ask, is this related to the Professor's work here at the University?'

'I am afraid I am not permitted to discuss this. However, you should be clear that the safe and intact arrival of the Professor at the Armament Corps is of vital importance.'

Kessler got the message. Mayer was now valuable cargo.

'Then I should also like to report an incident that occurred at the University last night: a break-in, and theft of some of the Professor's papers.'

'What? A theft you say?'

'Yes Admiral. It was late last night. Unfortunately, the perpetrator got away, but not before dropping a couple of pages of the documents he was stealing.'

'Pages? Pages of what?'

'I am not exactly sure yet, sir. Some kind of technical information.' Kessler stared at the mud-stained pages sitting on his desk. 'The Professor says the pages are some kind of fuel consumption calculation for a new projectile, called a rocket.'

Dönitz spoke urgently. 'Keep your voice down! It is not safe to speak of such things over the telephone, who else knows about this?'

'Only my orderly has heard the Professor speak. There is also the squad who searched the Professor's office.'

'Move them all to Berlin. In any event, the squad will be useful for providing armed protection on your journey. I will send you fresh replacements. Bring the pages of the document with you. There are other physicists here who could interpret this information.'

'Very good Admiral, it will be done.'

'Keep the papers safe… and the Professor.'

'Yes, Admiral, I will attend to this immediately, Heil Hitler!' Kessler snapped to attention as the phone went dead.

So, a change of duties: from interrogator to protector. The Professor would arrive safely in Berlin. He would make sure of it. Besides, there would be plenty of opportunities to quiz the Professor later. Nonetheless, it was odd; the theft from Mayer's office on the *same* day as the telegram arriving from Berlin. Had there been a security breach? Suspicious, Kessler headed for the telegraph.

Kessler scanned the layout of the radio room. It was a small box room with no external windows, crammed into the corner of the office. Everything seemed in order: a desk, chair, some notepaper, the usual communications log book, and the telegraph itself.

'Pass me the log.'

'Yes, my Commandant.' The fresh-faced radio operator extended a shaking hand with the log book.

Kessler flicked through the pages. Everything seemed neatly recorded.

'Has anyone else been in the radio room?'

'No, sir. Only me and I always lock the door when I leave, sir.' The radio operator swallowed hard, his eyes flickering with uncertainty.

'Move aside!'

The young radio operator vacated the box room. Kessler took his place over the desk. He ran his hand around the edge of the desk, then checked down the back of the telegraph. Nothing – a telltale layer of dust suggested no sign of tampering. Kessler rubbed the dust on his fingertips. 'Are you sure no one else has been in the room?'

'Yes Commandant, I am certain, only me.'

'And you have the only key?'

'Yes sir.' The radio operator stiffened.

Clandestine use of telegraph didn't seem plausible. There was only room for one person at a time in the radio room, and there was no hiding place for a private conversation.

'Tell me, how long have you been with us?'

'Three years, sir. Directly from the Signals Corps, sir.' The radio operator stood firmly to attention.

Kessler nodded, he remembered hand-picking the young

signals officer direct from the academy. The teenager was keen, and fresh from the tree; not yet corrupted by the spoils of the Wehrmacht. No, there *had* to be another explanation.

'Where does the telegraph cable go from here? How is it connected to Berlin?'

'Well, sir. The cable runs in the wall cavity to the ground floor, and joins the main bundle of cables under the building, and then into the street.'

'Could anyone tamper with the cable from outside?'

'Not likely, sir. The telegraph wire is bundled with a mixture of anonymous cables in the basement, and on leaving the building is further convoluted with more cables from all the other offices in the main street. Only a trained engineer could find the right wire, and even then, it would take some considerable time.'

Kessler nodded his appreciation. Nonetheless, he *would* have the entire length of the cables checked as a precaution. There was only one logical conclusion: the security leak must be in Berlin. If there *was* a leak? It could still be a coincidence. Was there some other chain of events that had brought the intruder to the Professor's office on the same day as the telegram from Berlin? He would find out, and hang the culprit for treason.

CHAPTER 11

Leipzig Railway Station

Commandant Kessler checked his watch. It was still early, but already the train station was busy with the first flush of commuters arriving off the tram lines that criss-crossed the main entrance. It was hardly a surprise; after all, Leipzig was an important rail head in the German railway network, with dozens of platforms for domestic travellers, and a large goods yard for freight. Closing the station had been out of the question. Instead he had to make do with a side entrance. Still, the men were busy unloading the three-ton truck that had been used to carry the Professor's papers to the station.

'How many crates left?'

The sergeant flipped the pages on his clipboard. 'Ten, we have already loaded fifteen crates onto the train, sir.'

'And the train is secure?'

'Yes sir, and arranged exactly as you ordered.'

Kessler was pleased with his shrewd plan – concealment in plain sight. Rather than commandeering an entire train he had opted for a couple of secure carriages on the early morning train to Berlin. The first train always carried a fair few soldiers heading home to their regiments. Nothing much would be out of the ordinary. With luck, most passengers wouldn't even notice his men on the train; as long as he could get his cargo of crates loaded before the public arrived for boarding.

Kessler checked his watch again. 'Let me see the secure cargo carriage, bring this crate.' Kessler patted the nearest crate with his leather glove. The sergeant gave more orders. Men moved efficiently to their allocated task.

The burly sergeant heaved the crate up the wooden ramp into the goods car. Kessler followed at a serene pace, checking the security measures. Everything was in place. Two men stood on guard duty, one at each door. They would remain at their posts inside the car for the entire journey; there would be no opportunity to interfere with the cargo. Kessler checked the manifest as several more crates arrived. 'Very good Sergeant, bring me the keys when everything is locked down.'

'Yes sir.'

'And the Professor?'

'As you ordered sir.'

Kessler smiled at his little ruse and headed for the first-class compartment in the adjacent passenger car. Once everything was secure, the public could board the rest of the train.

Nash took a welcome sip of hot coffee and observed the scene. To the average passer-by he was just another worker taking breakfast at one of the many cafes outside the station. So far the count was fifteen crates, and some thirty men; but no sign of Professor Mayer. The weapons they were carrying amounted to a fair arsenal: the latest automatic pistols, machine guns, grenades. These men were ready for a war, not a train journey. They were also professionals. The commander did not need to bark orders. Small gestures were enough to get the men moving quickly and efficiently.

One last crate appeared from the back of the truck. Still no Mayer. Had he missed something?

He would have to be careful.

After casually finishing up his coffee, he headed across the street towards the main entrance to the station. He shuffled the train tickets he had purchased earlier, while pretending to check platform numbers on the board. It was easy to blend in with the morning crowd.

The main concourse gave a clear view down the length of the train; exactly twenty passenger cars, with the goods carriage sandwiched between first and second class. Good news – nothing appeared to have been altered since last night. Two guards followed the last crate on to the train and the cargo doors were locked behind them. Another six heavily armed soldiers boarded the adjacent carriage.

Christ! Half the bloody German Army is on the train.

It didn't matter. Whether Mayer was on the train or not, his orders were to get the missing pages back at *any* cost. It seemed unlikely that such valuable pages would be locked away as cargo. If the papers were here at all, they would be on the person of the commanding officer.

A sharp blow of the station master's whistle announced boarding. Passengers filtered through the makeshift barrier onto the platform. Making like a commuter, Nash blended in with the bustling masses and soon found his seat; in the same carriage as the target. A bristling line of soldiers in the gangway gave the position of the German commander, hidden away some four compartments along the corridor. Nash estimated the distance: thirty feet or so away, a lot could happen over such a distance. It was a big risk, even for a trained assassin.

Nash sat quietly, ignoring the other passengers, taking comfort from the feel of the Colt Forty-Five pistol under his coat and the collection of stiletto throwing knives secreted about his person. All he could do now was wait. Everything depended on the small explosive charges he had placed under the first carriage last night, just enough to create a loud bang and damage some of the gearing, and hopefully noisy enough to draw the soldiers away to investigate. The window of opportunity would be narrow, very narrow indeed. Nash sat back, and to avoid striking up conversation with the locals, buried his head in a newspaper. It would be 'show time' soon enough.

The screech of brakes threw passengers forward, as the remnants of the explosion filled the air with smoke and the smell of cordite. Nash pushed past screaming passengers and burst into the gangway, catching a glimpse of the guards heading away up the corridor towards the explosion. Head down, breathing hard, pumping up the adrenalin, he charged, pushing civilians aside as they emerged from their compartments.

One… two… three compartments… he slipped a stiletto throwing knife into his hand and, at full tilt, piled through the door into the fourth.

Speed worked to his advantage as the knife instinctively found its target. A trooper dropped to the deck gasping for air as the blade penetrated his windpipe and spinal cord – that left only the Commandant. Allowing momentum to carry him over the body of the trooper, Nash landed hard, pulverising the Commandant's rib cage with his shoulder. Both men flew backwards onto the window seat.

Kessler drove his elbow into the side of Nash's neck, trying to catch the nerve endings that crossed the shoulder blade. It had the desired effect: Nash erupted in pain as the power to his right arm evaporated. Kessler was well rehearsed at close-quarter hand-to-hand combat, and knew how to damage his opponent.

'You cannot escape!' Kessler drove his elbow down again onto Nash's neck and shoulder.

Jarred by the impact, with nausea rising, and dizzy, Nash twisted abruptly.

'Guards! Guards!' Kessler bellowed, still raining down controlled blows on his adversary's head and neck.

Snorting blood, ignoring the pain, Nash arched his back, pulling out a second throwing knife. The blade danced around in his hand. He stretched his back some more to create a working space, then adjusting his grip, he drove the knife upwards, hoping to find the soft tissue of the lower jaw and then push the steel on into the brain stem.

'Arrggghhhhh!' Kessler sensed the danger, and using both hands halted the advancing blade, but too late – blood gushed from under his chin as the blade penetrated beneath his jaw.

'Arrrrggggghhhh!' Hammering hard, as if against an anvil, Kessler thumped both hands down on the hilt of the blade; a second gush of blood issued forth as the blade swept free.

Nash swung again.

Kessler blocked, but not fast enough. The knife opened a long gash up on his left cheek. Missing the eye socket, the tip of the blade glanced off his eyebrow. He screwed his face up against the pain, and raised his arm to protect the injury – it was a bad move.

Nash drove the blade hard towards his exposed jugular.

Instantaneously, Kessler responded, catching Nash in the stomach with his knee and sending the knife off target. The blade sunk harmlessly into the seat, a fraction of an inch from Kessler's head.

'Guards! Guards!' Kessler lashed out with his legs and, managing to get one foot squarely on Nash's stomach, he kicked hard. The blow forced Nash backwards onto the opposite seat. Kessler launched himself forward in attack but, as he did so, Nash dived sideways and grabbed the Commandant from behind into a headlock.

The men rolled frantically around the carriage, but with each jolt the headlock got tighter.

Rasping for breath, clawing at the vice-like grip across his windpipe, Kessler's vision began to blur. He tried to focus. Tunnel vision started to set in as the room slipped from reality. Kessler blacked out.

The sound of boots thumping down the corridor, and the barking of orders, marked the return of the soldiers. Nash flipped the Commandant over to expose the pockets on his tunic, and searched frantically. His instinct had been right. He grabbed the papers from the Commandant's inside breast pocket, then folding the sheets quickly buried them deep inside his own pocket. He wasn't about to make the same mistake twice; this time the pages would be secure.

Nash glanced into the gangway. Bemused civilians milled about in total chaos amongst the soldiers, lots of soldiers! It would have to be the window; this was becoming a habit. He smashed the butt of the Colt against the glass. It did the trick, shattering the window in an instant.

The train stopped dead as Nash jumped.

Luck was on his side for once. A steep grassy embankment offered a soft landing. A dense pine forest at the bottom of the bank beckoned. Nash rolled more or less uncontrollably down the slope, only just managing to gain his feet as he bounced into the first pine tree.

Shots rang out. Wood splintered next to his head. He dove into the dense tree line, and was suddenly swallowed by the damp and darkness of the tangled pines. He rolled into a semi-crouching posture, and plunged headlong into the woodland with his clothes ripping and branches slashing at his face – determined to put some distance between himself and the train. After about sixty feet, fatigue set in. The branches were just getting too dense for a belt and braces charge. Changing tack, he went down to an almost crawling position and, tucking his head in for protection, he drove on. It seemed to work, providing a bit more headway.

Instinct told him to change direction.

Always make the pursuit difficult.

He veered to the right, and ploughed onwards, desperately trying to keep tabs on time and distance. It would be all too easy to get disorientated, and with no view of the edge of the tree line, the last thing he wanted to do was to wander round in circles and end up back at the train.

He stopped to take stock in the darkness. Gulping deep breaths, Nash tried to calm his breathing; the noise rattled around inside his head. In the darkness, one needed to be able to *hear* or *smell* the enemy. Willing himself quiet, he tilted his head and opened his mouth wide; it all helped to focus on hearing. A few minutes of silence passed – nothing, no soldiers – he was in the clear, for now.

The corporal considered climbing out of the window after the assailant, but decided against it. The man was already in the tree line, and his orders were to stay on the train and protect the cargo. Besides, he had two casualties to deal with, and a crowd of panicked civilians. He resigned himself to the task as he put away his revolver.

Kessler groaned as he came to. He gradually focused his one good eye, and concentrated on breathing, then pulled himself onto a seat with some help from the corporal. He tried to shake his head clear. He needed to take command and assess the situation. Had he been out for just a few seconds, or was it longer? He looked down at the dead soldier on the floor. Huge quantities of blood had soaked into the cheap carpet from the knife wound on the soldier's neck. The corporal checked for a pulse, but both men knew their comrade was dead.

The papers!

Suddenly snapping to alertness, as if hit by a bolt of lightning, Kessler checked his tunic pocket; but he already knew the answer: the pages were gone. Boiling rage welled up. He controlled it, outwardly maintaining his composure for the sake of his men. He needed time to think.

He noticed the knife lodged in the seat opposite. He pulled out the blade, rolling it over in his hand. A commando's throwing knife; and well balanced. He gently ran a thumb on the stiletto blade. Razor sharp; but then he already knew that from the wound on his face. The injury pulsated. Blood dripped from above the eye. Ignoring it, Kessler continued to examine the knife. It wasn't Swiss, and there were no manufacture marks on the blade. English then? Or maybe American? He would find out.

The main problem now was deciding what to tell his superiors when he arrived in Berlin. Admiral Dönitz had specifically requested the papers. The security arrangements *had* been good. The operation *should* have gone smoothly.

Kessler smiled. At last a worthy adversary, a seasoned professional. The explosion had been a creative diversion. He would have his men collect any remains of the device, and samples of the explosive residue. It might at least give some indications of where the charge came from. He would also question the railway staff and his sentries at Leipzig station. How was the explosive device planted without arousing suspicion? Who was his attacker? Where did his attacker get his intelligence from? Who were his masters? Why were the papers so important? There were lots of unanswered questions.

CHAPTER 12

Princeton

Heinkel perched in the elegant Georgian-style armchair in the Governor Suite of the Princeton Hotel, while resting the bulging document wallet embossed with the US Patent Office logo on his lap. The edges of the once manila folder had discoloured into a rustic brown. Numerous worn pages protruded haphazardly from the bundle. He removed the red ribbon, turning the ageing cover to reveal the first page – new paper, dated 1st May 1933 – good, the contents would be up to date. The secretary had done well.

He glanced over to the bed.

The gaping corpse lay sprawled, with its head dangled over the foot of the bed; eyes rolled back in their sockets. The greying, cold skin contrasted with the cherry red lips of the young blonde.

Why did these American women insist on wearing so much make up? Or maybe it was just the after effects of the poison – it did that sometimes, bringing an eerie redness to certain parts of the flesh.

He turned the first page.

It was just a file note from one administrator to another. The second page looked more promising; a contents list of the patents filed by one Dr Robert Goddard from Princeton University. Things were on the right track. Goddard was some kind of American inventor who had turned his hand to the problem of vertical take off using liquid oxygen as a fuel. Goddard was a rocket man, one of the first. Ridiculed by his peers in the academic community, he had left Princeton and vanished into the fringes of society. The SS were still tracking him down but, for now, his old laboratory would do nicely.

Heinkel scanned the list: gas-propelled rockets, methods for producing hydrogen, titanium alloys for thermal stability – whatever that was – and then he saw it.

Liquid oxygen propulsion systems.

Dr Goebbels had specifically requested information on any and all uses of liquid oxygen, especially in engines or similar devices.

He flicked through the pages. Was it the right information? The morass of technical notes, calculations, equations, and schematic diagrams would have to be judged by experts back in Berlin. He turned over a page of mathematics, a technical drawing caught his eye. Was it some kind of prototype component of a fuel system? Part of a rocket engine? It certainly looked important. The technical drawing looked very intricate, some kind of metal alloy with flanges and connectors. The engineers back at Kummersdorf would figure it out. It was good intelligence. At least he would know what to look for.

He checked his watch.

After midnight, and definitely time to get going.

He carefully closed the document wallet and placed it in his leather satchel, then ripped down one of the drapes.

He could dump the American bitch along the way.

Heinkel adjusted the Princeton tie against the ill-fitting, crumpled blue shirt and then pulled on the cheap tweed jacket; the kind with the leather elbow patches sewn in. He looked the part as he stepped out of the beaten up Chevrolet parked up on the main campus. For good measure, he grabbed a couple of textbooks from the passenger seat. Nobody would take any notice, he was just another eager young professor working late.

He locked the car door, and walked purposefully along the

footpath, being careful to moderate his pace. Neon street lamps lit the way through the landscaped gardens. He paused at the first intersection in the pavement, glancing at the convenient campus map protruding from the neatly trimmed hedgerow. The Physics and Engineering Department was dead ahead, some fifty American yards.

The new red-brick building slowly emerged in the twilight.

He scanned the perimeter.

Lights were on in a few rooms, but that was to be expected. American academics seemed to keep the strangest hours. The glass-fronted lobby was deserted – all good – no sign of the night watchman. Not that some old, fat security guard would present any problems.

All the same, he thumbed the leather catch off the pancake holster under his jacket. The snub-nosed forty-five was a detestable American firearm; heavy, clunky, and with no range, but it would have to do.

He skipped up the steps and tried the front door.

It opened.

He moved into the freshly tiled lobby with its white walls and bright lights. The Yankees were obviously into modern architecture and minimalist clean lines. Contemporary furnishing provided a seating area in one corner near the reception desk.

He scanned the perimeter, listening for the telltale sound of footsteps.

Nothing.

He edged across to the noticeboard pinned to the nearest wall, flashing his eyes down the list of names and room numbers: the Rocket Science Laboratory was on the first floor. He ditched the school books on a convenient coffee table and, seeing a small illuminated sign on the far side of the lobby, found the entrance to the stairwell.

He worked quickly across the open-plan space, pausing to glance through the wire-meshed glass of the security door.

No movement.

He slipped into the stairwell, and climbed steadily up the steps, checking ahead constantly as he turned the corner onto the next flight. His shoes echoed off the concrete. The first-floor landing hosting a large number one on the breeze block wall soon appeared.

He peered through the door into the corridor; more white walls and tiled floors. Not much cover for a firefight, but then, he probably wouldn't need it.

He stepped into the gangway, moving left down the hall, hoping that he'd chosen the correct direction. He was in luck, the door numbers tallied and he soon found the right laboratory.

The white chipboard door gave the sponsor's branding: *Princeton Aeronautical Society, Rocket Science Laboratory*.

He paused, listening at the door, but it was no good. There was no telling what was on the other side. He would have to go in using his charm, or the forty-five.

He pushed open the door and moved silently into the laboratory.

The room was chaotic. The neat rows of parallel benches had long since been lost under mounds of debris. Engine parts, electrical components, wire and boxes of tools were heaped on every bench. The occasional paper-strewn cubby hole in the moraine of spare parts marked where the scientists, cave troll-like, were stationed during the day.

Heinkel walked slowly through the laboratory, checking each bench for life as he went. The place seemed deserted.

Suddenly, the sound of shuffling paper penetrated from the last bench.

He moved quietly, bringing the last bay into view.

A woman, or at least he thought it was a woman, sat hunched over some documents, scribbling away on a notepad. Her chunky frame stretched the white laboratory coat to its limits. Greasy, unkempt hair stuck to the collar.

One of the cave trolls was home.

Heinkel took out the forty-five.

The scientist stopped scrawling on the notepad and stiffened as the cold steel of the weapon pushed against the back of her skull.

'If you want to live, keep perfectly still and do exactly as I say.'

'I… who… what?'

He pushed the gun deeper into the matted scalp. 'Silence! Do not be alarmed. You must simply do *as* I ask, *when* I ask. Nod if you understand.'

The scientist nodded slowly.

'Good, I am glad we understand each other. Now, turn around slowly, but keep your hands where I can see them.'

The scientist swivelled slowly on the laboratory stool, hands in the air. Thick-rimmed glasses, and a pockmarked face stared back. Heinkel estimated the creature was in her late twenties. Obviously a laboratory assistant working late, but would she have access to the materials and documents he needed?

'I understand this is the Rocket Science Laboratory, and Dr Robert Goddard used to work here?' Heinkel waved the forty-five.

'Yes… yes it is. I… I… worked for Dr Goddard… '

'That's good, in that case you should be able to help me. Where are Goddard's notebooks?'

The assistant gulped, trying to keep her hands in the air. 'He… he took them with him… when he left.'

'You say you worked for Goddard?'

'Yes.'

'Then you will have your own notes of the work?'

She nodded slowly. 'Yes.'

'Where are they?'

The scientist titled her head stiffly towards the drawers at the end of her bench, hands still in the air.

'On your feet, get them.'

He shoved the assistant forward, driving the gun into the small of her back for good measure.

She opened the top draw, producing some moth-eaten hardback notebooks.

He gestured with the gun. She squeezed the pile of books onto the end of the bench. He flipped open the first notebook; it was full of scrawled numbers and equations. 'Tell me about these documents.'

'They're just my everyday work on Goddard's project.'

'Like what?'

'Err… err… ' The assistant closed her eyes.

Heinkel cocked the mechanism of the forty-five. 'Answer the question, be specific.'

'A record of my work for the last three years. Notes and calculations on several topics.'

'What topics exactly?'

Beads of sweat dripped down the assistant's forehead. Her mind screamed in terror as she fought for clarity. 'I… I have worked on fuel tank design, the oxygen mixing in the fuel lines, manifolds for the blending of the fuel and its burn time during flight.'

Heinkel raised the weapon, pressing the muzzle of the forty-five into her forehead. 'Now I have another question… ' He took a sheet of paper from his jacket pocket, one of the sketches from the Patent Office. 'Tell me, did Goddard make this?'

The scientist peered at the diagram, adjusting her glasses as she squinted. 'It's an injector manifold. Yes, it's Dr Goddard's design.'

Heinkel pressed the weapon home again. 'But has it been made? Do you have it here?'

'No… no… not exactly, only an earlier prototype.'

'Where?' He jolted the forty-five.

'Please, please! It's… it's on my bench!'

He gestured with the pistol. The assistant got the message and rummaged around on the bench, eventually producing a small but heavy component about the size of a grapefruit.

He took the weight of the flanged object and turned it over in his hand. 'Do you have other similar components?'

'No, Dr Goddard took them with him.'

He examined the expression on the assistant's face. The steady flicker of the eyes, the constriction of the pupils, and the submissive tilt to the head – she was telling the truth.

He crammed the metal object into his jacket pocket, and waved the assistant back to her stool.

'Sit.'

She complied.

'Now, I must be leaving.'

'Please, please… don't hurt me.' Tears streamed silently from under her glasses. Her hands shook as she struggled to keep them in the air.

Heinkel gave a neutral expression, and holstered the forty-five. 'I am not going to shoot you.'

The assistant sagged in relief on the stool, sobbing openly.

Suddenly, he grabbed a handful of greasy hair, forcing her head back. He pulled a knife from his back pocket. The assistant snorted, bubbles of snot mixed with the tears; she clenched her teeth, chest heaving for air.

He shoved the knife hard into her gullet, twisting the blade to hasten death. The blade jolted against sinew and bone, crunching on the resistance of the cervical column.

The assistant gargled, eyes pleading, arms clawing at Heinkel's chest.

He held firm, locking his victim against the laboratory stool. He gave a final nudge of the blade. The knife slipped deeper, severing the spinal cord.

The body went limp.

He propped the corpse against the bench. Blood pulsed onto the worktop from the neck wound. He wiped his knife clean on the edge of the laboratory coat, then turned to pick up the notebooks and headed for the door.

CHAPTER 13

German Rocket Programme

Commandant Kessler reported to the front gate of the Armaments Corps in the small village of Kummersdorf, a few miles south of Berlin. Kummersdorf was the traditional headquarters of the German artillery regiments and had been since the days of horse-drawn cannons in the eighteenth century. Things were a little different now with mechanised heavy artillery, but all the same, Kummersdorf was known in military circles for its big guns.

It also had a more clandestine role as the home for military research into ballistics and new rocket technology.

Kessler stretched his legs in front of the guard house, thankful to be out of the armoured car. He stared absently at the mini convoy; the armoured car sandwiched between two military support vehicles bristling with machine guns. That was all fine, but damned slow and uncomfortable.

At least the decoy had worked. The decision to send Mayer by road had been the right one.

Kessler checked his watch. 'How much longer? You've had our papers for some ten minutes now!'

The sentry smiled apologetically, telephone in hand. 'Sorry to keep you waiting Commandant, an escort from the main building will pick you up shortly.'

'As you can see, we have our own escort. Can't you just open the gate?'

'Sorry sir, visitors are not allowed to drive around the camp unescorted. My orders are no exceptions. I am very sorry, sir.'

'Just tell the camp commander I am here!' Kessler stamped off, and began pacing up and down in front of the main gate. At least the security measures seemed tight. He scanned the fence line – brand new, with fresh barbed wire along the top – someone had been investing in the place. Another two-man patrol sporting a German shepherd approached. The patrol moved purposely along the inside of the fence. It was only five minutes since the last walk-by. The dog barked and bared its teeth. Kessler flinched as the handler gave a stern voice command to silence the beast. German shepherds were proving to be obedient and reliable animals – Herr Hitler's favourite breed – and readily adopted by the army at the Führer's request.

Kessler lit up a smoke. Inhaling, he strolled in front of the main gate. The click-clack of a heavy-calibre machine gun being cocked greeted him. He nodded a smile at the nearest machine gun nest, and took another drag on his cigarette. A second heavy weapon cocked to his left. He gave another nervous grin; with bunkers on either side of the gate, the short approach road could be hosed down in seconds.

The sudden rumble of a three-ton truck announced the arrival of the escort. The truck swung round in a U-turn just inside the gate, bellowing diesel fumes, then stopped, with the engine still running.

A trooper scrambled down from the cab, and after ducking under the barrier, he snapped to attention.

'Commandant Kessler, I am to escort your convoy to main complex. If you could follow me… and err… sorry sir… no smoking… the aviation fuel you understand.'

Kessler took a final drag on his cigarette and climbed back into his vehicle as the escort waved the barrier open.

There was some open ground just inside the gate, and then another internal perimeter fence – a killing ground with a clear arc of fire – any intruder would be picked off easily. Anyone trying to escape would suffer the same fate. Kessler smiled to himself.

All this to house Professor Mayer?

Perhaps the Professor was much more important than he had originally thought? His orders were to deliver the Professor intact to Kummersdorf, so here they were.

The convoy trundled on for several hundred metres across more open ground – part of the artillery field – before arriving at a block of concrete buildings. Kessler's men were relieved from duty, and headed for the mess room for a well-earned break of bread, sausage and hot tea. Kessler and the Professor followed two smartly dressed soldiers into a long, box-like, new art-deco style of building. The walls were constructed of re-enforced concrete, painted white, and the building itself was sunk behind some earthworks. All built to withstand explosions, as well as the day-to-day rumblings of the artillery range. Kessler noted more sentry posts around the building.

Inside, the decor was plain and utilitarian, just like any other military base, but a transformation took place on entering the camp commander's office. His room was neatly decorated with wallpaper, plush drapes, and an ornate desk with symbolic flags of the Nazi Party perched on each corner. A picture of Adolf Hitler adorned the wall. An authentic Persian rug covered the floor. It was all tastefully done, and at some expense. Kessler approached the desk and snapped his heels in the Nazi salute.

'Commandant Kessler reporting, sir.'

The camp commander, Colonel Walter Dornberger, rose to his feet, crisply dressed in Nazi uniform.

'Welcome Commandant, I trust you had a good journey.' Articulate and very well educated, Dornberger was the real deal: a PhD in rocket science, with an illustrious career. He had already worked on several secret projects at the personal request of the Führer, including liquid fuels and rocket technology for the *Reichswehr*, the ballistics section of the German Army. His work marked a new milestone – rockets that exceeded the range and explosive power of all the current artillery technology. Test flights had already been conducted at Kummersdorf, the so-called *Raketenflugplatz* had been a huge success. In fact, Dornberger was now in charge of the entire army's weapons department (the *Heereswaffenamt*).

'… and welcome Professor Mayer.' Dornberger smiled and nodded in the Professor's direction. After all, he was a fellow scientist. 'Professor, I expect you are wondering why I have brought you here?'

Mayer shrugged. 'I was happy at the University of Leipzig. I have a position there and an active research group.'

'No matter, you are here now with many of your colleagues, and you have a duty to perform for Germany!' Dornberger grinned. 'I read your work on high octane fuel; most impressive!'

'My work is not finished. I need to get back to Leipzig… ' Mayer lowered his gaze to the floor.

Dornberger put on a friendly face. 'Alas, you need to forget about Leipzig. At least for a while. This is your home now, and there is much new work to be done! We have a fantastic programme! I am hoping you will join us.'

'What programme?' Mayer looked up, genuinely curious.

'Physics of course! Your research! We are both rocket men are we not? Anyway, how thoughtless of me! You must be tired after your long journey.' Dornberger snapped his fingers and, as if from nowhere, an orderly appeared.

Kessler sensed that Dornberger was being evasive, and wasn't going to answer any question about rocket technology. Perhaps that was no surprise; Kessler didn't have security clearance; at least not yet.

'There is a bunk for the Professor in number three barrack, please see to it… ' The orderly saluted and scurried off with the Professor in tow, leaving Kessler alone with the Colonel.

'Colonel, I have some items to report… some news… '

'Speak freely Commandant… ' The Colonel waved his arm in a sweeping gesture as he lit a cigarette.

'I think you already know about the break-in at Leipzig University… well actually, at Professor Mayer's office.'

'Not really, only that there was a break-in. What was stolen exactly?'

'Technical documents of some kind, I am not really sure, yet. The intruder was sloppy though, he dropped a couple of pages on his way out of the window.'

Dornberger stubbed out his cigarette prematurely.

'What?! On his way out the window! What on earth has been going on in Leipzig!? Did you catch this thief… this intruder?'

'Unfortunately… no… it was dark and the intruder slipped away… but… '

'This could be significant.' Dornberger wagged a finger in the air. 'The Reich has many enemies, and we like to keep our security tight here. It's a strange coincidence that this theft took place on the same day that orders were sent from Berlin to collect the Professor… ' Dornberger let the thought hang for a while. '… It could be a simple coincidence, or perhaps the telegram was intercepted?'

'Interception is *not* possible in Leipzig, the secure telegraph is inside our headquarters. I've already checked it myself.'

'Then Berlin perhaps?' speculated the Colonel.

'I have personal responsibility for the Führer's safety, and if there is a security leak in the telegraph office in Berlin, I will find it. It will be one of several checks on our communications systems.'

'Good, good, keep me informed on the investigation. Where are the papers you recovered? Do you have them?'

Kessler swallowed. 'Unfortunately… no, not any longer… there was an explosion on the train to Berlin… and the pages were taken.'

'What?! Explosion?! Taken?! How is this possible?!'

'The train was secure and well protected. I used some of our best men. A small explosion in one of the goods cars diverted attention, and within seconds an assailant was on me – a professional, highly trained – some kind of assassin or spy is my guess.'

'Assassin? Are you sure?'

'It was clearly planned in advance, the assassin knew exactly where to find us and when to strike.'

Dornberger shook his head. 'More evidence that communications between Berlin and Leipzig are breached.'

Kessler ignored the remark. 'He went straight for the papers.'

'Not after the Professor then?'

'No... I don't think so... if this man was here to assassinate the Professor he could have done that at any time in Leipzig. Besides, what for? No, he was after the documents.'

'Was this man a European? Did he speak?'

'Yes, white at least. Maybe American, could be the English.'

'So, a spy from the West is in our midst... then there is no time to lose, we need to find out what is so interesting about Professor Mayer's work that draws the attention of this spy. Find the security breach, and find it quickly.'

'Of course, Colonel, I will leave immediately, will that be all?'

'Yes, yes, please carry on.' Dornberger sank into his chair, rubbing his brow. There was so much to do, and so little time.

Kessler snapped to attention and headed for the door.

Professor Mayer sat on the edge of his wooden bunk, staring aimlessly into space. Was *everything* lost? Kessler *had* found the draft manuscript, or at least some of it. The last two pages! But where was the final version? Still hidden under the bookcase?

Mayer slumped. With his head in his hands, he mumbled to himself. 'Albert... I am sorry... so sorry... it's all my fault. You are in danger... everyone is in danger... ' The stump of his little finger throbbed. Mayer shivered and tried to switch his mind to more positive things.

The barrack room door suddenly swung up, and in walked a familiar face.

'Professor Hans Von Reichter! Hans, you are here too! I am so pleased to see you my friend!' Suddenly beaming, Mayer was up from his bunk.

'Gustav, you are here too? It's good to see you!' They shook hands. 'What happened to your hand?' Von Reichter saw the fresh bandage.

'An accident... ' Mayer changed the subject. 'Hans, you are still working at the Technical University in Berlin? Still working on... what did you call it? Electronics. The new electrical control system for rockets? Why are we here? How many others are here? What is going on?' Mayer fired questions.

'Take it easy, take it easy... I will try to explain. There is much to discuss.' Von Reichter gestured for them to sit. The two men huddled on the edge of Mayer's bunk.

Von Reichter spoke quietly. 'Well, what can I say? I have only been here a few days myself,' he glanced around the room before continuing, 'I was working happily in my office at the Technical University, when Colonel Dornberger arrived unannounced. He said that he was heading up a special research project and needed my expertise on guidance systems for some new projectiles.'

'What do you make of Dornberger?'

'Well, he's not one of those National Socialist thugs... I think he's like us; just a scientist trying to make the best of the situation.'

Mayer gave a sigh of relief.

Von Reichter continued. 'Anyway, it seemed a good chance for me to get involved in a new project. After all, Kummersdorf is only a few miles south of the city and within easy distance of my home. Dornberger indicated that the budget for the project had no limit, and that my work would be funded indefinitely!' He grinned like a schoolboy in a sweet shop;

then, his face soured. 'It wasn't until I got here… that I realised that I would not be permitted to leave…' Von Reichter tailed off.

'How are they treating you? You know, the soldiers?'

'Reasonably well. They leave us alone mostly. We have a bed each, and three meals a day. Albeit army food, but it's alright.'

'And what of the work? The laboratories?'

Von Reichter perked up. 'The main building has an extensive laboratory space in the basement. The facilities are superb! Lathes, engineering rigs, chemical containment areas, fuel-mixing platforms, electronic components; everything you could possibly imagine! With a laboratory like this I can do ten years of research in less than a year!'

Mayer gave a suspicious look. 'So what exactly are they asking us to build?'

'I haven't seen it all. I've been tasked with making a navigation and guidance system for a rocket. The rocket is being built on the base – a big one – bigger than anything any of us has worked on before. There's a test launch pad on site.'

'So much money… and so many men… why?… What are we *really* doing here? Scientific progress always comes at a price.' Mayer grabbed his friend by the lapels. '*Why* are we building rockets? *What* will Herr Hitler do with them? He will kill us all, start a war!'

Von Reichter spoke soothingly, concealing the start his friend had just given him. 'Gustav? Are you alright…? You are not yourself…'

Mayer released his grip.

'Hans… I am sorry, so much has happened…'

'Have no fear. Dornberger is a good man, and he has explained things to me. The Führer wishes only to see a strong Germany, strong in the sciences… strong in rocket science. You see, it's just a political statement to the world. German technology is the best and we are at the forefront of this new exciting field of rocket science.' Von Reichter believed his own naive optimism.

'No, I don't trust them.' Mayer shook his head. 'Who else is here?'

Von Reichter shrugged. 'Almost everyone, even Wernher von Braun.'

Wernher von Braun was a brilliant and dynamic young physicist, on the cusp of creating a new rocket that needed even more powerful fuels than before. In the world of rocket science he was an icon, a living legend.

Mayer furrowed his brow and gritted his teeth. 'This is no philanthropic science project. We're being used! I don't like it. Mark my words, once they have what they want, the Nazis will kill us all!'

CHAPTER 14

SIS Headquarters

Sir Hugh Sinclair sat at his desk in the bowels of the SIS building on the London embankment. He tapped his gold Parker pen on the notepad, and then checked his wrist watch for the third time in as many minutes. He eased back in the chair and exhaled, taking comfort from the rich smell of the leather.

Was this a good idea or not?

He wasn't sure.

In any event, things were in motion. Professor Einstein had come with a recommendation from Churchill; and the President of the United States, no less.

But he was still a *German*.

A timid knock on the door stirred Sinclair from his thoughts.

'Come!'

His secretary stepped respectfully into the doorway. 'Sir, Mr Einstein, sorry, I mean Professor Einstein for you.'

Sinclair stood up. 'Thank you, please show him in.'

The secretary ushered Einstein into the room with a smile, shutting the door behind her.

Sinclair stepped out from behind the oak desk and stretched out his hand. 'Thank you for coming to London, Professor.'

Einstein shuffled forwards in his ill-fitting dark suit, his eyes glazed over, as if detached from reality. He politely shook Sinclair's hand. 'Yes, yes, well I was already at a physics conference in Oxford.'

Sinclair held his grasp. Soft hands, a gentleman. He fixed his gaze on Einstein, and was met by the Professor's dark impenetrable eyes. It was as if… the weight of the world was on his shoulders.

Something didn't add up – was Churchill keeping something back?

'Welcome Professor, please, take a seat.' He gestured Einstein towards one of the more comfortable chairs on either side of the coffee table. 'So, how did you find Oxford? This is your first visit to England I believe?'

Einstein shrugged, 'It was fine. My colleagues there have treated me well.'

An empty pause filled the room. Sinclair decided to tackle the issue head-on. 'Professor Einstein, you are here because of the Leipzig situation.'

'Yes… the Leipzig situation,' repeated Einstein, shaking his head.

'I understand you know about the *document*… '

'Yes, the one we speak of… I read it in Leipzig. Mayer's work is astonishing.'

Sinclair glanced around the room, and dropped to a whisper. 'Let me give you my assurance. Our man has recovered the article in question.'

'Oh, thank God… ' Einstein closed his eyes, unable to conceal his relief, then sat upright, suddenly alert. 'There was a draft and a final copy. You have them both?'

'Yes. We have it all, both copies.'

'That's good, very good… ' nodded Einstein. 'Thank you, thank you… I cannot tell you how much relief this news brings.' Einstein let out a long sigh; he had not slept in days. His brow suddenly knotted. 'Who else knows about this?'

'Nobody, well, except Mr Churchill, and your friend President Roosevelt. Then, it's just *you* and *I*.'

'What about your man?'

'He was given strict instructions to recover the item, and read only enough to identify the correct document. He can be trusted and will take this secret to his grave. Anyway, he is a soldier not a scientist and would have no idea of the content.'

'Then it is safe?' Einstein studied Sinclair's face for reassurance.

'*Yes*, it *is safe*. In the personal possession of Mr Churchill, not even SIS will hold this information.'

'There is more... ' Einstein rubbed his brow. '... My friend, Professor Mayer, Gustav Mayer has gone missing. I am not sure where, but his life is certainly in danger. Soldiers have ransacked his office!'

'Yes, we know. Our man tapped into the secure telegraph in Leipzig. It seems the Professor will be transferred to Berlin: some military installation a few miles south of the city. That's all we have for now, except that he will be with other physicists and chemists. One of the other scientists is a fellow called Von Reichter. I believe you know him? What do you think this means, Professor?'

'It would seem the Nazis are building something. If Von Reichter is there, then it will be rockets, or something else that uses similar technology.'

'Do you think they know about Mayer's work?'

'No, Gustav would die rather than reveal this to the Nazis.'

'I don't know... ' Sinclair shook his head, '... every man has his breaking point. If they interrogate him enough... well... he will surely talk.'

'Interrogation! My God! We must get him out!'

'My team is drawing up some plans as we speak, we will do what we can.'

'Herr Hitler would regard that as an act of war if you used British soldiers to attack a German military installation on the edge of their capital city.' Einstein's shoulders slumped.

'Don't worry, we are well versed in this kind of work.' Sinclair gave a wry smile.

'Gustav *must* be saved. There can be no delay. The knowledge he holds is far too important,' affirmed Einstein.

'The military base is well defended, so a more subtle approach is needed, something that will not draw attention to Professor Mayer.'

'It all sounds very risky,' worried Einstein.

'My man is working up a plan.'

'A plan… yes… yes… good idea, an escape plan.'

'Professor Einstein, we will do all we can, but if what you say is true, should the mission go wrong… we *could* not let Mayer remain alive.'

'I cannot condone the killing of another human being.' Einstein folded his arms in protest.

'We may not have a choice,' warned Sinclair.

Einstein knew that the argument was logical, but he also knew that Gustav was his friend. A friend who had entrusted him with possibly *the* greatest discovery of the next hundred years. That was a trust that he could not break. 'Save him. Your man must find a way.'

'It seems that you have some influential friends. Mr Churchill has already reiterated the importance of the mission. We are putting all of our resources and our best man behind the operation. We will do everything we can.'

There was nothing more that could be said.

Einstein and Sinclair rose from their chairs and shook hands again. Einstein held Sinclair's grasp and stared into his eyes.

'Please, *please* save him. You *must* save him.'

Sinclair changed his estimation of Einstein. This was probably one of the most important operations the SIS was ever likely to conduct, or so it seemed.

Nash waited inside Braithwaite's tea shop. The Victorian opulence of Burlington Arcade filled the air with expectation. He fidgeted discretely in his chair, trying to relieve the uncomfortable itching of his Sunday best. It wasn't working; the starched shirt rubbed his armpits and neckline.

He tugged at his collar to loosen the stranglehold of the tie, and exhaled. It didn't seem to make any difference.

He stared at the flowery tablecloth, bone china cups, and the crisp white doilies. It was an idiotic idea, what the hell was he doing? Trussed up like the Christmas turkey, and for what?

His answer walked in through the door.

Dressed to perfection in a pink and white floral dress, her hair up in an elegant net. The pearls around her neck showed off her delicate features. She looked radiant; an English rose blossoming in the height of summer.

Nash's heart melted. Emily was the daughter of an English gentleman. She was out of his league – and he knew it – but at that moment it didn't seem to matter.

Nash jumped to his feet, and offered her the vacant chair at their cosy table.

'Emily… you look… well, lovely.' Nash smiled as she sat down. He inhaled gently, lingering on the fragrance. Her lavender scent soaked into his soul.

'Thank you Danny, I don't think I've seen you looking so smart in a long time.' She smiled back.

Nash took his seat, grinning like an idiot.

'Danny, I must say, this is a wonderful treat. I haven't been here for years… well not since Mother left.'

Her radiant glow faded a little.

Nash thought it best to change the subject. 'Darjeeling or Earl Grey?'

He beckoned the waiter over.

The young lad looked like a stuffed penguin in his serving outfit. Nash couldn't help a smirk at the thought that suddenly popped into his head: *You and me both pal.*

'Would you like your afternoon tea now, sir?'

'Yes, please. Emily, what will you have?' Nash beamed.

'Darjeeling please, thank you.'

The waiter nodded courteously, and scurried off to get their order.

'So, Danny, you've been away again?'

Nash shifted his gaze, trying not to look Emily in the eye. 'Yes, yes, I have.'

'I don't suppose you can tell me where. Another secret mission for my father?'

Nash absently picked up a silver teaspoon from the table and started fiddling it through his fingers. 'Something like that... you know how things are in Whitehall.'

'What happened to your face?'

She raised a hand to the scratches and splinter marks on his cheek. The silky touch of her fingers instantly raised his pulse.

Nash struggled to keep still. 'Nothing much, just some flack.' His mind flashed back to the dense woodland, and the scrape of the branches after diving out of the train from Leipzig. 'You should have seen the other guy!' Nash forced a comic cheesy grin.

'Oh, stop it Danny! It isn't funny!' She tilted her head in mock disbelief and laughed.

Nash joined in the laughter.

The waiter arrived with their tea and gingerly placed a silver teapot, a round of cucumber sandwiches, and a platter of the most delightful cupcakes that Nash had ever seen on the table.

The laughter subsided.

'Would you like some tea Mr Nash?' Emily blushed as she served him tea.

'Why, thank you, my lady.' He gave a theatrical nod.

They erupted into childish laughter.

Nash passed the sandwiches, and sunk his teeth into a neat triangle of white bread. The bite of the cool crisp cucumber filled his taste buds with pleasure. Suddenly hungry, he devoured a couple of rounds. His heart pumped as he watched Emily delicately nibble on a slice of bread.

'Tastes great doesn't it?' Nash grabbed another sandwich.

She chuckled between bites. 'Danny! Your manners!'

He tipped his non-existent hat. 'Sorry, my lady. It won't happen again.'

She smiled and gave a mischievous laugh. 'It's *will not*... not *won't*! We shall have to send you off for elocution lessons! Won't we!'

'Yes Madame, I'll be on the next bus to Eaton!'

Emily chuckled. 'Danny Nash, are you mocking me?!'

'Certainly not, my lady.' Nash dropped a sugar lump into his tea, and stirred it vigorously. Lifting the cup to his lips, he took a loud slurp.

'Danny, that's disgusting!' She tittered into her napkin. 'What would my father think!'

'I think... I think he would send me on another mission!'

Emily wiped her lips slowly. Her smile dropped. 'Danny?'

He grinned. 'What?'

'Danny, you're going away again, aren't you? That's what this is all about!' Moisture suddenly filled her eyes.

'No... no... it's not what you think.' Nash reached across the table and caressed the back of her hand. 'Emily, believe me. It's not what you think.'

'But you are going away?'

'Yes... yes, I am.' Nash lowered his head, unable to meet her gaze.

'Danny, why?! First Father, and now you! Why do you have to go away again?'

Nash paused. Reaching inside his breast pocket, he produced a small blue box.

Emily flushed. 'Danny, what are you doing?'

Nash flipped open the box.

'It's your mother's engagement ring. I had the diamonds reset, with your father's blessing of course... '

'Oh! Danny, it's beautiful!' Her white teeth shone through

her perfectly plump lips. She cradled the little box in her palm, admiring the diamonds.

'Emily, I… I have to tell you something, before… you know…'

Her face soured. 'Danny, say it… Danny!'

'You're right. I do have to go away again. I am not sure how long. But I thought…'

'You thought what Danny? You could marry me and then make me a widow the next day?! You're just like my father. All the damned wars! The sudden absences, not knowing whether he was alive or dead! It destroyed her…'

She began to sob.

'Emily, no, it won't be like that! I promise! I… I…'

'No Danny!' She abruptly closed the box and tossed it across the table. 'No Danny, I can't marry you! You see… you're already married to King and country – and my bloody father!'

She erupted in a flood of tears, and hastily pushed back the chair.

'Emily, please!'

'Danny, I can't… I am sorry…'

She dashed out of the tea shop, sobbing.

Nash slumped in the chair, the sound of the doorbell reverberating around his skull. The shop fell silent.

Numbed, he slowly picked up the blue box from the table, and dropped it back in his pocket. He closed his eyes against the pain, and reverted to type.

The shutters came down.

Emily was right: soldiering, King and country, were everything.

CHAPTER 15

Rescue from Kummersdorf

Nash checked his watch – three in the morning – not too bad considering. Things were more or less on schedule. He wound down the window on the stolen German staff car, sucking in deep breaths of the cold night air, and gazed up at the sky. Utter blackness. Thick clouds blotted out the moonlight. There was no sound, save the gentle creak of the pine trees and the odd scurry of wildlife. The narrow forestry track had been a good choice; concealed from the road but, equally, not far from the target area – Kummersdorf.

He fidgeted in the driver's seat, scratching at the stolen German uniform. It would have to do. He checked it over again for bloodstains. He wouldn't pass as a German officer with a dirty uniform. He brushed off a grubby mark on the labels, and glanced at the corpse in the adjacent passenger seat; the guy looked well and truly dead. It was all part of the deception.

Nash stepped out of the car, pulling the pistol from his pocket. He screwed the silencer into place and after instinctively checking the balance of the gun, he flicked off the safety. He popped open the trunk.

'Up, on your feet.' He waived the weapon, gesturing the half-naked officer out of the vehicle. Muffled protests issued through the gag.

'Silence.' Nash shoved the pistol against his forehead – instant compliance. He grabbed the officer by the scruff of his long johns, and frogmarched him towards the tree line. More urgent muffled protests issued through the gag. Straining at the rope binding his hands, the prisoner dug his heels into the mud.

Nash shoved hard. 'Just fucking move.' He lifted the prisoner by the scruff, as he made his way into the trees.

'Stop.'

The prisoner complied.

Raising his pistol to the back of the officer's head, Nash fired. The body slumped to the floor. Another double tap in the back ensured the outcome. He lifted the corpse by the ankles, and dragged the body into some brush. Nash dusted himself down. 'Christ!' he whispered to himself, shaking his head. He unscrewed the silencer and made his way back to the car.

He gave the car the once-over. Everything seemed ready. The neatly arranged bullet holes in the windscreen and those in the driver's body would be convincing enough in the dark. Exactly the sort of damage one would expect from a single burst of automatic gunfire. He repositioned the driver's body a little more. It had to look right. Something was missing – then he twigged it – fresh blood. He leant across to the corpse, and squeezed the wounds on the dead man's chest. It did the trick; a fresh upwelling of blood appeared on the tunic. Details were important if the plan was going to work.

London had sanctioned the job, but it was a calculated risk. The base was heavily defended, and the mission relied on stealth. There were many unknowns, not least the state of Professor Mayer. Escape depended on Mayer's mobility. Doubtless, the old boy would be slow, but they both needed to make it to the rendezvous point alive.

Nash flicked on a small torch, and checked his identity papers again. He had to admit, the boys in London had excelled themselves this time with a brilliant forgery. It would do the job.

He checked his watch – time to go – the charges would blow in ten minutes.

The car started first time, and bumped along the forestry

track without getting stuck in the mud. The headlights finally picked up the perimeter fence as the vehicle swung onto the road. If this was to succeed, it would need to be the performance of a life time. If it didn't; well, that came with the job.

Nash started the charade on cue. He switched on the main beam, and flashed the headlights, pressing the horn repeatedly as he swerved the car back and forth along the road. Hopefully the sentries on the main gate would get the message: a comrade in distress.

He pulled up sharply at the main gate and stepped from the vehicle, pacing urgently towards the sentries; chest out, with as much swagger as he could muster.

'I am Commandant Filsner! I have urgent orders from Berlin!' reported Nash in perfect German. 'We were attacked on the road, and my orderly has been shot! He needs medical attention, open the gate!' The sentries looked perplexed.

Right on schedule, the explosive charges went off. Flashes of brilliant, white light blinded the sentries for a few moments. Drifts of thick smoke and noise added to the confusion.

Nash shouted over the noise. 'Quickly! Open the gate, we are under attack!'

The two sentries, disorientated by the sudden change in circumstances, gaped at each other.

'See for yourself!' Nash waved his papers at the nearest sentry, and gestured towards the vehicle.

The sentry poked his head through the driver's door. One glance at the German orderly covered in blood was enough. 'Hans! Open the gate! Quickly!'

His comrade duly complied with a sudden burst of efficiency.

'That's more like it!' Nash headed for the car.

The sentry held the driver's door open. Nash piled in, revving the engine in an instant. At the same time the sentry started waving his arms at the machine gun post to signal his intent. He didn't need to bother; the machine gun was already turned away from the main gate and trained in the direction of the explosions.

Nash slammed the vehicle into gear, and sped through the main gate, across the open ground of the artillery field, following the short road to the main accommodation block. Lights flashed on in most of the buildings, as soldiers poured out of their barracks and into the small parade ground that marked the entrance to the laboratories.

There was still time – but not long – the soldiers would soon be organised; five minutes, maybe less.

He stepped briskly from the car and walked smartly to the first building in the accommodation block, hoping the Oscar-winning performance would hold.

'I have orders to escort some of the scientific staff to safety! Take me to Professor Mayer!' Nash spoke again in perfect German with a hint of the aristocracy for good measure.

The young soldier sitting at the reception desk stared back nervously and barely got his mouth open before Nash interrupted.

'On your feet soldier! Move! Quickly now! Take me to Professor Mayer!'

The soldier gulped as his spotty teenage face registered the order. Another explosion sounded outside. 'But... but sir, I... forgive me... I just man the desk and keep track of the domestic matters. I don't have the authority to move inmates... ' The desk clerk reached for the phone.

Nash pressed home the advantage. 'What is this?! Do you not salute a senior officer?! On your feet!'

The young soldier decided it was best to do as he was told. He jumped to his feet with a crisp Nazi salute.

'Good, now to your files, where is Professor Mayer? Hurry, the enemy is closing in!'

'Yes sir, his bunk is... ' The young soldier flipped through the register, hastily trying to find the right room.

'Quickly! Take me to him,' urged Nash.

'Ah! Here it is… bunk room number seven… ' The soldier memorised the room number and dropped the file on the desk. 'This way Commandant… ' Suddenly keen, the young soldier moved smartly along to the next block in the building.

Nash took over as the desk clerk pushed the door open to the bunk house. It was clean and tidy, with a row of eight bunks along each wall. Just like any other military quarters. However, all the occupants were out of bed and milling around, wondering what the noise was about outside.

'Mayer! Professor Gustav Mayer!' shouted Nash.

Silence – the gathering of scientists turned to face Nash, uncertain as to what was going on.

'Mayer! Professor Gustav Mayer!' he repeated.

This time he got a response from the back of the room.

'I am Mayer.'

The sea of bodies parted to reveal the Professor standing in his night clothes.

Nash stepped through the crowd. 'Get dressed quickly, you have one minute. Then you are leaving; dressed or otherwise.'

Mayer glanced at the officer's insignia – a commandant – there was no point arguing. His eyes studied Nash's face for a second. Had he met this Commandant before? It was possible of course; there were so many soldiers on the base.

Nash grabbed the Professor firmly by the arm and began to steer him out of the door before anyone could protest. The young soldier followed at a good pace, almost jogging to keep up.

'Commandant, beg my interruption… ' Nash kept walking. '… If you are taking the Professor… there are papers to sign… sir… '

Nash cut him off with a wave of his hand. 'No time for that now! Phone through to the main gate, let them know I am coming! Move!' He kept moving briskly towards the car with Mayer in tow.

The young soldier scurried off to find a phone as he had been ordered.

It was a long shot, but it might work. The access road would soon be clogged up with military vehicles. If they were going to escape, it would have to be now.

Nash opened the rear passenger door of the staff car, and pushed the Professor into the back. Mayer instantly recoiled at the sight of the dead orderly in the front seat.

'Don't worry about him… ' Nash smiled as he shut the driver's door and started the engine.

'What is going on? Where are you taking me?' Mayer glanced again at the dead orderly.

'I am here to protect you, Professor. Do not be alarmed,' Nash spoke reassuringly in fluent German. There would be time for explanations later.

He gunned the engine and moved off, keeping the speed to an urgent pace in a business-like military fashion; but not too fast to draw unwanted attention. They joined the main access road.

'Shit!' Nash cursed to himself. A small convoy of vehicles were already on the move. There wasn't much choice. He slipped in behind the lead car, just squeezing in front of two trucks. The vehicles headed for the main gate. With luck, he would simply be waved through with the rest of the convoy.

It was not to be. The convoy stopped at the barrier.

A sentry stood in front of the barrier, gesticulating with his weapon. A heated exchange started up with the driver in the lead vehicle, but the guard was having none of it, shaking his head and waving his weapon around. The convoy was going nowhere. A second sentry was on the phone in the small booth adjacent to the barrier. With lots of nodding down the phone, it looked like the sentry was taking orders from a senior office. No doubt, it was the order to close the main gate.

The sentry finished up on the telephone, and jogged out of

the booth, clicking off the safety on his machine gun. He planted himself squarely in front of the barrier, raising his weapon at the first vehicle in the convoy, and stood firm.

The game was up.

Suddenly, Nash slammed the car into reverse, crunching into the truck behind. Then, he hit the accelerator.

The car sped forward, miraculously swerving around the side of the lead vehicle without losing speed; but the nearest sentry was quick to act. Rounds thudded home, mostly into the dead orderly on the passenger seat. Realising his mistake, the sentry tried to adjust his fire – all too late – he was swept aside as the car smashed through the barrier at break-neck speed.

Nash brushed splinters of wood and glass from his eyes as the windscreen shattered. Seconds later a blast of steam engulfed him.

The radiator!

Flooring the accelerator, and ignoring the boiling radiator, he headed back towards the forestry track. A glance in the rearview mirror showed the headlights of the first truck already swinging out onto the road, only a few hundred yards behind.

He gunned the accelerator and switched off the headlights. Seconds later, he swerved the car off the road onto the forestry track. He put his foot down, ignoring the protests from the Professor being thrown around in the back. Both men bounced around violently as the car lumbered through potholes. A loud metallic whip announced the cracking of the rear axle – what the hell, they would ditch the car soon enough.

He checked the rearview mirror; as if right on cue, the first truck sped past the entrance to the track, closely followed by the second. Nash gave a sigh of relief; it would buy a couple of minutes at least.

Suddenly, he was thrown forward, with ribs burying deep into the steering wheel, his head slammed into the door frame.

Dazed, he glanced up at the tree trunk protruding from the now crumpled engine. Christ knows, they were lucky to have made it this far in the pitch darkness. The engine shuddered in a spout of steam and died.

'Are you injured?' The Professor seemed perplexed by the question. 'Any gunshot wounds?' repeated Nash in German.

'Well… err… no… I don't think so… ' Mayer patted himself down looking for blood.

'We have to go, follow me.' Nash pulled the Professor from the wreck. There was no time for etiquette. Shouldering the Professor to give him some support, Nash stumbled away into the woods.

The ground rose steeply and, with fallen branches hampering each step, Nash pumped hard, ignoring the cramp building up in his thighs. Adjusting his sweaty palm to keep a grip of the Professor's waist belt, Nash heaved; but it was no good, Mayer was a dead weight.

'Stop… please… stop.' Mayer puffed and panted. Despite the cold night air, sweat poured from his face.

Nash released his grip. Mayer collapsed at the base of a tree trunk.

'Professor, look at me! Listen to me, do exactly as I say!' Nash maintained perfect German.

'Where are you taking me? Who are you?'

Nash spoke calmly with authority. 'A full explanation will come later. For now you must trust me.'

'No, tell me now!'

Nash spoke in English. 'I come with a message from Professor Einstein.'

'Albert?! Message! What message?!'

'Come with me, you can ask him yourself.'

'Come where? Where are we going?'

'Look, I know it's been rough going, but about two

kilometres away over the next hill is a lake. That's our rendezvous point – someone will pick us up.'

'Someone? Who? Where are we going?'

'You're going to have to trust me… ' Nash smiled as he flipped open a compass to take a bearing. 'It's this way, not far… '

Mayer shrugged.

Nash hauled the Professor to his feet. Mayer wheezed as he gave him support.

'Look, we have to keep going.' Nash prayed they could cover the necessary ground in time; within less than an hour the place would be swarming with troops.

He hauled the Professor along, ignoring the discomfort of the stolen German uniform and the ill-fitting boots.

The Professor got worse as each minute passed. They were forced to stop again and again. They finally came to halt at a fire break in the tree line which seemed to mark the ridge above the lake. Both men collapsed to the ground.

'See… ' Nash pointed. 'The lake, and easier going from here: downhill.' He grinned. The Professor just wheezed. 'Come on, it's less than half a kilometre now. We can go straight down the fire break, and be there in ten minutes.' Nash gave another smile of white teeth in the darkness, and patted the Professor on the shoulder to give encouragement.

Suddenly, the sound of an officer barking orders broke the silence behind them. Multiple pairs of boots trampled through the woodland. Noise bounced around the forest as the soldiers fanned out along the hillside. Nash calculated the odds – *not good* – they would be on the ridge in no time. Even if it was only the two trucks from the convoy, it would be at least thirty or forty men.

He grabbed the Professor and started off down the fire break. Pushing hard, tripping over sticks and half-sawn timbers in the darkness, the loud crack of braking branches gave their position away.

'This way! This way! Cut them off!' The bright white of a

phosphorus flare lit up the shadows. A German officer stood silhouetted on the ridge. 'There! There! After them!'

Soldiers poured over the ridge and into the fire break as the flare petered out.

Nash tightened his grip on Mayer, almost lifting him off the ground, and increased the pace. Blundering down the fire break, with shouts going up behind, speed was now everything. Nash jolted his way down the hill, focusing hard on covering the rough ground, with his legs burning and shoulder aching under the Professor's weight.

The rough grass and timber finally gave way to sand as they stumbled on to the shoreline at the south end of the lake. Dumping the Professor to the ground, Nash stood over him, pistol drawn, firing controlled rounds up the fire break – it would slow them down – nothing more.

'Keep your head down!' Nash dropped into a crouching position to load a fresh magazine. The telltale noise of an engine rumbled in the distance.

'The plane!'

With renewed vigour Nash fired the next clip into the hillside. The tone of the engine changed as the seaplane touched down on the water.

'Let's go!' Pulling up the Professor, Nash sprinted for the water's edge. He squinted into the darkness; some white fuselage appeared about fifty yards away.

More shouts went up on the hillside; the breaking of branches signalled the rush of men down the fire break.

The first silhouettes came into view. Conserving ammunition, Nash gave a gentle double tap on the trigger. A silhouette crumpled to the ground. Another double tap, another soldier, then another.

'Can you swim?!' Nash fired again – another corpse.

'What?!' Mayer looked at Nash, then at the water.

'I said, can you swim?!' Another double tap; spent shell casings rattled onto the Professor cowering at his feet.

'Yes, but… '

The plane slowed to a taxi at the end of the lake, and went into a search pattern.

'Good. The plane will find us! Into the water – swim!' Nash didn't wait for a reply; firing one last burst, he pulled the Professor into the lake.

Suddenly stunned by the ice-cold water, Nash gasped an involuntary deep breath. With his heart skipping erratically, his limbs turned to jelly – cold shock immersion – he wasn't sure if the Professor could handle it.

Mayer flailed hopelessly.

'Breathe! Breathe! Fight it! Kick with your legs! Swim!' He gripped the Professor by the shirt collar, and kicked hard as the first few rounds zipped into the water.

The noise and white foam on the dark lake made an easy target; more bullets slashed into the water, much closer than the first volley.

'Swim! Swim!' Heaving with numb fingers and with the Professor struggling aimlessly, Nash lost his grip.

Mayer disappeared under the water, bullets danced around their position.

Ducking under, grabbing hair, Nash pulled Mayer to the surface. Rounds landed ever closer. Locking his arm around the Professor's chest, kicking with his legs and using his spare arm to get some kind of rhythm going, Nash headed into deeper water.

Suddenly, the plane loomed out of the darkness, only twenty feet away.

More rounds splashed into the water as the plane attracted gunfire. Not fancying an icy death, Nash kicked for the fuselage door.

The deafening noise of a heavy-calibre machine gun, the rattle of hot shell casings, and the smell of cordite greeted him as he touched the aluminium skid of the fuselage.

About bloody time! Some return fire from the plane.

There was no cover on the gravel beach. Screams went up in the darkness as the gunner found his mark.

A hand grabbed the Professor by the collar and unceremoniously hauled him onto the skid. 'Heave! For God's sake! Heave!' The crew man shouted over the din of the engines, rearranging his grip. The sodden Professor weighed a ton but, with purchase under the Professor's arms, and with Nash pushing from underneath, they bundled him through the small door into the plane. Nash hauled himself up onto the skid.

The crew man reappeared in the doorway, putting out a hand to assist. A thud of bullets sprayed blood from the crew man's chest, and punched holes in the surrounding airframe. He fell forwards, over Nash, and into the water.

Half hauling himself into the doorway, half lying on the skid, Nash poked his head through the door.

'Go, go, fucking go!'

The pilot didn't need a second invitation, and pushed the throttle forward. The plane accelerated, engines roaring.

Nash dug his hands into the lip of the doorway, desperately struggling to hold on as his feet dragged in the freezing water.

The soldiers on the shoreline sensed the departure and renewed their efforts. They were in luck. The cabin rattled to the popping sound of rounds hitting home; a real choice collection of small arms fire. A staccato of machine gunfire hit the cab. The pilot pushed the controls forward, flat out. Rounds clattered into the control panel; the pilot ducked instinctively as bullets peppered into the fuselage around his head.

The plane picked up more speed. The skids started to lift off the water.

Then it happened – a volley punctured the pilot's rib cage. His body danced like a rag doll as the shots rang home. Slumping forward onto the controls, the pilot was dead.

The plane responded by veering swiftly to the right, and then to the left. The passengers inside were thrown around the cabin. Nash lost his grip; flipping into the air like a wet fish, he bounced along on the water before coming to a hard stop in the middle of the lake. At that speed it was like hitting concrete. He lay semi-comatose on the water. Miraculously pockets of buoyancy in the ill-fitting German uniform kept him afloat.

The plane careered on across the lake, totally out of control, and swinging violently. Suddenly, the portside wing tip touched the water. It was enough to send the plane cart wheeling. The plane skimmed towards the shallows, spinning several times, scattering bits of fuselage along the way, before the mangled remains came crashing to a halt a few feet from the shore. The engine finally stalled. Then silence. No one stirred from inside the wreckage.

In the aftermath the troops focused on searching the plane and the immediate shore. It only took a few minutes before they were wading out to the wreck. The pilot and crew man were dead. The Professor, on the other hand, had been strapped into a seat. It had probably saved his life. He was badly injured, but nonetheless still alive.

In the gloom of the night, the semi-conscious body of Nash drifted away on the surface of the lake.

CHAPTER 16

Cape Town

Heinkel stood on the concrete pier, and took a deep breath. It was great to be on solid ground; the boat from New York to Cape Town had been a long haul. He flexed his toes, feeling the grip of the fine black soles against the firm substrate. A sudden breeze swirled a coating of fine dust onto his gleaming shoes and into his eyes. Blinking, he kept a firm hold on the leather satchel, and brushed down the lapel of his pinstriped suit with his free hand.

The weight of the bag tugged on his shoulder muscles. He curled his fingers more tightly around the handle and, tensing his frame, he attempted to walk evenly towards the customs house. His eyes flicked down at the satchel. It bulged a little more than one would like for a border crossing, but it was too late to change the plan now; besides the contents were important to the Reich.

He scanned ahead.

A wooden balustrade, some twenty feet tall, topped with rusting barbed wire demarcated the end of the pier. Strands of wire mingled into the chain mail fence on the edges of the pier, preventing any escape onto the adjacent rocks. The only way out was through the small timber construction that was the customs house.

Heinkel strained against the bright sunlight to see into the relative gloom of the customs shed. Thankfully, the shutters were wide open, letting air circulate into the space. Another dust devil spat grit into his eyes. Ignoring it, he assessed the threat.

A spartan office was occupied by one table, two chairs, and mostly empty shelving. A coffee pot sat on the stove at the far end of the room. One man stood in the corner, stirring something into a cup. Another leaned against the shutters; a worn green hat – the type an experienced hunter would wear – concealed his features. Thick cigar smoke curled from a cheroot in his hand. A third man occupied the passport booth at the end of the building.

Heinkel examined the booth. A fat American waiting in the queue bobbed to and fro, blocking his vision.

The passport controller sat on a stool. The open face of the booth gave easy access for travellers to hand over their documents. A pistol protruded from under his khaki uniform, but that was to be expected; such officials were always armed in South Africa. A door came into view behind the booth: the entrance to an office? Or a guard room full of soldiers?

The sweaty mass of the American tourist shuffled forward as Heinkel joined the back of the line.

The official read the American's passport, pausing to scrutinise the facial features of the holder. After some ten or fifteen seconds the American got his passport back – so far no bags or pockets had been checked.

Heinkel stepped forward, with his documents open at the correct page. He nodded a silent hello to the official.

The customs officer scrutinised his passport, flicking the pages. 'What brings you to Cape Town, sir?'

'I am here on business,' came a neutral reply.

'How long are you planning to stay, sir?'

'Ten days.'

The official looked up, checking Heinkel's face against the photograph in his passport. 'And where are you staying, sir?'

'The Table Mountain Hotel.' A precise and truthful answer.

The side door suddenly opened, the bushman's hat stuck out – an office door after all. A tall but stocky muscular frame filled the doorway. Smoke from the cheroot partly obscured the man's face. Dust and grime marked his green shirt; a packet of cigarettes protruded from his breast pocket. His bush fatigues sported a worn-looking Gurkha Kukri knife.

Heinkel stood fast, moving his eyes slowly between the two men. The official, he could drop in no time; but the big Africaan was a different proposition.

Rudy Temple stepped forward blocking any chance of escape.

'Would you mind stepping into the office, sir? A random bag check if you please,' Temple lied.

Heinkel stood firm. Gazing into the booth, he held out his hand. 'My passport?'

Temple spoke calmly to the official. 'I'll take that for now.'

The customs officer duly opened the rear of the booth and handed over the documents.

Temple escorted Heinkel into the back office.

'Take a seat Mr… ' Temple examined the passport; the pages were watermarked. It seemed genuine. '… Mr Heinkel… from Hamburg.'

Heinkel moved slowly and purposefully, gently lowering himself into one of the wooden chairs, his eyes fixed on Temple. He placed his satchel on the floor, against the table leg, the handle accessible for a quick getaway.

Temple puffed on his cheroot for a second, tapping the passport absently in his palm. 'Well, Mr Heinkel. What brings you so far away from home?'

'I am here on business.' Heinkel sat upright and firm.

'Yep, for sure Mr Heinkel, but what do you do for a living? Why are you here in Cape Town?' Temple stood towering over the desk, drawing on his cheroot.

Heinkel recognised the posturing, and smiled inwardly. 'I am in the manufacturing business. I am here to trade for raw materials.'

Temple nodded his appreciation, waving the cheroot. 'What's in the bag?'

Heinkel shrugged. 'Documents and valuables belonging to my employer.'

Temple stooped, picking up the bag. He dropped it on the table with a clank. 'Feels kind of heavy for a bunch of documents.' He eased off the leather straps and pulled out a manila file; he opened it onto the desk. 'What's this?'

'It's a list of supplies.'

'Go on… '

'Materials needed for my work.'

'What business?'

'Industrial components and engineering.'

Temple leafed a few of the pages. Mostly chemicals, machine parts, tools, and general supplies. The list seemed to tally with the man's story, but Temple wasn't buying it. He dug deeper into the bag, pulling out a heavy machine part.

'What do you call this?' Temple held the metal object up to the light. It was a heavy casing with a system of grills and flanges; a bit like the carburettor from an automobile. Perhaps he'd been wrong. Maybe this was just a straightforward business deal after all.

Heinkel sat calmly. 'Just a component from a machine in one of my factories.'

Temple studied the German's face. If he was lying, he was doing it well.

'Who are you visiting in Cape Town?'

'The Cape Mineral Company, and a couple of other metal smelters.'

'What for?'

'To place orders for the Weimar Republic. Germany is an industrialised nation, and I understand South Africa is open for business – I am here to buy metals.'

'I see Mr Heinkel, so your employer is the German government?'

Heinkel smiled. 'Something like that… '

'You've come in on a boat from America. What were you doing in the USA?'

'We have clients in America as well as South Africa. Germany has interests in many places.' Heinkel gave a majestic wave of his hand.

'I am sure you do.' Temple bounced the heavy flanged component in his hand. 'Did you get this in America?'

'I am sorry, that's confidential. Business is competitive, as I am sure you understand.' Heinkel forced a neutral expression.

'Yep, South Africa is dead keen on keeping things confidential. I am sure our Minister for Trade would be the first to confirm that… ' Temple leant forward and exhaled a huge cloud of smoke into Heinkel's face, '… but I *still* need to know where you came from in the USA and your route to Cape Town.'

Heinkel's lungs surged with irritation at the smoke, but he forced himself to keep still.

'I have come from the Rockefeller Foundation in New York.' Heinkel gave a wry smile. 'There is a letter of invitation in my jacket pocket. If I could take it out.' He gestured towards his own pocket.

Temple nodded and the German produced the letter. It was an embossed letter, inviting him to New York. The letter was genuine. It seemed that Heinkel was an industrialist doing some research on some new engineering techniques for manufacturing. The Rockefeller Foundation was partly sponsoring his research. It was possible. The Rockefeller Foundation was set up in 1913 by the immensely wealthy and philanthropic Rockefeller family. It was well known for sponsoring good causes all over the world, including scientific research.

The Rockefellers were also of German descent, so they probably had some legitimate ties with Germany. They were also immensely powerful, owning half the banking sector of

135

America, and international companies, including ones in South Africa. If this German was really a friend of the Rockefellers, then he might have friends in high places in Cape Town as well.

'Do you know Mr Rockefeller then?'

'I have met with him on behalf of the Weimar Republic. My business with Mr Rockefeller brings me here. An errand on my way home, if you like.'

'I see.' He nodded slowly.

This was no time for a diplomatic incident with Germany.

'An errand you say?'

Heinkel maintained a steady tone in his voice. 'As I mentioned, Germany has interests in the USA and now I have business in Cape Town.'

Temple suddenly spoke with polite formality. 'Thank you Mr Heinkel. It seems that everything is in order. You're free to go about your business in Cape Town, for now. However, since you are visiting on behalf of Germany, I am unable to return your passport just yet. Protocol you understand.'

Heinkel gave a hard stare. 'I appreciate your concern, but I will not be staying long.'

'Like I said, stick around and you'll get your documents back when you need to leave.' Temple drew on the cheroot and exhaled another thick smog.

Heinkel stood slowly and held out his hand. 'Please, my component… '

Temple handed over the lump. 'Stay in town, please, Mr Heinkel… for your own safety of course. The natives… '

Heinkel gave a blank look. 'You can count on it.'

'You are free to go.' Temple gestured towards the door.

Heinkel gathered his papers, and carefully closed the satchel. 'I will be back for my documents in a day or so… ' He turned on his heels and headed for the door.

Heinkel paced briskly into the baking sun, moving up the hill away from the customs house. It was interesting that no one else had been stopped. Did the Africaan know he was coming? If so, how? Was there a security leak or was it really just chance? Some prejudice against the superior German race was to be expected from officials. After all, the German colony of West Africa had been handed over to the South Africans after the last war. The damned Africaans had rubbed salt in the wounds ever since. German settlers in South Africa were on hard times; but not for much longer. The influence and power of the Reich was rising and, with these new weapons, the South Africans and their British puppet masters would be crushed.

Rudy Temple considered the situation. He had no choice. There was no evidence to detain the German; but he was a spy alright! It all made sense. If the Germans were making weapons and getting special materials, what better cover than a German industrialist with influential contacts of the likes of Rockefeller, one of the most powerful men in the world, and with some big investments in mining rights around the globe, including Africa. The Rockefeller connection was worrying. In fact, it changed the game completely. Either the heart of America's Wall Street was being conned, or the Rockefellers were in on it. The Rockefellers as German agents! Was that really possible? Either way, this German network was bigger and much more powerful than anyone had estimated. It might even explain the Nazi gold being deposited in banks around Southern Africa. Were the Rockefellers buying up Nazi reserves in exchange for industrial favours?

Temple smiled to himself. He would follow this Heinkel, if that was his real name, on his little tour of Cape Town. Then, it would be time to head back to London and break the good news to his buddies at SIS. Sinclair would be overjoyed at this latest revelation.

CHAPTER 17

Capture at Kummersdorf

Colonel Dornberger paced the room, perplexed by the events of the last twenty-four hours.

Somebody had attempted to abduct one of the scientists, but why?... And how? How in damnation did this happen? This was supposed to be one of the most secure military establishments in Germany: but evidently not!

'Commandant Kessler, tell me again, what happened last night.' Dornberger needed to understand. The implications could be critical to the rocket programme. Had the secrets of the German rocket programme been revealed?... And why Mayer? What was so special about Mayer? It didn't make any sense.

'My investigation is still underway, Colonel, but this is what I have so far.' Kessler tried to focus on the facts, the taste of failure stuck in his throat – it was strange and uncomfortable. He felt... emotions... felt... unusual... even a little human weakness... a blood-soaked iron cross flashed in front of his eyes.

Kessler dismissed his strange mood and snapped into report mode.

'My men are still sifting through the debris at the crash site, but at least I have a sequence of events. It was clearly a well organised attempt at abduction, and targeted at Professor Mayer.'

'Are you sure that Mayer was singled out?'

'Absolutely, the intruder had asked for him by name, specifically for him and no one else. The orderly on duty had taken the intruder, who he thought to be an officer, directly to the living quarters.'

'Surely, the orderly would have thought this irregular?'

'No, it was a professional job. The intruder had a genuine officer's uniform, and had spoken with authority.'

'In German, with no unusual accent?'

'Yes, fluent. His ID had even fooled the guards on the main gate.'

Dornberger could not blame the young soldier for unwittingly helping the intruder find his target. *But who was this imposter?* This was clearly not the work of local partisans or communists. He let his thoughts drift aloud. 'So, this was a professional soldier. Someone well trained – from the intelligence services perhaps?'

'All the evidence points to this, but there is more… ' Kessler paused to drop the next bombshell '… The way he handled himself, acquired the uniforms… our man is more than just a soldier. I would say he is a *trained assassin*.'

'Your friend from the train?' Dornberger could not see the connection.

'Yes, from the description; definitely the same man.'

'Well, the intruder clearly wasn't German. Who does he work for? The Americans, the Russians, the British?'

'We don't know yet, sir, at least not for certain.'

There were so many unanswered questions. How did the pieces of the puzzle fit together? None of this could be a coincidence. In all probability the intrusion on the base was linked to events in Leipzig, and the unfortunate incident on the train to Berlin. The explosion on the train had damaged some of the Professor's belongings and Kessler had also been attacked by a well-trained assassin – the *same* man. This assassin had taken papers. Why? Was there some secret that the Professor was keeping, or something in his notes of great importance?

'Commandant, tell me about the train, the explosive device – what do we know?'

'Well sir, a thorough forensic investigation of the explosive device and the train was carried out and has yielded some useful information. The explosive is a fairly common industrial mix that is used by any number of mining companies, and the like. I am afraid it provides no clues as to the perpetrator. However, we also recovered fragments of the timing device; and that was much more revealing.' Kessler at last had some good news to report. 'The device itself was simple and reliable. But whoever planted the bomb had made a mistake – the choice of materials for the timing device. It was made of some fairly sophisticated laminates; an unusual combination of materials. The outer casing was made of Bakelite, but inside there was also a thin layer of a new polymer called nylon. This is far from routine.'

'What are you saying? Are we dealing with a government-sponsored assassin?' Dornberger could not believe his ears.

'Yes, almost certainly.' Kessler was confident of the forensics. 'The Bakelite material was identified as British in origin, and is now also used in specialist industrial components. It will not be too difficult to source. Only a handful of companies use this particular type of Bakelite in Europe. The nylon composite was very novel. Only government-sponsored organisations have access to such materials. It must have come from either the British, or perhaps the Americans. Certainly both would have this technology.' Kessler concluded his report.

'I don't understand, what's the connection to Professor Mayer?' Dornberger was lost. It didn't make any sense; professional explosives experts, assassins, the theft of technical documents. Perhaps the papers taken from Commandant Kessler had much more significance? Dornberger followed the line of thought.

'Is the Professor spying for the Americans? The British? Or does he have something they want?'

'We do not know that yet sir, but we will when the Professor wakes up.'

'*If* he wakes up… I understand his injuries were severe.'

Dornberger didn't relish the situation. He much preferred

life as a scientist but, nonetheless, as the base commander he was responsible for the security of the rocket programme. That had to come first. The Professor was connected to something unsavoury and this called for an experienced investigator.

'I am making you personally responsible for the security of Professor Mayer. I need to know… ' Dornberger paused with trepidation, he did not necessarily approve of the brutal methods that Kessler sometimes employed, but on this occasion he needed results. '… I need to know what the Professor knows, I need him awake and well enough for questioning.'

Kessler stood, and clicked his heels in salute. This was a task that Kessler accepted with enthusiasm; after all he had a score to settle.

The chief medical officer had just finished his examination. There was no change in the Professor's condition. He remained deeply unconscious. The patient needed constant care, just to stay alive.

'The news is not good, Commandant. His chances of survival remain less than fifty percent.'

This wasn't what Kessler wanted to hear. 'What of the Professor's mental faculties? When can I question him?'

'Well… ' the doctor made his best guess, '… there's no real way of telling until he wakes up.'

'And when will that be?!'

He gave a shrug, ignoring Kessler's impatience; he had no idea. 'The Professor has broken some ribs, and his internal injuries will probably heal in time. However, there is a skull fracture; a nasty depressed fracture where parts of the broken skull are pushing into the brain. An operation is needed to rectify this. It is risky, it's a very complex procedure; the patient could die on the operating table.' The surgeon shuddered. If that happened, well, Kessler would not be happy. The alternative was just as grim. 'Without an operation it is doubtful the patient will ever wake up, so I think the operation should be done.'

'Well! Proceed with the operation!' Kessler shook his head; he was surrounded by fools.

'That is not so easy. He is alive and will need many weeks of rest to recover from his injuries. We have another operation to do on the abdomen to repair some tissue damage and stop some abdominal bleeding. That, I think will be fairly straightforward. Then, in an ideal world, he should recover some more strength. Only then will we see the final result.'

'Spare *no expense* Doctor, *keep him alive*. Do you understand?' Kessler hissed the words into the surgeon's face – he didn't need to – the surgeon was already terrified. Kessler's reputation for brutality was well known.

'Yes, of course Commandant, of course… but… I will need additional supplies… and the help of a specialist neurosurgeon. The head injury is complex. I have a colleague working at the main university hospital in Berlin. In fact, it may be better to move the patient to Berlin… '

'No! Absolutely not! For security reasons the Professor will remain here! My men will bring anything you need from the hospital in Berlin; anything at all. They are at your service.'

'Then bring me a neurosurgeon… ' The doctor paused, not sure whether he should break all of the bad news to Kessler. 'We don't have much time, perhaps only hours. We must do the operation on the skull this morning. Otherwise, the patient will certainly die.'

Kessler acknowledged the seriousness of the situation with a sharp nod, and then turned smartly towards the door. He headed back to his office and immediately set about the task, dispatching a fast car to collect the surgeon from Berlin and to bring any medical instruments that were needed. He would provide the Professor with the best possible medical care, for now at least.

The pigs squealed. Loud, shrill, urgent whining echoed around the damp concrete room. Chains rattled. Animals jostled for position, trying to escape the confined space, occasionally savaging each other, somehow sensing death. The smell of oil skins mixed with the metallic taste of fresh blood.

A loud bang, the hiss of a piston. A thrashing pink corpse falls to the ground.

The pig is heavy. Numb hands work a chain around its ankle. A tug on a pulley, a taut rope, the beast lifts off the ground. 'Put your back into it boy!' The words echo… Father's knife slashes open the bulging belly. The stench of gastric acid and faeces fill the air. I reach up, pull on the belly skin, but too late. An avalanche of warm, pulsating entrails fill my throat… blackness… echoing… blackness. 'Father!'

Nash coughed and spluttered the lake water from his lungs. Deathly cold penetrated his limbs. Faint voices slowly penetrated his skull. He lurched forward, thrashing, he opened his eyes and gasped in deep breaths.

He instinctively turned around in the water, looking for the shoreline. Suddenly he got his bearing; he'd been lucky and drifted towards the far shore away from the German troops. How long had he been out? A few minutes, an hour, maybe longer? In between coughs and bouts of shivering he tried to get a rhythm going; treading water would warm himself up.

With tremendous effort he rolled over onto his front and started a slow swim towards the shore, but his limbs wouldn't work; it was more of a pathetic doggy paddle. He was only fifty yards or so off the beach, but his legs were frozen lumps of meat.

Damn it! Swim!

Slowly, shivering, he managed to move, building up a bizarre rhythm.

Willing himself ashore, he stumbled onto the beach. Still shivering with cold, hallucinating, he somehow managed to get to his feet. He tried walking a few paces and collapsed. He looked down at his feet and instructed his toes to move – nothing. He prodded his thighs – no sensation. His legs just didn't feel like part of his body. They belonged to someone else; and they would not work.

'Fuck!' Gritting his teeth with frustration, he allowed his training to kick in. 'Okay, think! Escape and evasion: make a plan, always make a plan. Number one – fit to travel? No, not yet... ' he muttered to himself; but suddenly he knew what to do.

Reduce heat loss – yes, that's it! – get out of my wet clothes.

He staggered a few yards into the tree line to find some cover, and stripped off his soaking clothes. He brushed the water off his body as best he could with his bare hands to dry himself. Then wrung and twisted each item of clothing to remove as much water as possible. Then he got dressed. The clothes were still damp and cold, but at least he was losing less body heat than before.

Time to get going!

It would soon be sunrise, and the place would be crawling with troops by then. He wasn't about to let a little spell of hypothermia prevent his escape. The best option was to head east towards the Polish border. He took a compass bearing, not trusting his senses.

East – away from the lake – yes that was the right direction.

Drawing comfort from organising himself, Nash headed off.

The seaplane was obviously lost and the rendezvous with the ship in the Baltic Sea was now a pipe dream. The ship's commander would soon figure out that something had gone wrong, and would head back out into the more neutral waters of the North Sea. He would have to find his own way home. Fortunately, escape and evasion drills were second nature. The border was only one-hundred-and-fifty kilometres away, and even on foot in his current condition, he could cover that distance in three or four days. Once across the border into Poland, he could arrange a pick up.

The Professor's eyes went in and out of focus. His head throbbed intensely, with the most severe headache. A pain in his chest registered; it hurt to breathe. There were shadows moving around him, and voices, lots of voices. The smell of hospital disinfectant filled his nostrils.

Suddenly, the bright lights in the room came into focus. Mayer tried to shield his eyes from the light. He was unable to move his left arm. He tried the other arm; it worked but hurt like hell. He groaned on the edge of consciousness.

The doctor spoke with a sympathetic tone. 'Herr Professor, can you hear me? Can you hear me?'

The operation had been a relative success, but the head injury had caused some paralysis on the left side of the patient's body.

'You are in the hospital at Kummersdorf. You are safe. Just rest, please keep still.'

Mayer groaned a reply in acknowledgement.

The doctor was unable to conceal his relief. The patient had responded! The doctor looked at Kessler. 'He is coming round, but don't expect too much at first. It will be some days, a week or maybe longer, before he is well enough to be interviewed. I will keep you informed… '

Kessler nodded. There was nothing much he could do. He would have to wait until the Professor was well enough to give coherent answers to his questions. If he pressed him for answers now, it would kill him.

CHAPTER 18

Intelligence Review, London

Sinclair stared out of the office window, absently ignoring the hustle and bustle of the daily commute along the embankment of the River Thames. The mission in Germany had evidently gone wrong. Sinclair looked intensely at Nash. Both men wore grave faces.

'Danny, what the hell happened out there? I received a garbled message from HMS Belfast five days ago, indicating that the plane didn't make the rendezvous in the Baltic as planned.' Sinclair started pacing. 'I am going to have to tell Mr Churchill something, is there any shred of good news?' He turned to face Nash.

Nash sat hunched at the end of Sinclair's desk in a woollen sweater and an old pair of worn corduroy trousers. He gently probed the stitches in his brow, hoping that the bruising on his right eye would go down so that he could see out of it. A fresh dressing covered a wound on the back of his other hand. 'We were taking heavy fire at the pickup point; some fifty or sixty German troops; regulars not conscripts. I don't know… ' He rubbed his wound. '… I managed to bundle the Professor into the plane, and half got in myself. Then it all went bad.'

Sinclair nodded. 'Go on.'

'Munitions were incoming, bouncing all over the place. I am guessing the pilot took some rounds. Anyway, the plane flipped and the last thing I remember was waking up on the far side of the lake.' Nash closed his good eye, his head throbbed.

'Danny, what about the Professor?'

He shrugged. 'I don't know. The plane crashed on the lakeside. Mayer is either dead or captured.'

'We must assume the worst; that the Professor has been captured alive. Where would they take him?' queried Sinclair.

'Almost certainly back to Kummersdorf. It's the nearest location with high security. Besides, he knows too much about their facility. It would be a security risk to move him elsewhere.' Nash was sure.

'So, if we assume our man is still at Kummersdorf. What will happen next – interrogation?' suggested Sinclair.

'Yes, almost certainly, the Germans will obviously want to know why he was targeted,' agreed Nash.

'Then he will talk. Every man has his breaking point and the Germans will push him for answers.'

'I agree, that's the likely outcome.' Nash shook his head, and screwed up his brow against the next pulse of agony inside his skull.

'Militarily, I would say our options are limited. The Germans will not be fooled twice.' Sinclair opened his palms in a gesture of submission. 'They will strengthen their security quickly. The chances of another clandestine recovery will be much reduced.'

Nash sat up, stretching his back. 'A major ground assault is out of the question, and I agree; we can't make a second attempt to sneak into the base and grab the Professor. Besides, we're not even sure he's there. Even if he is, he may not be fit to travel. This leaves two other options: blow the place sky high, or do nothing – for now at least – and hope the old goat doesn't talk.'

'Not much of a choice.' Sinclair slumped into his office chair opposite Nash and continued. 'How about some carefully directed mortar fire from the ground onto the base?'

'Yes, that would be possible, especially if we use the communists or local partisans as cover. We would be unlikely to impact the main facility though. The buildings are mostly reinforced concrete secured behind steep earthworks. It would be a waste of time.'

'Yes, but the living quarters are not so well protected, and there must be plenty of fuel on site. A few well-placed rounds could be enough?' Sinclair leant forward on the desk, raising an eyebrow.

Nash looked up. 'It might work, but the odds are stacked against it – even for me – and I know the terrain. What if we do nothing? What can the Professor tell them?'

Sinclair shook his head. 'Let's face it. A man under interrogation will *eventually* answer *all* the questions he is asked.'

He was right, they both knew the score. It was a matter of fact that the interrogator *always* won in the end.

'So… ' Sinclair exhaled to clear his mind. 'What if we introduce some misdirection? We leak the idea that the Professor was targeted for some other reason… '

'Misdirection, so they don't ask the right questions?' Nash perked up.

Sinclair could see a way forward at last. 'Yes, precisely! It needs to be something that will infuriate the Germans to such an extent that it blinds them to other possibilities.'

Nash interjected. 'The Nazis despise the Jews and the Poles. Something with a race angle that will send them off the deep end. We could suggest the Poles were recruiting for their own weapons programme, or helping their Russian neighbours?'

'The Jewish idea is more believable.' Sinclair rubbed his chin and opened the draw on his desk, removing a file.

He threw the file open on the table. 'This came in yesterday from Rudy. The Germans are clearly up to something. I am not sure yet, but it looks like coercion: extorting funds from rich bankers in America. A German spy is shopping for precious metals in South Africa, and the Germans are stealing machine parts from the USA. But for what reason?'

Nash picked up the file, and scanned the first page. 'So… we let them.' He grinned for the first time. He paused as a plan began to formulate in his mind. 'We let them – and send them back to Germany with a believable story about a top secret rocket programme in the Middle East.'

'That will infuriate Herr Hitler for sure; the very idea that the Jews and the Arabs might be beating them at their own game!' Sinclair warmed to the suggestion.

Nash picked up a piece of paper from the file. 'What's this supposed to be?' He held the drawing up for Sinclair.

'We're not sure yet. Our technical team are working on it now, but we believe it's some kind of carburettor or mixing device from a new kind of rocket engine.'

'This could be useful intelligence for concocting a story.'

'Good idea, study the file. Misdirection is our best chance at the moment. Interrogation will be inevitable for Professor Mayer, but we should at least stack the odds in our favour. I am depending on you to create an elaborate hoax,' Sinclair ordered.

'Yes, sir. Do we still have an office in the Middle East?'

'Your best bet is our man in Cairo. It looks like you could do with a bit of sun.' Sinclair gave a wry smile.

'Yes, sir. You're not wrong on that score.'

Nash folded the file, and shoved it under his arm as he stood up.

'Danny… '

Nash paused.

'Will you see Emily while you're in London? She… well… she's not herself.'

'I don't know. I thought it best to leave it, for a while anyway.'

Sinclair nodded slowly.

Nash headed for the door. What the hell was he going to say to Emily anyway? Maybe it really was better to leave it.

Nash hobbled up the last flight of stairs, with a half-empty duffle bag on his shoulder. The musty, mildew odour of stale air on the top landing filled his nostrils. The bare floorboards creaked under his weight as he probed around the top of the door frame looking for his key. Eventually finding it amongst the accumulated dust, he wrestled with the deadlock. The mechanism finally gave a sudden click. He leant on the faded red paintwork, and shoved in the usual spot. The door sprang open. Nash stepped inside, dropping his bag on the moth-eaten rug, and closed the door behind himself.

He stared around the room, engulfed by loneliness.

This was the sum total of his personal life: a rented attic room with a rusty old bed, a wardrobe that had seen better days, and a battered old stove. In fact, not even that; the furniture belonged to his landlord, and he'd taken the stove out of a skip at the back of the NAAFI. Strictly speaking, the stove still belonged to the army. The only thing he could call his own were the clothes he stood up in and the contents of the duffle bag.

He sat down on the edge of the bed, and dragged over the canvas sack, placing it on the floor between his legs. He opened the drawstring, revealing the contents.

He pulled out one change of underwear, a clean but crumpled shirt, a pair of trousers – well, actually blue number eights, courtesy of the Royal Navy surplus store – and a set of stiletto throwing knives with an oil stone.

In the bottom of the bag he found the picture frame.

He lifted the small wooden frame gently in his palm. The light from the attic window above the bed seemed to bring out the colours of her face. Emily stared back at him from the photograph, standing all ladylike in her long dress and fine shoes. Her hair was tied back formally into a bonnet. It must have been taken on a Sunday morning before church.

Church – what the hell had he been thinking?

There was more chance of meeting the Pope than getting Emily, or any woman, to the altar.

He looked slowly around the room.

Desolation and death. What else did he have to offer her? Nothing.

A sudden gentle *tap-tap* on the door roused Nash from his thoughts. Who was it? Nobody knew he was here; except Sinclair of course. Maybe the landlady had heard him come in?

Nash exhaled as he struggled to his feet and shuffled two steps over the small rug to the door. He opened it.

Emily stood in the entrance, tears rolling silently down her perfect face. She tried to smile. Her cheeks dimpled as she curved her ruby-red lips.

'Danny… I am… I am sorry.'

Light flooded into Nash's world as she flung her arms around his neck.

CHAPTER 19

Espionage in Cairo

A dust devil swirled another blast of heat into the cafe. Nash adjusted his wicker chair; looking casually at his newspaper, he took a sip of the hot sweet tea; at least it was better than mouthfuls of dust, heat and diesel fumes. Cairo was always the same.

Still, it was a good spot, a side street near the central bazaar. More importantly, it gave a reasonable view of the thoroughfare and offered several escape routes into a myriad of alleyways. There was no point taking any chances. He took another sip of tea as a donkey overloaded with domestic goods shuffled past, closely followed by the hubbub of a small group of market traders, all dressed in rough-cut Egyptian cotton.

The brief was simple. He was to use his contacts in Egypt to create a mock-up production line for rocket engine components, take a few photographs, then let the information slip into German hands with the speculation that the Arabs and Jews had made significant advances in rocket technology. That would ruffle a few feathers in Berlin.

Nash casually glanced at his watch, as he took another swallow of the hot sweet tea. Playing the idle western tourist, his eyes scanned the crowd. Suddenly, a man dressed in rags sat in the chair next to him. Nash took a whiff of stale sweat and diesel oil; the last thing he needed was a beggar blowing his cover. He gestured discretely to move the beggar along.

'This way to meet Henry Ford, Sahib.' A toothless grin smiled idiotically.

Nash had found his contact.

His man moved off without saying another word. Nash glanced up and down the street. No one seemed to be watching. He casually dropped some loose change on the table, and followed at a discrete distance.

It was the usual circus: up and down several streets, through narrow alleyways, then doubling-back several times. Nash worked the crowd. Were they being followed? With the hustle and bustle of the market day it was almost impossible to tell. He moved at a natural pace, but maintained a visual on his contact.

They turned left away from the market, then took a right into a cobbled street. The crowds started to thin out. After another hundred yards, the contact slipped into an alleyway. Nash followed, ducking under laundry, stepping in between baskets, bags of rubbish and yapping dogs. Suddenly, the alleyway curved and widened. Nash emerged from the domestic paraphernalia of Egyptian life into an empty street. He followed the contact for another hundred yards. The man stopped at a nondescript door, and waved Nash forward. Both men quickly stepped through the doorway.

Nash squinted into darkness, and could make out his man ahead in the dusty corridor. He followed, skipping down a flight of stone steps into a basement.

He suddenly caught up with his contact; their path was blocked by a solid steel door. The man tapped on the door, and a spyhole quickly opened, followed a few seconds later by the metallic sound of several heavy iron bolts sliding. They were greeted by a person in plain Arabic dress sporting a Mauser rifle. He gestured for them to move down the single, narrow corridor.

The corridor took a zigzag with several right-angled corners. Ideal for muffling a blast in the corridor, or for fighting off intruders, noted Nash. They eventually arrived in a small reception room; if you could call it that. The room was poorly furnished with a moth-eaten armchair and a couple of upturned orange crates. A small stove sat in the corner, with tea on to brew. The room had two doors leading away from it, plus the entrance to the corridor. The contact gestured for Nash to sit and wait, and after a few minutes he returned with a westerner dressed in desert fatigues.

'Greeting Major, welcome to my shithole,' smiled Clarke Sanker.

They shook hands. Nash knew they would get along instantly.

Sanker worked for the Institute of Aeronautical Science (IAS) based in New York. The IAS often recruited engineers with military experience, and as luck would have it, the SIS had maintained contact with a few ex-servicemen who now worked in the private sector. One of these men was Clarke Sanker.

'Sorry about all the shenanigans, but one can't be too careful these days. Would you like some tea?'

Sanker offered Nash a brew.

'I have the photographs you requested.' Sanker passed a brown envelope to Nash.

He studied each photograph briefly. They showed flasks of liquid oxygen, and engine components under construction. Each photograph also had local artefacts that would enable the Germans to identify a Middle East connection: tea glasses, partial shots of men in local clothing. The pictures were a good start.

'I have something else.' Sanker handed over a metal object constructed of flanges and grills, about the size of a grapefruit, but much heavier.

Nash gave Sanker a puzzled look.

'What is it Major?'

'I've seen this before.' Nash was perplexed.

'Is that so?! Where?!' Sanker beamed, unable to contain his excitement.

'A drawing, obtained in Cape Town from a German with a heavy briefcase. In addition to documents, apparently the

German was carrying a piece of machined metal just like this one.'

'So, the Germans are working along the same lines,' offered Sanker. 'Where is this German now?'

Nash gave a shrug. 'Somewhere in Cape Town I guess. We had to let him go, but I believe he's still under surveillance. He was allegedly some kind of industrialist, being funded by the Rockefeller Foundation in New York.'

'New York! Rockefeller! Christ! We have offices in the same building!'

The IAS had its head office in the Rockefeller Centre, a huge tower block in the heart of the business district of New York. The institute had been invited to set up shop in 1930 during the construction of the Rockefeller Centre by Rockefeller senior himself. The IAS had remained there ever since.

'Do you think there is a connection? Are the Germans trying to infiltrate the IAS?' Sanker looked firm.

Nash rubbed his chin thoughtfully 'Probably not... I think it's a coincidence. Nonetheless, we are trying to keep tabs on our German visitor.'

'Did you keep the machine part?'

'Afraid not – there was no cause to make an arrest or confiscate the item.'

Nash studied the flanged metal again and passed it back to Sanker. 'What is it? Obviously not a machine part from a factory?'

'This... ' said Sanker as he turned the metal object over in his hand, '... is a prototype fuel injection system. It is designed to mix liquid oxygen in precise quantities with a hydrogen peroxide solution.'

Sanker was a brilliant engineer who had been working on rocket engines for a number of years. He had been hosting visiting scientists from the Middle East. In fact, the Arabs had just started their own rocket programme.

'You mean it's a part of the fuel injection system for powering a rocket?' Nash wanted to be sure.

'Yes, precisely,' confirmed Sanker. 'What's more, and this is the clever bit... ' Sanker headed into a technical rant about the injector system; after all, he was an engineer who loved his work. '... The inner workings are designed to cope with the corrosive nature of the ingredients. Hydrogen peroxide, as you know, is nasty stuff. However, we add a sodium permanganate catalyst to the hydrogen peroxide mix as well. The sodium permanganate speeds everything up by making the burn more efficient. We must not forget that pure oxygen is also very reactive and will oxidise and weaken the surface of the injectors.'

'So how do you protect the inner workings of the system?' asked Nash.

'With a thin layer of inert titanium coating the inside of the injectors,' Sanker grinned.

It was all starting to make sense now. Industrial chemicals! The Germans were after industrial chemicals in South Africa. Rudy Temple had been right; the Germans were up to no good. Hydrogen peroxide, sodium permanganate, and titanium were all on the Germans' shopping list.

'Tell me, why would the Germans want to buy these chemicals in South Africa, surely they have access to these in Europe?'

'Well, yes they do,' replied Sanker. 'But the purity of the material is critical to the burn characteristics, and some of the best permanganate deposits are found in Africa. Likewise, the purity of the titanium coating is also important. The best stuff comes from Canada, and we buy most of it.'

'So the Germans are buying top-grade permanganate in Africa, and getting Canadian titanium via the USA?' queried Nash.

'Yes, that's about the size of it.'

'So the solution is simple. We stop the sale of these chemicals and therefore bring the German rocket programme to a halt?'

'I wish it was that simple. Not so I am afraid… ' Sanker paused as he shook his head, '… the minerals market is controlled by international companies, some of them are German, and for others the Germans have significant shareholdings.'

'So, just close them down?' argued Nash.

'No can do.' Sanker gestured firmly with his hands. 'Raw materials are at the base of the global economy. If we pull the plug on one of the global metal giants, then the entire financial supply chain will risk collapse. The depression is fresh in people's minds, so I doubt the politicians in London or Washington would want to go down that road.'

It all made sense now. Nash could not believe what he was hearing. American institutions were wrapped up in the industrial food chain that supplied the Germans with raw materials for their rocket programme via Southern Africa.

'I am curious… ' asked Nash. 'I am pretty sure the drawing I have is identical to this prototype. How is that possible?'

'Courtesy of the US Office of Patent Applications.' Sanker smirked.

'What?' Nash was lost.

'One Mr Robert Goddard has filed a whole bunch of patents on the construction of a liquid fuel injection system to propel rockets in the last few years. The Germans have simply got hold of the patents and are copying the designs.' Sanker gave a wry smile.

'Unbelievable! I take it this Goddard works for the US government?'

'Actually no. Goddard made some early prototype rockets in his backyard. Homemade jobs – he's not a professionally trained scientist from the establishment. He managed a vertical lift of fourteen feet before his first rocket died. A few of the national newspapers in the USA got hold of the story and ridiculed Goddard as some sort of nutcase. After that, no one in the scientific community, IAS included, would take him seriously.'

'Where is he now?' pressed Nash.

'Not sure, last I heard he was in Nevada working on some crazy experiment.' Sanker wasn't a fan.

Nash sighed and shook his head in disbelief. 'Look, thanks for the photographs… I'd better get going.'

Sanker smiled as they shook hands. Nash took the photographs and the prototype fuel injectors, then headed out into the street. There was no time to waste. He needed to get the next flight to Cape Town.

CHAPTER 20

Kessler's Patient

The Chief Medical Officer flicked through the charts at the end of the patient's bed. The Professor was making very slow progress; but then this was to be expected for such a complex set of injuries. It was early days yet. The broken ribs were inflamed, which at least indicated that the bones were starting to mend. Examination of the abdomen had revealed a damaged spleen, which had been removed to stop the internal bleeding. This had complicated the recovery; without his spleen the Professor was more likely to succumb to post-operative infection.

The doctor lifted the dressing off the head injury to examine the wound. The surgery had gone according to plan, and they had managed to reposition the skull, and then close the wound. The Professor had done well on the first day after the operation, but became feverish and slipped back into unconsciousness on the second day.

The head injury was showing signs of infection with pus emerging through the stitches. The doctor cursed his bad luck and did his best to clean the wound. If this continued he would have to re-open the cut and clean out all the infected tissue inside the skull; and then stitch it up again. For now he would wait; after all, there was no point angering the Commandant unnecessarily.

'How is the patient today, Herr Doctor?' asked Kessler.

The doctor had been concentrating so hard on the patient that he did not hear the Commandant enter the room.

'I am afraid the patient is still very sick. He is unconscious most of the time, and in the short spells when he does come round, the patient is very confused.'

'Tell me Doctor, when the patient is awake, does he have the power of speech? Can he understand simple questions?' pressed Kessler.

'No, Herr Commandant, he is feverish and mutters to himself. He barely knows where he is, and cannot give any answers yet.'

'Well, perhaps you can administer a stimulant to wake him up!' Kessler suddenly produced a small leather box from his inside breast pocket. The doctor opened the box to find a glass syringe with a yellow liquid inside it.

'What's this? Adrenalin?' enquired the doctor, perplexed.

'Something to wake him up,' Kessler smiled.

The doctor folded his arms and huffed. 'I cannot! A sudden rise in blood pressure could rupture his wounds, even kill him!'

Kessler spoke evenly in a firm tone. 'Give the injection, or stand aside and I will do it myself.'

The doctor flushed and threw his hands in the air. 'Alright! Alright, I will do it.' He took the syringe. It was better than having some ham-fisted attempt by an untrained thug like Kessler. He swallowed and steadied himself. The idea of such brutal methods went against all his medical training.

He slowly administered the drug into the patient's arm. The effect was immediate. Mayer started to groan as he came to, opening his eyes to a squint; he was clearly disorientated.

Kessler slipped easily into interrogation mode, speaking clearly and softly, directly into the Professor's ear. He listened and watched the Professor's lips intently for any response. He tried a test question.

'What is your name?'

The Professor mumbled a reply. It was clear that he had understood the question. Kessler was spurred on.

'Who helped you escape?'

Mayer mumbled. The answer wasn't very clear, but the gist was that he did not know.

'Where were you being taken?' Kessler kept the questions simple, firm and clear.

The Professor mumbled again. This time the answer was inaudibly weak. The stimulant was wearing off quickly. A small spot of blood appeared through the dressing on the head wound.

'Enough!' shouted the doctor. 'If you kill him now, you will have no answers at all!'

Kessler conceded that the patient was not fit for interrogation. 'Good day Herr Doctor, I will see you the same time tomorrow.' Kessler stormed out of the room.

Furious that the prisoner had not answered his questions, he would come back every day and keep asking the same questions until he had some answers! Doctor or no doctor – he would do his interrogation.

In the meantime, he would continue his investigation of the plane wreckage and the corpses recovered from the scene. Several facts were clearly apparent. The bodies carried no identification and the clothing labels from their overalls had been removed. These were soldiers who wanted to remain anonymous. The plane itself was easy to identify; a Catalina seaplane. There were only a handful of manufacturers in Europe and most of these were in Scandinavia, or the United Kingdom. The various dials and emergency panels on the plane had instructions written in English first, and Norwegian second. So, perhaps this plane was made in the UK, and used by the Norwegians for a time? The weapons recovered from the bodies were definitely American. So was this some kind of Anglo-American operation? Kessler was determined to find out.

Mayer fell through space and time; as he did so, images leapt from the cosmos.

A meadow of wild flowers, a child in a pink dress… holding hands with a woman… the woman has red hair… Sophia! They are running happily in the pleasant sunshine. Bumblebees buzz from flower to flower, taking pollen from the foxgloves. Suddenly, the woman breaks. Skidding to a halt, she screams, and sweeps the child up into her arms. She runs in the opposite direction… but too late… the device hovers overhead. A sudden red glow lances forth from the machine… they are vaporized in an instant. Only scorched shadows remain.

Mayer screams, stars rush past.

Einstein appears, silhouetted against a boiling yellow inferno: the sun. He doesn't seem to mind the heat. 'Gustav… ' He smiles. 'Gustav… go back… go back… resist… fight! Do not despair. We are with you! Go back… fight!'

CHAPTER 21

Cape Mineral Company

Nash scratched at the stubble on his neck, eyeing the dark green boiler suit of the Cape Mineral Company up and down in the wing mirror. The battered pickup truck looked the part, but the boiler suit didn't. Something was wrong.

Too clean.

Nash stooped, picking up a handful of cement dust. He rubbed the dirt into his knees, and then liberally over the cuffs of his overalls. For good measure, he wiped his hands on the back of his trousers.

Much better.

He climbed aboard the pickup truck. The sweltering stale heat of the vehicle filled his lungs. He wound down the window quickly and exhaled.

The intelligence analysts back in Whitehall came up with some hare-brained ideas from time to time, and this was certainly one of them.

It had better work, there wasn't a plan B.

He flipped open the glove box and removed a brown envelope.

Would Heinkel take the bait? Passing false intelligence on the rocket programme in the Middle East up the chain to Germany would rely entirely on convincing Heinkel that the documents were genuine.

Nash slipped the photos from Cairo, and a few other random pages for good measure, into the back of the large brown envelope containing some Cape Mineral Company documents. He shoved the documents back into the glove box.

He took a deep breath and blew out steadily through pursed lips, relaxing his shoulders. It was time to slip into roleplay mode. He fished amongst the debris in the driver's well, retrieving a cloth. He smeared it across the windscreen, removing a fine layer of cement powder from the glass.

It would have to do. He tossed the rag in the back with the other working man's detritus and switched on the engine.

The rattle of diesel and the acrid exhaust added to the authenticity.

Heinkel would surely find the photographs, but would he report it to Berlin?

There was only one way to find out.

Nash rolled up outside the foreman's office in a cloud of dust. He leant out the window and smiled at the receptionist, who was already standing on the porch, clipboard in hand. She looked totally out of place in her high heels, black pencil skirt, and neat white blouse.

Nash spoke with the best South African accent he could muster. 'Is Mr Heinkel ready? I am here t'give him a tour of the mine.'

'I won't keep you a moment.' The receptionist smiled, and shuffled along the boardwalk towards the office door, being careful not to loose a heel.

Moments later she reappeared with a tall, well-dressed man – Heinkel.

Nash stepped down from the vehicle, and strode purposefully across the gravel towards the VIP. Heinkel was already offering an outstretched hand.

Heinkel looked in his mid-thirties, well groomed, and slim. The cut of his dark blue suit gave away an athletic physique. Nash assimilated a first impression of the man – disciplined, clean, and fit – just like a soldier. Heinkel even stood like a soldier: straight back, stomach in, chest out, and feet slightly apart. Yes, definitely, Heinkel had either seen military service, or was still a soldier now. There would be time later on to dig a little deeper into Mr Heinkel's past. Nash filed away a mental note.

They shook hands firmly.

'Good mornin', Mr Heinkel. I am the site foreman. Victor Lutz's the name, but everyone round here calls me Vic.'

Nash held the handshake for an extra fraction of a second longer – rough hands – so Heinkel didn't spend all of his time pushing pencils.

Heinkel smiled. 'Thank you for taking the time to show me around.'

'Oh, that's no bother, not at all, Mr Heinkel.'

Nash walked Heinkel back to the truck. 'Jump in, let me give ya the tour.'

Heinkel climbed aboard, loosening his tie slightly, to get some comfort in the blistering dry heat of the day.

Nash jumped in with a smile, and started up the truck. A cloud of black smoke issued from the rear as he gunned the throttle.

'Well, let's be on our way. It's not far to the open caste pit, just a few minutes along the track.'

The vehicle pulled away, bumping spasmodically over the stony ground.

'Ya' been in South Africa long?' Nash grinned.

Heinkel kept his gaze out of the windshield, bracing his knees on the sides of the seat to absorb the jerking motion of the pickup. 'A couple of weeks… '

'So, I hear ya' want t'buy some titanium… well you've come to the right place for sure. We make… I reckon… three hundred tons a month of the stuff. Finest money can buy – or at least that's what they say!'

'Very interesting… ' Heinkel stared out at the bush.

The terrain gradually steepened as the track filtered up the natural line of the valley, into a natural rocky bowl.

'It won't be long now… ' Nash pointed up ahead. 'Over that rise, and we're into the mine itself.'

The pickup truck rumbled on a few hundred metres and turned sharply over a rock bluff into the open caste mine. A huge white scar marked the landscape. The road disappeared in a zigzag down a steep slope into the bowels of the earth.

Nash found a convenient spot with a good view of the mine, and pulled up, generating another cloud of white dust.

'Well, here we are.' Nash gave a sweep of his hand. 'The largest titanium mine in South Africa.'

'Yes, certainly very impressive. What is the purity of the material you produce?'

'Ninety-five percent pure titanium dioxide ore.'

Heinkel stared blankly at Nash. 'And the impurities? What are they?'

Nash held on to the driver's wheel for a second, racking his brains for the technical details from the intelligence briefing. 'Yep, there are some impurities… but not so much… '

'Yes, of course, but perhaps you can brief me on some of them Mr Lutz?'

Nash struggled to find the information locked away somewhere in the depths of his skull. His mind raced.

This is a test? The bastards probing my cover!

'Manganese… yep, manganese at about one percent, some silicon… and a calcium mineral called hydroxyapatite.' Nash gave an inward sigh of relief, and forced a calm composure.

Heinkel stared at him, expressionless for a second.

'What about the mineral crystal structure of the titania? What form?'

Nash paused for a second time. *Think! Minerals… what crystals? Christ! Say something!* '… Crystal structure?'

166

'Yes, titania comes in three naturally occurring crystal forms. Which type are you digging from this mine Mr Lutz?' Heinkel scanned Nash's face for the telltale signs of deception.

Nothing.

'Oh! I see ya now mate. It's anatase. The crystal structure's anatase.' Nash surprised himself – *where the hell did that little nugget pop from?*

'Anatase?' Heinkel repeated, gazing at Nash.

'Yes… ' Nash swallowed the lump in his throat. Was it the *wrong* answer? A bead of sweat trickled down his brow.

'Forgive me, Mr Lutz.' Heinkel flicked his eyes. 'It may seem like a personal question, but I was wondering… that's the remains of quiet a nasty bruise on your face.'

'Oh! That's nothin' but a little indulgence.'

Fuck! The game's up!

Sweat erupted on Nash's chest, soaking into his overalls.

'Yes, but how did you get it?' Heinkel maintained an unreadable facade.

'Okay, you got me! Saturday night.' Nash shook his head and began to chuckle. 'Brawling with the blacks! I wouldn't be a good foreman if I didn't keep the coloureds in their place, would I?'

His sniggering subsided.

Jesus, what a bloody stupid thing to say!

Silence filled the cab for two or three seconds. It may as well have been an eternity. Finally, Heinkel spoke.

'It seems as if we can do business after all, Mr Lutz.'

Nash gripped the steering wheel, and smiled. 'Glad we can help, Mr Heinkel.'

Heinkel spoke formally and evenly. 'If you wouldn't mind, I would like some detailed geological reports on the titania, and also contact with your plant manager for making the subsequent titanium alloy sheeting.'

Still unreadable, this guy was good.

Nash saw his chance. 'As a matter of fact, Mr Heinkel. I have one of our brochures right here.'

He reached over to the glove box, retrieving the brown envelope. Nash raised the envelope for effect, studying Heinkel for the slightest reaction – nothing.

'Brochures you say?'

Nash offered the documents to Heinkel. 'Yes, take a look at your leisure later on. It contains some information on the minerals. I'll get one of the boys to drop some more geological details over to ya' hotel later t'day.'

Heinkel took the envelope.

Still nothing – poker face.

'Thank you Mr Lutz, that is very kind. Shall we be on our way?' Heinkel gave a slight controlled smile, just enough to show an amicable closure to proceedings.

'Yes, of course, Mr Heinkel. I'll drop ya' right back at the main gate.'

Nash drove back to the site office, using the ruts in the road to shake things up a little, and avoiding the risk of small talk along the way. He lurched the vehicle into a turn in front of the boardwalk, so that the passenger door would open onto the veranda. The secretary was dutifully waiting.

'Well, here we are Mr Heinkel.' Nash smiled.

Heinkel opened the door, stepping onto the walkway. He turned and leaned back into the cab, offering Nash his hand.

The two men shook. Heinkel held Nash's grip.

'I have a feeling we will be seeing each other again, Mr Lutz.'

'Yep, I expect so.' Nash stared back.

With that, the meeting was over.

Nash watched Heinkel walk away with the secretary.

He was a cool customer alright, and well trained. He must have been trained in the military, but what regiment? Was Heinkel SS? Either way, he was not to be underestimated. Perhaps Rudy Temple could shed some light on the comings and goings of Mr Heinkel during the rest of his visit to Cape Town.

Regardless, the task was done. The evidence was planted. It was just a question of waiting to see if he would take the bait.

Heinkel sat in the leather armchair in his hotel, calmly considering the situation.

This Mr Lutz clearly wasn't a geologist, but had the traits of some kind of professional; he certainly wasn't a rough neck working for the Cape Mineral Company. Far from it. So, who was he? A customs officer?

It seemed unlikely. He'd been dodging them for days, and besides the local police had no need for such an elaborate charade. They would simply call in their suspect for questioning, and make up a plausible excuse for the interrogation. No finesse. This man was smarter than that.

An intelligence officer of some kind, but from what agency?

The South African intelligence services were fragmented. It was possible, but not likely.

That only left the British.

But why would they show an interest? Had they been tipped off by the Americans? Were British agents waiting to intercept him on the return leg to Berlin? The British and their damned Commonwealth: the whole of Africa was awash with either the British Army or its military intelligence people. Whatever the reason, this was a situation that required care.

Heinkel smiled as he dumped the envelope on the coffee table. It usually paid dividends to think on suspect information. Ignoring it for a couple of hours would be a good precaution.

He allowed his mind to drift as he stretched out in the comfortable leather expanse of his chair.

A forest emerged into view.

The smell of bluebells, the gentle warmth of the sun, an inner peace as he rested the hunting rifle on the log. He looked through the cross hairs.

The wolf stood firm, almost majestic, snarling gently as the faint scent of human sweat caught its nostrils.

A steady voice of experience whispered into his ear. 'Feel the shot son, become one with the rifle. Take your time… '

Heinkel rested his chin against the stock of the rifle. The smell of linseed oil made him feel at home with the weapon. He worked his finger gently onto the trigger.

The beast snarled through the telescopic sight.

'That's it my boy… slowly… relax… a clean kill… '

Heinkel fired.

The wolf dropped to the ground.

'An excellent shot my boy! You've the makings of a fine gamekeeper. Your mother would have been proud.'

Heinkel surged with pride. At three hundred metres, not many sixteen-year-old boys could have made the shot. He looked at the rifle, admiring the elegant woodwork and craftsmanship of the weapon. Finally, he'd found his purpose in life.

It was early evening by the time Heinkel got to the brown envelope. After checking the blinds, he locked the door to his room. Carefully, expertly, he felt the edges of the brown envelope. There was no sign or smell of explosives. He gingerly worked open the sealed end, and laid the envelope flat on the desk.

He peered inside, trying not to disturb the contents.

The papers were as Lutz, whoever he was, had suggested; a brochure from the Cape Mineral Company, with some stapled inserts giving some recent geological data. Nothing looked suspicious.

He decided it really was just an envelope, and carefully emptied the contents onto his desk. The documents appeared to be genuine. He scanned one of the geology reports, the language looked technical enough. There were a few loose pages, and what looked like the edge of a couple of photographs protruding from the papers. The loose pages were letters of correspondence. A random collection of letters: one from a bank offering financial services in Cape Town, another concerning a hotel booking, and another relating to vehicle hire.

Heinkel pulled out the photographs.

He took in the details of the first photograph: liquid oxygen cylinders and men at work in Arabic dress.

A factory or installation of some kind?

He flipped to the second photograph: engine components, and what looked like a very large shell casing in the background. Maybe not a shell, it was too large, perhaps something else?

He wasn't sure. He picked up each photograph by the edges, and carefully turned them over. On the back, the photographic paper had an Egyptian watermark.

So, the pictures were either taken in Egypt, or at least, they were printed there. But what did the photographs represent?

Instinct started to churn in his gut. It was obviously a place where some very technical work was being done, involving some sophisticated engineering. The liquid oxygen was an interesting factor. Getting hold of liquid oxygen was not cheap, especially in Egypt. This was at least a well-funded engineering project, and certainly of military interest. But who would fund such an operation? It could be any number of governments with interests in the Middle East.

It was also possible that the photographs were deliberately planted amongst the papers – no not a possibility – definitely so. The question was really *who* put them there? And *why*?

Plant, or no plant, Berlin would want to see the photographs; but who should he use as the courier? He could do it himself, but that would blow his cover. He'd worked too hard over the last three years to infiltrate the Rockefeller Empire and its oil companies around the globe. No, he would get some local partisan to do it. There were plenty of African Germans looking for a better life back in the Fatherland. There were several captains in the merchant fleet who were loyal to the Wehrmacht, and any one of them could be the fall guy if things went wrong.

Heinkel smiled to himself as a plan formed in his mind's eye. Heinkel was a spy – no ordinary spy – but the best Germany had to offer.

CHAPTER 22

Mayer and Kessler

The doctor reviewed his notes. It was no use, he couldn't put Kessler off any longer. Professor Mayer had been at death's door and was simply unable to answer questions; but that was some weeks ago. The patient was still very fragile, and it was annoying that an SS thug could overrule the Army Medical Corp, but what could he do? He had already done everything that was possible.

The doctor stood at the end of ward, notes in hand, trying to speak quietly so as not to disturb his patient.

'Commandant Kessler, I must protest. As you know the skull injury has been infected and I have had to open the wound several times to drain the pus. I have only just finished re-stitching his skull back together again. I think it will heal this time, but the patient is too unwell to be interviewed.'

'It matters not. Time is now of the essence and the prisoner will answer my questions.' Kessler stood straight, towering over the doctor.

'I agree his fever is subsiding, but the repeated operations have resulted in some neurological damage. The patient has partial paralysis on the left side of his body – his left arm and left leg are very weak, and he may never walk again. His facial muscles are also partially paralysed. The patient can only mumble.'

'Paralysis or not, the prisoner is alive and I will interview him. What of the Professor's mental faculties?'

'He speaks with a terrible lisp, almost inaudible; I just don't know… please Commandant, let the patient rest for a few more days.'

'Impossible! We will proceed.' Kessler stormed off in the direction of the patient's bed. The doctor skipped along behind, still protesting.

Kessler sat on the end of the Professor's bed next to a nurse who was working intently on massaging the Professor's arm.

'Good morning Fräulein. How is the patient today?' Kessler smiled at the nurse.

'Improving Herr Commandant,' she dutifully replied. 'I have been giving daily physiotherapy, each day his arm is regaining some mobility.'

'Good and what of his speech?' Kessler watched as the patient drooled.

'This is not so good, Herr Commandant. His words are very slurred and broken, but I think I can now understand when he speaks.'

'Good, that is good,' Kessler smiled, patting the nurse on the knee. 'You will act as my interpreter.'

The nurse smiled back politely. Kessler turned his attention to Mayer.

'Good morning Professor, it is time for our weekly little talk. How have you been this week?' Kessler wasn't used to the softly, softly, approach; but he had no choice.

'Goooood… ' the Professor rasped in reply.

'I see you are being looked after well, and the food is good?' Kessler gave a sickly smile.

Mayer tilted his head forward slightly, not exactly a nod, but clear enough.

'Well I have some questions for you. I want you to think hard. I want you to think hard about the accident. Can you do that for me?'

No response. Kessler continued regardless.

'You remember the accident?'

Mayer tilted his head.

'Do you remember working in the laboratory before the accident?'

He tilted his head again.

So, the Professor does remember things before the accident.

'Good, good,' Kessler soothed. 'Think now about the day of the accident. You were in your sleeping quarters with all your colleagues. Do you remember?'

'Yeeeees... '

'There was some noise outside, and you were awoken in the middle of the night. Do you remember that Professor?'

Mayer gave a weak nod.

'A man came into your quarters looking for you; a German Officer who specifically asked for you by name. Picture this man in your mind, Professor.' Kessler paused to allow the patient to collect his thoughts. 'Think hard about this man. What do you see? Think carefully... picture this man in your mind. Is the man a foreigner?' Kessler tried to be soothing as he continued. '... Picture the man in your mind, think... and remember. He is dressed in a German uniform. Is this man a German... or a foreigner?' He waited a few more seconds for Mayer to focus his thoughts, then spoke clearly and calmly. 'Professor, is this man a foreigner?'

'Yeeeees.'

'Good, good... ' Kessler paused, '... now, what kind of foreigner? Is this man a Norwegian perhaps?'

Kessler remembered the instrument panel on the Catalina seaplane was partly in Norwegian.

'Nooooo.'

'Never mind, think hard Professor... ' Kessler paused, allowing Mayer to keep up, '... is this man American?'

'Maaaay beeeee.' Mayer gave a spasm and began to cough. The nurse attended to him, giving the Commandant a disapproving glance.

175

Kessler waited for the moment to pass, and then continued.

'Professor, do you know why this man, the foreigner, wanted to speak with you?'

Mayer gently shook his head.

'Was it about rockets?'

No response. Mayer went into another spasm and coughed again. Kessler pressed on.

'Was it about rockets? Did the foreigner want to know about rockets?'

'Maaaay beeeee… '

The reply was less audible. The interview was taking its toll.

'Did the man ask about rocket fuel?'

'Ca… can't… reee… member… ' Mayer muttered, less audible than before.

Kessler decided on a different line of questioning.

'Did this man carry a gun? An American pistol, perhaps?'

No response.

'Did he speak to you in English?'

No response.

The nurse interrupted. 'I am sorry Commandant, he is very weak. Perhaps we can try again in a few hours?'

Kessler gave a smile. 'You are right, Fräulein. We will try again this afternoon.'

Kessler hid his irritation. Every time he got to a critical step in the questioning the Professor would collapse. Was he really exhausted or was he just avoiding the questions? The game would continue later. Kessler rallied at the thought. He stood up and gave a polite nod to the Professor and the nurse, and headed back to his office.

Kessler gathered his thoughts as he walked towards the hospital for the afternoon session. The investigation at the crash site had eventually identified the origin of the plane thanks to the unique identifying chassis number and a manufacturer's mark stamped on the aluminium frame of the aircraft. It was a Catalina PBY mark 5 seaplane. This model was produced by an American company, but sold widely to the Australian Air Force, to forces in New Zealand, Canada, and England. The dual language on the dials suggested that the plane operated in Norway, perhaps between Britain and Norway. The small arms fired from the flying boat were American, but they had also found shell casings under the flooring grills from an older model Vickers machine gun. The Vickers was a giveaway – standard issue of the British Army. So this was clearly an American operation with a British connection.

Kessler burst through the doors onto the ward, walking briskly with a smile towards Mayer's bed. 'Good afternoon Fräulein. I trust the Professor has rested?'

She nodded and smiled.

'Good.' Kessler positioned himself on the bed, close to the patient. 'Professor, let us continue our conversation... ' he paused, '... we were talking about rockets. Did the foreigner ask you anything about rockets?'

Skipping the small talk, Kessler was determined to make progress this time.

'Nooooo... ' Mayer gargled.

'Did you tell him anything about rockets?'

'Nooooo... timeeeee... '

'So you would have talked if there had been time?' Kessler was curious.

The Professor shook his head and went into a coughing fit. Kessler ignored it.

'Did you know the man, had you seen him before?'

'Nooooo... ' Mayer coughed.

Kessler's senses worked overtime, something wasn't quite right.

'You *did* know the man! You *have* seen him before. Where?!' demanded Kessler.

'Nooooo… Nooooo… ' Mayer erupted into a violent coughing fit.

Kessler switched to a more soothing tone. 'Think Professor, where might you have seen this man before?'

No response. Mayer slumped.

'Think Professor, where… where have you seen this man before? Picture the man in your mind… where?'

'Deeee… ath… Der… Leib… haf… tigeeeee… ma… schine… ' The words struggled to come out. Kessler looked at the nurse for interpretation.

'Der Leibhaftige… maschine… ' The nurse looked puzzled 'He said something about death and the *devil machine* – does he mean the rocket?' She looked at Kessler for confirmation.

'Perhaps.' He turned to the Professor. 'What about the rocket Professor Mayer?' Kessler pressed for a reply.

'Deeeath!… Deeeath!… Der Leibhaftige… maschine!' Mayer forced the words out and collapsed back on the bed.

'What about the rocket Professor? Tell me? Tell me!' Kessler moved closer, desperate to hear the reply.

'Deee… ath… ' Mayer passed out.

'He must be delirious.' Kessler shook his head in disgust. 'We will try again tomorrow.'

With that the interrogation was concluded.

CHAPTER 23

Cape Town Harbour

Rudy Temple kept in the shadow of the fisherman's hut, and peered through a gap in the wooden slats to observe the quayside. The hustle and bustle of workers carrying boxes of fish, crates of coffee and other dry goods partially obscured his view. Heinkel was easy to pick out in his crisply pressed light tan trousers and clean white shirt. Temple flicked a glance along the concrete pier.

Good.

His men were in position, and would hopefully go unnoticed amongst the workers. He returned his attention to the target.

Heinkel walked at a steady pace, clutching a leather satchel. Temple squinted at the bag.

Yep, the same one from the interview at the customs office, and looking just as heavy. He had to admit, Heinkel was clearly a professional who paid attention to detail. The team had followed him for several days. He never used the same route twice, he doubled back to add detours, suddenly changed modes of transport, and was always alert. In fact, Heinkel had almost given him the slip on more than one occasion. Doubling the surveillance teams had kept the tail going, but that had its own dangers; it could make the target more aware. It was a risk worth taking to ensure the false intelligence was on its way to Germany.

But why was Heinkel putting everything on show now?

Heinkel suddenly stopped, and skipped up the

gangplank of a rusting German freighter, disappearing from view.

Heinkel stepped over the metal threshold into the Captain's cabin – if you could call it that.

The room was barely ten feet square. A beam of light fell through the one small porthole in the bulkhead, revealing a faded red carpet stained with a lifetime's worth of greasy boot marks. A small table sat in the corner, heaped with charts, worn notebooks, and navigation instruments. An impossibly small, narrow bench, partly obscured by a moth-eaten curtain marked the position of the officer's bed. The ever-present odour of diesel oil filled Heinkel's lungs.

'Captain, if I may, I have a small task that you can help me with.'

The Captain stood in a threadbare woollen jumper, unshaven, with his grubby calloused hands shoved deep inside his oily trouser pockets.

He shrugged. 'Maybe, it depends what it is and how much it's worth.'

'You will be rewarded handsomely for your services.'

'So, what's the job?'

'A package that needs to find its way to Berlin. Something of a delicate nature, one might say. A private matter for us Germans.'

'We're used to dealing with *private matters*. How big's the package?'

Heinkel opened the satchel, pulling out a parcel wrapped in brown paper.

'It contains some documents, and other matters of importance to the Reich.'

'Yes, well, that's not a problem. I can keep it in my safe.' The Captain nodded towards a metal box welded into the wall above his desk.

Heinkel stepped forward, examining the expression on the Captain's face. 'The parcel *will* remain secure?'

The Captain stood firm, his gaze fixed on Heinkel. 'We've done this many times before. Your package will be safe.'

Heinkel etched a small, sarcastic smile. 'Good. So, I can rely on you? *The Reich* can rely on you?'

'There's no love lost between my crew and the locals.' The Captain removed his hands from his pockets and folded his arms. He maintained a calm but hard expression. 'Yes, you can rely on me to get the job done. My men will need paying though.'

'Of course, on delivery. Five thousand reichsmarks.'

The Captain gulped, unable to conceal his surprise at the fee. 'On delivery is fine. The journey will take four days, maybe five, depending on the weather. The package will be in Berlin within a week.'

Heinkel kept an even, firm voice. 'See that it is.' His gaze moved towards the strong box. 'Open the safe.'

The Captain produced a heavy key from a lanyard around his neck, and calmly stepped up to the lock.

Heinkel eased forward with the parcel.

The Captain turned the heavy key in the lock and pulled open the door. 'Will you be travelling with us?'

Heinkel paused, checking the man's face for deception. 'No, just the package.' He placed it in the safe.

The Captain clanked the door shut, and turned the key.

'I have another small task for you... I have been followed by some customs officials. See that you depart in full view, and be sure to leave a passage plan with the harbour master.'

'You want them to know when and where we're going?' The Captain gave a puzzled look.

'Something like that.'

'Whatever you say mister.'

'Good, you will be met in Hamburg harbour – don't be late.'

Heinkel took a white envelope from his satchel; a thick wad of reichsmarks protruded from the paper. 'For your expenses... ' He held out the envelope. 'The rest you can collect in Hamburg.'

The Captain nodded. 'Consider it done.'

CHAPTER 24

Ambassador's Residence, London

The British Ambassador's residence in Kensington was luxurious with a thick red carpet and antique mahogany furniture. The trappings of empire were everywhere. A huge oil painting of the Battle of Waterloo hung above the fireplace, and on the adjacent walls hung portraits of Queen Victoria and Prince Albert. In between the paintings were trophies from various hunting expeditions: stags, wild boar and even a tiger's head. The piéce de resistance was a huge stuffed bear standing about eight feet tall in the corner of the room – reared up on its hind legs, huge claws and teeth at the ready. Doubtless, the bear had been shot on one of the Ambassador's many hunting trips.

Nash looked around the room, perplexed; didn't the aristocracy know this was the twentieth century? Maybe it was just a show to remind the minions of the British Empire? He smiled to himself as he waited for the Ambassador.

Lord Elgin-Smyth entered the lounge, and headed for the fireplace. He waved for Nash to remain seated, as he tapped a Mayfair cigarette from its silver case. He lit up and, after a couple of drags to get the embers glowing, he checked the gold pocket watch in the waistcoat of his three-piece suit, then turned to his visitor.

'Good day Mr Nash. Before we speak, I will mention a few rules of engagement.' Elgin-Smyth absently brushed some ash from his label and ran one hand through his neatly cut, but now greying, hair.

Nash nodded.

'As the British Ambassador, I cannot be seen to be supporting any kind of espionage from this residence, and especially not the kind that might compromise diplomatic relations between South Africa and Germany, which are rather delicate at the moment.' The Ambassador paused for thought. 'So we must tread carefully. Despite our little meeting in Whitehall, this time I think it's better that I don't know what you're up to. Do we have an understanding?'

'Agreed,' replied Nash.

'This arrived last night in the diplomatic bag from Germany.' He passed a large brown envelope to Nash. '… I almost forgot. Your orders from Sinclair; he's overseas wooing the Americans apparently.' The Ambassador dug into his breast pocket and handed over a telegram. 'My instructions are to let you open the package, read it, and then burn it.'

Elgin-Smyth politely turned to gaze at the flickering flames in the fireplace to give Nash some privacy. The Ambassador gently puffed on his cigarette and waited.

Nash opened the package. It contained a situation report on Kummersdorf, and some fresh aerial photographs. There were no surprises in the situation report, and it didn't really say anything beyond what he already knew. The Germans had recovered the wreckage of the plane, and had taken at least one survivor back to the base – probably Mayer.

He jolted in his chair as he opened the telegram with his orders. He re-read the telegram:

Most urgent. Terminate target. STOP. No rescue. Confirmed. Terminate target. STOP.

He slowly folded the telegram. This was an unusual request; killing other soldiers was one thing, but murdering civilians?

Nash studied the photographs for a few minutes to take his mind off the new orders. The Germans had already repaired the perimeter fence and the main entrance, but there was also some new construction. Evidently, earthworks were going up around the main buildings, and on the airfield some large containers had appeared. They looked like fuel tanks.

He stuffed the photographs in his breast pocket.

The Ambassador gave a disapproving look.

Nash stood from his chair and moved around to the fireplace. He dropped the remainder of the documents into the fire and waited for them to burn to ash. Everything else, he had already memorised. Nash turned to the Ambassador.

'We live in interesting times. This will be our little secret.' Nash tapped his breast pocket.

'If you insist,' grumbled the Ambassador.

Nash headed for the door.

The Ambassador called after him. 'Good luck old chap.'

Nash smiled back, and was gone.

Emily Sinclair worked cautiously down the new concrete steps, trying not to allow her footsteps to echo off the bare whitewashed walls; but it was no good, the high heels were hopeless. Coming straight from work in a tight pencil skirt had been a bad idea.

The stairs gradually gave way to bright lights, and more fresh white paint. The basement corridor of the SIS headquarters extended for some fifty yards under the building. It was a miracle to get this far without being stopped by a policeman, but then, having a father who was the head of the intelligence services came with its privileges.

Doors marked the length of the hallway at regimented intervals, unanimous, gleaming with camouflage green paint – all standard issue from the army stores. The smell of lacquer irritated her nostrils as she counted down the doors. 'One… two… three… '

She scraped a heel on the floor and, suddenly startled by the loss of balance, leant against the wall. She glanced up and down the gangway whilst rubbing her ankle. The muffled sound of voices issued forth from some of the rooms.

She moved to the next door and listened. Nothing. Holding her breath, she tried the handle.

It opened.

She slid through a crack in the half-opened door, being careful to close it quietly with one hand on the door frame, the other tensing on the doorknob. The lock gave the faintest of clicks. Perspiration marked her palms. She instinctively wiped them on her skirt as she turned round.

Evidently a small barrack room with four bunks – all unoccupied with just bare mattresses, except for one bed covered in kit. A man wearing a long grey field coat worked at a bench at the far end of the room.

She smiled and moved quietly between the bunks, sneaking up on the grey-coated figure. The back of his head moved slightly to the sound of metal clicking against metal.

She reached out to put a hand on his shoulder.

Suddenly the room whirled in mass bright lights and grey movement. A vice-like grip twisted her arm, pulsing discomfort bolted from her shoulder. The touch of cold steel pressed under her chin.

'Ouch! Danny, it's me! Stop, you're hurting me!'

The click of the safety catch going on echoed in her ears.

'Christ! Emily, I could have injured you.' Nash released his grip, hastily shoving the weapon in the back of his belt. 'How did you get in here anyway?'

She rubbed her shoulder, giving Nash a prudish look. 'I thought I would surprise you… '

Nash shrugged and smiled. 'Well, yes, you did!'

'I can see that. Danny, you're wound like a spring.'

'Sorry, I am just doing my kit prep for the next job.'

'So where is Daddy sending you this time?'

Nash grinned. 'Europe.'

She smiled. 'That sounds rather non-specific Major Nash.'

'You know how it is… '

'Yes, I do.' She edged up to him. Putting her arms around his waist, she removed the revolver. 'You won't be needing this for a few minutes, Major Nash.'

He gently took the weapon from her hand, his eyes fixed on her blue-green orbs as he eased his arm backwards to slide the Browning onto the bench.

He whispered as he backed up against the bench. 'Why's that Emily?'

She kissed him.

Nash welcomed the warmth of her body and the taste of her sweet breath; savouring the smell of her hair, he eventually broke the embrace. Breathing heavily, he leant his forehead against hers. He spoke softly. 'Emily… you shouldn't be here… I have work… '

She whispered. 'Danny Nash, you never did know when to shut up.' She smiled and kissed him more deeply than before.

Nash put all thoughts of packing his kit aside as he lifted her into his arms.

King and country could wait a few more hours.

CHAPTER 25

Photographs from Berlin

C olonel Dornberger sat in his office at Kummersdorf. He had spent the morning going over some lift calculations for liquid rocket fuels. The team had done well to identify the right mixture of liquid oxygen, hydrogen peroxide, and the other ingredients to get a controlled burn of the rocket motors. It was a real step forward, and would enable a steady lift on a rocket; and, more importantly, predictable control over the flight speed.

Dornberger revelled in the mathematics, lost in a world of numbers, probability theory, and calculus. The last remaining problem was to predict when the rocket would suddenly run out of fuel; and therefore where it would land. At such high speeds, a calculation error of only a minute would put the rocket miles off target.

He was suddenly roused by a loud, urgent knock on the door and, to his surprise, the adjutant did not wait to be invited in, but hastened across the room to his desk and snapped to attention.

'My Colonel, please forgive the intrusion! Admiral Dönitz has just come through the main gate! He will be here any second!'

In many ways Dornberger and Dönitz were kindred spirits; both cared greatly for the men under their commands. Dönitz had pioneered submarine warfare in the Great War, and was now busy rebuilding the U-boat fleet. It was a great opportunity to embrace new technology, and in the course of his work Dönitz had met Dornberger on several occasions in Berlin.

Colonel Dornberger stood up and checked the buttons on his tunic. He snapped to attention as Dönitz entered the room.

'Welcome to Kummersdorf, Admiral,' Dornberger saluted.

'Thank you, but please let us dispense with formality. I bring urgent news from Berlin.'

The adjutant took the Admiral's coat and closed the door on his way out, leaving the men alone.

Dornberger offered the Admiral a seat, and was so intrigued by the unexpected visit that he forgot to offer the Admiral some coffee or brandy. Dönitz went straight to business.

'What do you make of these, Colonel?' Dönitz dropped some photographs on the desk.

Dornberger was dumbstruck.

'Why Admiral, where did you get these pictures?'

'One of Wehrmacht's most trusted SS men obtained these photographs in Africa. They arrived by boat last night and were brought to SS headquarters. Herr Hitler is personally interested in this matter, and has asked me to report back.' Dönitz was matter of fact as usual.

'So, you want my opinion on the authenticity of these photographs?'

'Photographic experts at the Technical University have already confirmed that the pictures are genuine, and have not been tampered with. My question is, what do the photographs show?'

Dornberger nodded in understanding as he studied the photographs. He looked carefully at each one, placing them flat on the desk so that both men could lean over and scrutinise the images.

'You see this here.' Dornberger pointed. 'This is a liquid oxygen cylinder, and over here... ' Dornberger traced with his finger. 'This is a manifold for moving liquid fuels.'

'Could these be used for rockets?' Dönitz gave a concerned look.

'Yes! Yes!' Dornberger struggled to contain his natural scientific curiosity. 'See here... ' Dornberger pointed at one of the other photographs. 'This is the injector system and mixing chamber for rocket fuel. It looks almost exactly the same as our design.'

'A security breach? Do you think someone has stolen the technical drawings or components from Kummersdorf?'

'No, it's not possible. There must be another explanation?' Dornberger shook his head as he studied the pictures again. 'The dress of the workers, the tea glasses in the background... ' Dornberger paused, searching the Admiral's face; he looked just as puzzled. Dornberger continued. '... This is Arabic, possibly the Middle East. Is there an operation in the Middle East that I don't know about?'

'No, no, you are in charge of our only rocket programme.' Dönitz gave an assurance.

'Then someone else is building rockets and, judging by the injector, they must be at least as advanced as ours, if not more so.'

'Is there another way to copy the design of the injectors and fuel manifold?' asked Dönitz.

'Our work, at least on this component of the rocket system, is based on an American design. We got some drawings from the US Patent Office and developed things from there. It is possible that someone else has done the same.'

'Then this someone would need vast resources? Rocket development is not cheap.' Dönitz was stating the obvious, but wanted Dornberger's thoughts on who might finance such an operation.

'We have spent several million reichsmarks on our programme. There are very few with that kind of money. If the pictures were recovered in Africa, then perhaps it is a South African venture? Or a smokescreen? Perhaps it's really the British or an American government-funded project? Apart from a few diamond traders in South Africa, and perhaps some rich

Jewish bankers in the USA, few private organisations would have the financial resources, or the motivation, to fund such a project.'

'But you are confirming that these are pictures of a rocket facility, or at least the components of a rocket?' Admiral Dönitz wanted to give the Führer a technically accurate report.

'These are definitely rocket components.' Dornberger studied the pictures again. 'I would also say that, from the size of the oxygen tank, this must be for more than one rocket. So yes, we must assume it is a rocket facility of some kind.'

'What is the range on a rocket, could a facility in the Middle East threaten the German border?' Dönitz, as ever, was thinking of the bigger strategic picture around the world and whether or not this new threat could be directed at Berlin; or indeed the naval fleets in the north.

'It is hard to say. A few hundred miles, maybe five hundred. I don't think a rocket fired in the Middle East would make it all the way to Germany.'

'But it could threaten our oil interests in the Middle East?' asked Dönitz.

'Yes, definitely.'

'So, this also means our naval fleet, our cruisers, could be vulnerable targets in the Mediterranean Sea?'

'Yes, in theory... if the rocket had a good guidance system.'

The two men sat in silence at this new revelation for a few moments. Dönitz cut in, 'This could change military tactics and warfare in the Mediterranean. The Luftwaffe is getting most of its aviation fuel from the new oil fields in the Middle East. We must protect German oil exploration interests.'

'I am fairly certain that both the Mediterranean and Middle East could be threatened.'

'Thank you, Colonel. It's always a pleasure.' Dönitz stood up. 'There is no time to delay. I must report back to the Führer at once.'

'Admiral, I am pleased to help. But… ' Dornberger hesitated. 'It is also vitally important that we know how advanced the opposition is. Our programme has much work to do yet.' He didn't want to tell the Admiral that the rockets were nowhere near ready for test flights.

'I will recommend to the Führer that you should advise the High Command on all technical issues relating to this development. We will ensure you have all the facts as they emerge.'

'Thank you Admiral… and Admiral… another thought; if there is a rocket base in the Middle East, it should be visible from the air.'

'The Luftwaffe is already taking aerial photographs, but the Middle East covers a huge area. It will take some time to locate,' explained Dönitz.

'It must be near the coast. Liquid oxygen is shipped. It is rarely moved by road, and the heat of the desert will make the stuff evaporate quickly. Yes, look for a facility near the coast.' Dornberger paused to allow the Admiral to reflect on the information. '… And one more thing; it may be partially buried underground to keep the oxygen cool. There may also be a supply of aluminium sheeting nearby; look for an aluminium works of some kind. It is needed to make components and the rocket casing.'

Admiral Dönitz nodded his appreciation. 'Thank you, that will greatly narrow down the search area. We will find it. I will let you know when we do.'

With that, the two men shook hands firmly. Admiral Dönitz immediately took his car the few miles north, back into the city centre of Berlin. He could not keep the Führer waiting.

CHAPTER 26

Making Plans at Kummersdorf

Dornberger sat at his desk. His eyes flicked between the telephone and Commandant Kessler. The telephone rang. Dornberger snapped up the receiver.

'Yes, my Führer… ' Beads of sweat formed on his brow. 'It will be done my Führer… every effort will be made… ' Dornberger stiffened and gave Kessler a worrying glance. 'Yes, of course my Führer, we will double our efforts. I… '

A patriotic tirade blasted Dorberger's ear.

'Let me give you my assurance my Führer… yes… yes… I… of course… heil Hitler!'

The phone suddenly went dead. Dornberger gulped as he replaced the receiver. He loosened the top button on his tunic, then took a deep breath and exhaled.

'Well?' Kessler leaned forward in his chair, studying Dorberger's furrowed brow.

'Herr Hitler is not pleased. He wants us to increase production, and the pace of the experimental work. From now on, we are to work both day and night. We will introduce a night shift starting from tomorrow.' Dornberger rubbed his temple. 'I guess it would be more efficient anyway… '

'What about the Arabs? Do they have a rocket programme or not?'

'The Führer has made it clear. Politically and militarily, it is important for Germany to have absolute control over liquid-propelled rocket technology. There *must not* be any competition.'

'It is unthinkable that the Arabs and Jews could achieve

advances that we cannot.' Kessler shook his head in disgust. 'We will destroy this competitor. It is German policy you know – the Jews.'

'I guess it doesn't matter who the competitor is. The strategic purpose of the German rocket programme is to have a weapon that nobody else possesses. This would put Germany in a strong position on the international stage. The Führer is asking us to provide the ultimate deterrent.'

'And if we don't achieve this?'

'Failure… ' Dornberger shuddered. '… I've no intention of failing. Herr Hitler has given us unlimited resources; for now at least. We *cannot* fail. Besides, the Führer wants to declare to the world that Germany has the first fully functioning rocket. He wants to showcase German technology on the political stage.'

'Is that wise? Only yesterday the need for the utmost secrecy was the priority.'

'Yes, we should tread carefully, remain secretive. Politics is a fickle business; hopefully Admiral Dönitz will persuade the Führer to see sense. Still, our rocket motor should be a major scientific advance, albeit with military applications of course; but there will also be many civilian uses. We can even get one step closer to putting the first rocket in to space! Something to shout about… eventually… don't you think?'

'Please, Colonel, while I admire your enthusiasm for your scientific endeavours, we do need to move forward with a realistic plan.'

'Yes of course, we will need more men and materials to make things work around the clock.'

'That can be done.' Kessler gave a shrug. 'There are plenty of Poles and the like for manual labour; but finding more scientists… well that would seem to be a limiting factor.'

'I agree, and we need to give the research teams some motivation, some significant scientific advances to work on… '

'There is Professor Mayer… ' Kessler stared Dornberger in the eye. 'He holds some advanced technological knowledge – I am sure of it. If there was ever a time we need this information, it is now.'

'Alright, alright, I agree. We have no choice. The developments in the Middle East have added a new urgency that we cannot ignore.'

Kessler beamed. 'I will extract the Professor's thoughts onto paper. It may take a day or so, but you will have it.'

Dornberger slumped back in his chair. What choice did he have with both Admiral Dönitz and Hitler making demands on the rocket programme? The rather short chain of command from Kummersdorf to the Reich Chancellor didn't help matters. He was in the spotlight now, and the price for failure would be a bullet in the head. He pursed his lips with a regrettable decision.

'Find out everything that Professor Mayer knows, by all means at your disposal – and quickly.'

Kessler snapped to attention, delighted with his new task. 'Heil Hitler!'

Nash shivered and pulled his collar up in an attempt to keep out the cold night air. Time spent on reconnaissance was never wasted. He adjusted his binoculars, bringing the repaired perimeter fence into focus. Kummersdorf was clearly going through some changes. He scanned the binoculars towards the main gate: more good news, the Germans had installed another fortified machine gun post. It would be *much* harder to get into the base this time.

Suddenly, the binoculars picked up the perimeter patrol.

Christ! Only five minutes since the last one!

The Germans had doubled the patrols. Nash focused through the fence. Some new construction work came into view. One, two, three… four large mounds of soil, and only fifty feet from the perimeter fence. It would be useful cover. It also looked like the Germans were strengthening the earthworks around the main buildings. He zoomed in on the earthworks and some heavy machinery. A construction worker came into view.

Interesting – regular army engineers – so, no civilian labourers are being allowed on site.

That put pay to any ideas of sneaking in through the main gate.

He shifted his attention to the living quarters; more new earthworks, but still under construction. The binoculars picked out the infirmary building through a gap. Not good news. A sentry and a new machine gun nest. All the ground-floor windows were sporting new iron grills. The building was evidently very secure; that could only mean one thing. Professor Mayer *had* to be inside.

But could he do it? Could he kill a defenceless old man? A civilian as well. What exactly was it that the Professor knew? Whatever, it was clear that Whitehall now wanted him dead.

Commandant Kessler had a spring in his step as he burst through the doors into the infirmary.

'Good afternoon, Fräuline. How is the Professor today?' Kessler strutted over to Mayer's bed.

The nurse gave a disapproving look. 'Please, Commandant, this is a hospital. The patient is sleeping.'

'No matter, wake him up.' Kessler beamed.

'But, sir… '

Kessler's expression suddenly turned menacing. 'I said, wake him up!'

The nurse tried to gently rouse Mayer. Ignoring her efforts, Kessler roughly plonked himself on the bed. He gave Mayer's leg a hard slap.

'Wake up! Wake up!' Mayer groaned as he opened his eyes to narrow swollen slits. 'Good afternoon, Professor. Are you awake? Good! You have questions to answer!' Kessler gave him a second slap on the leg. 'I said, wake up!' Another stinging blow was administered.

Mayer groaned as his eyes opened. He tried to sit up using his good arm for purchase. He grimaced as a bolt of pain shot through his ribs. The nurse leaned over, stuffing pillows strategically to support his weight. Parched, unable to speak, Mayer put out a shaky hand. The nurse instantly responded with a glass of water – she knew the routine.

A few sips of water, and a bout of coughing seemed to clear his throat. Soreness pulsated from his voice box. He rasped an almost inaudible word of thanks, then took another mouthful of water as the nurse raised the glass. With his vision phasing in and out of focus, his head pounding, and an erratic heartbeat pulsing in his chest, Mayer tried to focus his mind on the present. Voice or not, he didn't want to irritate Kessler.

The nurse slowly took the glass away from his lips, knowing the interrogation would begin. For Mayer she was his lifeline; trapped inside his broken body, she remained the only person who could decipher his badly distorted ramblings.

'I will pick up where we left off. Let me see… ' Kessler gave his usual theatrical pause. 'We were talking about rocket fuel calculations; that was all very interesting. You do remember Professor?'

Mayer gave a slight tilt of his head.

'Good, good, and then you said something about *Der Leibhaftige maschine*… devil machine. Tell me, what did you mean by this?' Kessler's face hardened.

Mayer stared blankly into the distance.

Kessler smiled inwardly.

So the prisoner is trying to ignore the interrogator! A classic sign of defiance; and definitely hiding something of importance.

'Fräuline, a pencil and paper for the Professor, as quick as you can.'

The nurse promptly returned with a notebook, wondering what the Commandant had in mind.

'Now… ' He turned to the nurse for confirmation. 'The Professor is injured on his left side, but his right arm is working?'

The nurse nodded in agreement.

'Good, good; this means the Professor can write down the answers to my questions.' Kessler was warming up.

'Now… ready Professor… my first question… ' Kessler spoke slowly and clearly. 'Write down your name.'

Mayer complied.

'Write down the main ingredients of rocket fuel.'

Mayer paused, looking at the nurse for moral support.

'Please don't try my patience – write it down!'

Mayer scrawled down the names of a few chemicals.

'Good, good, now write the equation for kinetic energy.'

He scrawled out the well-known equation from Newton's laws of thermodynamics. $E = \frac{1}{2} mv^2$. Kinetic energy is equal to half the mass multiplied by the square of the velocity. Kessler recognised it as one of the equations he had prepared a question on for the interrogation.

Kessler paused to assimilate the responses.

So, no foolish questions, and the prisoner is able to document technical information. Clearly, he can hear and understand questions, and recall some basic scientific facts. He can write down mathematical symbols and recall details of equations. The prisoner is therefore able to answer more technical questions – questions of a more urgent nature that require answering.

'Professor, now I have a task for you. Before your little accident you were working here on the calculations for the precise mixing of oxygen, hydrogen peroxide, and sodium permanganate to make a steady burn of fuel.'

Mayer titled his head slowly. It was still the best he could do for a nod.

'Don't be surprised Professor. I have done my homework too.' Kessler gave a half smile. He continued. 'You will write out these calculations. The nurse will help you. I will return in two hours.' Kessler leant forward so his face was close to the Professor's. Kessler hissed, 'If the task is not finished, there will be severe consequences.'

Mayer sank back into the pillows, rasping and sweating.

'Commandant please, the patient is very distressed, he will need more time.' The nurse searched Kessler's expression for the smallest sign of compassion – and found none.

'Two hours! No more!'

Kessler stood up and turned briskly towards the door. The fuel calculations were essential. The photographs from the Middle East had shown the same injectors they were building at Kummersdorf. There was no more time. Dornberger needed to know exactly what rate of fuel injection was needed to get the fuel system to work. Mayer had spent much of his scientific career on such calculations, and could do it quickly, injuries or not.

Kessler strutted into the infirmary, checking his watch – exactly six p.m. The nurse quickly intercepted, waving with several sheets of paper, evidently trying to protect her patient. Kessler noted Mayer's slumped exhaustion on the bed.

Good the prisoner has been working hard. Kessler smiled.

'Commandant, I have spent the entire afternoon with the Professor. He is now very tired, but I am pleased to report that the task is completed. Here, take a look.'

She thrust the notes at Kessler again. He took the sheets of paper and carefully examined each page. There were detailed descriptions and calculations. The handwriting changed halfway down the page. Evidently the Professor had tired, and the nurse had written some of the notes for him. Kessler was pleased with the progress. Still, he was no expert and would need to get one of the other rocket scientists to check the calculations. But as far as he could tell, the Professor had at least done what he had been asked, and had made the required notes.

'This is a good start, Fräuline. However, I have another task. Wake the Professor.'

'But Commandant, he is exhausted. It is too much for him. Please, can this wait a little while longer? The patient will be stronger after a few hours of rest.'

Kessler wasn't in the mood. 'Wake the Professor! Now!'

The nurse went through the routine of waking Mayer again, propping him up on the bed with pillows. Kessler took his position at the Professor's side.

'Professor, a good start, I must admit. However, time is not on our side. We have to make some urgent progress. So, I am afraid, I have some more questions for you.' Kessler moved further up the bed to get closer.

'Now, I will take the calculations you have provided, and ask one of the engineers to check your calculations. We can discuss any amendments later. However, I have a few other questions now, different questions. Tell me about *der Leibhaftige maschine*. What did you mean by that? Are you working on something else?'

Mayer stiffened; suddenly breathing rapidly, pain flashed through his chest. He coughed involuntarily, wincing at new discomfort in his ribs.

Kessler smiled.

At last! A line of questioning worth pursuing.

He leant forward again so Mayer could hear between coughs.

'What kind of machine? Tell me Professor, what else have you been working on?'

Mayer stared back, taking deep breaths and snorting through his damaged nasal passage. Kessler sensed the challenge to his authority.

'Fräuline, a pencil and paper for the Professor, please.'

She gently passed the notepaper and pencil to the Professor, arranging his hands so he could grip the pencil against the paper. A tear rolled down her cheek.

'Professor, you will draw your machine. You will finish it today, and I will come back tomorrow morning to collect the drawing!'

Mayer grunted and, with a huge effort, threw the pencil on the floor. Kessler looked at the nurse. 'See that he does it. This is vital work for Germany.'

The nurse nodded in agreement as she brushed the silent tears from her eyes.

Kessler stood and, straightening his tunic, he stared hard at Mayer for a few seconds; then he turned smartly towards the door.

On his way back to the office, Kessler analysed the interview.

There was definitely an expression of defiance on the prisoner's face, but why the drama with the pencil? A small measure of protest is to be expected, but not this much. The interrogation has stumbled on something very important, something I've not considered before.

Kessler decided to check the case files on the Professor.

Perhaps some detail has been overlooked and there's some connection between this machine, if it is a machine, and the events in Leipzig?

A manuscript had been stolen from the Professor's office, but the thief had dropped a couple of pages. Then someone had gone to great lengths to get those pages back. Kessler recalled the fight on the train to Berlin – a professional soldier, an assassin no less. So, clearly the pages were of huge importance. Was there some connection between the manuscript and the Professor's machine? Was this the big secret that the Professor was hiding?

Kessler would find out soon enough.

CHAPTER 27

Mayhem at Kummersdorf

A dewy mist hovered a few feet above the ground. Nash busied himself with an equipment check, trying not to think too much about the grim task ahead. The risks were substantial. He would have to get in close to kill the Professor, and that meant by default a real chance of being captured. At least the German uniform looked the part. A regular foot soldier, the lowest of the low. The kind of rank that didn't look out of place on guard duty.

Nash secured his weapons and jumped up and down to check for noise: no clinking of metal on metal.

All good.

He leaned to the left and then to the right. The kit seemed reasonably balanced, given that his pockets were bulging with enough ammunition to start a small war. The bags of explosives and detonators inside his jacket dug into his ribs. It wasn't exactly ideal, but he needed to look reasonably like the average infantryman; and they didn't usually carry around big bags of explosives.

He poked around inside his jacket to make sure the detonators were kept clear of the main charges. It was a token gesture. One stray tracer round and he would be blown to smithereens. He jumped up and down again – still nothing jangling in his pockets. A last few delicate touches of black camouflage cream took the shine off his face; just enough to look like the great unwashed. The boots were suitably dull. What more could he do?

Patience was the name of the game now.

Nash moved forward, poking his head through the undergrowth. The coast was clear, and only a few yards through the long grass to the perimeter fence. He crawled forward, bolt cutters in hand. Resting the heavy pincers on the first chain link in the fence, he took up the strain – *snap*. No alarm – exhaling to relive the tension, he worked on the next link – *snap*. Then the next – *snap, snap*.

Suddenly, the dull sound of boots penetrated the mist. A patrol! He closed up the chain links as tidily as possible, and edged back a few yards into the mist. Mouth open, ears sharp, and utterly motionless – he waited.

The patrol passed.

He crawled back to the fence to resume work – *snap, snap*. He looked into the mist, checking left, then right – nothing. *Snap, snap, snap.*

He pulled back the mesh. Keeping flat, he edged under the fence. Methodically digging in his toes, and at the same time lifting his body a few centimetres off the ground, Nash gradually moved through the gap, cradling a rifle in his arms. Something tugged on his back.

Damn it! A snag!

He groped around, finding the errant loop in his belt kit. The loop suddenly released, sending a shimmer down the chain mail fence. He scampered through the hole, then paused to lay the fence flat again.

Sod it. It'll have to do.

The sound of soft footfalls and the panting of a dog drifted in his direction.

He dashed over the open ground in a monkey run, keeping low with his weapon against his chest, and threw himself against the edge of the nearest pile of earth. The sentries came into view. Chest heaving, willing his breathing to slow, Nash struggled to keep still. The guards chatted to each other. The dog barked, straining at the leash. The handler tugged back on the leash, cursing, as he directed the animal to heel. They moved off along the fence line.

Motionless, with his mouth open and breathing gently, he listened for signs of life on the other side of the earthworks: nothing. Perhaps the earth was just muffling the sound of dozens of soldiers on the other side?

What the hell, time to move off.

Nash started to climb. Loose dirt on the earthen bank dragged at his feet. Edging upwards, his feet suddenly slid. Clods of earth and stone rolled down the bank. He fell. Grinding to a halt, he repositioned his grip and started climbing again. With a snake-like rhythm he made it to the top of the mound.

Good, no reception committee.

He rolled carefully over the top of the bank and down the other side, coming to rest on the grass in a squatting position. He strained to take in the view as his night vision adjusted.

It was at least another two hundred yards around the base of the earthworks to the infirmary. He squinted into the distance: diesel storage tanks, but some way off along the edge of the earthworks.

After checking for noise, he moved along the mound in a monkey run; keeping low, but with one hand ready on his weapon. The diesel tanks loomed out of the darkness. He moved behind the first tank and, crouching low, he rested his back against the cool cast iron.

He quickly checked his map.

About half way to the infirmary, so far so good.

He stared at the corrugated base of the fuel tank, and smiled as a deviation from the plan formed in his mind.

He pulled two explosive charges from under his tunic, and wedged them at the base of the diesel tanks, setting the timers for a fifteen-minute delay.

He took out his pistols, then checked the silencers, before clicking a round into each chamber.

He moved off at a steady walk, casually shouldering the rifle, making like a bored trooper on guard duty. His boots soaked up the dew as he covered the last hundred yards around the curvature of the earthworks.

The side of the infirmary building came into view. Two sentries manned a fire door at the far corner. Dusting himself off, and straightening his tunic, Nash cut across onto the path at the side of the building.

All quiet, too damned quiet!

The soldiers stood outside the fire door, some forty yards or so along the building. The sentries seemed reasonably alert, but were shuffling their feet. It was a good sign; they had been on duty for a while. Nash placed his hands casually behind his back, and strolled along the footpath. Thirty yards… his hands gripped the pistols… twenty yards… safety off… ten yards… the sentries turned to greet their new comrade. Five yards… 'It's a cold night, eh? Soon be out of here and in a warm billet.' Nash spoke in fluent German, grinning like a fresh recruit.

Two yards… *close enough*… he pulled up both pistols simultaneously in a well-rehearsed, fluid movement, and fired.

Thud, thud.

Brains splattered up the wall. He lunged forwards to catch the corpses, slumping to the ground with a sentry in each arm in a tangle of kit and body parts.

He glanced around.

There was no follow up but, equally, nowhere to conceal the bodies. He rolled them out flat on the earth adjacent to the footpath. It would have to do. Hopefully, anyone glancing from the top of path would pick out the natural line of the building and not the corpses lying next to it in the darkness.

He dipped into the shadow of the doorway, and listened at the fire door – silence. He checked the pistols again, and tried the door handle. It opened up to reveal a crack of light – but still no sound, and no guard behind the door. He opened the door a fraction more, and peered into the dimly lit ward.

The warmth and smell of the oil lamps filled his nostrils. The ward was open plan, with the beds in neatly regimented rows along each wall. The gentle sound of snoring drifted across the room. Somewhere at the far end at least one patient was sleeping. All the beds in immediate view were empty. Nash inched in a little more; it was a big ward with not much cover. He caught sight of a desk at the far end of the ward. A nurse sat dutifully doing some paperwork, or so it seemed. Several of the beds about half way down the ward were occupied. With luck, one of these would be Professor Mayer.

Nash eased through the door, and crouched behind the nearest bed – definitely three patients, and the nurse – but no one else. It was a safe bet there were sentries just outside the ward, the slightest noise out of the ordinary would bring them running. He edged around the bed, pistol raised.

Working from bed to bed, he moved along the ward.

His wet boots gave a squeak on the hard, polished floor. The nurse looked up.

Nash broke into a sprint, cocking the pistol as he slid the last few yards into the desk. The nurse was already reaching for the telephone. Nash landed with one hand firmly gripping hers and pressing down hard on the receiver. The other hand pressed the cold muzzle of the pistol against her forehead.

'You're hurting me!'

'Quiet.' Nash gently released his grip on her hand, but at the same time pushed the muzzle of the pistol deeper into her forehead.

She got the message, and sat motionless at the desk.

Nash glanced around the ward. The three patients were still sleeping. One of them was badly injured, and bandaged up; he wasn't going anywhere. The other two were old men.

He eased the nurse to her feet and, with the pistol still firmly against her forehead, moved her across the ward to the first bed.

Nash glanced at the occupant – no luck. He sidled across to the second bed. The nurse moved in step, with the pistol pressing against her forehead.

Nash studied the patient for a few seconds. A frail, ashen shadow of a man lay in the bed. He picked up the chart on the end of the bed: Mayer! Or so the chart said. It was hard to tell through the gloom and bandages; he seemed to have aged since the plane crash.

Nash spoke quietly and clearly in fluent German to the nurse. 'Is this Professor Mayer?'

The nurse glanced at the bed, then at her assailant. 'Yes… yes it is.'

Nash nudged her forehead with the pistol. 'If you interfere, I *will* shoot you.'

'What are you going to do?' The nurse flicked her eyes towards the patient.

Nash drew his second pistol; raising it slowly, he took aim at the Professor.

The nurse interrupted in harsh whispers. 'I hope you feel proud of yourself. He's an old man and paralysed down his left side. Hardly a threat to a man like you… '

He stared down at the bed.

'Go ahead… shoot him… coward… '

Nash pressed his pistol into her forehead. 'Quiet, damn you.'

The nurse persisted. 'Look at him… how could you?'

Nash hesitated. 'Shut up. That's your last warning.' He pushed the barrel hard into her forehead.

The nurse moved her head in a small nod against the barrel of the pistol. There was nothing more she could do.

Nash clicked the safety on his second pistol; lowering his aim on the bed, he shoved the weapon in his waist band. Then, with a fluid movement, Nash twisted the nurse around, forcing her arm behind her back. Ignoring her squeals of pain, he restrained the nurse with one hand and pointed the now free weapon on the Professor. She gave an involuntary shudder and tried to look away – he couldn't blame her – this was brutal.

He took a fresh aim and applied gentle pressure to the trigger.

Suddenly, a shower of broken glass and gunshots filled his senses. Instinctively, he crouched and, turning towards the new threat, he peppered a few rounds of covering fire up the ward.

'Intruder! You are trapped!' Commandant Kessler clicked home another magazine in his machine gun and let rip.

Nash responded with pistol fire, but was off balance, still holding the nurse. She danced around like a rag doll as she took several rounds in the chest. Bullets ricocheted off the bed posts and light fittings. Nash lost his footing and toppled behind the bed.

He patted himself down for injuries whilst replacing his magazine. The German had the drop on him – he should be dead – but wasn't. He slapped the bottom of the magazine, clicking it home into the pistol, as another burst of gunfire showered his position.

Tossing the corpse of the nurse away, Nash swung round, finding a firing position. He screamed with controlled aggression as he laid down fire in Kessler's direction.

Kessler quickly replied with an equally controlled burst of fire as he slipped behind a concrete pillar. Nash ducked under a shower of brick dust and plaster.

Christ! The bastard's deliberately aiming high!

Nash fished for a fresh magazine.

Commandant Kessler spoke in English. 'American! American, yes?'

Reloading silently, Nash used the time to move into better cover behind the next bed – it was time to head for the exit.

'Why do you want the Professor?'

No reply.

'Well, no matter, you're too late!'

No reply.

Kessler reloaded.

'There is no escape you know. In less than a minute this room will be full of soldiers. You will be slaughtered like a pig. Give it up.'

Nash looked at his watch.

Kessler darted out from behind the concrete pillar, and fired an automatic burst.

Nash lost his aim as ricochets thudded into the mattress only inches from his head.

He rolled to his knees, ready to return fire.

He didn't get the chance.

The ground shook, windows imploded. A hailstorm of glass and timber filled the room. A fraction of a second later, the pressure wave was replaced by gushing flames of burning fuel, snaking through the windows and across the ceiling, engulfing the entire room. Nash fell into a foetal position, with his hands over his eyes, and his mouth shut. He waited for the fireball hit.

Seconds later, the backdraft sucked the hot flames from the room. The acrid smell of burning alcohol and other chemicals assaulted Nash's nostrils.

Jesus Christ! Not diesel tanks; but rocket fuel!

Nash remained on the floor, both terrified and impressed by the size of the explosion.

Kessler staggered across the burning room, peppered with glass and splinters from the blast. Blood dripped from his skin. Excruciating agony filled his ears. Kessler lifted a hand to his left ear – blood – lots of blood. A wave of nausea hit as he lost control of his balance; white noise filled his skull.

'American! American! You will pay for this! American!'

The room span as Kessler attempted to level his weapon. He fired random shots at the far end of the room, stumbling, and blinking smoke from his eyes.

He staggered down the ward towards Nash's position and kept firing.

'American! Come out and fight like a man! American!'

Kessler suddenly lunged forwards, sliding through the debris on the polished floor, adding to his cuts and bruises along the way. He came to rest at the foot of the bed and, rolling upright, he levelled his weapon at Nash – but he was gone.

Dazed by the explosion, with his ears ringing and smoke burning his lungs, Nash frantically rubbed his eyes. It was useless, everything was a blur.

'Fuck!'

He hunkered down in the fire escape, and waited for things to come back into focus. An amorphous, massive orange glow filled his vision. Half the camp was on fire. His eyes smarted. Shapes danced in and out of the orange-red molasses; large shapes, the edges of buildings perhaps? Coughing and spluttering, Nash poured water from his canteen into his eyes. It stung as he squinted into the heat, but it was enough.

The main features of the camp started to come back into view.

He lifted up his arm in an attempt to shield himself from the searing heat. An escape plan began to form. There was no chance of going back to the same hole in the fence – an inferno was in the way – but at least the barracks and most of the troops were on the other side of the fire.

He dashed across the grass and scrambled up the nearest section of the earth bank, then peered over the top. Absolute mayhem. The perimeter guards had abandoned their patrols and were busy pulling fellow troops from the fire. It was now or never.

Nash slid down the earthworks, and headed for the perimeter fence; or what was left of it. He picked a good spot, and clambered up the meshing, then dropped down the other side. He scampered a few yards into the undergrowth, pausing to stare back at the burning armaments base. The mission had been a success; nothing would survive the inferno.

Nash vomited into the bushes.

CHAPTER 28

Orders from the Reich Chancellery

Kessler absently picked at his wounds. It had been a close-run thing. A few more seconds and the outcome would have been very different. He remembered succumbing to the smoke. Fortunately, his troops had dragged him from the burning building.

Events had flushed out the assassin. He *was* a foreigner; likely an American, or maybe British. Professor Mayer was alive – protected from the explosion by his bed – and the fact that he was already lying down when the blast wave hit. The Professor had sustained only minor cuts to his face, and some smoke inhalation, but was otherwise unharmed. The sentries had gone back into the burning building and managed to drag the Professor, mattress and all, to safety. The other patients in the ward had not been so lucky. They were all dead.

Kessler surveyed the scene; broken glass and shards of wood crunched under his feet. The air reeked of wood smoke and soot. Most of the domestic buildings on the site had been damaged, but the army engineers could work miracles. The main reinforced laboratory complex was unharmed, apart from some cosmetic smoke damage.

The body of the nurse caught his attention, twisted and scorched. It was a pity, she had been a good interpreter. It was an inconvenience, granted, he would have to find another one. She was supposed to help the Professor draw his machine, and make any notes. Kessler squatted, observing the body. It was only chance that had delivered him to the infirmary at the right time so late at night: he couldn't sleep. Next time the American, the foreigner, whoever he was, would not be so lucky.

Kessler stood up, and inspected the remains of the Professor's bed. Had the Professor finished the task? There was nothing on the floor or bedside cabinet. Perhaps the drawings had been lost in the fire? Nonetheless, it was worth searching. He worked towards the nurse's station, poking around each bedframe to eventually arrive at the remains of the desk.

The surface of the desk was covered in glass and charred pieces of timber. Everything was soaking wet. The fire crews had worked hard through the night. Opening the top drawer revealed nothing – just the usual paraphernalia of a ward sister – keys to the medicine cabinets, a few instruments, and pencils. Kessler opened the second draw; and hit the jackpot. The papers were still a little damp, but it was written in pencil and still legible. Kessler smiled at his find and began to read.

The sketch on the first page was an outline of a rocket, with the outer covering peeled off to show the inner working.

So, the Professor was making a rough diagram of the inside of a rocket, but why?

Kessler peered more closely at the paper, starting at the bottom of the diagram. It looked like rocket motors, and the exhaust system. Above this were various fuel tanks, and at the top of the rocket was the nose cone. This was where the all-important explosive payload would go; but this was all well known to the engineers at Kummersdorf.

There's nothing new here. This is no good! Or maybe the drawing isn't finished?

Kessler turned over the page. Things were now looking more interesting – a few lines of scrawl, tricky to decipher; and a couple of equations.

Better, some fresh equations; but what for?

The Professor would have to explain.

Kessler carefully carried the damp pages back to his office.

They would dry out and be easier to read. Professor Mayer would be quizzed on their contents. Kessler smiled to himself again; he was looking forward to it.

Admiral Dönitz sat at his desk in the Reich Chancellery. The room was a perfect rectangle containing an art-deco style fireplace at one end; an expanse of carpet filled the room. The neat lines of the new style of civil engineering shone through; cleanly dressed stone, with large windows at precisely regimented intervals. Dönitz stared at a map of Germany on his desk. Shaking his head, he tossed the photographs from Egypt onto it. The meeting with his supreme commander, Adolf Hitler, had not gone well. The evidence of competition in the Middle East, and the news of the attack at Kummersdorf, had sent the Führer into a rage.

The long drive back from the Führer's private residence, the Berghof, had left Dönitz stewing on a mixture of poor military strategy and sheer lunacy. It was madness. Why spend millions of reichsmarks on a project of limited military value? Nonetheless, Dönitz still believed in the importance of the chain of command. So that was that. He would do his duty.

A knock at the door roused Dönitz from his melancholy.

'Colonel Dornberger to see you Admiral,' the orderly announced.

'Good, good, show him in.'

Dornberger paced smartly into the room. The orderly closed the door behind him, leaving the two men alone. Dornberger came to attention in front of the desk, giving a sharp click of his heels.

'Please Colonel, sit down, please... let's dispense with the formalities.' Dönitz gestured towards the chair in front of his desk.

'What news from your meeting with the Führer?' Dornberger searched the lined expression on Dönitz's face. He had never seen the Admiral look so concerned.

Dönitz took a deep breath and exhaled. 'Well… to say that the Führer is displeased would be an understatement.'

'And?' Dornberger leaned forward, on tenterhooks.

'We both have some new orders, with immediate effect. The armaments base at Kummersdorf is simply not secure enough for such a special project. We must move the rocket programme to a new, secret location.'

'What?! Where?'

'Good question… but I have a suggestion… ' Dönitz leaned over the map, '… I know of a more secure location, and very remote. At least your scientists could work on the rocket programme undisturbed.'

'Any improvement in security is welcomed; perhaps a change of location would help.'

Dönitz pointed at the northern coastline with his finger. 'Here… it's currently a small place, on the Baltic Sea – Peenemünde. There is an access road, and a few small buildings where the navy used to keep supplies. It's rundown now, but shouldn't take long to convert things and build up the facility for the rocket programme.'

'There will be logistics in moving things, adding delays, and what about the cost?'

'The Führer has made it clear. The relocation is an absolute priority, you are tasked with making bigger and better rockets than before. Colonel Dornberger… apparently you have all the resources of the Reich at your disposal for this task… at least for now.'

Dornberger swallowed. 'And if we fail?'

'We are already on thin ice, you *must* not fail. We are… ' Both men stared at each other. It didn't need saying – Hitler was adept at removing commanders who displeased him. Dönitz broke the silence.

'Well, from a military viewpoint, it is defended on at least two sides by the sea. We can reinforce it quickly from the naval base in Heligoland.' Dönitz traced a finger across the map.

'At least that's some comfort to have the navy close by; how long do we have to make the move?'

'Effective immediately and to be completed within a matter of months. We have no choice; the Führer demands a rapid timetable. I will draw on men and resources from elsewhere in the navy to facilitate things.'

'What about building the fleet and the U-boat programme? This will continue? Rocket technology is potentially many months away from providing any strategic value to the defences of Germany.'

'The U-boat fleet remains part of my grand strategy for naval defences, but Herr Hitler has other ideas. He wants weapons of assault. We are to have command of the seas with the U-boat, and the rocket will give us command of the sky – apparently.'

'I see… ' Dornberger swallowed, a cold sweat formed on his brow, '… then I had better make progress.'

'For all our sakes, you *must* make things work. Hitler has pledged millions of reichsmarks; but he wants results.'

'Tell the Führer that he will not be disappointed, we will double, no triple, our efforts.' Dornberger stood and saluted.

With that the meeting was over. Both men knew the consequences of failure. Dönitz was a submariner at heart. He would do what he could to help his friend, Dornberger, and the many good officers under his command.

CHAPTER 29

Mayer's Delirium

Kessler sat on a chair next to the Professor's bed, studying the papers he had found in the infirmary. Mayer was suffering from smoke inhalation. The doctor, admittedly, was doing his best to keep the prisoner stable, and at least things were more secure in the main complex. The Professor had his own private room with constant medical support. Nonetheless, he was still weak.

'Professor, this is an interesting drawing. It is a sketch of one of the prototype rockets, is it not?'

Mayer gave a feeble nod.

'Take a look at the drawing.' Kessler held the paper close to the Professor's face. 'Is it finished?'

Mayer studied the sketch as best he could. He remembered now. It was just a simple plan of a standard rocket. He needed to convince Kessler that this was his machine. In a moment of delirium he had obviously mentioned something about his new theories, but what? Was it just garbled information, or details of the device? Mayer had no idea.

'Professor, is the drawing finished?'

Mayer nodded.

Kessler turned over the page and studied the notes on the second page. One of the engineers had confirmed that they were basic mass calculations, showing the amount of force required to lift a given weight of rocket fuel. In the grand scheme of things, this was schoolboy physics. Had Mayer sustained brain damage to such an extent that all he could do was recall basic physics? If this was the case, the interrogation would be a waste of time.

'Professor, the calculation on the second page has an equation. $F = ma$. What does this mean?' It was a test. Kessler knew the answer.

'Foorceee… Foorceee… is… maaass… times… accel… ' Mayer erupted into a coughing fit. The strain was obviously too much, but Kessler got the gist of the answer. The Professor *did* recognise the simple equation. Kessler waited for the coughing fit to subside.

'So, you can remember your physics. That is good. Now, I want you to write down some real equations – not this schoolboy nonsense!' Kessler leaned forward into Mayer's face. 'Write down the exponential calculus for a rocket burning one hundred kilograms of fuel. What is the resultant lift and how long will the fuel last?'

Kessler raised the game: one of his engineers had prepared some questions, some calculations, all about rocket fuels. He had the answers in his pocket. The calculations were way beyond the average person, but a rocket scientist who had spent all his life on such calculations would find them easy to complete. Kessler passed a pencil and paper to Mayer, and held the notepaper up to the Professor's good arm so that he could write.

He repeated the crucial information. 'Write down the calculation; one hundred kilograms of fuel, what is the lift and burn time?'

Mayer worked slowly. He wasn't trying to stall. His brain could do the calculation easily. He had solved it in seconds; but his body would not let him write the answer down on the paper. It took incredible concentration just to get his right arm to transmit the thoughts into words and numbers on the paper. Slowly the calculations appeared, in between violent coughing fits.

Kessler examined the scrawl. It matched. The Professor had given a correct answer.

'Good, so you remember your calculus. Now let us focus on your machine. Is it some component of a rocket, or some advanced prototype?'

'Yeeeees,' Mayer lied.

'Then draw it!'

Mayer thought for a minute. He needed to draw something technical that Kessler would not recognise and have to verify with an engineer. It would need to be convincing, and keep the engineers busy for a while. It would need to be a real technological advancement in the rocket programme. Mayer considered the options. He had several new ideas about manifold designs and fuel mixing that he had not shared with his colleagues.

That's it!

He could throw Kessler off the scent by giving him a new, improved, manifold design. Mayer began to sketch, and hoped that his body was up to the task.

Kessler sat waiting: what else could he do? The prisoner was a wreck.

Mayer pressed the pencil to the paper, drawing slowly, with his hands shaking so much that he needed to repeatedly go over each line. A rough sketch slowly formed on the page.

'What is it?' Kessler was genuinely puzzled.

Mayer was exhausted and, lacking the energy to speak, he gestured for the paper and wrote a few words. He had drawn a rough sketch for the very first turbo thrust pump; in effect, a turbo charger for a rocket engine. It would take the engineers a few days to figure it out, but it would increase the initial acceleration of a rocket off the launch pad by at least two hundred percent. That would be a major technological advancement by anyone's reckoning.

Kessler stared at the diagram, clueless. The engineers would need to read it.

'Is there anything else, Professor?'

Mayer gave a half shrug.

'Are you sure there is nothing else, Professor?'

Mayer tried to shrug again, but it just started off another coughing fit.

'Is there more? Professor, is there more?!'

Mayer continued coughing violently, unable to answer. Spots of blood emerged from his mouth and nose.

'Herr Doctor! Herr Doctor! Attend the patient!' Kessler called in the doctor who had been waiting outside.

Mayer passed out.

Dr Steinhoff examined the sketch, eyes wide. 'My, my… this is very exciting!… This is… I think… a new type of booster… yes, I think so, a turbo booster!'

'So what? How significant is it?' Kessler asked.

'This is *very* significant. You see, if this is a booster – and I think it is – then we will be able to make our rockets go *much* faster!' The rocket scientist beamed.

'Then I suggest that you get your team of engineers to make it and test it.' Kessler stared at the scientist.

'Of course, of course, there is so much work to be done! We will need to make proper technical drawings, then to prepare a mould in which to pour hot aluminium to cast the turbo device. Then fan blades will need to be added, and made at a very precise angle, length, and flexibility.'

'How quickly can you make this, within a couple of days? Professor Mayer is very ill. His capacity to answer questions is… shall we say… becoming limited. We may not have much time.' Kessler was being realistic.

The scientist shook his head. 'Not a chance. The task is a real challenge, and will keep dozens of scientists and engineers hard at work for several weeks. This task is at the frontier of precision engineering.'

'But you *can* make this?'

'Yes, in time. I must say, this is a work of genius, simple, yet elegant... '

'I am sure it is – just get on with it!'

'Of course, Commandant, will that be all?' Steinhoff swallowed, and returned his gaze to the sketch. A cold sweat trickled down his back. What if he couldn't make the booster? The design was intricate and Commandant Kessler was not a man to displease.

Steinhoff clenched his jaw as a new emotion hit home.

Envy.

He had toiled on the design of rocket engines for years. Recognition for his work was long overdue. Why hadn't he seen this before? How could a sick man sketch a work of genius in minutes? The hand of providence had given him Mayer. He would do well to use this advantage, and keep Mayer alive as long as possible.

'Commandant, I must protest! The patient is *very* sick. We *must* let him rest,' the doctor whispered in harsh tones, standing outside the patient's door, desperately trying not to disturb the calm. Despite his best efforts, Mayer was in decline. 'Please Herr Commandant! The smoke from the fire has compounded a number of medical problems with the patient. He has a *serious* lung infection.'

'No matter, you will assist me during the interview. I want to know what *he* knows. The Führer wants to know what *he* knows!' Kessler towered over the doctor.

'Look, I can give the patient pain relief and keep him comfortable, but that is all. He really needs to rest; he's on death's door.'

'Herr Doctor, that is precisely why the interrogation must continue!'

Kessler stormed into Mayer's room with the doctor in tow.

Mayer had a high fever and muttered periodically – even Kessler had to admit that he was probably wasting his time – but still, a round of questioning wouldn't hurt. As a precaution he had brought the senior rocket scientist, Steinhoff, along to take notes and listen just in case the Professor garbled some nugget of pure genius. The turbo device had been a good step forward. Maybe he had been wrong, perhaps there was no new machine after all? On the other hand, if a sick man could sketch out such a revolution in engineering as the turbo device, then there must be other technological advances trapped inside his head. Kessler reasoned that the interrogation was worth continuing.

'Professor, can you hear me? How do we control the turbo device? How do we feedback the signal from the device to the fuel tanks?'

Kessler was asking ridiculously complex questions, but the engineers needed answers. With luck, he might blurt them out between bouts of delirium.

'What is the feedback signal?' Kessler persisted.

Mayer mumbled nonsense. Any chance of a reasoned conversation had long since slipped away.

'What is the feedback signal?' Kessler repeated, shaking Mayer by the shoulders.

'I know… Albeeert… '

Both Kessler and the rocket scientist leaned in close to catch what the Professor was saying.

'Albeeert… friennnnd… save… meeee.'

Kessler looked at the rocket scientist. 'Dr Steinhoff, who is Albert?'

'Albert, that will be Albert Einstein,' answered the rocket scientist.

Dr Steinhoff was a physicist, as well as a fine engineer. Everybody knew of Einstein; his equations and ideas had turned the world of physics upside down in the last twenty years. If the situation had not been so grave, Steinhoff might have been lightly amused by Kessler's ignorance.

Mayer continued his delirious mumblings.

'Mass… to energgeee… quan… tuum… fast… so fast… '

Kessler glanced at Steinhoff for explanation.

'Mass to energy; he must be recalling one of the field equations. Maybe $E = mc^2$. Fast, something is fast – it could be light – the speed of light.' Steinhoff was intrigued.

'Noooooo… Nooooooo!' The Professor dissolved into a coughing fit. Then, out of the blue, came a moment of lucidity. Mayer opened his eyes, and spoke clearly.

'Wave number equals two *Pi* over *lambda*. Quantum energy, quantum energy!'

Mayer collapsed back on the bed.

'What is he talking about?' Kessler could see things were moving into new ground.

'I have no idea,' Steinhoff shrugged. 'Something to do with wave energy and quantum mechanics.'

'We must know more!' Kessler turned to the doctor. 'Wake him up – you have the adrenalin shots. Do it!'

The doctor produced a box of glass syringes with long needles. 'I have prepared a dose of adrenalin, as you requested; but please understand, the hormone is a strong stimulant. It will wake the patient up for a few minutes only.'

'Do it!' Kessler ordered.

The doctor complied. He carefully took out the first glass syringe containing adrenalin, and instinctively tapped the glass to remove any air bubbles and to check the contents. With the syringe raised in the air, he pressed Kessler for confirmation. 'This will be only a temporary boost to energy levels. It is a hefty dose – too much and we risk heart failure or a massive internal bleed.'

'Proceed!'

The doctor took the Professor's arm and delivered the

injection. The effect was immediate. Kessler wasted no time in resuming the interrogation.

'Professor, what about wave energy? Tell me! Is this something to do with your new machine?'

No answer.

'Answer! Answer the question!' Kessler slapped the Professor across the face.

The doctor didn't bother to protest on behalf of his patient. Kessler continued with a few more blows. Blood poured from the Professor's nose.

'Gooooo toooo heeeeeell.' Mayer snorted his own blood and clasped his lips tight.

'Answer!' Another slap.

'Gooooo tooooo heeeeeell.' Mayer was in turmoil, he *had* said something about his idea! 'I'll see yoooou in heeeeell… ' Mayer coughed up spots of blood and prayed for death.

Kessler looked at the doctor. 'Give him the *other* drug, the truth drug – give him the mescaline – do it now.'

Mescaline was a new mind-controlling drug, developed by the SS, for just such occasions. When it was mixed with cocaine and heroin in the right proportions, a prisoner injected with the concoction would answer anything.

'No! It cannot be done! It will be a potentially lethal cocktail. There is adrenalin already in his veins!'

The doctor, reluctantly, prepared the mescaline syringe. A few hundred milligrams in the syringe – an educated guess – he didn't know if the dose would fry the patient's brain, or make him sing like a canary.

He injected the dose.

Mayer gasped into a spasm with the rush of cocaine and heroin. Then after a few seconds his muscle tone relaxed as the mescaline kicked in. He gave a crooked smile, as his eyes wandered aimlessly around the room.

'Tell us about two *Pi* and *Lamda*,' Kessler asked quietly.

The Professor gave a gargled half smile.

'Nooo... toooo diffi... cult for you... ' Mayer half giggled. Blood dripped from his nose.

Kessler could not believe it; Mayer was arrogantly refusing to reply because he wasn't smart enough!

'Then talk to Dr Steinhoff. You remember Steinhoff? You worked on the fuel tanks together.' Kessler tried to motivate his prisoner as he passed the control of the interview to Steinhoff.

'Gustav, please, we want to help you. Please help by answering my questions. Do you agree?'

'Yeees, you know... you know... ' he muttered an approval.

'The wave number, tell me about this. Why is it important, what is it for?'

Mayer chuckled in his delirium. Blood frothed at his lips as he spoke. 'Wave number... particle energy... same thing!' Mayer tried a smug smile, but couldn't.

'What? No! Impossible? Are you sure?!' Steinhoff's mind reeled. This was scientific heresy! This was like saying the earth was flat, or the sky was green. It didn't make any sense at all. He needed to know the logic steps. How did the Professor's mind go from A to B, and then make a sudden leap to Z?

'Gustav, how can this be? I don't understand? How can wave energy and particle energy be the same thing?'

Mayer gave a satisfying half nod and continued.

'Planck... made... mistake... constant not constant.'

Steinhoff absorbed another monumental intellectual blow. Planck's constant was a number, a fixed number that was used in numerous scientific calculations. It was a universal rule, something that did not change, and something that *could not* change. It was a number that described a fundamental physical property of the universe – it could not be wrong. Everything that science did, or was, depended on this. Steinhoff was perplexed.

'Why is it not constant, Gustav why?'

'Not sooo… fast… wavelength… momentum… same.'

'When are they the same?! Gustav when?!'

'Small… veeery… very small… ten… minus… nine… '

Steinhoff didn't understand.

'Gustav, are you saying that wavelength and momentum are the same? But only when things are small?'

'Yeees.'

'I don't understand, what has this got to do with rockets?'

'Nothing… better than… rocket… faster… travel… to stars… '

With that Mayer slipped into unconsciousness, blood dripping from his nose and lips.

Steinhoff gazed at Kessler as he tried to rationalise what he had heard. 'I am not sure. I think the Professor has come up with some completely new propulsion concept based on quantum physics, but it doesn't make sense. I cannot see how this idea has come about.'

'Then wake him up! Find out! Doctor, more adrenalin and more of the truth drug! Now! Quickly!' Kessler flashed a menacing look at the surgeon.

The doctor gave the Professor another shot of adrenalin, and immediately followed this with another shot of the mescaline mixture. It took longer to take effect this time, and the adrenalin only just brought Mayer back to some kind of consciousness. It was a massive dose of adrenalin, and the doctor dared not give another injection.

'Gustav, is it a novel propulsion system, how does it work?'

'In part… more… much more… ' Mayer coughed a fine spray of bloody saliva. His skin turned ash-grey from the effects of the drugs and oxygen deprivation.

Mayer collapsed into silence.

'Another injection! More adrenalin!' ordered Kessler.

'I cannot, another injection *could* kill him!'

'Do it anyway!'

The doctor did as he was told, and injected another syringe full of adrenalin. It was an enormous dose – he was surprised to see Mayer survive the injection.

'Gustav, what is the engine made from, what material?'

'Carbon… small… small… carbon cage… '

'Carbon; how small? What do you mean by cage?' Steinhoff wasn't following the idea.

'Sixty… carbon… atoms.'

'How do the carbon atoms work?'

'Time… of flight… mass… to… energy… '

Mayer started to slip away. Steinhoff was overwhelmed by what he had just heard. He grabbed the Professor by the shoulders and desperately tried to shake him awake.

'How do the carbon atoms work? What else do you need?'

'Electric… field… '

'An electric field? What does the electricity do? How much voltage? Where does the carbon go?' Steinhoff fired questions.

'Acceleration… the… key… '

The last few words faded away as Professor Mayer slipped into a coma.

Mayer fell through the dark chasm. Cool, moist air freshened his face. Walls of granite twinkled as they flashed by. He continued to fall, further and further into the earth. He did not seem to mind. Suddenly a crimson light issued from the pit, miles below.

Mayer focused on the redness and accelerated through the gloom.

Suddenly, a cave floor rushed up to meet him. Winded, but unhurt, he sat up.

'Where am I?'

'Hell, welcomes you… Professor Mayer!' the beast roared, raising his whip.

Crack!

Searing pain erupted in his chest, blood welled up from the flesh wound.

'Arghhh! What do you want from me?!'

'Nothing. It's not what *I* want from you, but what *you* want from me!'

The beast laughed.

'I don't want anything. Let me go!'

'Now, now… Professor Mayer… ' The beast crouched closer, its foulness and stench filled Mayer's nostrils. The creature spoke quietly. '… Search your feelings… there is something you want, isn't there?'

Mayer's head slumped in shame. 'Yes… yes there is… my Sophia… '

The devil cackled, cracking his whip in the air.

'I can return her to you… put everything back as it was. I only ask for one thing in return.' The devil snorted vileness and smiled.

'What would you have me do?' Mayer dabbed his fingers into the blood on his chest.

'Give me the secret… give me the secret of your device!'

The devil's face suddenly transformed. Kessler stared back at him.

'Give me the secret Professor Mayer… then everything will be yours… home… wife… even children.'

Mayer yelled in defiance. 'No! No! Never!'

'Very well. If we cannot bargain… ' The devil growled a deep belly laugh that echoed around the cavern. He clicked his fingers.

A gangly wrath appeared, dragging his beloved Sophia towards oblivion.

'Sophia! No! Leave her! Please, I will do anything… anything!' Mayer sobbed.

'The secret… the secret… and everything you love can be saved.' The devil cracked his whip, opening another wound on Mayer's chest.

'Arghhh! Alright! Alright! But let her live… please… just let her live.'

He beckoned the beast closer; sobbing, he whispered in its ear.

The devil bellowed with laughter.

Mayer stared into the abyss of his mind's eye and despaired.

CHAPTER 30

Peenemünde

Colonel Walter Dornberger called the team together in his new office at Peenemünde. The last few weeks had been a period of rapid change. Admiral Dönitz had chosen the new site well; remote from any big population centres and easily defended.

Peenemünde sat at the end of a narrow spit of land on the Baltic coast. The spit was low-lying and exposed to the elements, but provided a natural defence. The new rocket base was essentially surrounded by water; with the sea to the north and the Peene River to the south.

The beach along the spit stretched for miles at low tide. The sand flats were ideal for the test firing of rockets, and repelling any potential invading force. The river mouth of the Peene was equally well defended, with anti-aircraft batteries and machine gun posts concealed from the air by a dense line of pine trees. It would take a heavily armed flotilla to break through into the river, and even if they did, they would never make it ashore.

Dönitz had provided Dornberger with ninety extra scientists and technicians to help establish the new rocket programme; including the brilliant physicist, Wernher von Braun and other top engineers from the Reich.

Kessler made his report.

'On domestic matters first of all, gentlemen... ' He checked the figures in his notebook. 'Yes, well, I can report that construction is more or less complete; including all the main laboratories, outbuildings, and quarters for the troops.'

'That is good news; as you know, we are under some pressure from the Führer to keep to the new timetable,' Dornberger interjected.

'Well, we are on schedule. It also means we don't need the slave labour anymore.'

'What will happen to them?' Steinhoff queried. Hitler had provided hundreds of Jews and Poles, slave labourers who worked to build the base.

'My men will deal with it,' Kessler smiled.

'What does that mean?' Steinhoff gave him a flat look.

'Gentlemen, enough.' Dornberger raised his hands. 'Commandant Kessler will see to it that the prisoners are returned from whence they came.'

Kessler nodded.

Dornberger looked Kessler in the eye. '... And Commandant, there are to be no more summary executions... your men... I don't approve of their methods.'

'We are merely doing our Führer's bidding. The labourers needed discipline; how else were we meant to hack this massive test facility from the wilderness in only a matter of months?' Kessler gave a polite smile.

Steinhoff changed the subject.

'The new turbo booster is working well. As you know, it has taken some considerable time to figure out the details from Professor Mayer's rough sketch; but it was worth the wait. A work of genius, I might add.'

Dornberger nodded his approval.

'We now have a precise method to control the rate of mixing of the rocket fuel ingredients; simple, but elegant, and with very few moving parts.'

It was a real breakthrough. A major stumbling block in rocket technology had been overcome.

Steinhoff continued. 'We have run numerous static tests on motors fixed in the lab. It's all good, smooth acceleration and deceleration. The main fuel of alcohol burns steadily in the stream of liquid oxygen, and with a couple of key catalysts for the reaction – sodium permanganate and hydrogen peroxide – we can keep the burn going.'

'How much lift did you get on the bench tests?' Dornberger asked.

Steinhoff smiled. 'A motor with a full set of turbo injectors can easily lift several tons; we can now offer plenty of payload to the nose cone.'

'How much payload?' Dornberger wondered what sort of punch the new weapon could pack.

Steinhoff checked his notes. 'At a maximum... four hundred pounds of high explosive, several hundred would be routine.'

Germany was now set to build huge rockets with enough fire power to level a small town.

Steinhoff continued. 'There's more. This is no longer a bench test. We have more or less completed our first rocket in the *Vergeltungswaffe* series. We will call this the V1. The fuel booster has enabled us to launch rockets from a sloping ramp – rather like sending them off the end of a large ski jump. It works well. The rockets get away cleanly, and the small wings on the side of each rocket stop it rotating in flight, so we have forward thrust. It makes good acceleration and can gain height quickly. Things are proceeding well, but we still have a few more test flights to do.'

'Good, that is settled then. We will do some test flights and I will report to the Reich Chancellor next week,' Dornberger summed up, wanting to get onto other matters.

'Dr Steinhoff, what of the other device?' Hitler had asked for a detailed technical report on the interview with Professor Mayer.

'I am afraid I cannot report much progress. I have been over and over my notes. I simply do not understand what Professor Mayer was alluding to.' Steinhoff shook his head in frustration.

'He is still in a coma, and has barely stirred since the move from Kummersdorf. Everything is locked inside his head.'

Dornberger raised an eyebrow. 'The surgeon has made no progress?'

'No, I am afraid not, we simply have to wait; there is a chance Mayer will *never* recover.' Steinhoff shook his head.

'No matter, what progress have you made?'

All eyes turned to Steinhoff.

'We have two major lines of investigation. The first is on the theory. We have reviewed all of Plank's original equations from the 1870s that used the notations of *lambda* and *Pi*, and many derivations of these terms by other scientists since then. The fact is, we cannot figure this out.' Steinhoff had to admit defeat. Whatever was going around in Mayer's head was way beyond him.

'Then we need to get a specialist in this area to help,' Dornberger reflected.

'There are no specialists really. There's Mayer of course, and... ' Steinhoff racked his brains trying to think of another scientist who might be able to solve the riddle. '... Einstein? What about Einstein?' Steinhoff smiled.

'That's rather difficult. He is living overseas now. How would we get him to come back here?' Dornberger was aware of the high profile Einstein was now getting in England and America for his work on atomic physics.

'He is the only one who can solve this problem; besides, he worked with Mayer. They are friends,' indicated Steinhoff.

The conversation was going nowhere. There was no hope of attracting Einstein back to Germany. He had made thinly veiled hostile remarks about the human rights record of the Reich to the media in the USA. It was clear that Einstein would not come to Peenemünde voluntarily. Dornberger tried a different tact.

'You mentioned a second line of enquiry?'

'Yes, the other is the structure of the device. Professor Mayer mentioned something about carbon structures, and electric fields.' Steinhoff was struggling to keep his report optimistic. 'We have done some research into carbon-based materials and their properties in electric fields. Every schoolboy knows that the graphite in your pencils is made of mostly pure carbon, and that it will conduct electricity, but there's no logic as to how or why these properties might be used in a propulsion device.'

'What about other forms of carbon?' asked Dornberger.

'The only other crystalline form of carbon of any significance is diamond – and that's as hard as nails and chemically stable – unreactive.' Steinhoff had to concede failure. 'I cannot make this carbon without Mayer!'

Progress on the device was at a dead end.

Colonel Dornberger stood to attention in the Admiralty office of the Reich Chancellery, while Dönitz eagerly opened his report.

'It looks like good progress... ' Dönitz nodded with satisfaction as he scanned the first few pages. 'Colonel, sorry, where are my manners... please, be seated.'

Dönitz waited until his guest was duly seated, then looked at Dornberger.

'So Colonel, the Führer wants to know about his *Vergeltungswaffe* – the vengeance weapon is almost ready? Tell me about the payload. How much explosive can it carry?'

'Our test flights have improved the payload. Now, in theory, more than one thousand kilograms,' Dornberger replied.

'You have done well it seems; this should keep the Führer happy. What is the blast radius of the weapon now?'

'The payload will detonate on contact with the ground. The immediate explosion will flatten everything within one hundred metres, and the shockwave that follows will cause damage for hundreds of metres around the epicentre.'

'I see… Herr Hitler is thinking about offensive uses of this weapon. If the weapon was used on the battlefield, how effective could it be?'

Dornberger paused before replying, imagining an explosion on open ground amongst a line of troops, with armour.

'If the weapon was detonated amongst an advancing column it would cause devastation. The blast would penetrate armour, destroying tanks and other vehicles. The shockwave would shatter internal organs and burst eardrums. Any troops in the proximity would take heavy casualties and be incapacitated.'

Dornberger could barely imagine the horror. He continued. 'Do you think the Führer would actually sanction the use of such a weapon against troops on the ground?' He shook his head in despair.

'Perhaps I can persuade the Reich Chancellor to keep the weapon for defence, but I doubt it, he has already made up his mind. He wants the capability to attack other cities in Europe, especially London, and wants to target the Americans too.'

'This is madness! There are no substantive forces that could threaten Germany's borders to justify the use of such a weapon, at least not yet!'

'I know, I know… ' Dönitz rubbed his forehead. '… Let's hope the Führer only uses it as a political deterrent to prevent the British and Americans from interfering in our European affairs.'

'And if he doesn't? What then?' Dornberger struggled to conceal his revulsion. He had built this weapon for defence, not for assault on civilian population centres. 'The rocket can fly at several hundred miles per hour, and could reach London in less than an hour, depending on the location of the launch site.' He paused; at least that part was true. 'However, dare we tell Herr Hitler that we are still refining the flight controls so that we can precisely target the rocket? The reality is that we still have more test flights to do.'

'We need to be pragmatic… ' Dönitz drummed his fingers on the document, '… the report needs to show some progress on the guidance system and the range of the rockets, but I am reluctant to include any suggestions about the targeting of civilian population centres.'

'I couldn't agree more… ' Dornberger looked gloomily at the Admiral.

Dönitz looked at Dornberger. 'What of America? The Führer will ask. What are the prospects of developing a weapon that can hit the Americans?'

'No, not yet. This would require a bigger rocket with more fuel, or a better propulsion system,' Dornberger was certain.

'That brings us neatly to the other matter… ' Dönitz lowered his voice to a whisper. 'The Führer asks about progress on the… well… shall we say… other device?' Dönitz glanced around the room as if looking for conspirators.

Dornberger spoke in a harsh whisper. 'My report indicates that we have several lines of investigation, but the technology is very advanced and we do not yet fully understand the concept of how it works. Professor Mayer hides many secrets inside his head. He is still in a coma.'

'Please understand, the Führer is *totally obsessed* with this new device,' Dönitz hissed back. 'Christ! He says this is a super weapon beyond compare and we are to gather the finest minds in Germany to solve the problem!'

'The finest minds in Germany *are already* gathered!' Dornberger countered.

'I know, I know… I tried to explain… but that's no good. He wants Professor Mayer – and if that's not possible he wants Professor Mayer's friend – *he wants* Einstein!'

Dornberger sat in stunned silence at the news. Staring into space, Dornberger finally spoke.

'But… but… I don't understand… I mean… how? Einstein is a figure of international standing. He has spoken out, at least in a roundabout way, against National Socialism. He will not come to Germany of his own free will.' Abduction was unthinkable. Dornberger was sure he had misunderstood.

Dönitz closed the file and folded his arms, his gaze firmly fixed on Dornberger. 'I am afraid it is out of my hands. Herr Hitler has already given instructions to the SS. Einstein is to be repatriated to Germany at *any* cost.'

CHAPTER 31

Abduction

Oliver Heinkel drove slowly through the quiet, leafy suburbs of Oxford. Even in the darkness the pleasantly arranged Georgian houses exuded tranquillity, the sort of place one could raise a family. Oxford had become popular with the middle classes, being only a short commute to London. It was also the temporary residence of Albert Einstein. The Leipzig office had issued him with a travel permit. Einstein was renting a house while he was on sabbatical in Oxford for some physics event at the University. It was all very convenient.

Heinkel checked his watch, everything was on schedule. He peered into the hedgerows and picket fences, looking for signs of anything out of the ordinary – nothing. He turned right into Einstein's street, cruising at a steady speed. There were no celebrity mansions, just more slices of the idyllic suburban dream.

He drove past the front gate. There were no obvious signs of security, and no policeman on the doorstep, but that didn't mean anything. British intelligence were adept at hiding in plain sight. The place could be crawling with agents.

He made another right turn, and drove around the block; satisfied with the reconnaissance, it was time to go on foot. He parked the Jaguar under a leafy tree, choosing a spot next to a mature garden that offered plenty of cover, and turned the engine off. He sat in silence, his heart raced a little. It was an honour to be personally selected by Dr Goebbels for this special task.

He checked his dark clothing again for labels, and then weighed the Webley revolver in his hand. It felt clunky and unbalanced, but would do the job. The superior engineering of the German Sauher 38 automatic pistol was preferable, but the forensics situation dictated that there could be no trace of any German involvement. He holstered the British weapon, and stepped out of the car.

Nothing moved on the street.

He pulled up his black raincoat, and detoured back around the block.

Einstein's place was close to the river with good tree cover. He moved cautiously through the trees, following the curve of one of the narrow footpaths. The sound of a train's whistle echoed in the distance; the occasional flash of car headlights lanced into the tree line. The chug of a canal boat faded along the waterway, leaving only the heavy night air for company.

Suddenly, the sound of twigs snapping and rustling in undergrowth broke the silence. Heinkel levelled his weapon: a fox. He eased off the trigger and, taking a crouching position, he listened – nothing. He moved forward slowly, searching for targets with his weapon.

The tree line abruptly stopped and was replaced by a thicket of rhododendrons, demarcating the back garden of Einstein's rented property. He worked his way through the bushes, taking up a position behind a convenient rhododendron stump with a good view of the lawn. He sat, breathing calmly, with his mouth open and ear titled towards the ground. A maple tree grew at the side of the house, obscuring most of the street lighting. Mature shrubs encircled the entire garden, with sections overgrowing onto the porch. He scanned the shadows looking for movement.

Silence.

He moved his eyes up onto the roof of the house, following left to right, systematically checking each window all the way to the ground floor. The house was in relative darkness, apart from the small glow of a lamp coming from the study on the ground floor. A dark-haired figure sat at a desk. It had to be Einstein.

Heinkel checked the chamber on his Webley; then rubbed some dirt on his face to dull his complexion. Suitably blacked up, he circled through the rhododendrons, heading for the path at the side of the house. A branch cracked underfoot. He froze, then moved his weapon in a steady arc, but there was no target. He moved off, breathing gently, easing his footing with each step to minimise the noise.

He edged carefully along the side of the garden, emerging onto the footpath at the corner of the house; hidden from view, but only a few feet away from the rear porch. He peered around the corner. A wicker chair sat at the far end of the porch. The glow of the lamplight broke the shadows on the wooden decking. Heinkel moved carefully onto the wooden steps, his weapon at eye level, tensing on the trigger. The boards creaked; instinctively he rolled the ball of his foot with each step to ease the load on the planks. Inching along like a black ghost, Heinkel made for his target.

He reached the back door. He leant his back against the wall and tried the handle. The door eased open with a barely audible squeak of the hinges. He rolled into the doorway, weapon trained down the hall – nothing.

He moved forward, checking the open door to his right – a dining room – all clear. He edged down the hall to the kitchen, weapon scanning for targets – all clear. Satisfied, Heinkel moved back up the hall to the study door. A slit of light shone under the door. He eased the door open, weapon up, and moved silently into the room.

Einstein puffed on his pipe, literally contemplating the universe, lost in his thoughts. He would have scarcely noticed a herd of elephants charging into the study, never mind a trained assassin.

Einstein stirred, as the cold steel of the revolver penetrated his thoughts.

'Good evening Professor Einstein.' Heinkel pushed the nozzle of the revolver into the back of Einstein's head.

'Who are you?' Einstein remained calm. 'Have you come to kill me?'

Heinkel was surprised by the response. Usually his victim would be in a flap, big time, but not Einstein.

'No I am not here to kill you, are you alone?' Heinkel already knew the answer, but wanted to judge the temperament of his new friend.

'Alone? What is it to be alone? Are you alone?' Einstein replied quietly.

'Your services are required Professor – in Germany.'

'Service to Germany? What possible use can I be?'

Heinkel lowered his weapon. It was worth trying the softly, softly approach. 'Professor, I do not know. I am just the messenger, and I am asking you to come to Berlin,' he lied.

'Berlin? No, I cannot go there. I am morally bound by my ethical stance. Freedom and the sanctity of human life.' Einstein paused. 'No I cannot go back to Berlin, at least not now.'

'I understand, but you can do a great service to the German people.'

'If only that were true. I fear that any service I might give would go towards supporting a morally corrupt regime. Thank you for the invitation, but I am afraid I will decline.' Einstein remained perfectly calm.

'I am sorry Professor.' Heinkel waved the revolver. 'This is not really an invitation. You must come with me.'

'Now?'

'Yes, now.' He pressed the gun against Einstein's chest.

Einstein shuffled to his feet.

'Do I have time to pack?'

Heinkel was mildly amused by the bumbling Professor. 'No, we leave now.'

'At least let me get my coat and lock the door.'

Heinkel nodded in agreement. A missing coat and a locked house would suggest the Professor had gone for a walk and failed to return. The police would waste days searching the riverbanks.

Einstein calmly put on his overcoat and locked the door. Both men stood on the porch.

'This way.' Heinkel pointed the gun in the direction of the back lawn. Einstein moved off, walking calmly across the grass.

'Where are we going?'

'No more questions, silence.' Heinkel poked the gun into Einstein's back. 'Head for the wooded path, we're going down to the river.'

'Why are we going there?'

'No questions, just move.' He prodded Einstein with the gun.

Nash checked the number plate on the Jaguar. Not surprisingly, it was stolen. Missing from the driver's pool at the Bank of England. The team had been following him ever since Cape Town. Heinkel had taken a plane from Cape Town via Nairobi to Alexandria in Egypt. It was a relatively new commercial route for Imperial Airways. A short hop on a flying boat to Southampton completed the journey. They could have picked him up as soon as he set foot on British soil, but Sinclair had decided to run with it.

Heinkel had visited several diamond traders and bankers in London. What the hell was he doing talking to bankers? Was this something to do with his connections to Rockefeller in America, or his activities in Cape Town? It was certainly looking like Mr Heinkel was on a grand tour to fill the German coffers alright, but what for? Then there was a sudden departure from his routine, with several visits to Oxford in the last few days. What was he doing in Oxford? It didn't make any sense – there weren't any big banks in the sleepy little town.

It would have to wait; there were more pressing matters. The parked vehicle was empty. Heinkel was on foot; but where?

Nash spoke into his radio. 'The target is foxtrot. Does anyone have eyes on?'

'That's a negative, sir,' a voice crackled back.

'Run another check, how many VIPs within a mile radius of our position?'

'Will do, sir.' The earpiece turned to static.

Nash moved to the rear of the car, searching around the door seals with his torch, then around the boot. He took a knife from his belt, and wedged it into the lock, forcing the trunk open. He shone the torch inside. Nothing much, just a small holdall. He unzipped the bag: a used shirt, a tie, and some polished shoes.

Nash spoke into his radio. 'Be advised, the target has changed clothing, stand by.'

He shone the torch around the edge of the trunk, out of habit, rather than searching for anything in particular. Then he noticed it – a thin slither of gun paper sticking out from the internal upholstery. He tapped the side panels inside the trunk – *chink, chink* – the unmistakable sound of metal on metal. He stabbed his knife into the lining, and tore open a hole in the upholstery. Instantly, the material collapsed as a huge cache of weapons tumbled into view.

'Be advised, we have weapons, lots of weapons in the boot of his car,' the radio crackled. Nash shone the torch over the pile, and picked up a rifle that caught his attention. An Arisaka type 99 sniper rifle. He let out an involuntary whistle. All the way from Japan, one of the finest weapons money could buy. He scanned the torch over the rest of the hoard: a Browning automatic rifle, a bunch of top-of-the-range pistols, and specialist boxes of ammunition. These were weapons of some considerable finesse; it could only mean one thing. Heinkel *was* trained by the military, and an assassin. What was more, he was on foot and looking for a target!

The radio crackled into life. 'We have that VIP check, sir.'

'Go ahead, any names connected with science and technology, or big banking?'

'There is one sir.' The radio went to static for a few seconds. 'Sir, the next street over, number 52, Professor Albert Einstein.'

Nash drew his service revolver, and started running.

The direct route across the back gardens of the adjacent houses would be quicker.

He leapt over the first garden fence at a full sprint, then the second. Abandoning any notion of a tactical advance, Nash ploughed across garden lawns to emerge on the next street. Weapon up, breathing heavily, he scanned the street – no contact – just the leafy suburban vista. He sprinted the last few yards down the street. The screech of tyres sounded in the distance – back up from Scotland Yard. There was no time to wait; fully expecting a burst of automatic fire, Nash flew up the garden path to the front porch.

He panted, utterly breathless, struggling to concentrate and level his aim. He swung into a crouching position, doing a three-sixty turn; weapon at the ready, he scanned the immediate area – no target. The house was all quiet, no lights were on. He tried the door handle.

Locked. Maybe no one's home?

He smashed one of the small glass panels in the front door, and found the door latch. Then with the mini flashlight from his pocket, weapon up in a secure hold, he dove through the door. His blood pumped as the torch beam bounced off the walls. The slightest lapse in concentration at close quarters, and he could easily shoot the wrong target. Nash worked down the hall, with sweat dripping from his brow.

The sudden noise of boots sent Nash pivoting in an instant, training his weapon back towards the front door. Flashlights dazzled his eyes.

'Hold! Hold!' he shouted as he raised his weapon in clear

view. The crash of glass and more boots sounded from the kitchen. Armed police filled the hallway. Boots thudded up the stairs in short order.

'Sir, we've done a sweep of the house, ain't no one here.' The officer holstered his weapon.

'Any sign of a struggle?'

'No sir, nothing sir. The broken glass is all ours.'

Nash barked orders. 'Fan out! Search the grounds at the back of the house! Alpha team; secure the perimeter! Bravo team; on me, towards the river! Move!'

Armed officers scattered purposefully in all directions.

The darkness and undergrowth hampered the search. Nash moved at a steady pace into the surrounding woodland, heading down the small footpath towards the river. Weapon up, scanning the tree line, he listened. What else could he do? An assassin in tree cover could take him out anytime.

Suddenly, the faint noise of an engine filtered through the woodland. The noise grew steadily.

An outboard engine – a boat!

Nash sprinted towards the river.

He burst through the tree line on to a green; the grass sloped gently, giving way to a patch of gravel that marked a small landing area cut into the riverbank. It was just possible to make out two shadowy figures splashing around at the water's edge. A small motorboat approached the shore. Nash raised his weapon at the shore party and took aim. The silhouetted figures shimmered in the moonlight – which one was Einstein?

It was too risky.

Adjusting his aim, Nash fired six rounds at the boat instead. The telltale thuds of bullets driving home into the woodwork indicated that the shots were on target. A lucky shot might even take out the helmsman.

He dropped to his knees to reload. He flipped open the weapon, tapping out the empty shells onto the ground. He

245

pushed fresh rounds into each slot, ignoring the return fire now thundering over his head. The rhythmic shower of bark and splinters was informative – automatic weapons. He clicked the revolver shut, and rolled to his left, recovering into a knee-firing position.

Nash focused on the boat and opened with rapid fire. A scream went up – his lucky shot. The engine revved momentarily and, with a burst of speed, the boat skewed the final few feet towards the gravel.

The two figures on the shore moved haphazardly towards the craft. One of the participants seemed to be dragging his feet, slowing down the proceedings. Einstein!

Bellowing, Nash charged down the grassy slope. With no time to avoid incoming fire, he lunged forward in a short zigzag, praying he would make the distance.

Heinkel raised his pistol, while holding onto Einstein with his free hand. He squinted into the blackness of the tree line and fired two shots. The bullets went wide as a sudden tug from Einstein sent his aim adrift. He tugged back, and adjusted his grip on Einstein's collar, then fired off a couple more rounds. The sound of the boat revving its engine blasted into his ear. More shouts came up from the tree line: reinforcements. It was time to run.

Heinkel waded into the freezing water, dragging Einstein with him, as the boat slid nose first onto the gravel. Ignoring the cold and gunfire, he grabbed Einstein around the waist and shouldered him roughly over the side onto the available deck space. He then heaved himself aboard. The small boat pitched up. Heinkel landed in a tangle of limbs with Einstein on the tiny wooden floor. There was barely room for two people on board, but at least the outboard was still idling.

Heinkel leapt to his feet and revved the throttle. It gave a satisfying throaty sound as fresh fuel flowed into the engine. He threw the gear lever into reverse. The propeller dug into the riverbank instantly, and a cloud of foam formed in the shallow water. He tugged on the throttle a second time. Another shower of sand and foam went up in the air, but the boat didn't move. He powered up the engine again; the foaming suddenly subsided as the propeller bit into slightly deeper water. The boat lurched slowly backwards.

Nash hit home and, diving forward with a precarious grip, he landed flat across the bow. His extra weight pitched the bow downwards. Heinkel lost his footing. Nash clambered forward, his feet slipping continuously on the wet woodwork of the bow. The boat rolled, pitching Nash onto the short windscreen, but sending his gun sliding from his grip. With one hand on top of the windshield, Nash stretched out for his weapon – too late – it slid over the side.

Heinkel braced himself on the slippery deck, trying to level his revolver. Water splashed across his face as his firing arm wandered with the roll of the boat. He fired regardless. His target disappeared in a sudden gust of spray.

'No, stop it!' Einstein pushed Heinkel's arm away, sending the next round harmlessly into the water.

Bellowing with rage, Nash leapt forward, bundling himself and Einstein over the side. The two men hit the water in a melee of arms and legs and disappeared below the surface. Heinkel slid across the deck, catching the gear lever on his clothing and sending the boat screaming in reverse. He clambered to his knees and, using the starboard rail to steady himself, he scanned the water for his next shot. The water foamed in the darkness – too late – the backwards momentum from the engine had pushed the boat a good ten metres away down the river.

Frantic splashing and shouting announced the arrival of Nash and Einstein back at the surface. Nash gasped a lung full of air, then another, and feeling a tug on his arm realised in the confusion that he was still holding onto Einstein. The Professor coughed and grunted, evidently still alive.

Nash span round, looking for his adversary, but there was no need. Rounds zipped over head from the shore party. The cavalry had arrived. The silhouette of the motorboat, with water bouncing over the transom and the engine whining, made a good target. Covering fire from the shore party snaked along the foamy trail, peppering towards the boat.

Heinkel ducked as rounds pounded into the woodwork around him. Lying flat on the floor with one hand on the wheel, he expertly allowed the engine to blast the boat in reverse, and downriver. An eruption of splinters penetrated his leg; ignoring the pain, he concentrated on keeping the stern downstream. More water billowed over the transom, but it was better than being dead.

Nash switched to lifesaver mode as the boat disappeared into the darkness. He grabbed Einstein around the shoulder, and ploughed the few yards to the riverbank. Police officers piled knee-deep into the water, lifting Einstein from his grasp, and laying covering fire into the dark water.

Nash sat at the water's edge panting. He automatically felt his holster, looking for his pistol, then remembered: he'd dropped it. He coughed some putrid water, cursing under his breath.

Heinkel resigned himself to the situation. The flooded boat and freezing cold were the least of his problems. He peered over the bow towards the shore. It wasn't worth it. Going back against overwhelming fire power would be suicide. There was nothing more he could do. Incoming rounds were at least dropping short into the water. He was out of range. Survival mode kicked in. A quick inspection picked up a few wounds, nothing major.

Expertly, he dropped the engine revs and manoeuvred the boat around. He headed downriver. He could ditch the motorboat and rendezvous with the German freighter back in Southampton as planned. But the mission had failed: the prime target was lost, and his cover story was blown. The assailant on the bow of the boat was also strangely familiar. Had their paths crossed before in another war? Perhaps? No matter, he would use failure to strengthen his resolve. He would be back to even the score.

CHAPTER 32

Devil Machine

Doctor Steinhoff sat at his bench in the laboratory at Peenemünde, surrounded by a clutter of half-machined engine components, tools, and rolls of numerous technical drawings. He flicked through the pages of his notebook. It just didn't make any sense. Maybe he had missed some small but crucial detail? Or perhaps things were on the wrong track completely and the device would never work? More likely, Mayer's delirium had just created a fanciful suggestion that was nothing more than the mixed up ramblings of a dying man – a complete fiction. The whole thing seemed a waste of time.

On the other hand, his superiors had given considerable store to the work of Professor Mayer. Commandant Kessler had gone to great lengths to extract information and keep the Professor alive. So maybe there was some scientific credibility in the Professor's garbled comments after all: but it *just* didn't make *any* sense at all.

Steinhoff reviewed the logic steps.

Professor Mayer had mentioned a machine; something different, but it didn't seem to be a rocket. But then Mayer had also mentioned the stars, travelling to the stars – his exact words. So, this machine was some kind of rocket or propulsion device powerful enough to leave Earth's atmosphere and go into space. But to what end? How could it be made? Mayer had said, and this point was clear; that wave energy was converted to, or somehow created, particle energy. Impossible!

Steinhoff reasoned through the argument in his head for the hundredth time.

Back to basics. Mayer must have been talking about Einstein's work. The idea that energy is related to mass. His now famous equation predicted this, $E = mc^2$. It made sense, brilliantly simple, but nonetheless it made sense. If the speed of light, c, was constant, then energy, E, would be related to mass, m – it was inevitable from the math. So, what next? How did that help? Well in theory, it might therefore be possible to turn mass into energy, and this energy would take the form of an electromagnetic wave; some kind of light. But what kind of light? An energy wave like radiation? Or something new?

Steinhoff remained perplexed.

The device was made of carbon, and that something involved sixty carbon atoms. The Professor had also mentioned something very small. What the hell did that mean? Was it that carbon atoms were very small? Everybody knew that. He must have meant something else, but what?

Steinhoff considered the comment on *sixty carbon atoms*. He had already spent hours on this, sketching out different ways that carbon atoms could be arranged into a sequence of sixty atoms. There were lots of possibilities. Carbon atoms joined together in chains, like some long atomic snake – or in a square lattice to make graphite – pencil lead. Carbon could also be structured into a diamond lattice. This amused Steinhoff. He would be a rich man indeed if he could discover a way to synthesise diamonds from charcoal! Of course it was impossible. There had to be some other way of joining up sixty carbon atoms.

Suddenly, Steinhoff had a moment of true inspiration.

Mayer had mentioned particles, *so maybe the particles were made of carbon?*

That was it! He needed to draw a spherical carbon structure!

Steinhoff worked feverishly, trying to think of ways to join up carbons and bend them into the shape of a sphere. A square lattice would never work, the geometry was all wrong. A long chain of carbons would be flexible and, like a snake, could be coiled in many different ways but would never make a sphere.

Then he had it – it wasn't a solid sphere at all – but a hollow one! A carbon cage of hexagons, just like a soccer ball! Desperate for confirmation, Steinhoff sketched his idea – sixty atoms! That was it! Carbon particles so minute, so impossibly small, that they would be invisible to the naked eye.

Steinhoff had reasoned his way to carbon nanoparticles.

But there was a problem. He had absolutely no idea how to make these new carbon nanoparticles, and even less of an idea of how they could be fabricated into a propulsion device. He was completely stumped.

CHAPTER 33

Progress – Mayer Wakes

Kessler and Steinhoff sat on the edge of Mayer's bed in the new purpose-built hospital wing at Peenemünde. The steady flow of oxygen into the face mask supplemented Mayer's regular breathing. Oxygen was apparently good for healing head injuries. Kessler gently lifted the Professor's forearm; it was warm, and pink. He let the arm drop back onto the bed.

'Tell me Doctor, has the patient showed any signs of stirring?'

The doctor flicked through the medical charts at the end of the bed. 'Well, yes, he is improving. The chest infection has cleared. His breathing is good, all things considered. We've been keeping a close record of his vital signs; they appear to be stable now. There are short periods of semi-wakefulness, not long, mostly less than a couple of minutes. We have noticed an increase in rapid eye movement. My best guess is that he will awake fully, possibly within the next few days.'

'Few days… we don't have time to wait *a few days*.' Kessler gave the doctor a hard stare and tossed a small box of syringes onto the bed.

The doctor stiffened. 'What's that?'

'Mescaline, a new formulation,' Kessler smiled.

'Commandant, I cannot administer this. It was probably the mescaline and heroin mixture that sent him into a coma in the first place.' The doctor took an involuntary step away from the bed.

'Like I said, this is a new formulation. It contains some… shall we say… new stimulants.' Kessler stood, holding out the box. 'Herr Doctor, I am giving you an order.'

Steinhoff interrupted. 'Please make the injection. We need the Professor to be fully awake. He has rested for some time. We are lost without his help.' Steinhoff gently passed the box to the doctor, 'Please… '

'Alright, alright; but I cannot be responsible for the outcome. New stimulants you say?'

Kessler nodded.

The doctor lifted a glass syringe from the box; the needled glistened as the thick liquid oozed from the tip. He hesitated. 'Perhaps only one trial dose: agreed?'

'Doctor, the SS have approved the new formulation – proceed!'

He carefully fed the syringe into the Mayer's forearm, pushing gently on the plunger.

Nothing happened.

'Give him another dose,' Kessler ordered.

'No wait! Look!' Steinhoff pointed at Mayer's face.

Muscles twitched as his eyelids flicked open for a few seconds; a groan issued from underneath the oxygen mask.

The doctor leaned over the bed. 'Professor Mayer… Professor… ' He gently shook his shoulders. '… Can you hear me?'

Another groan; this time his eyes wandered, but stayed open.

'Don't be alarmed Professor Mayer, you are in hospital. I have been looking after you. Can you hear me?'

Mayer slowly nodded.

'You have been asleep for a long time, but don't worry. You are safe.'

Mayer croaked and coughed as the world swam in and out of focus.

White light.

His eyeballs throbbed. He instinctively turned his head away from the bright ceiling. Stiff muscles stretched. Ligaments found new life as the popping of unused tendons vibrated through his skull. It was somehow refreshing.

A dark, blurred figure sat on the edge of the bed. Ghostly movements filled his peripheral vision. Mayer tasted the dusty, leathery foulness of his mouth; swallowing, his throat grated. 'Water…'

The doctor leaned over and, after removing the face mask, he offered a drinking straw. 'Take a sip… carefully… not too much… just wet your lips.'

The water flashed a sudden wave of coolness through his chest; his eyes started to focus. He gulped down several mouthfuls of the refreshing liquid. He stretched his right arm, there was no pain. He took in a deep breath. It was a little awkward, but effective.

The room came gradually into clear view. Mayer absorbed the scene. A clean white room, the smell of disinfectant, the hum of medical instruments. He took another good breath and flexed the digits of his right hand. His strength seemed to be returning.

A doctor hovered attentively to his left. He heard the doctor's voice in his ear.

'Just rest Professor… you are in hospital…' The doctor smiled, repeating himself. 'You will be a little stiff; you have been sleeping for a long time… just rest.'

Hospital? Mayer remembered.

The crash. No, not a hospital, but a prison!

He turned his head slowly to the right.

A Nazi uniform, a commandant?

He gritted his teeth. Vague recollections of questions filled his mind. This man had asked him so many questions. Mayer sensed danger. Who was this man?

He gazed at the Nazi, searching for recognition. The mind is a strange thing, he could see the man asking questions.

What is his name?… What is his name? Kessler! His name is Commandant Kessler. Yes, Commandant Kessler from the SS.

Mayer met Kessler's gaze head-on as it all came flooding back.

What have I told him? The rocket design! The turbo booster! My God!

He remembered making the sketch. He *had* told Kessler about the turbo booster. Had he told Kessler anything else?

Mayer wasn't sure.

Well, there wouldn't be anymore.

Mayer clenched his good arm into a fist on the bed and waited. His strength seemed to be returning with each passing minute.

'Welcome back Professor, I've been waiting for you.'

Mayer opened his mouth to speak, but then decided not to. Silence would be his weapon.

Kessler asked another question.

Mayer ignored it, and instead assimilated the details of the room. The door was a few metres away. He tried to wiggle his toes. The right leg responded. Nothing from the left leg. He wouldn't be escaping anytime soon.

He searched around the bed with his eyes.

Fight back… fight back… but how? The oxygen cylinder maybe?

Oxygen would burn, but he didn't have anything to rig it up with. Regardless, it was just out of arm's reach, too far from the bed. He didn't have the strength.

Kessler spoke again.

Mayer blanked him out, and concentrated on the room, looking for a more realistic option.

Then he spotted the box of syringes.

It was worth the chance, but he needed a distraction.

'Professor Mayer, you *can* hear me? Am I right?'

Kessler's voice penetrated his thinking.

Mayer decided to respond. 'Yes.'

'That's good, we can resume our last conversation.'

Mayer feigned undue weakness. 'Con… versation?… What… con… versation?'

He gently gripped the bed clothes with his right arm, inching the box of syringes closer.

'You spoke of a machine. Tell me about your machine.'

'Fever… must have been… the fever,' Mayer lied.

The box edged a little closer.

'Yes, you spoke of a machine… '

Mayer touched the edge of the box with his fingertips.

'Mach… ine… what… machine?' Mayer kept his gaze fixed on Kessler.

Kessler hissed. 'Professor, *no more games*! Tell me about your new equations!'

'Equation?… Lots of… equations.'

Kessler sat forward. 'Tell me about carbon, Professor. What type of carbon? How do you use it?'

'Carbon… yes… there are… many forms… of carbon.' Mayer stalled.

He worked his fingers into the box, and around one of the syringes.

'What do you do with the carbon to make your machine?'

'Come… come closer… listen… '

Kessler leaned in.

It was just enough.

Mayer took a deep breath and, tensing his grip on the syringe, he thrust the needle upwards with all his strength. The needle rammed home into Kessler's flesh, deep under his lower jaw. The metallic lance sat buried to the hilt, only stopping when the glass end of the barrel met the skin. Shaking with effort, Mayer frantically pushed on the plunger.

'Arghh!'

Kessler lashed out.

Mayer absorbed the blow; his head rattled with the numbness of the impact.

Kessler staggered backwards. 'Arghhh!' He pulled the hypodermic from under his jawbone. Gazing down at the broken syringe, he saw that it was empty.

'I *will* break you!' Kessler produced a crisp handkerchief and mopped at the wound under his neck. His face turned pink with rage. 'You *will* tell me everything. Then you will beg for death!'

He stormed out of the room, holding the wound under his neck, as the drugs took effect.

Kessler staggered down the corridor as a wave of heroin and mescaline pacified his muscles. His eyes registered the impossible.

The walls pulsated with iron crosses.

He reached out to one shiny black cross; as he did so, the medal dissolved into blood. He took another. The metal became effervescent, and vanished from his palm. Blood dripped through his fingers. He grabbed desperately at the wall; each cross turned crimson red.

Death oozed forth from the plasterboard.

His father's voice echoed inside his skull.

'Iron cross? No… only heroes deserve such honours. It is beyond your reach… murderer… murderer!' The voice boomed with laughter, then hissed, 'Remember your grandmother. Remember the Sabbath!… Jew… '

The ceiling sagged like an overweight blancmange. Sandbags and a machine gun nest came into view. His father stood, skeletal, with his rotting flesh holding onto the weapon. He pulled back the cocking mechanism of the heavy-calibre gun.

'Be a real hero boy… be a man… '

His tattered Imperial uniform flapped as he opened fire. Empty shell casings rattled into the treasure chest of medals at his feet.

Kessler screamed as he dived forward into the hailstorm of bullets, hoping for just one medal from the box.

CHAPTER 34

Making Carbon

Mayer sat up in the bed, trying to hold still. He felt the fresh air against his scalp, and a certain claustrophobia lift with each turn of the crepe bandage. The doctor unwound the dressing.

'How does that feel, any pain?'

Mayer replied. 'Feels fine, tender but no pain.' He lifted his right arm to feel the healing wound on his head.

'No, no, don't touch it.' The doctor gently blocked his movement. 'We need to keep it clean. The scar tissue looks pink, a decent scab has formed, and no puss. I think you're on the mend at last. Any headache?'

The constant dull throb in his head provided the answer. 'Yes... most of the time.' Mayer rubbed his eyes with his good arm.

'But improving? Less frequent?'

Mayer half shrugged, and moved his attention to the rest of his body. He worked his right arm and tensed the muscles in his good leg. It seemed reasonable, even good enough to stand on. The left arm and leg remained mostly numb. Paralysis. He wondered about escape. 'My left side?'

The doctor tried to keep a neutral expression. 'Look, I am afraid I don't know if it will improve. In time, perhaps, but you can expect some disability.'

Mayer looked the doctor in the eye. 'You... you can get me out of here?'

The doctor paused and lowered his gaze to the floor. 'No... no, I wish I could, but I can't. I am truly sorry... '

The door burst open. Kessler stood in the doorway. The doctor suddenly fussed with the bed clothes, going red in the face.

'Why was I not informed that the patient was awake?'

Mayer interrupted before the doctor could reply. 'Because the patient... is... civilian... not a convict.' He stared daggers at Kessler. Hatred, yes, it was hatred. It was alright though. In these extreme circumstances it was possible, even acceptable, to hate another human being. But then, where did Kessler score on that scale? Did he count as human? Mayer's resolve strengthened.

Kessler moved briskly towards the bed, pulling up a wooden chair. A small plaster covered the cut on his neck.

Mayer stared. 'Wound hurts... doesn't it?'

'Yes, well, your little stunt yesterday,' Kessler resisted the urge to rub the bruise under his jaw, 'tells me that you are fit for interrogation.'

'Go to hell.' Mayer turned away, focusing on a blank spot on the wall.

'Oh, I can assure you Professor, you *will* go to hell, but *only* after answering my questions.' Kessler slapped him across the face.

His good side stung from the blow. The scab on his head cracked, oozing a fresh crevice of blood.

'Go to hell... '

Mayer reeled from another slap, his head jarred. The wetness of fresh blood dripped from his nostril. Pain shot through his scalp as the scab on his head lifted.

Kessler spoke with an edge in his voice. 'You *will* answer my questions.'

'No... you will kill me anyway.' Mayer turned away.

Kessler looked at the doctor. 'Hold out his arm.'

The doctor stood motionless.

'Do it now, hold out his arm!' Kessler took a fresh box of mescaline syringes from his breast pocket.

Mayer thrashed, snorting through gritted teeth, as Kessler's fingers locked around his wrist. The pressure hurt the wrist bones; he tried to pull back, but it was no good. The muscle tension failed as Kessler forced the arm flat against the bed.

'Arghh! Nothing... you get... nothing!'

Kessler dropped the box on the bed and, with his spare hand, took one of the syringes. Unceremoniously, as if darting a wild boar, he thumped the syringe into Mayer's arm.

'Arghh! I... will not!' Mayer took the pain through gritted teeth and turned his head away.

A rush of coolness shot up his arm, and fanned out across his chest. He gazed at the wall, snorting in deep breaths.

Fight it... fight it... fight!

A tug on his arm, a second pinprick. Violation, a needle moved around in his flesh. A deluge of anaesthesia and euphoria swept through his veins.

Pain. Perhaps pain would hold the tide back?

Mayer bit his lip.

His lip throbbed for a moment, then was lost as heroin and mescaline pulsed through his skull. His brain fogged; a primeval force seemed to erupt from his brain stem, taking control of his body.

Mayer foamed at the mouth; his eyes rolled back in his head as the mammoth dose of mescaline took over.

Kessler waited.

The doctor protested. 'How can you be so brutal? This... ' he waved his arm at the pitiful scene, '... this is not what Germany is about.'

Kessler whispered harshly, 'You *will* assist me, or if you prefer, you can be reassigned to the labour camps in the east: *as an inmate!*'

The doctor blanched.

Both men watched as Mayer writhed about on the bed. Slowly, he calmed to a drunken stillness. Kessler gave a satisfying smirk. It was good to be in control.

Kessler barked an order. 'Steinhoff! Where's Steinhoff? Steinhoff, we need to start. Get in here!'

Suddenly, Steinhoff appeared at the door. He glanced at Mayer, then at the doctor.

'Commandant... I... I am at your disposal, sir.'

'Pull up a chair, take notes. I need your assistance.'

Steinhoff nodded, as he sheepishly took out his notebook.

Kessler composed himself, and delivered a test question, leaning in close so that Mayer could hear. 'Let us begin... the substance graphite is made of carbon? Made of carbon... think about carbon Professor Mayer... answer yes or no... is graphite made of carbon?'

'Yeeeessss.'

'Good, good... another question. Diamond is made of a carbon? Yes or no?'

'Yeeeessss.'

'So you understand carbon structures. Now, let's talk about carbon particles.'

Mayer suddenly snorted, his eyes wandering.

'Ah! I thought that would touch a raw nerve,' Kessler smirked. 'Don't worry, let me rephrase the question. How do you make carbon particles?'

Mayer gave a spasm, thrashing his good side pathetically in the bed. 'Ummmhhhh!... Ummmhhhh!'

Kessler baulked at the surprising resistance to the drugs, but took care to conceal his reaction. 'Please answer, how do you make carbon particles?'

'Ummmmhhhh!'

'Never mind, don't trouble yourself Professor. You see... our clever Dr Steinhoff has already figured it out. You remember Steinhoff don't you?'

Mayer wheezed, snot dribbling from his nose. 'Ummmhhh!... Ummmhhh!'

Kessler leaned closer to Mayer's ear. 'That's it... that's it!

Feel the despair! Feel it!... You have *already* given your secret away! What harm can it do now... tell us the detail... tell us the rest...'

'Ummmmhhh! Ummmmhhh! Noooooo!'

'It is carbon sixty that we need, yes or no?!'

'Ummmmmmhhhhh!'

'Okay, I will take that as a yes! How do we make carbon sixty?'

'Nooooooo!' Mayer contorted; stiffening his face, a trickle of blood issued from his nostril.

'Herr Doctor, more mescaline for the patient if you please.' Kessler smiled.

'Commandant... please...'

Kessler cut him off with a wave of his hand. 'Now! You can clearly see the patient is resisting! More!'

The doctor duly administered a third massive shot of the drug. Mayer relaxed back into the pillows with the sudden rush of euphoria. Kessler waited a few more seconds for the fresh dose of mescaline to penetrate.

'Now, that's better...' Kessler continued, '... how do we make carbon sixty?'

'Nooooo... you... can't...' Mayer gave a crooked smile, his head flopped uncontrollably. 'Nooooo... not... possible...'

'Tell Steinhoff... tell Dr Steinhoff... how do we make carbon sixty?' Kessler waved Steinhoff forward.

'Gustav, it is me, Steinhoff. Please, how do we make carbon sixty? Please tell me, then you can rest.'

'Burn...'

'Burn what Gustav?'

'Burn... veeerrrry high... temperature...'

'Gustav, do you mean burn carbon at a very high temperature? How high? Gustav, how hot does it need to be?!'

'Hot... veeerrrry hot...'

Steinhoff leaned forward. 'Tell me! Tell me! How hot?!'

'Hot... hot... as... heeeelll!' Blood flowed from both nostrils as Mayer went into a seizure.

'Enough! Enough!' The doctor pulled Steinhoff away, 'Stop! Stop! There is nothing more to be gained here today – look!'

Mayer gurgled blood from his mouth and nose, squirming with delirium; the smell of excrement penetrated the room.

'Alright! Alright! I am sorry... I... we... just needed to know,' Steinhoff shook his head.

'Do you have enough to make the carbon structure?' Kessler pressed.

'It is possible, yes, I think I so.' Steinhoff tried to clear his mind. 'Mayer was into burning all sorts of materials at high temperature in his search for fuels and catalysts; perhaps he stumbled on something? I can try burning some ordinary carbon at very high temperatures. Yes, that would seem a good place to start.'

Kessler, satisfied with the plan, stayed to watch as Mayer went into another seizure.

Dr Steinhoff whistled a merry tune as he examined the latest carbon sample on his microscope. The idea of burning wood in a blast furnace at high temperature to create fine carbon particles had worked! The resulting soot contained a mixture of different types of carbon, including a small fraction of the ultrafine carbon nanoparticles that were needed for the device. But there was lots of crap in the sample. It needed cleaning up; what's more, the process was very inefficient. Nonetheless, the principle was sound; but where could one find a bigger fire?

That's it! Why make your own fire when Mother Nature has already done it for you? Fires! Forest fires!

It was just a question of locating regions where forest fires were common and digging up the ash containing the carbon. A little bit of cleaning and washing would soon yield the required volume of material. There were arid parts of Europe that sometimes suffered extensive natural fires: Greece, the Russian Steppe.

But why wait for a recent forest fire? What about carbon and charcoal deposits in the geological record? There had been vast global fires in the past. Perhaps ancient charcoal deposits could be mined for the all-important nano carbon?

Steinhoff grabbed the telephone.

'Operator... yes, Dr Steinhoff... put me through to the Department of Geology at the Technical University of Berlin.'

The line cracked for a few seconds, then started ringing.

'Hans, how are you? It's Steinhoff... yes... yes... I am well, and you?' A bit of small talk seemed only polite. 'Listen, Hans, I need a small favour... some information. I am looking for high-quality carbon deposits that contain ultrafine material... ' He checked his words carefully; there was no need to explain about the device. Steinhoff explained his requirements. '... You know the kind, very fine dust, burns cleanly.'

'Well let me see... yes, there are some. We have companies working the new oil fields in the Middle East; most of the reserves are capped off by a good quality coal seam. Then there's Central America; some good stuff there. Recently, my team also excavated some new deposits in the diamond-mining regions of Southern Africa.'

The latter was particularly interesting. Germany already had strong interests in the region.

'Hans, thanks. Do you have geologists in the field now? Could they bring back some samples from Southern Africa, and the other sites?'

'We certainly do, in fact, I have some samples in the lab now. I can send you some over, you can expect them in a couple of days. I see you're not at Kummersdorf anymore, where should I send them?'

'That's very generous, but I will send our man to collect the samples today.' Steinhoff neatly avoided the question; the fewer who knew about Peenemünde the better.

Steinhoff worked through the last of the geological carbon samples supplied by his colleagues in Berlin. The sample preparation had been fairly straightforward. It was simply a matter of grinding up each sample into powder, and washing it with industrial alcohol; there was no shortage of that at Peenemünde. The resulting carbon and alcohol mixture contained the ultra-fine remains of the ground-up carbon.

He examined each one carefully on the microscope.

The deposits from the Middle East were not that great. The high oil content in the coal had made the extraction of carbon less efficient. However, the material from South America gave a good quality carbon sample; certainly worth working on an industrial scale. But the quality of the South African deposit was absolutely stunning. The carbon came from a seam that was apparently close to the surface, and only a few metres thick. It would be easy to dig up. What was more, the sample was perfect; an almost pure source of the right kind of carbon.

Steinhoff leapt from his chair, and rushed towards Dornberger's office.

'We have it! We have it!' Steinhoff burst into the Commander's office without knocking. Dornberger looked up from his desk.

'You have what?'

'The carbon! We have the carbon particles!' Steinhoff waved a test tube of the stuff in Dornberger's face.

Dornberger gave a large grin, and leapt to his feet, shaking his hand. 'Well done! Well done! Where did you find it?'

'In Southern Africa. There's a deposit running close to the surface in the wetlands on the east coast, Zululand apparently. It's mainly swamp and mangrove, but we can get the natives to dig it up. The muddy deposits can be cleaned up on site, and we should be able to collect enough material for several devices. It could be shipped directly to Germany the same week!'

'This is fantastic news! We should make arrangements immediately!' Dornberger gave a huge grin and shook his hand again. Both men beamed at each other. A major hurdle had been overcome.

Now Steinhoff could build his device.

CHAPTER 35

Cape Mineral Company, Head Office

Heinkel, pleased with his new orders after the fiasco in England, rehearsed the deception again. He stood on the steps of the Cape Mineral Company Headquarters, absently gazing at the ornate stone facade. The straps on his leather satchel strained; he ignored the weight of the bag. The mining company was obviously doing well to afford such an iconic building in the centre of town, and right next to the South African Reserve Bank – that might come in useful.

The charade had to be perfect; otherwise the chairman wouldn't fall for it. He had to admit; it was a remarkably devious plan. One of his best.

He skipped up the steps into the lobby; the hard soles of his shoes echoed off the polished marble as he made his way to the elevator. He studied the signage for a few seconds, identifying Director Krumbach's office on the fourth floor. He pressed the big brass call button. The clank of cables and mechanical parts sounded in the shaft as the lift approached. Suddenly, the door opened.

Heinkel stared at the white face of the bellboy.

'What floor would you like, sir?'

He stepped into the elevator. 'Fourth floor please.'

Rudy Temple peered out from behind the carved stone pillar.

So, Mr Heinkel was back in town, and paying another visit to the Cape Mineral Company.

Temple watched the numbers light up above the elevator… second… third… fourth floor.

Interesting, it seems Mr Heinkel has some business with the director.

Temple lit up a cheroot, checked his watch, and headed for the street.

Heinkel smiled at the receptionist, still clasping the heavy satchel with his left hand.

'It will not be long now sir, Mr Krumbach will be with you shortly,' she smiled back. The company accounts had made interesting reading. Krumbach was living the dream, but for how much longer? The Cape Mineral Company had been through a period of rapid expansion, buying out German interests in West Africa, and was now overstretched. It was an impressive debt: some ten million US dollars. It was a simple matter of exploiting this weakness.

The deception was already in motion; the idea of getting Himmler to write a personal letter to Rockefeller was a stroke of genius; both men were on the board of the Schroder Bank. The rich capitalist had taken the bait easily with Himmler exalting the difficulties of German land and mineral wealth being absorbed into the colonial interests of the British. The imperial dogs had squandered hard-earned German wealth on lavish residences and hunting trips, and allowed the business to fall into ruin. It was an ideal opportunity for Rockefeller to buy some mineral prospects in South Africa and, acting indirectly on behalf of the Schroder Bank, he could also return shares back to their rightful owners: the German people.

The personal assistant roused him from his thoughts. 'Mr Krumbach will see you now, sir,' she beamed at Heinkel.

The plan was working.

Heinkel entered the room and was assaulted by the smell of stale tobacco and furniture polish. Krumbach waddled out from behind his mahogany desk, cigar in hand. The buttons on his expensive waistcoat strained against his portly midriff.

'Ah! Mr Heinkel, it is very nice to meet you at last. I hear you have been buying titanium from us, is that right?'

Heinkel shook the flabby outstretched palm, concealing his disgust with a polite smile. 'Yes, I have been making some purchases for my employer.'

'Well good, good, please take a seat.'

He waved Heinkel towards one of the green leather chairs in front of the desk, whilst puffing on his cigar.

Heinkel ignored the putrid odour, and sat down with the satchel on his lap.

'So, how can I help? You want to purchase some more titanium?' Krumbach chewed on his cigar.

Heinkel maintained his neutral but polite expression. 'Yes, I will be making another purchase, and also some orders for a few other metals: manganese, aluminium and so on.'

'Well, we have the finest materials around. It shouldn't take too long to get you everything you need. Your employer?… You represent one of the big manufacturing industries in Germany?'

'Yes, something like that. You might say that I am expressing interests on behalf of a large consortium of industrialists and government departments.'

Krumbach's eyes expanded at the prospect. 'Well, that makes you an important customer indeed!'

Heinkel dropped his polite smile slowly. 'Perhaps, but I am also here on another… shall we say… more delicate matter.'

Krumbach stopped drawing on his cigar. 'Delicate matter?'

'Well, it's a question of politics really.' Heinkel gave a controlled smile and continued. 'You know how it is, politicians always seem to interfere with big business.'

Krumbach snorted. 'You're not wrong there. Sharks, the lot of them.'

'Quite so, you are Dutch I think, not British?'

'Yes, my family was from Amsterdam originally.'

'And I hear the British investment in the Cape Mineral Company hasn't gone so well?'

Krumbach furrowed his brow. 'Where did you hear that?'

'Come now, Mr Krumbach, one has only to look at your share price.'

'Alright, so it's slipped a little, where is this conversation going?'

'The people I represent would like to offer you a business proposition.'

Heinkel took the letter from his breast pocket and tossed it onto the table.

Krumbach flicked his eyes at the envelope, then at Heinkel. 'What's this?'

'Open it. It's a letter of introduction from Mr Rockefeller.'

'What, *the* John Rockefeller?'

Heinkel smiled as he folded his arms. 'Yes, one and the same. Read… please.'

Krumbach removed his cigar, depositing it smouldering in a glass ashtray. He slit open the letter with an ivory-handled paper knife, then blanched at the contents.

'This is an aggressive takeover? You want to buy out the British shares to give a Germany consortium control of the company?'

'Strictly speaking, no. It's a re-investment, and technically the shares would belong to Mr Rockefeller. The British and Americans are allies, surely the board will not object to an American investor of such calibre.'

Krumbach shrugged. 'Perhaps not.'

Heinkel leant forwards and spoke in an even tone. 'Persuade them, you are the director of the company.'

Krumbach rubbed his fingers across the sweat forming on his brow. 'Well, that's not so easy. The current investors are mainly British gentry, Lord this, and Lord that – powerful men with the ear of the British Prime Minister. Rockefeller's sympathies with Germany are well known.'

'Please consider the proposition.' Heinkel paused to open his satchel. He took out a gleaming bar of gold, stamped with the emblem of the old Kaiser's Imperial Germany. He held it up to the light for a few seconds and gently placed the block on the table.

Heinkel gave a reassuring smile. 'Your cooperation is appreciated, Mr Krombach.'

Krombach stared at the gold bar, then at Heinkel.

'And all I have to do is persuade the board to take Mr Rockefeller's offer?'

Heinkel maintained a passive facade. 'Yes.'

Krumbach leant over the desk and slid the gold bar towards himself. 'Then perhaps we can do business after all.' He picked up his cigar and gave a couple of sucks to get the embers going again.

'Good, good. There is one other minor logistics detail you can help me with on my current visit.'

'Logistics?'

'Yes, we would like to do some prospecting on the east coast, around Zululand.'

'What the hell for? There's nothing but swamp and yellow fever to be had there.'

Heinkel nodded appreciatively. 'I know, but please indulge me. The terrain is rough going, and I need a crew of local workers... as well as some permits... but done discretely.'

'Discretion is my middle name. I can find you a crew of blacks, no problem.'

'Thank you Mr Krumbach.'

Heinkel stood, concluding the meeting with another flabby handshake, before heading for the door.

The greedy fat oaf had been easy to bribe, and would be so distracted by Rockefeller's apparent offer, enabling the little venture in Zululand to go unnoticed. Heinkel could spirit the real prize away, and secure some essential rare metals for the German rocket programme. Mr Himmler would be pleased.

CHAPTER 36

Mfolizi River, Zululand

Nash took a swig of the warm, rank water in his canteen. It was better than nothing in the heat and humidity. At least the lush jungle undergrowth was good cover.

A distant chugging sound caught his attention.

Nash swung the binoculars up stream. It was just one of the natives – only three small boats had idled along the river all day. It was definitely a quiet backwater.

The perfect place for going about one's business unnoticed.

Nash zoomed the binoculars towards the task in hand, and tried to concentrate on the dilapidated house boat moored only a few yards away.

The noise of insects buzzed in his ear. He absently scratched his neck; the full strength mosquito repellent had stopped working hours ago. It was hard to tell what was worse; the heat and humidity of the day, or the insect fiesta that seemed to start with the approaching twilight. Thick clouds of mosquitoes were already hovering over the water's edge.

To hell with it.

He wiped the sweat off the binoculars, and focused on the boat.

There was movement at the stern, with men gathering around a small table and chairs on the open deck.

He scanned forward. The binoculars picked up the square bulk that constituted the cabin area. He ran the binoculars over the cabin, but it was impossible to see through the small grubby windows. Nash shifted the binoculars up to the open-top wheelhouse. The guard was still sitting there, but that was no surprise; it was the highest point on the boat, giving a good view over the river.

A sudden splash in the water.

Nash swung the binoculars, tensing his muscles.

Just a catfish.

He exhaled.

The binoculars followed the waterline of the hull. It was a very shallow draft, ideal for coping with the muddy tributaries that fed into the Mfolizi swamp forest. The jungle was relentless. Tangled masses of mangrove roots gave way to knee-deep mud effervescing with the stench of stagnant water. The mangrove swamp merged seamlessly with mile upon mile of dense jungle, riddled with sodden malaria-infested ditches, and humidity – going by boat was the only civilised way to travel.

'Gentlemen, be seated.' Heinkel spread the map out on the table as he beckoned the men forward.

Briefing time!

Nash tuned in, trying to stay alert. It had taken hours to inch through the undergrowth to get within a few yards of the target. It was close enough to hear everything, but also close enough to get caught.

Making fine adjustments to the zoom, Nash picked out the details of the book spine sitting on the table.

A geology text? What were they looking for? Gold? Diamonds?

It didn't make any sense.

'Dr Steinhoff what is your assessment of the situation?' Heinkel paused, offering the floor to his companion.

Nash assimilated the mystery guest.

Late forties, average height, slouching a little, certainly not fit – a civilian of some kind, probably a geologist or scientist going by the textbook. But why is he here in the middle of the jungle?

A third man appeared. Tall and muscular, in the peak of

physical fitness. He sported a side arm, several clips of ammunition, and a large knife. The third man was clearly a soldier; very professional, very alert.

Boots clanked on the stairs.

Two men appeared in the wheelhouse.

Scruffy, dark oily skin – they must be locals. The skipper and his mate perhaps?

The waterways could be treacherous. It made sense to hire local people who knew the river. The guard gave them a disdainful look of tolerance.

Yes, definitely, just the hired help.

It was probably their boat.

The *click-clack* of a weapon being cocked drew Nash immediately back to the main deck. A fourth man stood towering over his companions, lean, very alert, and carrying a machine gun. He was obviously on patrol duty around the deck, but also gave close interest to the proceedings.

This gathering is getting interesting. Some kind of German agent, a scientist, and what looked like two guys from Special Forces, or at least very disciplined mercenaries. What the bloody hell is Heinkel up to?

Nash was sure about one thing. There would be no boarding the boat tonight; the machine gunner would hose him down long before he made the gangplank. Observation was the name of the game right now.

'Gentlemen, we have found what we were looking for.' Steinhoff took a small glass vial from an ornate box on the table. He held it up in the lamplight, pausing to watch the dark crystals twinkle, before passing it around. 'There's more… '

Steinhoff placed a shiny black rock sample in the centre of the table.

Nash was perplexed. Whatever was being passed around the table was of great interest – that much was clear – each man took the opportunity to study the contents of the tube. But what was in it? And what was the rock sample? Nash had to concede: he had no idea.

He strained to catch the conversation.

'Well gentlemen, you see we are looking for a very special sub-type of carbon deposit. I had a local ranger bring some samples to me; the ones you just examined. From my initial analysis I have identified this location as the best source of the material.' Steinhoff duly pointed at the map.

Heinkel interrupted. 'Dr Steinhoff, excellent work! Our instructions from Berlin are to recover as much of the material as possible, and without attracting too much attention.'

Steinhoff continued. 'Yes, well, the main deposit is located here on the Mfolizi strata. Millions of years ago this area alternated between a shallow sea and lush tropical forest. The mud on the seabed was compressed over geological time to create the mudstone deposits we see all around in this area today. However, the brief periods of tropical forest also created some thin, but exquisite, seams of carbon.'

Heinkel wondered. 'How much carbon are we talking about?'

'Each deposit is about a metre thick, and sandwiched between much thicker layers of mudstone.'

'Are the deposits accessible from the surface or do we need to dig?' Heinkel was full of questions.

'Well, providence is on our side. Part of the riverbank has collapsed, revealing the rock strata for us. Here on the edge of this bend in the river. The geology is nicely exposed.' Steinhoff pointed at the map again. 'There is a nice rock face that we can simply dig the material from. There is no need for subterranean mining. We can drive a coal barge right up to the shoreline, and simply load the material directly from the rock face into the boat.'

Heinkel raised an eyebrow. 'Will this not attract attention?'

The huge soldier replied. 'No, the boat traffic around the

site will be minimal, just the odd fisherman. There is nothing of interest here for the locals.'

Heinkel gave the soldier a fixed stare. 'All the same, we will keep tight security on this operation.'

'The position will be easy to defend. The riverbank is steep, and the dense jungle behind means that any attack would most likely be an amphibious assault from the river. The perimeter will be secure,' the soldier confirmed.

'What about the work force, the miners?' Heinkel turned to Steinhoff.

'We will use a small gang of locals. They will live on site until the operation is completed. There will be no leave for them, but they'll be well paid. It's easy to buy a man's silence when he can earn a year's pay in a month.'

Heinkel gave the soldier another hard stare. 'The cargo must be returned securely to Germany.'

'The coal barge will drive down the river to the main port, and the cargo will be transferred to a steamship. We will be hidden amongst the routine activity of the quayside. The steamship will then depart for Hamburg when it is loaded. With luck, we can send a boatload of the stuff back to Germany within the month.'

'Good. You will escort Dr Steinhoff and the cargo all the way to its destination.' The soldier nodded. Heinkel's decision was final.

With that the meeting was over.

Nash lay in the undergrowth dumbfounded – what the hell was going on? Some kind of top secret geology trip financed by Berlin? But it didn't make any sense – digging up gold or diamonds – that *would* make sense. But carbon? What was so special about carbon? How was this tied to the Cape Mineral Company? Nash was clueless. The geologists and chemists back in London would have to figure it out.

Then there was the clandestine mining operation. Whatever

was being dug out of the ground was extremely valuable to the Nazis – important enough to use Special Forces for its security all the way back to Germany.

What about Heinkel? He was clearly up to his neck in it. Heinkel *was* the main architect for the attempted abduction of Einstein. Was this job in Zululand connected to Einstein in some way? The logistics were well planned; but who was this Dr Steinhoff? A geologist? Was there some technology angle that had been overlooked?

Whatever was going on, time was short.

CHAPTER 37

Zululand Swamp Forest

Nash hunkered down in the amphibious assault craft, waiting patiently for the men to get into position. It was only a mile up the river to the target area, and bobbing around at the mouth of the estuary was a risk, but with some luck the plan would work. The last few days had certainly been hectic, and the details of the assault a bit too hastily thrown together. The information on carbon deposits had somehow hit a raw nerve in London. No less than a direct phone call from the Prime Minister to Sinclair had set the wheels in motion for an immediate assault – not the usual way the chain of command worked. There had been so little time to prepare.

Nash stared up at the stars, and murmured, 'Hey, Emily... so here we are... I know you're hurting and when this is done... well... keep an eye out for me.'

He shook his head. This was no time to get sentimental, but the whole thing left an uneasy feeling. What was it about his report to London that had stirred up so much interest? Was it this Dr Steinhoff fellow? Apparently from Berlin, and with some expertise on rocket engines; that tied events in South Africa firmly to the German rocket programme – but why? Heinkel was SS, a German spy, for sure. Then there were the soldiers on the boat. German Special Forces, or just more SS?

Whatever was going on, Sinclair's orders were very clear: stop all carbon shipments from Zululand at *any cost* and bring in the key players for interrogation.

Nash looked around the boat at the men. The navy's finest.

They had already proven themselves on reconnaissance missions to the target area these last few nights.

'Okay, listen up.' Nash spoke quietly. The three small assault craft bobbed together on the water. 'We are going in against a well-armed and determined enemy. The shoreline is steep, and well defended. The only way in from the water is via a wooden jetty, but luckily for us, we're not all using the front door… ' Nash grinned in the darkness.

Behind the mining camp was mile upon mile of the toughest jungle imaginable. The Germans had worked on the assumption that no attack would come from the rear. Nash hoped this error would play to his advantage. Nonetheless, it was a risky assault plan – and the teams were new: elite army and navy troops from the hastily commissioned Cape Amphibious Training Base; the first true generation of Naval Special Forces in the region.

'The damned weather is not on our side for going ashore.' Rudy Temple flashed a smile from one of the other boats.

It was good to have him along. Nash looked through the clear night air at the full moon. 'Rudy mate, I thought you had a direct line with God and could arrange the weather.'

'Afraid not!' he grinned. 'Hey, but don't worry, us Africaans will save your limey arse if you get in the shit.'

Nash shook his head. 'Thanks mate, that brings me no end of comfort.'

At least the low profile of the flat-bottomed assault craft would help. Hopefully no one would notice their little aluminium boats.

Nash gave a harsh whisper to the three boats in the landing team. 'Stay sharp. We don't want to be caught out in the open. Radio silence from here, move out.'

Would three boats with a grand total of eighteen men be enough? Time would soon tell.

The men instinctively took up firing positions, lying flat on the cool aluminium plate. Nash teased the engine forward, revving gently, barely raising the nose of the boat more than a foot above the waterline. He soon found a steady rhythm, satisfied that there was minimal foamy wake behind the boat. The engine was almost silent, with the exhaust manifold on the outboard motors being especially designed to vent below the water line.

The boats moved through the darkness, with men peering into the gloom; weapons at the ready. Gradually the river mouth engulfed them. The boats made a tactical advance upriver, as the silhouette of mangroves on the shoreline grew larger.

Nash cut the engine some five hundred yards from the target area; Temple and the coxswain on the other boats did the same. They would paddle the rest of the way.

Nash focused the binoculars on the shoreline. It was pointless – just a mass of dense blackness – swamp and jungle. Nothing seemed to be stirring, but that didn't mean anything. You could hide a battalion in the undergrowth and still not see them.

He signalled for a final weapons and camouflage check. The enemy would only see the whites of their eyes, and even then, only at close quarters. He checked his kit for noise and weaponry: two automatic pistols, machine gun, belt kit with spare ammo, daggers, and grenades – all present and correct. Last, but not least: one machete, dangling on a length of parachute chord. An essential piece of kit for working through the jungle, but still, a pain in the arse to keep tucked away. Nash shoved it under his belt kit as best he could, and did another weapons check. It wasn't necessary, but every man had his quiet little habits. It was all about being mentally prepared for the assault. Besides, these guys were the best of the best, a good impression was needed.

The paddles dipped gently in and out the water, pushing the boats steadily towards the mangrove fringe. This was the danger zone. If there was a trap to be sprung, it would come now.

It didn't.

Nash sensed the gentle shudder as tree roots scrapped under the hull: shallow water. A storm of sand flies leapt from the branches of the mangroves. With the safety off and adrenalin pumping, each man piled silently ashore over the bow, taking up defensive positions amongst the mangrove roots. Nash followed the last man over, and waded to the head of the formation. He fanned his weapon back and forth, mouth open, with eyes and ears straining.

Good news, no battalion hiding in the bushes.

Nash whispered, pointing towards the jungle. 'Boats away, form up, move out in two minutes.'

The men complied, drawing the lightweight craft into the mangroves, and stashing them under the dense foliage.

'Come on, come on, let's move!' Nash pressed himself against a salty tree trunk, wedging his submerged boots onto some mangrove roots to stop himself sinking in the mud. Weapon up, staring into the darkness, he waited for the men to form a column. The sooner they were through the mangrove fringe the better.

'Rudy up front, gunner to the rear,' Nash whispered. It was better to have the best navigator lead the head of the column – and Rudy Temple was a master craftsman; the bush would test everyone's skills to the limit. The beefy gunner with his high-calibre machine gun took up the rear. Anyone following their trail would be hosed down in seconds.

Nash moved gently forward into the mangroves, trying not to disturb the water, only to be instantly engulfed by blackness drenched with humidity and mosquitoes. His eyes started to adjust to the darkness; the shadow of the man in front went in and out of view. The buzz of mosquitoes filled his ears.

The men moved in unison, silently through the swamp.

After fifty yards of counting time and footsteps, the water started to recede; giving way to muddy, lush jungle. Temple stopped and checked his compass for direction. Satisfied with the compass bearing, he tapped the man behind on the shoulder, and started counting footsteps in his head as the column moved off again. He stopped every fifty yards or so, took another bearing and repeated the process. It was painstaking work; but completely necessary. Getting turned around and lost in the bush was not an option.

The assault team worked its way inland for two hundred metres and then turned parallel to the shoreline, heading towards the mining camp. The dense bush tore at their clothing, and every man was drenched in sweat. Yet, they moved silently forward in good order.

Eventually the jungle began to thin out.

Nash tapped the man up front on the shoulder; the column duly stopped. 'Rudy, how far?'

'Two hundred metres, over the rise,' he spoke quietly in Nash's ear.

'Okay, weapons check and water, we move in two.' The message went down the line. Each man took a few seconds to recheck their weapons, stow machetes, and gulp down a few hard-earned mouthfuls of water.

'Listen up.' The men gathered round. 'We go as planned; in three squads with my team down the middle. Remember flanking positions – if these bastards get behind us we're finished. The enemy is alert and professional. Go in hard and fast.'

The men nodded in agreement. It didn't need saying; every man knew his job, and the job of the man next to him.

The team moved silently up the slope, weapons at the ready.

Nash peered over the rise. Good news: mostly quiet with only two guards patrolling the makeshift perimeter at the back of the camp. He followed the roll of barbed wire with the binoculars; all strung out like a great snake along the rear perimeter. It was a token gesture about waist height. He waved the men forward. Sliding over the rise, moving in a commando crawl, he went head first down the bank, trying to keep his weapon out of the mud.

The teams moved efficiently down to the perimeter, each leaving a man behind on the ridge to lay down covering fire.

Nash held his breath, lying flat and motionless against the wire. Boots clumped past in a rhythmic plod – the two guards – they would be back soon enough. Sweat dripped from his palm. He adjusted his grip on the wire cutters.

Click! The first cut.

The wire gave a quiet snap. *Click, click, click*, more cuts. The tension in the barbed wire gave a little. He crawled forward into the roll of wire. Then, putting pressure on the cutters, with his free hand ready to dampen the vibration in the adjacent coil, he made ready for the last cut. Muffled foot falls approached from the distance.

Snap! A clean cut.

Nash eased the wire back with his free hand and stowed the cutters hastily in his breast pocket. The footfalls suddenly got louder – guards!

He leapt through the gap, commando knife drawn, and piled on top of the first man, shoving his hand over his mouth and simultaneously plunging the knife through his neck. Pushing down firmly, desperate to silence the guard, he dug in the knife and twisted. The guard gave a few spasms as blood gushed from his jugular. Nash kept the pressure up.

The body went limp.

A gentle thud caught Nash's attention. The second guard dropped to his knees momentarily, before falling face down in the mud. He registered the gaping hole in the guard's forehead, and glanced a nod of thanks to his left. Temple smiled back, with a small trail of smoke still rising from his silencer.

The assault team needed no second invitation, and fanned out through the gap in the wire. Nash surveyed the scene as the men quickly took up flanking positions along the perimeter.

'Number One,' he hissed at Temple, pointing towards the nearest cover – a couple of tool sheds and a pile of gasoline barrels.

The team went forward, moving silent and swiftly. Nash's nostrils filled with the smell of gasoline as his slid behind a few drums.

'See that.' He pointed to the right. 'Tents – they must be sleeping quarters for the workers.'

Temple nodded, and dispatched two men to keep the workers under wraps. There was no point having civilians screwing up the line of fire.

Nash peered over the top of the gasoline barrel to get a better view of the camp. Further down the slope, a larger shack perched at the end of the jetty; likely the main guard room and the reception for boat landings.

'How many guards do you count?'

Temple whispered back. 'Two outside the guard room, four on the beachfront, and we can expect some at the far end of the jetty; at least eight men.'

'Plus whoever's inside.' Nash nodded towards the light burning brightly in the guard room; with luck that would include Steinhoff and Heinkel. 'Remember, we need the scientist alive.'

Temple duly nodded.

It was a good twenty yards across open ground towards the guards' shack; and no chance of making the distance without a firefight.

Nash tapped Temple on the shoulder. He got the message and raised his pistol. With luck they could take out at least one guard, maybe two, with the silencer.

'Alarm! Alarm!' A shout broke the silence – so much for the element of surprise.

A headshot dropped the first guard outside the shack. Rolling off the decking, the second guard found some cover on

285

the riverbank, and instantly returned fire. Simultaneously, weapons trained up the hill on Nash's position.

Rounds thudded into the drums. He ducked down behind the gasoline cans. Fuel spewed from the bullet holes.

'We need to move!' Nash screamed as he tossed two smoke grenades into the open ground. Green smoke filled the air.

Moving forward, the six-man team worked in pairs, providing covering fire for each other.

Nash sprinted in a zigzag shooting from the hip, then rolled up onto his knees in a defensive firing position, providing a hailstorm of covering fire for the next pair in the team. Machine guns rattling, the sound of splintering wood penetrated the smoke as the rounds found their target. A guard staggered through the smoke, blood pouring from his chest. He danced like a rag doll as ammunition filled his torso, then collapsed to the ground, dead.

Nash felt a rush of movement to his left. The second pair from the team zigzagged past, firing rapidly. They didn't make it – ignoring a shower of blood, bone and splinters – Nash pressed forward.

Suddenly, with the smoke clearing, a German screamed into view.

A deafening shower of hot shell casings poured onto Nash's shoulder. He ducked as Rudy peppered the German full of lead. The body bounded across the mud landing close by. It was good enough; Nash dived behind the corpse for cover and returned fire. Rudy Temple landed in the mud next to him.

'Fuck! We can't stay here!' Nash bellowed the obvious and let off another targeted volley. A body dropped in agony a few yards to his left – one of his men rolled around in the mud minus a leg.

A burst of fire hammered into the ground, showering Nash with earth. Rolling over, he pulled a smoke grenade from his webbing.

'On three! Give me covering fire!'

Temple duly slapped home another magazine, pouring firepower on the wooden shack.

Nash lunged forwards, and tossed the smoke grenade through the nearest window. The shack erupted in a cloud of thick orange smoke. For good measure, he tossed in another; it had the desired effect.

The front door of the shack burst open.

Despite the choking smoke, the guards kept in formation. A burst of fire – move – a burst of fire – move. The guards worked as a team to make an orderly retreat to the river, whilst still pinning Nash's men down in the exposed ground.

Nash issued new orders over the din. 'Left flank, give covering fire! Number One keep those bastards down on the riverbank!'

The enemy still had plenty of fight left in them, but with luck they could be held. Nash was sure Heinkel would be among them.

Out of nowhere, a boat engine roared into life.

'The jetty!' Temple pointed towards the water.

Nash poked his head around the corner of the shack.

Steinhoff and Heinkel!

Heinkel expertly hacked at the mooring lines with a machete, and returned fire with his automatic pistol. Evidently, he and the scientist were doing a runner and leaving their comrades to it.

Nash took a careful aim, trying to pick out the engine compartment. He fired, suddenly flinching as fragments of wood exploded next to his head.

'Shit!' Nash rammed home another pistol mag and clicked a round in the chamber.

Too late – Heinkel was already on the move!

The engine revved violently to the sound of crunching gears as Heinkel threw the boat into reverse.

Nash lunged forward into the open, firing rapidly at the

stern. It paid off: thick smoke billowed from the engine compartment.

Choking on the smoke, Heinkel pushed hard on the throttle, sending the boat downriver. The stern disappeared from view.

Suddenly, a heavy burst of machine gunfire erupted from behind the shed at close range. Nash was perplexed – why wasn't he dead? Then he realised the shots were not directed at him, but at the assault team holding the rear. Sparks flew as shots bounced off the oil drums; then his rearguard was gone in a fireball of hot diesel.

Nash threw himself to the ground, the scorching heat whisked inches over his head. As the blast wave receded a familiar sound registered in the back of his mind: the *click clack* of someone reloading a heavy-calibre machine gun.

Catching a glimpse of a huge muscular German – the guy from the boat, standing tall, weapon at the ready – Nash tensed and waited for death as another surge of heat passed overhead.

The German disappeared from view behind the orange glow. Nash dove back into cover on the other side of the shed, hitting the dirt hard.

'Fuck!' he curled up into a ball. Shards of wood and hot metal screamed inches above his position. The steady whir of the heavy-calibre weapon filled his ears.

He risked a glance up the hill.

Flames and mayhem; there was no chance of making cover. That left only one choice; take the fight to the enemy.

He rolled over, pulling the pin from a grenade, and hurled it through the shack window. He buried himself into the ground.

The explosion showered more shards of timber and glass in all directions.

Jumping to his feet, he piled through the first window to be met by a turbulent mass of splintered furniture, dust and blood; but no soldiers. Where was the German giant?

The remains of the front door suddenly burst from its hinges.

The German stood looming in the doorway, with large splinters of wood down his left side. He limped forward. Blood poured around a shard of timber impaled in his eye, his face ached with the pockmarks of numerous shrapnel wounds. Inflammation would soon close his remaining good eye, and the pieces of wood jutting from the back of his hand would make it awkward to hold his weapon – but none of that mattered – for now, killing the enemy was good enough.

The German screamed as he lifted the machine gun.

Click – the magazine was empty.

'Shitze! Shitze!' He leapt forward, discarding the heavy weapon.

Nash wheezed as the air was driven from his torso. The weight of the huge German sent a sharp pain through his chest, ribs fractured.

The first punch hit home like a block of cast iron, crunching teeth together. Blood filled his mouth. Dazed, Nash flailed his arms in a frantic attempt to defect the next blow.

Smash! Cartilage shattered on bone, blood gushed from Nash's face; with his eyes puffing up under the assault, his vision began to close. He bucked violently, but it was no good, the German was simply too heavy.

'Die! Die! Die!' The German rained down more vicious blows.

'Fuck you!' Nash bellowed with remains of his strength, then twisted his body whilst fishing in his belt kit for a knife.

The German landed another devastating punch and, sensing the end, grabbed Nash by the throat.

'Time to die now, American!'

Nash choked on the vice-like grip. The German expertly pressed his thumbs into the Adam's apple – Nash knew the technique – a very efficient way of crushing a man's airway. He hunted for air, but found none; his pulse pounded surreally inside his head.

The grip tightened.

Nausea began to rise and, with his lungs bursting, his eyes beckoned the fog of unconsciousness.

Miraculously, Nash found the blade, and with the last of his strength, he rammed it home.

The German bellowed at the pain in his chest, distracted enough to release his grip. Nash sucked in lungfuls of air.

'Shitze! Shitze!' The German pulled the knife from his own chest. 'My turn, American scum!' He powered down with the weapon.

Parrying, Nash somehow managed to deflect the steel tip into the floorboards.

Thud!

The impact echoed close to his head.

'I said die, American!' The German reigned fists down on the helpless Nash, then pulled the knife from the floorboards.

This time the knife landed on target.

Pain erupted in Nash's shoulder. For good measure the German twisted the blade.

'Arghh!' Blood gushed from the wound and, with his vision blurring, Nash knew he would not be able to deflect the blade again.

'American swine!' The German bellowed another stream of obscenities as he pulled the knife from Nash's shoulder, raising the blade high, cursing through clenched teeth as he swung the knife down again with all his bodyweight behind it.

Nash waited for the end.

Gunfire filled the room.

The huge German erupted in an explosion of bone fragments, blood and internal organs. He gave a confused look, then dropped the knife and slumped forward.

He was dead.

Gagging underneath the weight of the blood-soaked body, Nash thrashed his legs, with panic rising.

Suddenly, the dead weight was lifted. Nash gasped in air. He opened his eyes, blinking; a shadowy figure began to emerge.

'You alright boss?' came the welcome voice of Rudy Temple.

Nodding, unable to speak, Nash sucked in air.

Temple smiled. 'Told you I'd save your limey arse!'

Nash heeled the corpse in the head. 'Fucking Englishman, not American! Nazi bastard!'

Temple pulled Nash to his feet. 'Take it easy mate, he's well and truly dead.'

Nash rested against Temple, holding his shoulder wound, relieved to be alive.

Outside the fight was all but over. The last few guards on the riverbank surrendered with dignity. The assault team rounded up the workers from the tents up the hill. Then scouted the remains of the jetty and beachfront for prisoners. The miners were a ragged bunch; all locals. No doubt they would have been worked hard on the promise of a good wage, before being ruthlessly dispatched. There was no sign of Heinkel or the scientist.

Later that evening a steamship left South Africa for Germany. It carried a precious cargo. Not as much as they would have liked, but enough, just enough for the task ahead. Dr Steinhoff nodded to himself with satisfaction as he checked the purity of the batch; the nano carbon was perfect. His superiors in Berlin would be pleased.

CHAPTER 38

Headway at Peenemünde

The pieces of the puzzle were coming together at last. Steinhoff worked carefully with the nano carbon from Zululand. Awestruck by the properties of this new material, and feeling the hand of history on his shoulder, he worked on, checking his calculations.

What was it that Professor Mayer had said? Wave energy being converted to particle energy; or maybe it was the other way round. It didn't matter, either way it was a revelation – like stepping out of the Dark Ages and finding a spaceship.

Steinhoff flushed with another rush of adrenalin.

Mayer had also mentioned electricity. It made sense now. The device needed an electric field to work. The nano carbon had some very special electrical properties. The first few experiments had been simple, a kind of 'proof of principle'. If Professor Mayer had been alluding to some kind of propulsion device then it would need to be made of light but strong materials – aluminium sheeting – just like a rocket. There was plenty of that lying about the workshop. It had taken a few attempts, but eventually he was able to make aluminium sheets coated with nano carbon.

The results were astounding.

Steinhoff checked the calculation again – *this couldn't be right* – but it was.

The carbon coat conducted electricity better than any other material known to man. The optical properties of the material also changed, going from a matt black to an eerie fluorescent green glow when it was charged with a small amount of electricity. Amazingly the colour changed even more, from green to yellow, to orange, and then to a bright fluorescent red as more electricity was passed through the material.

Where did these optical properties come from? Were they important?

Steinhoff had absolutely no idea; but he did understand electricity.

That's it! A giant dynamo! Electromagnetism!

The material was super-conducting, it would make a fantastic giant dynamo; an electric motor that would propel a new kind of rocket.

Steinhoff set about the task immediately.

He wrapped up one of the carbon-coated sheets in a copper coil. Sure enough, when electricity was passed through the copper coil, the carbon was magnetised. Steinhoff felt the sheet trying to move. But even so, the movement was not that strong, not enough for a rocket. Maybe it was just a question of more carbon, or more electricity?

He needed more aluminium sheets; it needed to be bigger.

He skipped meals and, with no need of sleep, adrenalin kept his mind working through the night. As the first rays of morning light filtered into the workshop, he stepped back to examine his handiwork – it looked good.

The latest design made much more sense. It incorporated several long sections of nano-coated aluminium sheeting for more power. The sheets were bent and bolted together on a frame to form a hollow tube. In effect, the inside of the tube was a bunch of carbon plates.

He checked the power cables attached to the device.

All good.

It was time to give it a go.

Tentatively, he turned up the dial on the power supply; a sudden flash brought the device to life.

Steinhoff jumped.

The plates immediately gave a bright fluorescent red glow; but there was no movement.

'But what's this?… Yes… ' Steinhoff muttered to himself. Something *was* happening in the middle of the tube. A fine carbon dust began to form – a kind of long thin line of red carbon plasma appeared in the middle of the tube.

He smiled. *Progress!*

The electricity in the plates was somehow vaporising the nano carbon from the surface to form the plasma in the central core of the tube.

He stared at the glowing plasma, the stuff of science fiction.

But how could he make it move?

He kept his eyes on the red glow down the middle of the tube and, walking slowly around the prototype equipment, he carefully examined each part of the tube.

How to make it move?

Lost in thought, he made another full circle around the prototype, and ended up staring down the tube. He shook his head, lost; he took the pipe from his pocket in resignation. He lit the tobacco and took a few puffs to get a good glow in the bowl. It seemed to help.

He absently sucked away on his pipe, blowing clouds of smoke into the open end of the tube.

Suddenly, as the tobacco smoke hit the red plasma, there was a brilliant white flash. The whole structure jolted forward. The force was enormous – it moved the tube, and the bench it was sitting on; even smashed the retaining bolts that were holding the bench to the concrete floor.

Steinhoff's jaw dropped, dumbstruck; his pipe clattered to the floor.

What had just happened?

The impossible.

He stared at the pipe, then at the wrenched bolts.

How could a couple of puffs of tobacco smoke create such a massive force?

He examined the bolts.

Completely shattered – only a force of at least several tons per square inch could do that. Steinhoff's brain kicked into overdrive.

This was monumental. If a few puffs of tobacco smoke could create a lift of several tons, what would a steady stream of smoke into the plasma tube do? Lift hundreds of tons? This was wild! There was nothing like this!

It made the last five years of effort on the rocket programme look stupid. They had spent half a decade making a rocket engine that would lift a couple of tons, and by today's standards that represented a fairly large rocket. But this was in a different league. This was a whole new way of thinking that could power an enormous rocket. Maybe it could lift a rocket that was a hundred metres tall, ten times the size of their current efforts.

Steinhoff considered the payload.

How much damage would a hundred tons of high explosive do?

The current payload was a few hundred kilograms, and that was devastating enough, easily capable of destroying an area about the size of a football pitch. What would a hundred kilograms, or a thousand, of high explosive do? Destroy a small town? Destroy a city? It could certainly be used to devastating effect on the battlefield.

Steinhoff changed tack.

You don't have to use all that force to lift something very large. There was an alternative – move something smaller – but move it very fast.

Maybe they could make their current rockets, travel a few thousand miles an hour instead of a few hundred? The rockets could reach New York in thirty minutes, instead of just London! The Reich would have a weapon that could target any location, anywhere in the world!

Steinhoff smiled, nodding to himself; his chest surged with

pride – he had done it! He had *really* done it. He threw a triumphant punch into the air.

'Yes! Yes! Yes!'

His grin broadened. At last, recognition would come – and *he had* toiled for so long. There would be honours for sure! The saviour of the Reich! Decorated by the Führer himself no less! Then there would be globalisation of the Reich, with all and every possible resource available for science; maybe even a Nobel Prize. Steinhoff beamed.

But there was a problem: no one had ever made anything fly that fast before. What would be the stresses of the massive acceleration on the fuselage of the rocket? Would the carbon coatings survive at such speed? What about the guidance system? It was challenging enough to get the rockets to fly in a straight line at only one hundred miles an hour. How on earth could they make a guidance system to direct a rocket to a specific target when the speed of flight was over a thousand miles an hour? The slightest error would put the rocket off target by many miles, missing the objective completely.

It was time for another little chat with Professor Mayer; but this time he would do it alone.

Mayer stirred from his sleep, sensing a presence in his room. He opened his eyes. The dim glow of the sidelight told him it was still night-time. His head thumped. He reached up to the wetness around his neck and registered the clammy sweat soaking through his hair. His pyjamas soaked in salty dampness. The fever had returned.

Suddenly, he spotted a figure at the end of the bed. Standing motionless, dressed in a white laboratory coat.

'Steinhoff?'

Mayer tried easing himself up on to a pillow; his good arm took the strain, but ached. He wedged a pillow under his armpit and half sat up in the bed.

'Steinhoff? Is that you?'

The white-coated figure remained silent, almost monolithic in the lamplight.

'Steinhoff? *It is* you?' Mayer coughed.

No response.

'What do you want?'

No response.

'Steinhoff?' Mayer rubbed his thumping brow. The bruises on his face throbbed. He looked at the silhouetted man again. Perhaps it was a dream?

The pain of wakefulness told him it wasn't. Mayer stretched towards the switch next to the bed and, with his muscles aching, flicked the main lights on.

Steinhoff remained fixed to the spot.

Mayer glanced him up and down. Unshaven, oil-stained laboratory coat, and pockets full of tools. 'Steinhoff… please… '

Steinhoff responded. 'I have it. I've built my first prototype.'

Mayer gasped. 'No!' He made a fist with his good arm and punched the bed. 'Steinhoff, stop, it is not too late. Please stop!'

Steinhoff spoke evenly, as if detached from the world. 'You know I cannot do that. The prize is within my grasp.'

'You *must* give it up.' Mayer went into a coughing fit; he rasped between breaths. 'You don't know what you've done!'

'Done?… Done? I have made a great discovery, possibly *the greatest* discovery; but to make it complete, there are details.'

Mayer flushed with fever, sweat dripped from his brow. 'I cannot help you.'

'But you will. You know how it goes; a little work here, some adjustment there… one prototype follows another… until perfection is achieved. Yes, perfection. That's it… perfection… '

'Perfection?… No, just perfect madness.'

'I will start work on a second prototype device tomorrow. I need to know about torsion, the stresses on the aluminium frame. How fast will the device go?'

'How fast? Forget it!' Mayer rolled back flat on the bed to relieve the ache in his good shoulder. His skull pounded as the blood rushed to his head. His stomach churned.

He stared at the ceiling as Steinhoff spoke.

'Faster than the speed of sound?'

'You do the math.' Mayer rubbed his abdomen, with cramp rising in his gut.

'*How fast?*' Steinhoff moved forward, taking a wrench from his lab coat pocket.

Mayer flinched as the cool weight of the steel pressed against his belly. 'Very… fast.'

'The speed of sound?'

Mayer gasped as the wrench pushed deeper into his stomach, then yelped as the wrench was twisted. 'Yes… yes… obviously!'

The weight was suddenly lifted. Mayer recoiled holding his gut.

'How do I get the carbon sixty to give a stable coating, and stay intact at the speed of sound?'

'No, I cannot… help you.' Mayer remained curled up.

'How do I get a stable carbon sixty coating at high speed? *How?!*'

Steinhoff's voice echoed around the room. Mayer tensed as the wrench rested on his head wound.

Steinhoff rolled the tool clumsily over the bandage.

Mayer gritted his teeth against the pain. The sound of the scab cracking, and the moistness of fresh blood soaked into his bandage.

'Steinhoff… it is not too late… turn away… ' Mayer's gullet burned with rising vomit; his intestines tightened in unison with the fresh pain in his skull.

'How do I fix the coating at high speed?!'

The sudden *thump, thump* of the wrench against his skull sent a sharp, lancing pain through his body. 'Arghh! Arghh!…

Do you not see it?' Mayer covered his head with his good hand, and gritted his teeth. The wrench smashed into his knuckles, closely followed by a wave of pain. 'Arghh! Electrostatic... you work it out!'

Steinhoff's voice boomed through the pain 'Electrostatic? Very clever. *How?* How exactly?'

'You're the genius... your twisted mind... will never the find answer!'

A deep thud, pain, and the rush of vomit registered as Mayer passed out.

CHAPTER 39

Sir Hugh Sinclair, Whitehall

S ir Hugh Sinclair poured over the maps in the cabinet
office briefing room and the latest reconnaissance
photographs from Peenemünde with General Gort, the
head of the British Army. The political situation in Eastern
Europe was deteriorating rapidly, with Herr Hitler showing
aspirations to annex parts of Austria and the strategically
important Sudetenland on the Czechoslovakian border. Perhaps
Mr Churchill had been right all along about Hitler, but nobody
had listened – until now. The threat from Peenemünde *was*
significant. The Germans could potentially target any major city
in mainland Europe, perhaps even London. Regardless of any
intent, the mere existence of the facility gave Hitler a political
advantage.

Sinclair worried, but kept an outward air of calm efficiency.
Any substantial military intervention at Peenemünde by the
British would be seen as an act of war. Equally, doing nothing
was not an option.

The German fleet was still anchored in the Heligoland
Bight, in the north west of Germany. This was a natural harbour,
and the towns along the River Elbe that fed into the massive bay
had a long history of shipping and ship construction. Hamburg
in particular had all the heavy steel industry and infrastructure
needed for making weapons. The military significance of basing
the German fleet in Heligoland was not lost to the sharp military
mind of Sir Hugh Sinclair.

Not only could the German fleet move freely westward into

the North Sea, but it was also only a short hop eastwards around the Schleswig Peninsula into the Baltic Sea. The fleet could quickly mount a defence of the rocket base at Peenemüde.

'What about a bombing raid on Peenemünde?' asked Sinclair.

'Out of the question. Too overt, and politically it would be too risky. Britain is in no shape to go to war.' General Gort shook his head.

'Sometimes one has to take risks to win,' Sinclair countered.

'I agree, but the risk is simply too great. Besides, any bombers would have to fly direct to Peenemünde, and that would take them over the heavily defended Heligoland. The German cruisers with their big guns would chew us to pieces. There are also substantial air defences at Peenemünde.'

Sinclair threw another idea in to the mix. 'What about a high-altitude bombing raid?'

'No good.' Gort rubbed his brow. 'The planes are not up to it. They would burn more fuel than they can carry. In any event, Peenemünde is a small target area. They need to fly low to be on target.'

'Then, what about a ground assault with regular troops?'

'That would be political madness, and militarily we simply don't have enough men and equipment. The only route in is by sea, and the Germans have the area well defended. We would have to defeat the German Navy first, and then battle ashore at Peenemünde. There would be heavy casualties and little chance of success.'

'I thought that would be your answer,' Sinclair paused, 'I have been discussing options with the Secret Intelligence Service. Our boys from Section D are going to have a crack at the Hun.'

Gort stiffened with surprise. 'Bloody hell old chap, are you sure?!'

Section D was a newly formed part of MI6 and its specialty

was undercover operations behind enemy lines. Its sole purpose was sabotage and destruction of the enemy's infrastructure. Or indeed, any other little job they were asked to do.

'The operation has already been approved by Mr Churchill,' Sinclair continued as he pulled up an aerial map of Peenemünde.

General Gort raised an eyebrow, murmuring to himself.

'Clearly, the facility is well defended from an assault by sea or by air; but there is one weakness.'

Gort gave a cautious look. 'Go on, I am listening.'

'The base is at the end of a narrow strip of land that is serviced by one road. The route is not well protected. The Germans are simply not expecting an attack from within Germany.'

'What are you suggesting? That we simply walk up to the front door and knock?'

'Yes.' Sinclair stood up and lit his pipe, puffing absently on the mellow tobacco. 'The enemy is arrogant. That is their weakness. They will not be expecting such a daring attempt.'

Gort had to admit – Sinclair had a point.

'We will use a small team with lots of high explosives. You can see from the photographs that there are four main areas to attack. The main living quarters housing the scientists and the guards, a cluster of buildings that, for now, we think are workshops. There is also the main experimental station. The latter is surrounded by concrete bunkers and is partially buried in the ground. We would need to get a man inside to do any significant damage.'

Sinclair seemed to have it all worked out.

'What's the escape plan? How do we extract the assault team?' asked Gort.

Sinclair looked grimly at his colleague. 'There is no escape plan. This is a one-way ticket for some very brave men.'

General Gort fell silent, and furrowed his brow.

'General, I know... I know... but understand this;

disrupting the German rocket programme is pivotal. It is essential to morale in the British Isles that no rocket ever makes it onto our soil. It is also critical from both a political and military point of view. The simple fact is that the Germans have rockets and we do not.'

'And if the men are captured?'

'Nothing will identify them as British. They know the score.'

'Very well, then I agree… I just hope Mr Churchill has made the right call. This could turn into a pretty old mess fairly easily.' General Gort collected his hat from the coat stand in the corner of the room. 'Good luck. Obviously, we can provide anything you might need… just let me know.' Gort gave a rare smile.

Sinclair nodded as Gort left the room, then waited. Alone at the large oak table, Sinclair dialled an internal number.

'It's on… '

He hung up the receiver and re-lit his pipe.

Emily Sinclair snuggled under Nash's arm, listening to the steady rhythmic beat of his heart. Her full warm breasts pressed against his rib cage. A sweet perspiration moistened her cleavage as Nash gently stroked her golden brown hair. He kissed her on the forehead and sighed.

Emily smiled, gazing up into his eyes. 'I love the sound of your heartbeat… so strong… reassuring.'

Nash smiled back, running his fingertips over her left breast; the nipple instantly hardened. 'I love everything about you too… ' Nash leant over, and kissed her tenderly on the lips. She responded, pulling him in closer, feeling the undulations of the firm muscles covering his ribs.

The taste of perfume and moist lipstick filled Nash's palate. He ran his fingers around her waist finding the small of her back. The softness of her skin tantalised his senses; with his heartbeat rising, he kissed her deeply. Her breathing increased, chest heaving; her tongue darted in and out of his mouth between gasps.

'Oh Danny! I wish this could last forever…'

Nash eased her back into the pillow, breaking the embrace; he smiled. 'I wish it could too… but I have to go to work soon.' He brushed his index finger across her fringe, tracing it lightly over her eyebrows and down to the tip of her nose. He whispered. 'Such a perfect, perfect face. You're beautiful… you're funny… you make me smile… you're everything a man could ask for.'

He kissed her deeply on the lips and sank back onto the bed, relaxing his whole being. He exhaled gently. All the tension had gone; she somehow made him complete. But would it last?

A pigeon landed on the skylight window of the attic room. It purred gently, pecking absently at the glass.

Nash grinned. 'Pigeon pie… have you ever eaten pigeon pie?'

'Oh Danny stop it!' Emily giggled. 'The poor thing!'

'Sorry, force of habit… survival rations and all that…'

'Yuk! Is there nothing you haven't eaten?' Emily stared up at the window, watching the bird patter across the glass.

The pigeon suddenly evacuated a white-green splurge onto the window.

They burst out laughing, then gazed into each other's eyes.

She drew her leg over Nash's. The warmth of her damp groin pressed against his thigh. Her hips pulsated involuntarily; rubbing herself against his calf muscle, her breathing became shallow and erratic. She opened her mouth, searching for his, pushing herself harder against his leg.

Nash responded, and drew her closer.

She eased herself onto him, drawing in a deep breath as a wave of pleasure pulsated through her body. Her fingernails dug into his chest, stretching the stitches on the knife wound in his shoulder.

'Ouch!' Nash gave a playful smile.

She writhed on his waist with increasing force, breathing more deeply than before. 'Sorry, sorry, I forgot about the wound... Danny... I... Danny!' She pulsed wetness onto his groin. Nash responded with increasingly deep thrusts.

Emily gave a spasm and smiled, working harder, beads of sweat formed on her neck. Nash ran his hands firmly on her breasts.

'It's okay. Don't worry. Let yourself go.' He thrust deeper, squeezing her nipples, feeling the tension rise in her body.

Emily writhed with pleasure, gripping Nash's manhood with her pelvic muscles. A flush of heat and wetness issued from her groin.

She gasped and fell forward, whispering in his ear. 'Danny, I love you, I love you!' She flicked her tongue on his earlobe as another spasm of delight wracked her body.

Nash felt her firmness, and warmth; unable to hold back, he thrust deeper, arching his back and almost lifting her off the bed.

Surprised by his own passion, a wave of muscle tension pulsed through his body. They came together and collapsed into each other's arms back on the bed. Her wet breasts heaved against his chest; he ran his hand gently through her hair, taking deep breaths of her perfume.

'Emily, I can't stand to be without you. Stay with me forever.'

She gasped. 'I will... I will... ' She kissed gently onto his pectorals, slowly catching her breath. She worked up to the knife wound and placed a tender kiss over his stitches.

'Does it hurt?'

'No, not any more,' Nash lied.

She buried her face against his chest, drawing a finger over the scars on his body.

She whispered as she caressed his skin. 'So many cuts and bruises. You poor man. I will look after you... just come home safely.'

'I'll always be here for you Emily… always… ' Nash kissed her forehead. She snuggled deeper into his chest.

'Will you Danny?… ' She ran her index finger absently over his scar. 'I so worry, when you're away. It's so dangerous. I fear that one day you will not come back.'

'I know… I know… but would you change who I am?'

She kissed his chest. 'No, I wouldn't change a thing.'

'I only know soldiering. What else would I do?'

'You've been in the field a long time. Perhaps it's time to think about a less active role. You could take a desk job, be in charge, or a training job at the barracks?'

Nash chuckled. 'Me, driving a desk?! Now, that's something I'd like to see!'

'Okay, not a desk then, but what about training? Daddy needs good men like you to instruct the next generation. There are younger men out there now… '

'Maybe one day, but not just yet.'

'Why not just yet? It would be ideal.'

'There's something I need to do.'

'Another job for Daddy?'

Nash tried to conceal his concern, but his voice wavered. 'Yes, another job.'

'Danny, what are you doing? It's a dangerous mission, *really dangerous* – isn't it?'

'Yes it is, but what else would you have me do?'

'Stay here with me.'

'I wish I could,' his arms tensed into a hug, '… but I am a serving soldier, and orders are orders.'

'Let me speak to Daddy, maybe he can send someone else?'

'No!'

'Why not?'

Nash shrugged. 'If it's not me, it would be somebody else anyway.'

'Danny, please, then let it be somebody else!'

Nash kissed her on the forehead and stared into her beautiful blue-green eyes. 'You know that's not possible. I have to go… whatever the danger.'

'Oh Danny, promise me you will consider the training job. Promise me… '

'Okay, when I get back… we can talk about it… '

'Just come back in one piece, alive and well.' A tear rolled down her cheek.

Nash kissed away the tears and drew her closer to his chest. 'Emily, I love you. No matter what, I promise, I will return. Then we can be together… forever.'

Nash fell silent. It was a promise he couldn't keep – and he knew it.

CHAPTER 40

Special Operation D

Nash thumbed the mud off his watch – six a.m. – that made the eighth patrol along the perimeter fence in the last hour. Peenemünde was well guarded. The cover from the undergrowth was a bit sparse, but so far so good. The clump of ferns was doing its job. Anyhow, it would soon be time to go, another half an hour at the most until it all kicked off.

Sinclair had been very clear; discuss the mission with no one and report directly to him, and him alone. So be it. This one was so secret that the normal chain of command was completely bypassed. Only Sinclair and the First Lord of the Admiralty knew the true purpose of the mission. This was something beyond top drawer, ultra-top secret.

He had to admit, the odds for success were fairly modest. He would need a bit of luck on this one. The only saving grace was the hired help. Sinclair had done a good job of cooking up a diversion – an assault on Peenemünde by a larger force of men; this time on the books at Whitehall with the general objective of causing mayhem and destruction. The assault team would certainly do that with demolition experts from Section D of British Intelligence and some South African Special Forces. What was it Sinclair had said? Nash smiled at the thought: *a diversion of sufficient magnitude*, to enable him to slip into the base undetected.

That was all fine and dandy, but the assault team were completely unaware of his presence. The prospect of being killed by friendly fire wasn't uplifting; but then they *must not* know, *could not* know, the true purpose of the mission, or even of his presence. It was better that way. There was a good chance that some of the men would be injured, perhaps captured alive. There would be nothing they could give away under torture, apart from the obvious: being ordered to blow the place up.

Still, the orders were a bit cryptic: the destruction of any carbon-based device and anything that looked out of place in the workshop building. What did that mean? What did the device look like? How big was it? There wasn't much to go on. Apparently, Churchill's orders to SIS had used the phrase *imperative to humanity*. It was at least clear that any, and all, such devices should be utterly destroyed, along with the scientists who built them – the very knowledge of its existence wiped from the face of the earth.

The thought sent a chill down his spine. Nash buttoned up his overcoat some more to keep out the morning air. The bulky civilian clothes weren't ideal for the job, but were completely necessary. Staying incognito in similar attire to the captive Polish and Jewish labourers at the base was all part of the plan. Blend in with the natives.

He looked at his watch again, and pushed back the ferns to get a better view of the perimeter fence. All quiet, for now. The clock was ticking, the German troops would be up and about soon. Why the hell hadn't the fireworks started?

Rudy Temple marched smartly towards the main gate at Peenemünde. The clicking of heels resonated on the road, breaking through the quiet of the early morning air. The German uniform grated on his skin; he ignored it – the ruse had to work – they couldn't get into the camp by force alone. But would the sentries fall for it? The oldest trick in the book: pretending to be something you're not.

The men looked convincing enough in their German

uniforms, not too neat and tidy, but that worn look of a soldier busy with the day job. This time, escorting a delivery of new workers for the camp. The 'workers' were the boys from Section D, and they'd outdone themselves this time, playing the role beautifully with their stinking, ragged civilian clothes. He only hoped the sentries wouldn't notice the somewhat baggy nature of their rags; each man carried a shedload of concealed weapons and explosives. Temple tried not to grin. These likeable British guys didn't do anything in half measures. Just in case, there was also an insurance plan. The workers pulled a couple of handcarts stacked up with shovels, picks, and other tools. Hidden underneath the tools were a couple of heavy machine guns and enough explosive to start a major firefight – after all, that's what they were here for.

Temple focused on the main gate.

Only fifty yards to go.

The gate looked flimsy enough, just a wooden frame with some simple wire mesh. The sentry post to the left and the machine gun nest to the right were exactly as expected from the aerial photographs. Two sentries shared a smoke in front of the gates. The machine gunners looked bored in the nest, having probably been there all night. For once, the intelligence had been right. The entrance to the camp had only modest defences; but getting in would require all the brass neck and balls his men could muster. If the game was up before they got through the gate they would all be dead: machine gunned on the open ground.

So far, so good, only a few yards to go.

Temple kept a steady pace. Sweat trickled down the back of his neck as he quietly clicked the safety off his machine gun. The column came to a halt.

One of his men moved forward, greeting the guards in fluent German. 'We have a delivery of new workers for you.' Temple's linguistics expert handed over their papers with a smile.

'We are not expecting any new labourers until tomorrow?'

The guard glanced at the papers and then at the trooper standing before him.

Temple's heart missed a beat. It wasn't just the German accent that needed to work; the papers forged by the British had to be up to the job as well. If they weren't they would soon find out.

Temple faced towards the nearest machine gunner, sprung like a coil.

If things go noisy now this guy will die first.

Muttering and the exchange of papers went on at the sentry box.

What the hell is taking so long?

The conversation went back and forth. Temple moved his forefinger under the trigger guard – he would only get one shot at the machine gun nest before they returned fire.

Laughter erupted at the sentry box. Temple gave them a glance.

Christ!

The linguistics man was handing out cigarettes.

Come on get through the damned gate!

Suddenly, all relaxed and casual, the lead sentry waved a hand at his comrade and the entrance was duly opened. All the same, Temple kept his finger on the trigger as they marched through the gate.

The approach road continued on into the base, more or less in a straight line, but running parallel to the shore some hundred yards or so up from the beach. The buildings were clustered into three groupings along the road; the main barracks and living quarters were first, the workshop was another fifty yards down the road, and at the far end sat the main experimental station. Each cluster of buildings was surrounded by trees, so there was plenty of cover to be had.

The plan was brutally simple.

The men would march down the road and be dropped off as three separate work details; one for each cluster of buildings.

It was still fairly early in the morning, and with luck, they could contain most of the German forces in the barracks. They had to – they were outnumbered by ten to one. If the German troops could break out in force it would all be over.

Temple took the first and largest team of South African Special Forces to hold the barracks. The demolition crews moved onto the workshop and the experimental station. Each four-man unit consisted of two Sappers with the explosives and the engineering know-how to maximise destruction, and two Special Forces guys armed to the teeth to lay down covering fire.

Temple held his work detail in the road outside the main barracks. He felt vulnerable in the open, but had to wait the agreed two minutes while the other teams got into position. Temple made things look busy by issuing shovels to the work detail; it also cleared the cart sporting the heavy machine gun, which was now positioned nicely in front of the main door. It would just be a matter of quickly removing the tarpaulin and then pouring hundreds of rounds per minute into the barracks. The men inside would not stand a chance. For good measure, some of the work detail moved to flank the building. Feigning a bit of gardening with the shovels, they were ready to toss grenades through the barrack windows.

Temple checked his watch. The two minutes were up. He ripped off the tarpaulin from the heavy machine gun: that was the signal to unleash hell.

He pulled back on the cocking mechanism, the first belt of large-calibre rounds clunked into place. He'd barely cocked the heavy weapon when the first explosion went off, followed closely by several more rapid explosions: the grenades were doing their work.

Dust, splintering timbers, and bloodcurdling screams issued from the barracks. Temple waited at the ready.

The barrack door swung open as a group of men, dazed and confused by the smoke, tumbled down the short wooden step onto the street.

Temple opened fire.

A hailstorm of bullets took them out instantly, and pulverised the door. He arced the weapon to the left, and then to the right, spraying rounds through the front windows; methodically trying to kill as many as possible. The advantage of surprise wouldn't last for long.

Suddenly, the weapon clicked.

'Stoppage! On me!' Temple yelled at the nearest trooper. Ducking down behind the cart for cover, he desperately fished for a fresh ammo crate and tried to change the feed on the machine gun.

Rounds danced in the road a few inches from his position. Small arms fire. Off centre for now, but with the dust clearing, the rounds would soon find their target.

The magazine clicked into place. Temple leapt to his feet. He pulled back on the cocking mechanism, unleashing another storm of bullets into the front of the building.

Timbers splintered into match wood as the German troops were caught in the deadly tirade. Bodies piled up in the doorway as men were trapped in the confusion. Others dived for cover as best they could.

Hot shell casings bounced and clattered rhythmically onto the floor around him; so many that he risked losing his footing in the debris.

'Feed me! Reload!' Temple dropped the firing rate to heavy bursts. A trooper slid up to the cart, grabbing a fresh ammo crate. Temple let out another burst.

'Come on! Come on! Feed me!'

Click – nothing – the belt was empty.

The trooper lunged forward, slapping another belt into the feed. Temple didn't wait. He hit the trigger, showering the trooper with hot shell casings as more rounds thundered home into the barracks.

Temple shouted, 'Hold them! Hold them!'

He glanced down at the empty ammo crates: only two crates left. At best they could hold out for another four or five minutes. He hoped it would be enough.

'About fucking time!' Nash whispered to himself as he heard the first explosions issue from the camp. He slapped the plastic explosive on the fence post, and lit the fuse – not much finesse, but it would do the job. He threw himself into the nearest depression and waited for the bang.

One... two... three... four... *thud*.

Fragments of fence post and soil flew into the air. Not bothering to wait for the dust to settle, he jumped through the gap. There was no time to waste engaging the enemy; getting to the workshop was the priority. He skirted through the pines, ignoring the assault and the rounds ricocheting amongst the trees, and sprinted in the right direction.

He pulled up behind a pine tree at the back of the workshop, breathing heavily; instinctively changing the magazine in his weapon, Nash observed the scene.

It wasn't looking good.

The four-man demolition team were out the front, pinned down by machine gunfire from within. The workshop was well guarded.

It was time to move, with adrenalin pumping, Nash ran at full tilt towards the side wall of the workshop.

He piled into cover at the side of the building, thankful to be alive. He tossed a grenade through the nearest window, and ducked for cover. The gun battle raged on at the front of the workshop: it at least kept attention away from the rear.

Boom!

A cloud of dust issued from the remains of the window frame. Nash dived in.

Rolling to his feet, he sprayed the room with an arc of fire, taking out two of the guards near the front door in the process.

The weapon juddered in his hands until the click of the trigger reported that the magazine was empty. He dropped onto one knee behind a solid workbench, quickly changing the magazine. A slap on the bottom of the casing told him the magazine was firmly home. He clicked a round into the chamber, and peered over the bench top.

Mayhem.

The demolition team were still laying fire into the front of the building, but they had their work cut out. The last two remaining guards were dug in behind some upturned oak benches at the front windows. Surrounded by spare ammo and with heavy-calibre weapons, the guards had the advantage; but their full attention was out front.

Orders were orders. The job was to take out the device, not to interfere with the fighting. Ignoring the gun battle, he scanned the workshop.

Just the usual crap: bits of metalwork, machine parts, what the hell is it supposed to look like?

Suddenly, an odd-looking cylindrical tube came into view at the back of the workshop. A strange reddish-green plasma glowed from its centre. It was certainly out of place with all the other bits of engineering. That had to be it! The carbon device!

Nash moved towards the back of the workshop, scuttling in a monkey run along a row of workbenches, with his head down. Stray rounds bounced off the benches. Keeping low was the best option; besides it was a good twenty yards across the open workshop to the device.

He arrived at the end of the first row of benches, and peered across the gap: it seemed all clear. He dove across the gap into the next row, instantly rolling up into a three-sixty arc with his weapon. He checked the vicinity.

Ten yards to go, and one more row of benches.

He froze.

Movement caught the corner of his eye. He peered at an

angle back across the workshop: a leg. It belonged to one of the guards, who was still busy pouring rounds out of the front window.

'Fuck it.' Carefully aiming the Browning, he fired a shot at the back of the guard's knee.

The man twisted around cursing at the pain, raising his weapon, seeking out the new threat. A big mistake. Machine gunfire from outside peppered the man's chest full of holes.

Nash mumbled to himself. 'That's one down for the home team, now let me get on with my job!' Satisfied, he turned his attention back to the carbon device.

Lifting his weapon ready for another monkey run, his brain just about registered the swift dark shadow heading his way – but too late!

Pain exploded in his forehead, and by reflex action his arm somehow managed to deflect some of the blow. The sound of a heavy wrench pounding into the concrete floor caught his ears, as blood gushed into his eyes. Sensing a gap and, despite blurred vision, he raised the Browning pistol; and then fired.

Another blow from the wrench sent the shot wide.

He scrambled to close the gap with his assailant, and kicked out with his feet.

Nash got lucky, his attacker slipped and crashed to the floor. A wild swing from the assailant sent the wrench thudding into the bench, fractions of an inch above his head.

'Fuck that!'

He grabbed hold of the mystery wrist, and heaved down with all his might against the side of the bench. Bone crunched on the woodwork.

'Arggghhhh!' The opponent dropped the wrench.

Swivelling round, still unable to see, Nash planted his boots squarely in the middle of the man's chest; and pushed. It was enough to momentarily pin his attacker against the bottom of the far bench.

He raised the Browning, hoping for a headshot, and fired. The reverberation through his feet, still firmly planted in the man's chest, told him the rounds had struck home. He quickly wiped the blood from his eyes, and levelled the weapon for another shot.

His vision finally cleared, revealing a man in a white coat staring into space with the top of his head missing: a dead scientist.

'Jesus!' Nash kicked the body aside. He'd nearly been taken out by an egghead!

Get yourself together!

He wiped the blood from his weapon and checked the magazine, before grabbing a field dressing. It was worth spending a moment tidying up his head wound; after all, he couldn't set the explosives with blood running into his eyes.

Tugging on the bandage, satisfied that it was secure, he scampered out of cover towards the device. More bodies in white coats – it looked like a few more scientists had been caught up in the crossfire.

He slid across the floor, keeping in the last of the cover, and came to rest directly underneath one end of the strange tubular device.

It was time to finish the job; he only hoped the new high-tech explosives would work. Pulling off his rucksack, Nash produced a Mark I Bee Hive demolition charge. The unusual conical shape of the explosive was designed to funnel the blast in one direction: ideally onto the object it was attached to.

He checked the three sharp metal prongs on the base of the charge and hoped they would hold; it all depended on wedging the charge securely. He rammed the Bee Hive in between some carbon-coated aluminium plates, letting the metal prongs dig in.

Now for the time pencil – not exactly the greatest detonator – but it would have to do. Nash carefully pushed the time pencil into the top of the charge.

The time pencil was an ingenious idea consisting of a firing pin held back inside a small copper tube by a thin wire. The wire was surrounded by a glass vial containing acid. The deal was simple: crack the glass vial by squeezing the outer copper tube with a pair of pliers, and be long gone by the time the acid has eaten its way through the firing wire. The trouble was, the acid never worked at the same rate. A fuse might take two minutes, three minutes, or even four to blow.

He *had* to be sure the device was destroyed.

Sweat erupted in his palms as he picked up the pliers; and for good reason. Squeeze too hard and the thin wire holding back the firing pin would break, causing an instant explosion. But if you don't squeeze hard enough – no acid – so nothing happens at all.

He lifted the pliers to the time pencil, then suddenly stopped.

Photographs!

In the heat of the moment he had nearly forgotten the photographs! The boys in Whitehall loved their intelligence briefings; it wouldn't do to return from a top secret mission without photos. It was hardly the best way to keep a mission secret, but apparently Churchill had asked for some pictures.

Nash snapped away with the camera, working his way around the device. One side was still under construction, evidently the device wasn't finished. But then he noticed something; another bench with similar mounting and retaining bolts.

Was there a second device? The bench had a depression in the surface from something heavy, and a light dusting of black powder marked out the shadow of a long object. The bench had definitely been used to make a device, but where was it now?

Nash glanced around.

Nothing.

He took photographs of the bench and stowed the camera in his rucksack.

It was time to set the detonators.

He focused on the pliers, ignoring the mayhem outside. He adjusted his grip, feeling the pliers firm up on the surface of the time pencil.

Crack – the vial broke.

Still alive!

The countdown was on.

That left two, maybe three minutes, to set some other charges. The orders were to stay and confirm the destruction of the device, and blow up anything else that looked important along the way.

Nash set about placing a second Bee Hive on what looked like a complex fuel injection system being constructed on a bench a few feet away. He wedged the charge into one of the manifolds and pushed in a time pencil as before, then working carefully with the pliers, he crushed the copper tube.

The charge was set.

Pain erupted in the back of his head.

A powerful metallic blow sent him sprawling to the deck.

Nash rolled over, willing his eyes to focus; fighting down nausea, his head started to spin.

'Well, well, if it's not my American friend from Kummersdorf!' Commandant Kessler stared down at Nash. 'If I remember correctly, I did promise to kill you – and I always keep my promises.'

Kessler swung the metal pipe again.

Nash rolled. The pipe gouged a three-inch dent in the floor instead.

Kessler raised the pipe for another swipe. It was a pity he couldn't use his Luger pistol, but it was too risky; the intruder had pockets full of explosives. Besides, the second prototype needed to remain intact.

'No more games, American.' Kessler swung wildly, using the heavy pipe to good effect.

Crab-like on all fours, Nash scuttled backwards, trying to keep out of the path of each blow. The pipe struck home. Pain issued from his ribs.

Instinctively, he grabbed the pipe with both hands; rolling and twisting, Nash tried to liberate the pipe from his attacker.

Success!

The pipe clattered to the floor.

Kessler shrugged, and with a sadistic smile drew his SS dagger.

'So, a knife fight… ' Nash returned the favour, drawing his commando knife.

The two men locked together in close quarter combat.

Kessler hissed, 'You're too late! Mayer has told us everything!'

'You lie! Mayer's dead. I was there remember!'

Kessler gritted his teeth. 'No, I think you'll find Professor Mayer is very much alive.'

'No…! ' Nash pushed forwards with his knife.

Kessler used the thrust to put Nash off balance. Rolling to the left and then to the right, Kessler tried breaking Nash's handhold on his wrist. Nash strained under Kessler's larger weight; the SS blade inched closer to his throat. Kessler sensed the advantage.

'You *must* die!' hissed Kessler. He renewed his efforts. The blade nicked Nash's neck.

'Not today!' Nash screamed, suddenly finding the strength to twist his commando knife down towards Kessler's abdomen. He would let the weight of his assailant find the blade.

Kessler was quick to respond, arching his back to create room for the knife; the blade swept dangerously below him.

It was enough, Kessler was off balance. Nash forced his knee into the gap and, finding Kessler's stomach, he pushed like hell.

The two men parted but, despite the exertion, both sprang to their feet quickly, ready for the next round.

Kessler had a longer reach. He swiped out with his blade. A patch of blood welled up on Nash's chest.

Ignoring the pain, Nash readied for the next swing. Kessler lunged. Rolling under the thrust, Nash expertly slashed his own knife across Kessler's ribs: a superficial wound opened. At least they were even – both men bled from the chest.

They squared up for the next rally.

'You cannot escape, my men will be here any second, and you will be captured!' Kessler stabbed out with his knife.

'I don't think so!' Nash returned with an underarm swing towards Kessler's stomach, but with lightning agility Kessler grabbed his wrist, directing the knife point away.

Kessler kept twisting. He gave a hard tug and suddenly drove Nash's arm into the side of a bench.

The commando knife clattered to the floor.

Kessler struck out, opening the wound on Nash's chest. Nash staggered back under the blow, stumbling over a toolbox. Kessler wasted no time in diving forward, this time firmly pinning Nash to the ground. He raised his dagger for the mortal blow.

The first Bee Hive exploded.

The shockwave sent a shower of hot metal shards and debris across the room. That was enough to set off the second charge. This time much closer, the explosion threw Kessler into the air, and sprawling into the far wall, unconscious.

Nash closed his eyes against the heat as the blast wave went overhead; with his ears ringing, hot debris rained down; but the bench took the worst of the explosion. Perplexed by his sudden change of fortunes, but glad to be alive, he tried to stand.

Not good: the room swam, a wave of nausea hit home. White noise filled his ears. A wet trickle filtered into his consciousness; his head was bleeding again. He gingerly fingered his chest. More blood, but it was just a muscle injury; the knife hadn't penetrated the chest wall. He ripped open a field dressing and pressed it over his ribs.

He struggled through the debris towards the back of the workshop. He *had* to inspect the remains of the device. He needed to be sure: was it completely destroyed?

He need not have worried.

The Bee Hive was more than enough for the task. The device was shattered into hundreds of pieces, with just scorch marks signified where the machine had once stood. He picked up a fragment of the device and shoved it in his rucksack. Sinclair would want experts to analyse the material.

He glanced around for anything else that might be vitally important. Conveniently, the explosion had also ripped a hole in the rear wall. A couple of desks sat in the far corner, heaped with notes and technical drawings.

He hobbled over for a closer look.

He scanned through the large rolls of paper and, grabbing a selection, he pushed them into his rucksack. It would slow the Germans down considerably if they didn't have their technical drawings. He picked up a handful of photographs; they showed pictures of the device. He flicked through them quickly, then stopped; a picture of the two benches, each with a device.

So there *was* a second weapon!

But where is it now? Not here.

It had to be in the main complex.

He shoved the photographs into his bag and picked up a can of white spirit from the nearest workbench. He splashed it around. A quick flick of a match soon saw the remaining documents ablaze.

A sudden clatter of metal drew his attention to the gap in the rear wall.

Kessler!

Pivoting round, and simultaneously drawing his pistol, Nash fired. Wood splintered from the opening as Kessler disappeared from view. Weapon up, edging forwards in a tactical advance, he followed Kessler through the gap.

Seconds later a massive explosion ripped open the front of the building. The demolition team had finally made it through. The crew looked strangely puzzled. Someone had started their work for them? The two Sappers shrugged at each other. They set about wiring up the main concrete supports in the middle of the workshop and the gable ends. A few well-placed explosions would bring the house down.

Temple held on for dear life as the last rounds powered out of the heavy machine gun. A dull click and the hot whirl of the barrel told him that the last round had been spent.

They were out of ammo.

Temple sounded the retreat. 'Withdraw! Move, on the double!'

He tossed a last grenade through the barrack room door, and splashed the few remaining smoke canisters on the road to cover their withdrawal. He pulled out his pistol, and headed for the tree cover.

A loud thud announced a series of explosions further along the road. The demolition teams were still hard at work. But what could he do without ammo? Besides, his forces were split at the three locations; each team would have to make their own way out.

That was the plan. The aim was to rendezvous twenty miles down the coast, and wait until dark for a British submarine to pick them up. Hopefully, a few of them would make it.

His men, at least, had trained hard for the long haul, and were well rehearsed at escape and evasion from behind enemy lines. The British Sappers on the other hand were engineers, fit, but not trained in the fighting withdrawal methods.

The Sappers had other ideas.

An almighty explosion levelled the workshop building sending debris in every direction for hundreds of yards. A huge dust cloud formed over the camp. Temple paused in the tree line; his British comrades had sacrificed their lives to cover his escape. Truly humbled, he would mourn them later. For now, determination to survive was everything, he headed for the rendezvous.

He had a submarine to catch.

CHAPTER 41

Main Complex

Smoke swirled amongst the burning trees and remains of the wooden buildings. Nash stalked after Kessler, with his ears still ringing; the pistol weaved to and fro, searching for a target. The zip-zap of occasional small arms fire flicked dangerously close. Ignoring it, he studied the hazy vista ahead. A sudden eddy in the smoke revealed a lone figure. He took aim, and fired two rounds.

Kessler disappeared into the foggy blackness.

Damn it!

Nash half-jogged after his quarry, slapping a fresh magazine into his pistol as he went.

He stepped into the acrid smoke, holding his breath. His eyes burned with the tang of chemicals and soot. He kept the weapon up all the same. A shadow shifted a few yards ahead. He fired two controlled rounds, adjusted his aim, and then fired again.

Nothing.

He shuffled forward, coiled, ready for the attack, his weapon still searching for a target. The smoke gradually cleared. A building emerged into view: the back of the main complex.

But no Kessler.

A monstrous diesel engine, akin to one of Brunel's great Leviathans of the Victorian age, sat firmly attached to a large concrete standing. Several huge cylindrical steel containers some thirty feet high, perched in regimented order next to the diesel; together the construction lined the back of the building. The diesel engine and steel tanks were attached to each other by a spaghetti of industrial pipework.

A sudden muzzle flash issued forth from amongst the pipework. Rounds zipped into the concrete around Nash's position.

Instinctively, he dropped to a knee-firing position, and poured rounds in the direction of the muzzle flash.

The click-clatter of bullets on metalwork gave way to a loud hiss. A jet of steam erupted from a damaged pipe; but no Kessler.

Nash searched the gantry along the diesel engine with his weapon, following it up some steps, then along a first-floor level amongst the tanks. One of the tanks was liquid nitrogen, the warning label said so. At minus two hundred and seventy degrees Celsius, it could freeze-dry a man to dust in seconds.

Still no Kessler.

'American! You cannot have the device! You have already lost!'

A short burst of machine gunfire sent Nash diving for cover behind a low concrete plinth. He pulled a grenade, and tossed it towards the diesel engine.

Boom!

Shards of hot metal flew into the air, hot oil spewed onto the concrete. Smoke and steam flashed up the side of the building.

Ignoring the billows of smoke, and the whiz of hot steam, Nash zigzagged at break-neck speed across the open ground. He crunched into the concrete standing next to the diesel, and went into a crouching position. Slipping on the oily debris, he searched for Kessler.

Jets of steam blocked his vision.

The sudden clank of feet vibrated on the gantry.

Nash darted forwards, and let rip a short burst. Rounds flecked off the handrail of the walkway. Kessler jumped, and disappeared from view under the liquid nitrogen tank.

'Bollocks! Well, there's more than one way to flush the bastard out. To hell with it!'

Nash reached for the remaining Bee Hives in his rucksack.

Steinhoff stood over the bed. The rattle of machine gunfire echoed outside the main complex. The occasional grenade blast made the internal windows vibrate. The smell of cordite drifted into the room.

Mayer lay semi-conscious on the bed, but despite re-dressing the head wound, he seemed to be going downhill.

Steinhoff felt a pang of regret in the pit of his stomach, not for exacerbating the head injury, but for the lack of time. The fighting seemed to be getting closer.

Boom!... Boom!... The walls vibrated with another blast. A fine spray of concrete dust shook off the ceiling.

Yes, there was so little time.

A steady flow of oxygen hissed from the face mask. A drip fed life-saving fluids into the emaciated body.

Steinhoff sat on the edge of the bed. The stale dampness of sweat, acrid urine and disinfectant suddenly mixed with the cordite to assault his nostrils. The brick dust only added to the ashen paleness that was Mayer's face.

Steinhoff opened the small box, and stared down at the syringes.

Silver lances of truth, or purveyors of death?

Lifting out the first syringe, Steinhoff gingerly punctured the rubber tubing on the drip. He pushed the plunger steadily, watching the dense liquid mix with the fluids in the bag.

He waited.

Nothing.

He checked his watch – two minutes – still nothing.

Boom!

Steinhoff flinched.

More brick dust.

He lifted another syringe, and injected a second dose.

Mayer gasped as his eyes flicked open.

'Hello Gustav, it's me, Steinhoff. Can you hear me?' He leaned close to Mayer's ear.

Whumph! The walls gave a heavy vibration. Glass cracked.

Mayer rasped.

'I have been working hard… very hard you know?' Steinhoff searched the blank expression in Mayer's eyes. The oxygen whooshed under the face mask.

Mayer gave a muffled sound.

'I have finished it. The device! I *have* finished it. It is a thing of beauty, so… so elegant… '

'Ummmhhhhh! Ummmhhhhh!'

'Sorry, what was that?'

Steinhoff removed the oxygen mask.

'Nooooo! Nooooo! Nooooo!' Tears began to roll down Mayer's face.

'Of course, I understand now… you mentioned *travelling to the stars* once. Well, naturally I assumed it was just the delirium. But it wasn't was it?'

'Goooo… to… heeeeeellll… '

'I must ask you again. Just exactly how far and how fast do you think your device can go? Oh, I am sorry… *your device*… I should say *my device*, after all I built it! Answer the question: how fast can it go? Ten times the speed of sound, a hundred? How fast?!'

'Fuck… yooooou… '

'Not really the answer I was looking for, but that's easy to fix isn't it?' Steinhoff injected a third dose into the drip bag.

Mayer snorted, spasms shot down his right arm as the fluid hit. His brain fogged over with a wave of psychedelic euphoria.

Whumph!

A sudden rush of air filled the room with broken glass. Thick smoke began to roll through the windows.

Steinhoff shouted into Mayer's ear over the din. 'Now, how fast?!'

'Suuuper... sonnnic... yeeeeees.'

'Yes, supersonic, but how fast?'

'Maaaaach... fif... teee... '

'Did you say Mach fifty – fifty times the speed of sound? Are you sure?'

'Faaaaaster... faaaaaster... '

'My God! Faster? How much faster?!'

Mayer coughed violently as he took in the heavy smoke; fragments of lung tissue and blood spewed onto the bed clothes.

'How do I make the fuselage hold together at Mach fifty?! How can I make the nano carbon coating secure at that speed? How?!... How?!'

Mayer stiffened as his eyes rolled back into their sockets; foaming at the mouth, a seizure took hold.

'No! No! Answers! I need answers!' Steinhoff injected the last syringe into the drip.

Mayer thrashed, arching his back. The spasm passed and he sunk back onto the bed.

A machine gun rattled, loud and crisp, outside the door.

Blood dripped from Mayer's ears and nose. Sinews of congealed blood clots dangled from the corner of his mouth.

Steinhoff grabbed Mayer by the pyjama shirt, lifting him up off the bed. 'How do I make it strong enough?!'

No answer.

'How? How?!... How fast will it accelerate?! Enough to achieve escape velocity? Can we put a rocket in space?! How do I hold it together at that speed?! How fast?! How fast will it accelerate?!'

Mayer gave a spasm, his eyes glazing over, 'Acceeeeelerate... toooo... God... '

With that Professor Gustav Mayer was dead.

Nash took stock. Three Bee Hives, and three time pencils remaining; one with a ten-minute fuse, the others just four minutes. It was enough. The explosions would take out Kessler, and with luck, bring the back of the building down. Perhaps the second device was on the other side of the wall? The explosion would at least do some damage.

He worked his way around the smouldering diesel engine onto the metal gantry. He wedged the first Bee Hive into the fuel inlet; some five hundred gallons of pink diesel would certainly get the show on the road. He took out the ten-minute time pencil, pausing to rub the sweat and oil off his palms. He pushed the detonator gently into place, then fished around in his pockets for the pliers.

He took the strain, feeling the copper tube flex under the bite of the plier.

Crack!

Ten minutes.

Suddenly, machine gunfire sparked up the side of the engine. Nash slipped. The pliers clanked haplessly onto the floor of the gantry. He rolled onto his belly and, with a double-handed grip on his weapon, emptied the magazine in Kessler's general direction. Instant jets of super-cooled nitrogen sprung from the bullet holes in the nearest tank.

Vibration on the gantry?

Kessler was on the move.

Nash pushed a fresh magazine into place and, recovering the pliers for safekeeping, he pulled himself upright. He searched along the gantry with the pistol.

Nothing.

More resonating footfalls issued from the metalwork.

He edged forwards, finding the aluminium steps leading up the side of the first gas tank. He dodged an arctic blast of nitrogen gas. The muzzle of his pistol caught a split second flash of liquid nitrogen, and instantly frosted over. Icy numbness penetrated his hand from the freezing weapon. Tiny splashes of liquid nitrogen stung the back of his hand like a thousand hornets.

Ignoring the pain, he methodically worked up the steps, cautiously following the curvature of the vessel. He swept the pistol wide, craning his neck. It was no good; at best he could only see a couple of yards around the curve of the tank.

He moved forwards, one step at a time, weapon up.

No Kessler.

He emerged onto a landing, and swiftly searched the gantry and pipework for a target.

Nothing.

An iced-up valve on the side of the tank caught his eye. He took out the second Bee Hive. The ice crackled under protest as the prongs on the Bee Hive dug into the frozen metalwork. He worked the explosive charge behind the valve, hoping for maximum effect. He took out a second time pencil and pushed it into place. The charge felt cold. Would the sub-zero temperature slow the acid in the time pencil down so that the charge wouldn't go off? Or would the ice cold make the firing mechanism brittle, breaking the thin command wire to cause an instant explosion?

He wasn't sure.

He set the pliers around the already cooling copper tube, and took up the pressure.

Suddenly, a dark figure appeared in his peripheral vision. Dropping the pliers, Nash reached for his weapon.

Too late!

Kessler's full bodyweight piled into his rib cage. Both men rolled down the steps in a devilish embrace.

The pliers clattered, bouncing off several pipes below, before disappearing from view.

Nash jarred heavily against the gantry as they bounced; flailing his fists, he registered the crunch of his knuckles on the fleshy ligaments of Kessler's jaw.

Kessler returned with a solid punch to the diaphragm.

Paralysing breathlessness, and pulsing abdominal pain, sent Nash's next punch off target.

They cascaded down the last few steps, separating on the flat of the gantry.

Kessler drew his SS dagger.

Nash reached for his trusty stiletto. 'Bollocks!' The knife was gone.

Kessler lunged, taking the advantage.

Nash stepped back in a defence posture; he blocked the knife with a double-handed blow to Kessler's wrist.

'Let's finish this, American!' Kessler swung again.

'Arghh!' Nash registered a sharp pain. Blood flowed from his forearm. He bellowed. 'Come on then! Come on!' He whipped off his rucksack, fending off Kessler's next blow.

The bag ripped open, spilling the last Bee Hive onto the floor.

Nash kicked out, finding the soft tissue on Kessler's inner thigh. He kicked again, reaching for a handhold on Kessler's knife arm.

Kessler crumpled onto one knee.

Leaping with all his strength, Nash focused on the German blade and, twisting Kessler to the floor, he landed on top of him.

Kessler gritted his teeth and, with sheer determination, maintained a vice-like grip on the dagger. He kept control of the blade, sweeping it under Nash's abdomen.

Blood gushed from the wound.

Kessler, sensing a sudden gap, pushing his knee into his assailant's sternum, he kicked hard.

Nash flew backwards, landing with a jolt onto the gantry, next to the wayward Bee Hive. He picked it up, half stooping against the agony in his gut. He menaced the sharp prongs at the base of the explosive towards Kessler.

Kessler stepped forwards and, with an underarm swing, aimed for the abdominal wound.

Nash blocked, locking Kessler's forearm against his body, while still grasping the Bee Hive in his free hand.

The diesel engine exploded.

The detonation sent both men over the side of the gantry. An orange glow of red-hot fuel engulfed the walkway. Still locked in combat, both men rolled about under the flames.

Nash felt blisters form on his face as the fireball receded; with his clothes scorched and smoking, he held onto Kessler's knife arm.

Kessler flailed onto his back, moving his shoulder up and down wildly.

It was his only mistake.

Nash powered down with the Bee Hive, planting the sharp metal prongs into Kessler's chest.

Kessler arched in agony, hissing through clenched teeth. 'Arrghhh! Germany will prevail! You cannot win! You cannot win! The Reich will prevail!' Kessler coughed, blood splattered from his mouth and nose.

Nash stood, holding his stomach wound.

'Fuck the Reich!' He stamped his boot hard down on the Bee Hive, driving the prongs deeper into Kessler's chest.

Kessler frothed blood.

Nash knelt down next to his victim. 'Where is the second device?'

Kessler smiled; blood dripped from the side of his mouth. 'Behind reinforced concrete... with dozens of men... well-armed men. You have... lost.'

Nash grunted. He took the last time pencil, and pushed it gently into the Bee Hive. He stood up.

Kessler squirmed.

'Goodbye Commandant, and just so you know... British... not American.'

Nash walked away.

Thrump!

After only thirty yards, the Bee Hive on the liquid nitrogen tank went off.

Nash turned as the strangely muffled explosion gave way to gushing liquid. Metal creaked and snapped, as the tank toppled over, sending a wave of liquid nitrogen in Kessler's direction.

Kessler registered the immense freezer burn as the boiling liquid washed over his feet. A brittle snapping sound crackled in the air as his flesh froze. He lifted his leg; curiously, he examined the frosted stump where his foot had once been.

Kessler smiled to himself, as he snapped the time pencil embedded in the explosive on his chest.

At last… a hero's death… an iron cross after all.

CHAPTER 42

Epilogue: Aftermath at Peenemünde

Colonel Dornberger brushed the debris from his desk, and hastily arranged a pencil and paper as best he could to make ready for the Führer's phone call. The operator would only be a few moments – not much time to gather his thoughts – bad news travels fast. Somehow Berlin knew of the attack in no time at all. Perhaps it was no surprise with SS men and party political officers snooping around in every building at Peenemünde. No doubt one of them had radioed news of the assault to the Reich Chancellery.

The phone rang.

Dornberger glanced across the desk at Steinhoff. He looked worried too, and for good reason; both their necks were on the line.

Dornberger picked up the receiver.

'Yes, my Führer... yes, that is correct... the base has been attacked... yes, of course my Führer we will double our efforts. We... of course my Führer... yes my Führer. No stone will be left unturned... yes, yes... he is with me now... yes, it will be done my Führer.'

The phone went dead. Hitler had hung up.

'Well?' Steinhoff stared at the ashen-faced Dornberger.

'He is furious... and had ordered that the defences be strengthened.'

'And?' Steinhoff probed to stir Dornberger to his senses.

'... And the Führer orders the security to be tripled on the perimeter and main gate. There is to be no opportunity for a second ground assault, or further sabotage.'

335

'We are allowed to continue?'

'Yes, but… we are to move your project.'

'What? Now?!' Steinhoff was perplexed.

'Apparently, we are to move you and the device in total secrecy to a new underground complex in the Carpathian Mountains, near Reisebirge. The Führer called it his *Wolfsberg*.'

'I've heard of it, only whispers and rumour, an impregnable fortress dug deep into the mountainside… I didn't realise the Führer had actually built the thing.'

'Apparently so, what's more, he will be here in forty-eight hours to inspect our repairs and preparations.' Dornberger steeled himself at the thought.

'How bad is the damage? My work must continue.'

'Details are still coming in… ' Dornberger absently dabbed at a cut on his forehead; everyone was in bad shape. '… The barracks have been hit hard, almost totally destroyed by heavy fire. We have over one hundred casualties.'

Steinhoff spoke logically. 'Yes, but the army will send more men?'

Dornberger sensed no sign of remorse at the loss of so many men. He decided not to comment, but continued. 'The main laboratory has taken a few heavy blasts. Mostly superficial damage to the outer wall, and as you know several of the inner concrete buttresses are cracked. Many of the windows are shattered. Fortunately, the engineers indicate that the structural damage can be repaired, and the damage to the windows and interior is mostly cosmetic.'

'What about the workshop?'

'That's the main problem. It's been totally destroyed.'

Steinhoff sunk back in his chair. 'No! I can't believe it! We have to rebuild… find new labourers… work day and night… we have to do it.'

'You should have heard his voice… trembling with rage… the Führer doesn't share your optimism.' Dornberger shook his head. 'It's also possible that they weren't here for the rocket programme.'

'What?'

'Think about it. The workshop was specifically targeted. Clearly the assault was made by professional soldiers, probably Special Forces, and their explosives experts knew exactly where to place the charges for maximum effect. This cannot be coincidence.'

Steinhoff shrugged. 'Perhaps the workshop was just an easier target? It is, or rather was, just a simple brick and timber building. Nothing like the reinforced concrete used in the main laboratory complex.'

'No, that would be too convenient.' Dornberger went with his gut instinct. 'No, they were after you, Steinhoff. Look at the evidence. The second prototype device and most of your notes have been completely destroyed. Charges placed deliberately for maximum destruction of the device.'

'So, what are you saying?' Steinhoff wanted to be sure.

'The Americans, the British, someone knows about your machine – and want to stop it – bad enough to risk some crack troops on an assault deep in our territory.'

'Do you *really* think they were after me?'

'Yes, definitely. At the time of the attack you were deep inside the main complex, and reasonably well protected. It is only by chance that you survived the assault. However, many of your technical assistants have been killed.' Dornberger was unable to conceal his annoyance. 'Damn it! I should have insisted that *all* of your project was moved into the main building.'

'It's not your fault. You gave into my requests on the mark II model. I just wanted the flexibility to be close to the machinery in the workshop; with so many small adjustments to make, it made sense to be near the lathes and cutting tools.'

'Nonetheless, they were good scientists, and now all are dead because I did not think of the security implications.' Dornberger shook his head wearily. 'Look… Steinhoff… it's best that you stay in the main complex from now on, and with an armed escort. We can't take any more chances. We will make careful preparations, and then move things to the Führer's *Wolfsberg*. The transportation of the remaining device, the few surviving technicians, and whatever remains of your notes *must be* secure.' Dornberger was deeply concerned – physicists were now a valuable commodity and in short supply.

Steinhoff nodded in agreement.

There was so much to do, and so little time to do it.

Sinclair sucked in the bad news as he studied the documents from Peenemünde. There was only one conclusion: the Germans had more than one device. The latest aerial photographs also showed a hastily constructed railway line, going right into the camp.

So, the Germans were looking to move the device to a more secure location?

It was the logical thing to do.

But where?

Sinclair picked up the phone. 'Margaret, bring me the most recent report on the recognisance along the Czech border.'

The secretary dutifully replied and seconds later appeared with the report.

The Czech Resistance had paid with their lives to get this first-hand intelligence. It was certainly a massive construction project by any measure, and underway in the remote Carpathian Mountains. The Germans were tunnelling into the hillsides and setting up heavy defences. The secrecy and complex defences pointed to military weapons development. The rumours were that the Germans were moving their uranium work from Berlin to a new facility. The proximity of uranium ore in the region was also too much of a coincidence. This had to be it.

If this location was good enough for the uranium weapon,

it would be secure enough for the device, and God knows how many other secret projects.

It looked like an impenetrable fortress. If construction of the device was moved to Czechoslovakia, then it would all be over. There could be no successful attack against such a well-defended underground facility.

There was only one brutally simple solution: kill as many German scientists as possible *before* they get to the complex. Destroy every train and every convoy heading in that direction. *Nothing* from Peenemünde would get through to the Carpathian Mountains.

Sinclair picked up his pipe. Sabotage, murder and mayhem were the unsavoury tools of clandestine warfare. He had another job for MI6 and the boys from Section D – after all, the D was for *destruction*.